NEW MEXICO!

The twenty-second hard-fighting episode in the *WAGONS WEST* series—a blazing adventure into the unexplored regions of a nation and into the darkest corners of the human heart as men and women of America's old West push onward to make this land fulfill its promise to be—great, strong, and proud.

9-12-90

★ ★

WAGONS WEST

NEW MEXICO!

**THE WIDE OPEN SPACES LAY TANTALIZINGLY BE-
FORE THESE ABLE YOUNG PIONEERS OF A GROW-
ING AMERICA AS THEY WENT FORTH INTO THE
UNKNOWN WHERE ADVENTURE WAITED**

TOBY HOLT
Secret orders would once again plunge him into the direst of
risks as this bold, stouthearted young man dons the disguise
of an outlaw to trap the wild comancheros in their own lair
. . . or die trying.

CINDY HOLT KERR
Her heart already broken by betrayal and tragedy, this blond,
blue-eyed Western gal would astonish all Paris as she fought
for her dreams and desires.

CAPTAIN HENRY BLAKE
Held by chains of loyalty and lust, his liaison with a German
baroness is dragging him deeper into a dangerous intrigue
and toward a deadly rendezvous.

CALUSA JIM
A man as cruel as he is cunning, the leader of the comancheros
relishes evil, feasts on debauchery, and hungers to kill the
good, the innocent, and the enemy he loathes—Toby Holt.

★ ★

MARJORIE WHITE
Unable to tame the wanderlust in her soul, she will dare to sail aboard a whaling ship, never guessing that her wild spirit will lead to a harrowing captivity . . . and heartbreak.

TED TAYLOR
Crossing half a world in search of his missing bride, he will enter distant ports, fight bloodthirsty pirates, and face one last moment of truth . . . for love.

JUANITA
Kidnapped by the comancheros, she is trapped in a life of degradation and horror until one man rides into the outlaw camp . . . with a promise of freedom.

JANESSA HOLT
Proud inheritor of the Holt courage and her Indian mother's gift of healing, she has brought new hope to the sick . . . and a new beginning to one hard-drinking, aimless young man.

ANDREW JACKSON BRENTWOOD
Acting undercover amid Europe's most treacherous men, he finds unexpected danger in the laughing eyes of a beautiful woman . . . willing, wanton, and married.

LYDIA VON HOFSTETTEN
Breathtakingly lovely, she is an irresistible temptation to a dashing soldier whose heart can be forfeited in a cruel game of sex and seduction.

HERMANN BLUECHER
The diabolical head of German military intelligence, his ambitions put the leadership of Prussia within his ugly, relentless grasp . . . if he can kill an American named Henry Blake.

Bantam Books by Dana Fuller Ross
Ask your bookseller for the books you have missed

WAGONS WEST ★ TWENTY-SECOND IN A SERIES

NEW MEXICO!

DANA FULLER ROSS

BANTAM BOOKS
TORONTO · NEW YORK · LONDON · SYDNEY · AUCKLAND

NEW MEXICO!

A Bantam Book / published by arrangement with
Book Creations, Inc.

Bantam edition / September 1988

Produced by Book Creations, Inc.
Lyle Kenyon Engel, Founder

ISBN 0-553-27458-9

Published simultaneously in the United States and Canada

PRINTED IN THE UNITED STATES OF AMERICA

O   0 9 8 7 6 5 4 3 2 1

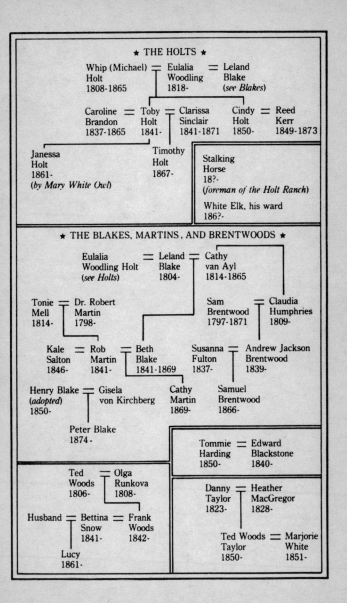

★ THE HOLTS ★

Whip (Michael) = Eulalia = Leland
Holt   Woodling   Blake
1808-1865   1818-   (see Blakes)

Caroline = Toby = Clarissa   Cindy = Reed
Brandon   Holt   Sinclair   Holt   Kerr
1837-1865 1841- 1841-1871   1850-   1849-1873

Janessa   Timothy
Holt   Holt
1861-   1867-
(by Mary White Owl)

Stalking
Horse
18?-
(foreman of the Holt Ranch)

White Elk, his ward
186?-

★ THE BLAKES, MARTINS, AND BRENTWOODS ★

Eulalia   = Leland = Cathy
Woodling Holt   Blake   van Ayl
(see Holts)   1804-   1814-1865

Tonie = Dr. Robert   Sam   = Claudia
Mell   Martin   Brentwood Humphries
1814-   1798-   1797-1871 1809-

Kale = Rob = Beth   Susanna = Andrew Jackson
Salton Martin Blake   Fulton   Brentwood
1846-   1841-   1841-1869 1837-   1839-

Henry Blake = Gisela   Cathy   Samuel
(adopted)   von Kirchberg Martin   Brentwood
1850-   1869-   1866-

Peter Blake
1874-

Tommie = Edward
Harding Blackstone
1850-   1840-

Ted = Olga
Woods Runkova
1806- 1808-

Danny = Heather
Taylor MacGregor
1823-   1828-

Husband = Bettina = Frank
          Snow   Woods
          1841-   1842-

Lucy
1861-

Ted Woods = Marjorie
Taylor   White
1850-   1851-

NEW MEXICO!

I

When he saw smoke rising from the mountains ahead, Alvin Mosely knew he had found the right place. At Encima, a village nestled in a valley, buildings were burning. A moment later, Mosely heard gunfire. It was the sporadic sound of shots meant to mock and to terrorize, not the steady volleys of a battle. He was positive he had found the right place.

Early spring had brought warm days to the Chihuahuan desert of Mexico, but a shiver passed over Mosely as he rode toward the mountains. He was on his way to see the leader of a band of comancheros that had been raiding across the border and ravaging the New Mexico Territory during the past months. Now, to while away the time, they had left their secluded hideout and taken over Encima.

A motley collection of Mexicans, Indians, and bandits from north of the border, the comancheros were more savage than the fiercest Indians. And the band now in Encima was the most feared of all the comancheros because it was led by a man who was as cunning as he was brutal. He was known as Calusa Jim.

Mosely turned his horse and pack mule onto a narrow road leading into the mountains. On the mule were two large cases filled with assortments of thread, needles, lace, and other notions. Mosely was a peddler, which was not an extremely lucrative occupation, but of late he had handsomely supplemented his income by searching out targets for the comancheros, recruiting drifters to join their ranks, and delivering the products of their raids to markets in Mexico City. Although he worked with the

1

outlaws, Mosely still feared them. Most of all he feared Calusa Jim.

That day, especially, he had even more reason to be afraid, for something had gone amiss on the trip from which he was returning. These days, much of the money the comancheros made from their raids came from the sale of captured women. Mosely took them to a dealer in Nogales, who drugged them, beat them when necessary, and in turn sold them to an exclusive bordello in Mexico City, where foreign women were in great demand. Mosely also drugged the women, to make them easier to transport, but this time one of them had died en route to Nogales.

The narrow, rutted road led back into a high mountain valley that contrasted sharply with its arid surroundings. Watered by springs, it was lush with vegetation in shades of bright green that stood out dramatically against the dull brown of the mountains. The town of Encima, comprising some fifty adobe buildings surrounded by crop fields and pastures, sat in the middle of the valley.

Mosely could see fires in the distant town square; pigs and fowl were being roasted to feed the comancheros. Smoke also rose from the ashes of houses burned as a punishment for their inhabitants—because of attempts to hide young, pretty wives or daughters, Mosely guessed, or because some other form of resistance had been offered.

The Mexican Army posed little danger to the comancheros, but Calusa Jim took no chances, and a half-dozen men were posted as guards on the road ahead. Mosely recognized the one in charge, a half-breed named Camargo. Large and muscular, with knife scars on his hawkish, unshaven face, he was walleyed and always seemed to be looking in two directions at once.

No one, not even Camargo, argued with Calusa Jim's orders, but the six men were obviously disgruntled over being placed on guard while the others enjoyed themselves in the town below. Like all comancheros, they were grimy and dressed in tattered, mismatched clothing that had been looted from houses during raids, but they were heavily armed with the best of weapons.

Mosely grinned anxiously as he rode up to them. "Howdy, Camargo," he said, with feigned confidence. "Has anything important happened while I was gone?"

The man jerked a thumb toward the town. "Are you *un idiota* or only blind? You can see what we are doing. We don't have anything better to amuse ourselves with, because you haven't found us any good places to raid."

"I had to go to Nogales," Mosely protested uneasily. "I can't do two things at once."

"You can't do even one thing at once," Camargo retorted. He casually took a knife from his belt sheath and traced an imaginary line over his own forehead. "If you don't find us some good places to raid, you had better have a wig to wear the next time I see you."

The other five men—three of whom were Indians—chortled appreciatively, but Camargo continued glowering. Mosely laughed nervously, trying to pass it off as a joke. "Where is Calusa Jim?"

"In the cantina." Camargo spat in the dirt and resheathed his knife. "Go on, get out of here, Mosely."

Needing no further urging, Mosely spurred his horse on. His uneasiness, however, only increased as he neared the town, for the few townspeople in evidence avoided his gaze and wore terrified expressions. Old women and men stood cooking in the square for the comancheros. Tears of despair streamed down their cheeks, and two of the men, to keep the fires blazing, were breaking up furniture that had been thrown out of houses.

In a building across the square from the cantina, women screamed and wailed as comancheros laughed raucously. A few comancheros sat around the plaza, eating and drinking, while others strolled about aimlessly, as if looking for some hapless target for their amusement. Avoiding them, Mosely dismounted in front of the cantina and went inside.

The owner, pale and trembling in fright, stood behind the bar. All the tables had been thrown into the street except one, where Calusa Jim was sitting. A girl of about sixteen, her pretty face stained with tears, sat rigidly beside him. Against the wall nearby was a bed that had been dragged in from another room.

Calusa Jim eyed Mosely briefly, then ignored him. Big, heavyset, and meticulously neat compared to his men, the comanchero leader looked to be about forty. Because he spoke both Spanish and English with a heavy French accent and always wore a French officer's tunic, Calusa Jim was rumored to be a deserter from the French forces that had been sent to Mexico a few years before to prop up the short-lived regime of the Emperor Maximilian. Calusa Jim's attitude discouraged personal questions, and Mosely was wise enough not to ask him any, although the peddler was intensely curious about the gleaming steel hook that the fiendishly cruel outlaw leader had in place of a right hand.

"Howdy, Calusa Jim," Mosely quavered, approaching the table warily. "It's mighty good to see you again."

Calusa Jim gestured Mosely to come closer. "Where is the money?" he demanded.

Mosely quickly opened his shirt and removed the money belt beneath it. "Calusa Jim," he blurted, "one of the women died. She was acting up a lot, and maybe I gave her too much opium. But for some reason she just up and died on me."

With a swipe of his hook, Calusa Jim snatched the money belt before Mosely could even flinch. The belt dangled from the shiny, sharpened tip as the man glared at Mosely. "Perhaps one did not die," he suggested in a soft, dangerous tone that made his French accent more distinct. "Perhaps you have kept part of the money."

"No, I'd never do that! I'd never try to cheat you! Call your men in to search me right now."

"I am not as stupid as you are," the outlaw leader sneered. "If you have kept part of the money, it would be hidden somewhere."

Mosely shook his head rapidly, his terror mounting. "Honest, I haven't, Calusa Jim. I know better than to try to cheat you."

An eternity seemed to pass before Calusa Jim answered. "Do not let it happen again, Mosely," was all he said.

"No, I won't, I promise," Mosely assured him, weak

with relief. "From now on I'll be real careful with that opium."

A glass and a tequila bottle with its neck broken off were on the table, and with a sudden swipe of his hook Calusa Jim sent them crashing to the floor. "More tequila and glasses!" he shouted.

The cantina owner rushed to the table with a bottle and two glasses, and Mosely sat in the one empty chair. The owner started to open the tequila, but Calusa Jim jerked the bottle away with his good hand, and with a slash of his hook he shattered the neck, causing the girl beside him to jump in fright as glass scattered over the table. Calusa Jim splashed tequila into the glasses, and the cantina owner retreated to the bar.

After draining half his glass, the outlaw leader opened the pockets on the money belt. "Did you mail that package?"

"Yes, just like you said," Mosely replied between gulps, grateful for the tequila. "But it seems to me we're already having plenty of trouble from the army without riling them further. That Colonel Hamilton will be like a mad bull when he opens that package."

Calusa Jim gazed somberly at his hook for a moment. "I want them to feel the same anger I do," he said quietly.

The remark suggested that the man blamed the army for the loss of his hand. Calusa Jim counted the money, then pushed Mosely's share and the belt across the table. "I want you to find good places."

Pocketing the money, Mosely nodded. "I'll do my best. But you know how things are in New Mexico now. Everyone is on guard because of your last raids, and there're no easy pickings. What about crossing the river into Texas? You haven't raided there, and they won't be expecting—"

"No!" the bandit leader interrupted angrily. "I have not raided in Texas because the Texas Rangers would follow me back into Mexico—but the federal cavalry will not. I do not need advice from you, Mosely. All I want you to do is find some good places to raid."

"Then that's what I'll do," Mosely agreed quickly. He took a swallow of tequila.

Calusa Jim refilled the peddler's glass. "Find me a place where we can capture many women. We need cattle, too, for provisions at the hideout. And fodder for the horses."

"I heard that some ranchers are settling on the Rio Hondo," Mosely remarked. "I can look around there, and on my way I could stop at the Indian reservations to see if I can recruit a few more men."

Calusa Jim seemed satisfied with the idea. "All right— but I also need something for them to do. Go to Rio Hondo, and also look around west of the Rio Grande, in the vicinity of Acoma."

"Right, Acoma. Whatever you say, Jim." With tequila in his belly, money in his pockets, and his worries about the dead woman now behind him, Mosely enjoyed a sense of well-being. "I'll rest up and leave first thing tomorrow morning—"

The gleaming hook darted out, snagging Mosely's coat lapel, and the little peddler's contentment changed to raw fear as Calusa Jim dragged him across the table. "You'll leave now!" the man hissed in Mosely's face. "Find me some ranches to raid, and they had better be good ones!"

"All right, Jim, all right!" Mosely stammered. "Whatever you say! I'll leave now."

Calusa Jim disengaged the hook, and as Mosely hurried toward the door, the bandit leader stood up, yanked the girl to her feet, and shoved her toward the bed. She began sobbing, and the cantina owner turned his pale, trembling face away from them. Mosely hurried outside.

It occurred to him as he mounted his horse that both the girl and the cantina owner had heard the conversation between him and Calusa Jim. But neither of them probably understood English, and in any case, Calusa Jim never took unnecessary risks. By the time the comancheros tired of the pleasures that Encima had to offer and left to return to their hideout, the girl and the cantina owner would be dead.

In Santa Fe, the capital of the New Mexico Territory, Colonel Wayne Hamilton stepped out of his quarters and strode angrily toward the town plaza. In his hand was a package he had received in that day's mail.

The commander of the United States Army units stationed in the territory, Hamilton was a tall, graying professional soldier who had spent most of his career in the West. He had been in countless battles and skirmishes in the Civil War and with renegade Indians, and he was not a man easily moved to rash action, but the contents of the package in his hand had sickened and infuriated him.

On any other day, Hamilton would have enjoyed his walk down the narrow, stone-paved streets to the plaza, for Santa Fe was one of the pleasantest places he had ever been stationed. The crisp, clear air had a tangy scent from the piñon trees dotting the high, rolling desert plateau, and to the north the snowcapped peaks of the Sangre de Cristo Mountains sparkled in the bright early spring sunlight.

As Hamilton neared his destination, the tile-roofed adobe buildings lining the street gave way to a wide flagstone plaza where local Indians were selling baskets and earthenware goods. It was a market day, yet the activity in the plaza remained at its usual sedate, timeless pace. Indeed, back in the early 1600s, when Virginia's Jamestown colony had still been a raw frontier settlement struggling for survival, Santa Fe had been a thriving, well-established town.

Colonel Hamilton crossed the square to the Palace of the Governors, a simple adobe structure that had an unimposing façade but which dated from 1610 and was said to be the oldest public building on the North American continent. The palace now housed the territorial administration, and Colonel Hamilton went straight to the office of the governor, a dedicated public servant of forty-five named Patrick Mills. Hamilton knew Mills well and liked him, but on this occasion, instead of returning the man's polite greeting, Hamilton dropped the opened package on the governor's desk. Mills took one look at its contents, and his face turned pale.

"Good Lord!" he exclaimed, standing up. "Where on earth did you get this, Wayne?"

"It came this morning in the mail," Hamilton replied grimly. "They had the gall to use the United States mail! You'll notice that the hair is brown, with some gray in it. One of the men killed in the last raid near Las Cruces, a storekeeper named Jones, had hair just like that. The scalp is undoubtedly his."

The governor sighed heavily and picked up a paper from his desk. "This arrived from the State Department this morning. It's a reply to the messages I've been sending them about the comancheros."

"I hope it's good news," Hamilton said, his mouth set in anger.

"I'm afraid it isn't." Mills tossed the paper back down. "Our ambassador in Mexico City has once again obtained assurances that the authorities will look into the matter, but his private sources indicate they intend to do nothing. Their garrison in Chihuahua is poorly manned, and the last thing they want is more trouble with the comancheros. That's the way it stands, with no promise of changing."

Shaking his head in disgust, Hamilton stepped to the window and gazed out at the plaza. The muscles in the sides of his lean, tanned face were tense as he clenched his jaw. "Then it's up to us, Patrick. Give me authority to take a cavalry troop across the border, and I promise you an end to this trouble."

"I only wish I could," Mills said wistfully. "But that's outside my jurisdiction as territorial governor. I agree entirely with your feelings, Wayne, but we can't settle the problem that way."

"That's the only way to settle it!" Hamilton snapped, turning around. "And jurisdiction be hanged! Why do you think they aren't raiding in Texas? It's because they would have a company of Texas Rangers on their heels all the way to Mexico City, if necessary!"

"Texas is a state," the governor pointed out, "with considerably less federal control over it than a territory. If you took the cavalry into Mexico, our prospects for attaining statehood would be set back for years. This is a serious problem, but attaining statehood is more important to the long-range interests of our citizens."

Hamilton stabbed a finger toward the package on the desk. "Is statehood more important than that? People are dying, Patrick!"

"I'm simply trying to be as good a territorial governor as you are a soldier," Mills said calmly. "We each have our responsibilities. I realize your men are being stretched very thin in patrolling the border. How is their morale?"

Hamilton shrugged. "Good enough, considering. The heavy patrols are wearing them down, and I suspect that the comancheros have informants on this side of the border—they always manage to evade us. I intend to alter the patrol routes some, so we may get lucky and catch them. But it's a long shot."

"Let's hope you do," Mills said. "And we still might get some help from Washington. As soon as I received this message from the State Department, I sent back an urgent appeal to the Secretary of the Interior. I explained that the situation has become intolerable and requested that he give the problem his personal attention."

Hamilton smirked skeptically. "I wouldn't hold my breath. In any event, what can he do?"

"I'm not sure." Mills, disheartened, stared at the package on his desk. "From our standpoint, it appears that all the possibilities have been exhausted. Mr. Caldwell is a member of the President's cabinet, however, and a department secretary. Perhaps he can come up with some new ideas or pressure someone into doing something."

In fact, the urgent message from Patrick Mills had already resulted in a conference in Secretary Caldwell's office at the Department of the Interior in Washington. The meeting was attended by Caldwell's key subordinates, together with representatives from two other departments.

Speaking for the State Department was a nervous, intense undersecretary by the name of Peter Holman, who seemed the complete opposite of the representative from the War Department, Colonel Frank Bolton. A reserved, stolid soldier, Bolton had an impressive display of decorations on his uniform, and his presence in Washington rather than in the field was mutely explained by his left sleeve, which was empty and pinned up.

The men had been arguing for some time, and the air in the room was thick with tobacco smoke. Secretary Caldwell used all his diplomatic talents to soothe fraying tempers while prodding those present for a solution. The message from Santa Fe had struck a personal note with him, for his own family was from the West, and he knew the hardships of life on a half-civilized frontier.

The inaction by the Mexican government was mentioned several times, and the discussion turned to that subject again. "It seems an unavoidable conclusion to me," one of Caldwell's subordinates volunteered, "that the problem must be dealt with by Mexico City. There must be some way we can pressure them to take action."

Undersecretary Holman, squirming in his chair as the man spoke, shook his head. "We've done everything we can. We're constrained by the need to maintain harmonious relations. No, the solution lies with the War Department. More soldiers are needed in New Mexico."

"Find me the funds," Colonel Bolton rejoined calmly, "and I'll put a soldier every ten feet along the border. But you know Congress won't give us the money for that, and in my opinion we already have more than enough troops stationed there."

Everyone looked at him in surprise. Holman voiced what they all were thinking: "If more than enough soldiers are there, why can't they stop the raids?"

"Because they're not being allowed to do their job," Bolton replied. "I could order Colonel Hamilton to send a company to track those comancheros down, and that would be the end of it."

"Invade Mexico with a military force?" Holman reddened. "That isn't a solution, it's an act of war against a friendly nation. It—"

"I'm sure," Caldwell interjected, "that the colonel was speaking theoretically. You say a single company could attend to those comancheros, Colonel?"

"Yes, sir." Bolton's tone was confident. "The bandits number fewer than a hundred men, and they would be no match for trained cavalry in a pitched battle. But even fifty companies wouldn't be enough to wage a *defensive* campaign in that remote, rugged region."

"That rules out a military solution," Caldwell concluded. "We've also ruled out bringing pressure to bear on Mexico City. There must be another answer."

After a momentary silence, one of Caldwell's subordinates spoke up. "Perhaps we could ask the governor of Texas for his assistance. Texas Rangers aren't military forces, but a company of them could probably do the job."

"That's out of the question!" Holman erupted. "There's no difference between that and sending soldiers into Mexico."

"I must agree with Mr. Holman," Caldwell said. He looked across the room at one of his aides who was trying to draw his attention. "Did you have something to add, Mr. Bailey?"

Bailey, a gangling, meek-looking man, cleared his throat. "Yes, sir. I was thinking of an incident that happened last year, when I was in the Treasury Department. An assassination attempt against the President was discovered and squelched. The man who took care of that might be able to help with this."

Holman was running his fingers through his hair nervously. "You mean turn it over to the Secret Service? That's out of the question."

"Well, actually this man is a civilian," Bailey continued. "There was some concern about who might have been involved in the plot, so the investigation was turned over to an outsider. He tracked down the guilty parties and handled everything very capably."

"A plot against the President?" Caldwell shook his head. "This is the first I've heard of it."

"It was kept very quiet, sir," Bailey explained. "I was friends with several Secret Service men, but even they knew very little about it. I did find out the name of the man, however. It was Toby Holt."

"Toby Holt?" Bolton pondered. "I've heard that name."

Bailey smiled thinly. "That's quite likely. Mr. Holt was governor of the Idaho Territory, and he's served the government in other capacities. He might be able to help with this. A man working alone can accomplish things that are impossible for a regiment of soldiers."

"I'm not in favor of giving official sanction to a civilian to stir up trouble in another nation," Holman remarked. "It's completely contrary to acceptable diplomacy."

"Some civilians from Mexico are giving us no end of trouble," Caldwell pointed out frostily. "There's a fine line between proper caution and negativism, Mr. Holman. Now, do you have a specific objection to offer against Mr. Bailey's suggestion?"

Holman hesitated, then reluctantly shook his head. "No, I don't have a specific objection, sir."

Colonel Bolton spoke up. "Mr. Bailey is correct in saying that a man working alone can do things that are impossible for a regiment of soldiers. In fact, Calusa Jim appears to have a very good network of informers, while we know next to nothing about him. A man working alone could correct that. But he would have to be the right man. This would be an extremely dangerous undertaking."

Caldwell stood. "You're absolutely right. So before we go any further with this, we should contact Mr. Holt and get his reaction. Could I ask you to do that, Colonel?"

"It would be my pleasure, sir. Do you know where he lives, Mr. Bailey?"

Bailey shook his head. "Not exactly. I understand he has business interests in Chicago, but I'm not sure he lives there. He has friends in the Secret Service, though, and they'll probably know. I'll introduce you to them."

"Good." Bolton stood. "Now we're getting somewhere."

In the office of the North Chicago Lumber Company, one of two businesses he owned in the city, Toby Holt sat at a desk, scanning papers and signing them. Only minutes before, he had arrived on a steam launch from his logging camp up Lake Michigan, and his business manager, taking advantage of Toby's presence, had urged him to sign a backlog of contracts.

When he had finished, Toby replaced the pen in the inkwell. "What else do you have, Dieter?"

Dieter Schumann, a big-boned, red-haired man in his late forties, who had done a superb job of looking after Toby's business interests for the past year and a half, handed him one last document. "This is a revised royalty contract with the inventor of that barbed wire our iron-works is manufacturing. I believe you'll agree with its provisions, but perhaps I should explain—"

"If you negotiated the contract," Toby cut in, "I know I'll be satisfied with it." He signed the paper and stood, offering Dieter back his chair.

The business manager smiled appreciatively. His employer's trust in him was something he took pride in, and in any case he knew that Toby was impatient with the humdrum details of business.

A lean, muscular man with sandy hair and blue eyes, Toby Holt was far more at home in wide open spaces than in a business office. His strong, tanned features were those of a man who could and would deal with trouble, and the livid scar on his left temple and his somewhat stiff walk were reminders of his latest brush with danger. Only a few months before, he had been shot in the head and side by gangsters who had left him for dead—which had been their fatal mistake. Toby was almost healed now, although he still favored his left side because of lingering pains where a bullet had grazed his ribs.

The trouble had occurred in Kentucky, where criminals had been trying to gain a foothold in the horse-racing circuits. They had attempted to take over a horse farm belonging to distant relatives of Toby's and had killed Alex Woodling, the father of the young woman Toby loved and intended to marry. Alexandra—she had been named after her father—had since leased the farm to friends, and Toby had taken her to his Wisconsin logging camp, where he hoped she could recover from the tragedy.

Dieter touched on a related subject before Toby left. "Concerning Miss Woodling's horses—" He opened a desk drawer and took out a folder of papers. "We've been receiving the bills on the ones you sent to your ranch in Oregon. I've been paying them, as you instructed, but it hasn't been cheap."

Toby glanced through the bills, then handed them back. "It's money well spent, as far as I'm concerned." He picked up his carpetbag. "I have to talk to an estate agent downtown about some good stands of hardwood that Frank has his eye on. Did you make reservations for me at my usual hotel?"

"It's all taken care of." Dieter walked with Toby to the door. "I was hoping that you would be my guest for dinner. Abigail would enjoy it as much as I would, Toby."

The tall man broke into a wide grin. "You know that's an invitation I can't turn down, especially if Abigail is doing the cooking. I always look forward to seeing her and the boys."

"At seven, then," Dieter said. "I'll send my carriage to the hotel for you."

Outside the lumberyard's gate, Toby hailed a carriage to take him downtown. Each time he visited the city these days, the new construction on all sides stirred memories of the Great Chicago Fire of 1871, when chance had put him in a position to help the authorities prevent the fire from utterly destroying the city.

At the hotel Toby checked in and left his bag, then went back out into the bright midafternoon sunshine. He walked in the general direction of the estate agent's office, although with an additional purpose in mind. He wished to get a present for Alexandra, but he was at a complete loss as to what to buy her.

Even though she had only just turned nineteen, Alexandra was independent and practical for her age, having been brought up by her widowed father. She was also something of a tomboy. She cut her hair short and had no particular fondness for jewelry. Indeed, she wore riding trousers, boots, and a jacket most of the time. Still, there were many other facets to Alexandra's personality.

Her mother had been a Bradford, a direct descendant of the governor of the *Mayflower* settlers at Plymouth Colony in 1620. On her father's side, she was a Kentucky aristocrat. She liked bright, pretty dresses and hats, but Toby knew nothing about choosing clothes for a woman, and entering a dress or hat store without knowing exactly what he wanted was an adventure he did not relish. Gazing at the signs and shop windows as he strolled through the city, Toby tried to think of a gift that would please her.

He had met with no success when, hearing a commotion across the street, he saw a scene that annoyed him: Two women carrying signs—members of a temperance organization, protesting the sale of alcoholic beverages— were involved in an argument in front of a saloon. One of them, a stout, middle-aged matron, was struggling with a man who had seized one end of her sign. He was pushing and pulling it, trying to wrestle it away from her or shove her into a mud puddle beside the curb.

Three other men were standing outside the saloon, shouting encouragement to the fellow, while the heavyset bartender in his white apron stood in the doorway and watched with amusement. Passersby were glancing in disapproval, but no one was doing anything to stop the trouble. Toby strode rapidly across the street.

Seeing Toby's expression as he approached, the man released the sign to give his attention to the tall intruder. Meanwhile, his three friends fell silent. All had been drinking heavily, and the one who had been tormenting the woman looked ready for more trouble. Clenching his fists, he lunged at Toby to strike the first blow.

Brushing the punch aside, Toby hit the man in the stomach hard enough to knock the breath out of him. As the man doubled over, Toby gave him a little shove toward the curb. In his drunken state, the man teetered, his arms windmilling, then sprawled into the mud puddle with a splash.

"Pick him up and get out of here. Take him with you," Toby ordered the other three men. They glanced at one another, then began edging away. "Hold it!" Toby snapped, pointing to the man in the puddle. "I told you to take him with you."

The men sullenly waded into the water to help their staggering friend. Toby crossed the sidewalk to the bartender. "You should be ashamed of yourself for letting that go on. Those ladies have as much right to express an opinion as you do to run a business."

"They're driving some of my customers away," the bartender growled.

"Then those customers probably have bad consciences,

buying liquor with money they should be using to support their families. In that case they have no business being in a saloon."

The bartender, muttering, went back inside, and the two women, resuming their protest, called out their thanks to Toby as he walked away. He doffed his hat in acknowledgment and had hardly put it back on when a large shop sign half a block ahead captured his attention. Suddenly he knew what to buy for Alexandra, and he wouldn't even have to set foot in a women's clothing store. With a lightness in his step, Toby continued down the street.

II

Adela Ronsard tried to control her trembling as she gazed out at the lights flickering past the train in the night. The second-class carriage was drafty, with a damp chill seeping through cracks around the sooty windows, but Adela was trembling in terror, not from the cold.

A courtesan whose clients included some of the wealthiest and most powerful men in Germany, Adela had made a foolish, perhaps fatal, mistake. She had been caught reading secret papers she found in the bedroom of a client named Hermann Bluecher, a feared official in German military intelligence. The butler had run to inform his master, and realizing that her life was in danger, Adela fled the house in panic.

With no family or friends on whom she could rely, and certain that the border crossings and major stations would all be watched, Adela grasped at the only recourse left to her. The secret papers she had read had mentioned an American captain named Blake, who lived outside Frankfurt am Main, and it seemed that he might protect her in exchange for the information. Without delaying to change clothes or pack a bag, Adela had hurried to the Berlin station and boarded the first train south, intending to throw herself on the American's mercy.

Now, as the train began slowing near the village of Grevenburg, her destination, Adela dreaded leaving the carriage, for the lighted car and other passengers gave her a sense of security. Danger could lurk in the dark night outside, for if Bluecher had guessed where she had gone, he could have dispatched someone to kill her. But she knew she had to leave the train and ask directions to the estate of Grevenhof, where, according to the papers, the American captain lived.

Men glanced at Adela as she stood and walked down the aisle toward the door, but she was used to such looks. The daughter of an Egyptian mother and a French father, she had a striking, dark beauty that set her apart from most German women. Priding herself on being a courtesan rather than a simple whore, she dressed in stylish, expensive clothing.

The train almost stopped, then continued inching forward. Peering nervously out the windows, Adela noticed a freight train on the sidetrack, apparently waiting for the passenger train to pass. The carriage screeched to a standstill, and Adela climbed down the steps behind a young couple—villagers, from the looks of them. Steam swirled around the platform, and the couple disappeared into the darkness before Adela realized she should have asked them for directions. After glancing around the dimly lighted platform, she started toward the station office, where a railroad employee and an older woman were talking. Her train was already moving out of the station, and the sidetracked freight chugged into motion.

As if in a nightmare, a man hidden behind a baggage cart only yards away suddenly stood, lifted a pistol, and aimed it at her.

Adela screamed and ran toward the office. Smoke puffed from the pistol, but both her scream and the report of the weapon were lost in the noise from the departing trains. The bullet struck her shoulder, spinning her around. She struggled frantically to stay on her feet and reach the office.

The man fired again, and Adela felt a stabbing pain in her neck. Numbness seized her, and her legs collapsed under her. Even as she fell, she tried to will herself toward the lighted office. She saw the office door open, watched the stationmaster come out, look at her in astonishment, then shout at someone behind her. Adela tried to lift a hand to him, tried to call out, but she could not, and she knew that she was dying.

The butler came into the carpeted study with a telegram on a silver tray. Hermann Bluecher, who had spent the past hours waiting in unbearable suspense, wanted to leap up, snatch the envelope, and tear it open. But since he weighed over three hundred pounds and was not agile, he was forced to wait as patiently as he could while the butler crossed the room.

When the telegram was finally in his hands, Bluecher ripped it open and scanned it quickly, then settled back in his chair with a sigh of relief. The woman was French, so he had taken the logical precaution of alerting agents at the border crossings into France to watch for her. But after he reread the papers she discovered, it occurred to him that she might go to the American captain, and he took appropriate action. Now he was pleased that he had done so, for she had been found and executed at the Grevenburg railroad station.

Bluecher licked his dry lips. The past hours had been so nerve-racking that he had even lost his appetite—an extremely rare occurrence—but now it returned in full, ravenous force. "Bring me a repast," he ordered the waiting butler. "Quickly, man!"

The servant bowed and hurried out, and Bluecher reread the telegram in satisfaction. It had been foolish of him to leave the papers in his bedroom, he reflected, but such a small oversight was understandable, given his preoccupied state during the past days. The papers pertained to the most daring scheme he had ever devised, and he had been carrying them around constantly as he refined his plan of action.

Informants planted in key government offices had told Bluecher that the new head of German military intelligence—General Hans Fremmel, his direct superior—had suggested to Chancellor Bismarck that he, Bluecher, should be replaced as head of internal security. Worse still, Bismarck had agreed.

The suggestion had not been implemented because Bismarck and Fremmel were aware that Bluecher had powerful friends in the Reichstag and the bureaucracy, as well as in banking and industrial circles. Bismarck and Fremmel would doubtless make their move as soon as they could justify his dismissal by catching him red-handed at some shadowy or illegal activity.

Such an opportunity would probably present itself because Bluecher frequently pursued private projects contrary to government policy. Politicians such as Bismarck had to cater to the masses, whereas Bluecher proudly worked for what he viewed as the best interests of Germany. The results sometimes drew unfavorable publicity, which he directed elsewhere, but Bismarck and Fremmel were powerful enough to accuse him openly if he misstepped.

Bluecher had decided that the crisis called for extreme measures: Bismarck, then Fremmel, would have to be assassinated. Political turmoil and an international crisis might result, but that did not faze Bluecher. He would survive and thrive, as he had always done, and if he were very clever, he might himself take General Fremmel's place—or even Bismarck's.

The butler returned, carrying a tray laid out with a platter of finger-sized strudels and a mug of thick, sweet cocoa. Cramming the pastries into his mouth, Bluecher chewed rapidly, crumbs spilling from his lips. He gulped down half the cocoa, then reached for another strudel. As he chewed, a troubling thought occurred to him, and he snapped his fingers to stop the butler, who had started to leave. The man stepped back into the room and waited patiently until Bluecher finished chewing.

Sending an agent to Grevenburg had been an afterthought, and the agent was far from Bluecher's best man. The telegram had claimed success, but if that was not true there was a potential for trouble. Experience had taught Bluecher that the American army captain was not to be underestimated and that every eventuality must be guarded against.

"Tomorrow," he said after swallowing, "go to the police. Tell them that the woman who was here stole some expensive jewelry and then fled. Give them a full description of her, but tell them that I want no publicity. After all, the woman is a prostitute."

The butler bowed and left, and Bluecher, satisfied,

popped another pastry into his mouth. Even if the woman
had somehow survived, she would represent no danger to
him or his plan. No one would believe anything said
against an important government official by a prostitute
who was wanted by the police.

Gisela von Kirchberg was dreaming of Henry Blake,
and she smiled as she felt the touch of his lips on hers.
Then a noise caused her to wake up and open her eyes.
She was intensely disappointed to find that her lover was
not in bed beside her.

The lamp on her nightstand was turned low, illumi-
nating the photograph of Henry beside it and casting dim
shadows over the large, high-ceilinged room. Gisela sat
up, wondering what had disturbed her sleep, and was
slightly annoyed when she heard a horse stamp restlessly
in front of the mansion. It was the middle of the night—
certainly not a time for visitors—but thinking that it might
be Henry returning, she sprang out of bed.

Looking out the window to the drive below, Gisela
saw a wagon parked in front of the steps, and the butler
and another man were carrying some long, apparently
heavy object inside. That seemed odd, yet Gisela's dashed
hopes for her lover's return outweighed any curiosity she
might have felt.

Returning to the bed, Gisela picked up Henry's picture and gazed at it longingly. She replaced it carefully
and lay down, settling herself with her eyes on the picture. Faint noises came from downstairs, but she ignored
them. The next morning would be soon enough for her to
find what had been brought in the wagon.

Just when Gisela was drifting back to sleep, there was
a knock on the bedroom door, and it opened quietly.
"Madam Baroness?" her personal maid said in a soft,
apologetic voice.

"What is it?" Gisela asked, an edge to her voice.

"The stationmaster is here, madam," the maid replied. "He has brought a woman with him—a woman who
was shot at the station."

Thinking she had misunderstood, Gisela told the maid

to repeat what she had said, then interrupted impatiently before the woman had finished. "Why did he bring her *here*? This is a private house, not a hospital!"

"Perhaps it would be better for the stationmaster to explain, madam," the maid suggested.

Grumbling resentfully, Gisela donned her robe and slippers and stalked down the hall, with the maid at her heels. The sound of her footsteps wakened the baby in the nursery at the other end of the hall, but Gisela ignored her son's cries, which of late had become irritatingly frequent. "Let the nurse earn her keep," she muttered under her breath.

As she descended the wide marble staircase, she saw the white-haired stationmaster, along with several hastily dressed servants, hovering outside the drawing room off the entrance hall. The servants shrank back at her approach, and Gisela fairly pulled the stationmaster into the room with her. The household physician, Dr. Ian MacAlister, wearing only his nightshirt and trousers, was bent over a woman on a couch. One glance was enough to convince Gisela that the woman was not respectable—her skin looked ghoulish in contrast to heavy application of cosmetics. Her neck and shoulder were bandaged, but she appeared to be breathing normally.

The stationmaster was apologizing and trying to explain what had happened.

"Perhaps you misunderstood her," Gisela suggested when he had finished his incredible tale.

"No, Madam Baroness," the man quavered. "When the smelling salts awakened her, she spoke quite clearly. She said Captain Blake's name twice, then the name of your estate, Grevenhof."

"And you say she was shot? Who shot her?"

"I don't know. I—I didn't see him, Madam Baroness. My wife saw a man shoot the woman, then flee. A freight train was leaving for Frankfurt, and he probably climbed onto one of the cars."

Falling silent, Gisela glanced again at the woman on the couch. Despite her gaudy makeup, she was undeniably attractive—a sultry beauty. Moreover, she was young, probably about Henry's age, while Gisela herself was thirty-seven, uncomfortably close to forty.

Unreasoning jealousy swelled within her, but she suppressed it as Dr. MacAlister straightened and looked at her inquiringly.

"Who else knows about this?" she asked the station-master.

"Only my wife, Madam Baroness," the man answered. "No one else was at the station when it happened. I warned her not to tell anyone else. I know that you value your privacy, Madam Baroness."

"You did well. If anyone else, including the police, needs to know about this, I will tell them myself."

"I understand, Madam Baroness. The entire matter is already forgotten."

Gisela led him to the door. "I will express my gratitude in a concrete way within the next day or two. Good night and thank you."

After closing the door behind him, Gisela turned to the doctor. "In the future, remember that you are in my employ. If others are brought here, *I* will decide whether or not to treat them. Will she live?"

Although he was accustomed to Gisela's heavy-handed manner, the doctor was still taken aback. He returned her glare, his thick side-whiskers bristling and his chin jutting resentfully. "I believe so," he said in his Scots-accented German. "I've stopped the bleeding, but there's a bullet in her shoulder that I'll have to remove. And, madam, as to whom I will or will not treat, I took an oath that requires me to administer aid to whoever needs it."

"Then have them taken to the stables," Gisela returned furiously, "where they can bleed on the straw instead of on my furniture! Now remove the bullet, and do whatever else is necessary. I want that woman to live because I wish to question her!"

The doctor, the only household employee who would argue with her, also knew when to drop an issue. His face was flushed, but he merely bowed in reply, then stepped to the door and summoned servants to carry the woman out.

"Isn't she beautiful?" an older maid murmured as she watched from the doorway. "The poor dear, it must have been a lovers' quarrel. One of her sweethearts probably became so jealous of her that he—"

She broke off abruptly when she saw her employer's expression. Gisela stood by the door impatiently, then pushed it closed behind the departing procession.

Alone in the room, she stared at the wall without seeing it. While the circumstances behind the shooting remained a mystery to her, one essential fact was clear. Henry, her husband, the only man she had ever loved and whom she would die for, was involved in some way with the woman. And that was all that mattered to Gisela.

Before she met Henry Blake, she had never known real happiness. He had transformed her life and filled her with joy in countless ways, but Gisela was aware that her newfound happiness was not free.

Its price was jealousy, in the form of a gnawing doubt that constantly threatened to grow to raging force within her. In her mind, Gisela could still see the woman's olive skin . . . smooth, soft olive skin, and large, firm breasts, which she had no trouble envisioning Henry caressing.

Gisela clenched her fists, tightly trying to control her growing panic. What the maid had said had started a train of thought, leading to an almost logical explanation of why the woman had been shot.

Over a year before, Gisela recalled, someone had tried to shoot Henry, too, and that incident had also taken place at a railroad station. Until now, the reason for the shooting had remained a mystery. But couldn't it be possible, she wondered, that the man who was behind that attack was the same one responsible for shooting the woman tonight? If the woman and Henry were lovers, surely the gunman—the victim's husband or another lover?—would have been jealous. . . .

Trembling, Gisela tried to dismiss the thought. Yet it was clear that Henry, who was always scrupulously honest with her, had refrained from telling her something. He had never mentioned a dark-complexioned woman, even though the woman apparently knew him and where he lived.

She corrected herself: He had always been scrupulously honest with her *before*, but their relationship had recently changed. A few weeks before, she had yielded to Henry's concern about their son's status and agreed to a wedding. It had been a quick, simple ceremony, performed by the burgomaster of Grevenburg, and now they were married. Could Henry be taking her for granted already? she wondered.

The butler came into the room, started to speak, then, seeing her agitated state, quickly bowed and hurried out. Gisela barely noticed him. A lifetime of maintaining iron control had never prepared her to face the helpless terror of loving someone and losing him, and her reaction was to strike out in any way she could.

She ran to the fireplace mantel, where a number of expensive crystal vases were displayed. One by one she slammed them down onto the stone hearth, where they exploded into bits. As the shards from the last vase scattered, she darted to a large, ornate china cabinet against the wall. Gisela grasped the side of the cabinet and tried to rock the heavy piece of furniture off balance.

A few ornaments rattled, but the cabinet barely budged. Her determination fueled, Gisela slid her fingers behind the cabinet, put a foot against the wall, and pulled with all her strength. Ornaments spilled to the floor as the cabinet slowly leaned forward, then fell with an ear-splitting crash of splintering wood and breaking porcelain.

Gisela stalked into the hallway from where the butler and servants had wisely disappeared. Near the foot of the stairs was a thin wooden pedestal on which stood an exquisitely carved alabaster bust. Gisela grabbed the bust by the neck and heaved it across the entryway, threw the pedestal after it, then dashed up the stairs.

Little Peter was still wailing, and Gisela put her hands to her ears as she ran to the nursery. She opened the door to see the buxom nurse cuddling the baby. The woman cowered at Gisela's presence.

"Quiet that baby!" Gisela shouted, then slammed the door. The baby screamed even louder, and Gisela stalked down the hall toward a tall Chinese vase on a side table. Flailing out savagely, she sent the vase flying. It shattered

into dozens of pieces that went sliding along the polished
floor.

She finally stopped outside Henry's rooms, her anger
gradually fading and leaving in its wake suffocating despair. Half-blinded by tears, she walked into the sitting
room between their bedrooms, passed the couch where
the two of them frequently sat, and crossed to her bedroom. She climbed into bed, pulled the covers over her
head, buried her face in her pillow, and sobbed bitterly.

Henry Blake and Clifford Anderson were leaving the
new State, War, and Navy Department building in Wash-
ington, where a conference had just taken place to decide
Henry's future in the army. The meeting had pitted two
War Department officials, for whom Henry had worked
during recent years, against representatives from the State
Department, including Henry's close friend, Anderson.
Henry had met Clifford Anderson in Europe, where Henry
was now assigned as a military observer at the Mauser
Arms Works in Frankfurt.

As he walked down the wide flight of granite steps
leading to Pennsylvania Avenue, Henry was insensible to
the beauty of the southern spring day, for his mind was
still racing over the consequences of the meeting. Although Anderson and his colleagues had argued long and
hard to have Henry permanently assigned to the State
Department as a roving military attache—an intelligence
agent, it amounted to—the War Department had asserted
its authority over him and said no. In a matter of months—or
sooner, if a suitable field assignment became available—
Henry would have to leave Germany for duty as a line
army officer.

Pennsylvania Avenue teemed with midday carriage
traffic, and Henry and Anderson weaved their way across
the street toward Lafayette Park. An army lieutenant wearing a campaign hat with a cavalry insignia on it rode by
them, and Henry returned the offered salute. The rider's
rank and apparent age did not escape Henry's attention,
for although the man was clearly several years his senior,
Henry was already a captain. His select assignments in
Europe and the influential friends he had made there had

provided him with opportunities he never would have had in the peacetime army at home, and he wondered, as he often had done before, what paths his life might have followed if he had never left the United States.

Anderson must have sensed Henry's mood, for as they walked across the park toward a restaurant, the older man asked him if he was disappointed at the results of the meeting.

Henry admitted that he had mixed feelings. "As was mentioned, I'll never be promoted to senior grades without line experience. I feel an obligation to serve in a line unit. I had a close friend in the cavalry, a man named Reed Kerr, who was killed in combat not long ago. But I don't look forward to being separated from my wife and my son." Henry did not mention that Reed had been married to Cindy Holt, the woman he himself had once been engaged to. Although Henry loved Gisela and was enthralled by their tiny son, he often thought about Cindy and wondered how she was faring.

Anderson shook his head ruefully. "If you're saying that you feel obligated to serve in the cavalry to accept your share of danger, then I'll argue with you. Few cavalry officers, regardless of where they're stationed, undergo more danger than you have."

Henry patted his friend on the shoulder. "No, I wasn't saying that, Clifford. But line organizations are the real army, and that's what I went to West Point for. I feel an obligation to be a part of that."

"I understand," Anderson replied. "Still, you're uniquely qualified for what you're doing right now. What other army officer is a personal friend of the king of Spain? What other officer has a friend whose father-in-law is the head of German military intelligence? I only hope that the War Department is sensible enough not to stick you in some godforsaken post in the middle of nowhere and then forget about you."

Henry smiled weakly, realizing that that was indeed a possibility. He and Anderson fell silent as they entered the crowded restaurant. After they were seated and a waiter had taken their orders, Anderson suggested that

Henry check on ships scheduled to depart from Baltimore, if he was in a hurry to return to Germany.

Henry agreed that was a good idea, for he was indeed impatient to see Gisela and Peter. And after the tension-filled meeting and the noisy congestion of the restaurant, he reflected, it would also be a pleasure to get back to the sedate, serenely ordered atmosphere of Grevenhof.

The sun was rising over the harbor at Belfast, Maine, as a radiant Marjorie White stood talking on a pier with her friend, Cindy Kerr. Marjorie, who had achieved world-wide fame with her photographs of the Great Chicago Fire, was now setting out to fulfill what for many years had been her greatest ambition: She was embarking on a whaling vessel, to photograph its voyage to the South Pacific.

A gig from the whaler was waiting for her beside the pier, while the young sailor manning the oars shivered in the breeze sweeping Penobscot Bay. It was an unusually cold spring day, and the two women were huddled in thick coats. As they talked, Marjorie reflected that Cindy appeared to have adjusted to her husband's death a few months before. The young, attractive sister of Toby Holt was as vivacious as always, her blue eyes sparkling with life.

When Cindy warned about the dangers of the coming voyage, Marjorie had to laugh. "My greatest danger is being thrown overboard by the first mate," she confided in a low voice, so that the waiting sailor could not hear. "He's a horrid little man named Horatio Cade, and he was moved into the second mate's cabin so I could have his for my equipment and supplies. And of course he's superstitious about having a woman on board."

"Do sailors still believe that old tale?"

Marjorie shrugged. "Not all of them. Captain Tench is very pleasant and a perfect gentleman. So is the second mate, Ned Baylor."

"Well, I certainly hope the voyage will be enjoyable for you," Cindy said, still sounding concerned.

"I'm sure it will," Marjorie assured her. "And instead

of worrying about me, you'd better have a thought for yourself. The nightlife of Paris is notorious for ruining young, beautiful women."

It was Cindy's turn to laugh, and she waved a hand dismissively. "I intend to enjoy Paris, but I won't forget why I'm going there."

"No, I'm sure you won't," Marjorie said in all seriousness. For the past winter, Cindy had been studying with a retired newspaper etcher. She had been introduced to him by the famous American artist Gilbert Paige. Paige had taken Cindy on as a protégée after seeing her pencil sketches, and now she was going with him to Paris. "I just hope you get along with his Russian friend better than I do with Mr. Cade. What is her name?"

"Anna Ivanova Kirovna." Cindy looked uneasy. "Gilbert says she was one of the foremost etchers in the world, but she has never let anyone work with her."

"If you can't convince her to be your teacher, I'm sure you'll be able to find someone else in Paris to help you. And just think—you'll be there to enjoy part of the season."

Indeed, Cindy's ship would be leaving in a matter of days and was scheduled to arrive before the onset of summer. This would be her first trip to Europe, and Cindy had admitted to some misgivings about being so far from her family and friends. The independent Marjorie had reassured her; after all, Marjorie's husband, Ted Taylor, was all the way across the country in Nevada, and she would probably not see him again for years.

The two friends hugged each other tightly, then Marjorie picked up her carpetbag. "Well, the tide will soon be turning," she said, "so I'd better be on my way. I'll write when I can, and I'll send the letters to Toby's ranch in Portland. I'm sure you'll be settled in by then, and Janessa can forward my letters."

Cindy kissed her friend on the cheek. "I only wish I could write to you. Take care of yourself."

Marjorie got into the gig and looked back to wave as the sailor rowed toward the ship. In minutes, Cindy and the pier were left far behind, and Marjorie turned to face the sailor at the oars. Hardly more than a youth, he was gazing back forlornly at the town. Marjorie guessed it was his first voyage.

"My name is Marjorie White."

"Yes, ma'am. I'm David Cornell."

"Pleased to meet you, David. Is this your first voyage?"

"Yes, ma'am. I've been up and down the coast on small vessels, but this will be my first blue-water voyage."

Marjorie's attention was drawn to the ship, which loomed ahead. Named the *Beluga*, she was an impressively large sailing bark of presteam vintage, just over one hundred and fifty feet in length. With her towering rigging sooty from the brick-and-iron tryworks—the furnaces behind the foremast in which the whale oil was rendered from blubber—the whaler was easy to distinguish from the cargo vessels lying at anchor nearby.

The gig drew alongside a rope ladder hanging from the deck, and Cornell suggested to Marjorie that a bos'n's chair be rigged to lift her aboard.

"No, thank you," she replied, not wanting to start the voyage by asking for special consideration. "I'll climb the ladder."

The young sailor tried to steady the gig as Marjorie stood, shouldered her bag, and took hold of a rung; but when she made her first step and the ladder swayed perilously from under her, she wondered if she had made a mistake. Cornell quickly grabbed the bottom of the ladder and held it taut, politely averting his eyes as Marjorie's skirt lifted in the wind and she clambered on up.

The sailors were lounging in the waist of the ship as she stepped on board, and not one of them stood up to assist her. The thin and wiry first mate, his sharp features drawn in a dark scowl, was leaning against the rail nearby. Some two inches shorter than Marjorie, Horatio Cade tried to compensate for his lack of stature with a bull-like disposition and the voice of a foghorn. He roused several of the men to haul in and secure the gig.

"Captain Tench, sir," he turned and announced in a stentorian tone, "I beg to report that the entire ship's company has now mustered and is ready to put to sea. Our bad-luck lodestone has just heaved aboard."

The sailors laughed, and Marjorie reddened. Despite

the rancor in the first mate's voice, she knew she had to treat the remark as a joke and thus forced herself to smile. The captain, aft on the quarterdeck, winked at her approvingly and touched his cap. Marjorie bade him good morning and crossed to the companionway leading to her cabin.

The cabin, small to begin with, was so crowded with her equipment and supplies that she could hardly move about. Securely lashed down against the motion of the ship, the cases and crates were stacked to the ceiling. Marjorie squeezed around them, deposited her carpetbag on the tiny bunk, then went back out and climbed the ladder to the quarterdeck.

Isaac Tench, in his fifties and a veteran of many whaling voyages, was a tall, angular man, with a face leathery from decades of exposure to the elements. Affable and even-tempered, he had bowed to the inevitable with good grace when Marjorie prevailed upon the *Beluga*'s owner to provide her a berth on the whaler.

Tench chatted with Marjorie, asking her general questions about photography, but broke off in midsentence as the ship's timbers groaned and the vessel shifted noticeably. He went to the rail and looked down at the water. "Mr. Cade! The tide is ebbing. Let's weigh anchor, make sail, and stand out to sea!"

"Aye, aye, sir!" Cade roared. "Port watch, man the capstan! Starboard watch, into the rigging! Move yourselves! Move! Move!"

The ship suddenly came alive, with men scrambling up the shrouds and others stamping in unison around the capstan, singing a chantey while Cade bellowed orders. The bow anchor came free of the bottom with a jerk, and the ship started to drift in the seaward flow of the tide.

A quick string of orders was issued from the captain, then relayed by the mates in turn, but the terminology was meaningless to Marjorie. Her attention was riveted on the men high in the rigging. Clearly many were novices, hesitant and awkward as they edged out to the end of the yards to release the furled sails. Marjorie gasped as she saw David Cornell lose his footing and almost fall, but he caught himself just in time. Marjorie released her breath. To her chagrin, she realized that Cade had also observed the mishap, but he simply grumbled a curse and left David and the other young, inexperienced sailors to do the most perilous tasks in the rigging.

Sailors on other ships called out and waved as the *Beluga* passed them, her unfurling sails rumbling and snapping in the wind. On deck, lines of men chanted at the mates' bidding, hauling on the brace lines to trim the yards. A favorable breeze enabled the ship to make good headway down the bay, and Marjorie was able to relax as the young sailors descended from the rigging.

Her relief was short-lived, however, for Cade soon thundered more orders, all directed at the novices, who were forced to scurry aloft again and again to make some minor and seemingly unnecessary adjustment to the sails. By midday, when the cabin boy brought a plate of cheese and ship's biscuits to the quarterdeck, it was clear to Marjorie that Cade took cruel pleasure in tormenting the young sailors and forcing them to risk their lives. She thought it strange that Captain Tench either failed to notice or declined to interfere in the small man's brutality.

Marjorie was relieved, at least, to discover she was not prone to seasickness—as were some of the sailors—and by late afternoon, with the *Beluga* plowing through the rolling waves of the open sea, she joined Tench, Cade, and Baylor in the officers' mess for dinner.

The fare was plain but substantial, a thick stew over rice, and at first Marjorie enjoyed the meal, for she was hungry, and Tench and Baylor, if not Cade, seemed to be in good humor. Baylor, a stout, jolly-looking Irishman, expressed interest in photography, a subject that Marjorie never grew tired of discussing.

As Baylor grew expansive, Cade fixed him with a steely glare, causing him to fall silent and concentrate on his food. Cade and Tench began discussing needed repairs and other matters having to do with the ship, and Marjorie, like Baylor, ate in silence.

When the meal was over, the cabin boy came back in to refill the tin cups with coffee and gather up the plates.

Captain Tench remarked in satisfaction about the smooth passage out of Penobscot Bay. "I only wish," he said wistfully, "that we could weather Cape Horn in as handy a manner."

Cade grunted sourly and looked across the table at Marjorie. "With our sure source of ill fortune aboard, the winds will undoubtedly be contrary every foot of the way."

Marjorie, having watched Cade tormenting the young sailors since early morning, was unable to keep silent. "As far as the younger crewmen are concerned, Mr. Cade," she said tartly, "the most dread source of bad luck could bring them no greater misfortune than being commanded by you. My heart was in my throat all day as I watched you place them in dire peril for no apparent reason beyond your own cruel satisfaction."

Cade's eyes grew wide, and Baylor pushed his seat back, looking at her in astonishment and alarm. The cabin boy, who had come back in for something, turned and fled in terror. Only Captain Tench, calmly sipping his coffee, seemed unaffected by what Marjorie had said.

Cade leaped up from the table, his face crimson. "I will be greatly obliged," he hissed between clenched teeth, "if you will leave the crew and my affairs to me! Kindly attend to your own business, *Mrs.* White, which is bringing bad luck to this ship and all who sail in her!" He wheeled and stamped out, slamming the door behind him. Baylor stood and quietly followed him. The captain continued placidly sipping his coffee, seemingly oblivious of the incident.

At length he put his cup down and stood up. "Mrs. White," he said as calmly as if he were talking about the weather, "you must get along with Mr. Cade during the voyage."

"But how can I! You saw what he was doing as well as I did, and I can't—"

She broke off as the captain lifted a hand and shook his head. "Mr. Cade doesn't try to tell me what course to set, how to search for whales, or anything else to do with my duties. And I don't try to tell him his duties because he's the best first officer I've ever had." He paused at the door. "Make peace with Mr. Cade and try to get along with him during the voyage." He went out and closed the door behind him.

Abashed, Marjorie sat back in her chair and stared into space. What she had said to Cade, she now realized, had been unwise, but to apologize was out of the question.

As she sat there, a chilling thought possessed her: Cade might even be so inhumanly cruel that he actually *wanted* to make one of the young sailors fall from the rigging and kill himself. Then he could blame the mishap on her, citing it as evidence that she had brought bad luck to the ship.

Marjorie feared that a very long, difficult voyage lay ahead.

III

Chopping at brush to widen a trail through the forest, Frank Woods restrained his temper as he listened to the four lumberjacks with him grumbling as they worked. His years as a logging camp foreman had taught him to be judicious in exerting authority over lumberjacks.

Standing six feet, six inches tall in his bare feet, and with a muscular frame to match his height, Frank was fully capable of backing his authority. Yet lumberjacks, in his experience, were a breed apart. Regardless of how much they were being paid, or how easy the work was, if they believed too much authority was being exerted over them, they would pack up and leave.

Frank knew they were grumbling now because they considered the task before them frivolous. In fact, the reason he was working alongside them was to get them to do this particular job. The lumberjacks respected him and usually completed his bidding, but there were limits.

After a while, the men's complaining became too much even for Frank to bear. He straightened and glared at them. "If you'd put as much effort into your axes as you do into your jawbones," he barked, "we'd get twice as much done! Now shut up, and let's get this work finished!"

"Work?" a man named Kelly shot back. "Making a road for horses to run back and forth through the woods ain't work! This is something for a little kid to do, not men!"

"Do I look like a little kid?" Frank demanded, dropping his ax and squaring his shoulders. "If I can do this, you can too!"

An imperturbable man named Grubbs, short but built

35

like a gorilla, shifted the wad of tobacco in his mouth and spat. "We're on the wrong trail anyways."

"Why do you say that?" Frank asked.

Grubbs waved in the direction from which they had come. "That bank on t'other side of the curve there. A horse couldn't get down that without going heels over teakettle."

"No, we're on the right trail," Frank told him, picking up his ax. "Let's get this section done, then we'll call it a day."

"All right, but we're on the wrong trail," Grubbs insisted as he recommenced chopping at brush.

Frank gritted his teeth and let the remark pass, knowing it was useless to argue. The other men grumbled but continued working, and Frank tried to set an example by increasing his pace.

Actually, Frank detested the work as much as the lumberjacks. But the trail was being cut for Alexandra Woodling, which made all the difference to Frank. His admiration for the young woman grew with each passing day.

When Frank first met Alexandra, he concluded that Toby Holt had finally found the right woman. She had all the vitality of youth, plus the charm and poise of a woman twice her age. Of course, Frank had been a bit embarrassed when his thirteen-year-old daughter, Lucy, had begun following Alexandra around—Alexandra was, after all, in mourning, and he respected her privacy—but Alexandra had quickly become fond of the girl and didn't seem to mind.

The only drawback was that Lucy, in emulation of Alexandra's habit of wearing riding breeches, had started wearing trousers, which she had sewn herself. Frank didn't approve of this, but he tried to keep an open mind. Lucy, always painfully shy, had developed such a severe stammer that she rarely tried to speak, and Frank harbored the hope that the newfound friendship with a young woman she admired would help her overcome the impediment. At the isolated camp, Lucy had few enough friends of her own sex.

Frank and the lumberjacks chopped brush until they had worked their way down into a shallow dell, where a large fallen tree blocked the path. Alexandra had blazed the trail for them, putting red paint on trees, bushes, and other objects she wanted removed and white paint on obstacles she wanted left in place. The tree trunk rested several feet off the ground where it blocked the trail, and although it appeared much too high for any horse to jump, there was a spot of white paint on it.

The lumberjack named Willard eyed the trunk and put down his ax. "Well, I seen Miss Woodling's horses, and a body could might near fly a kite under their bellies. But not even one of them animals is going to jump over that."

"Of course not," Grubbs agreed, and spat tobacco juice. "This has been the wrong trail all the time."

"I've been out at a work camp," Kelly grumbled, "and I would've stayed there if I'd knowed I was coming back to this."

The fourth lumberjack, Lars Jacobsen, took off his cap and scratched his head. "Frank, that young lady must've got her paints mixed up. That tree is a lot higher than any of those jumps you constructed for her at camp."

Frank had built a fenced training and exercise course at Alexandra's request when she first arrived at the camp. "Yes, but that's different. That's for daily workouts, and this is for giving the horses a good hard run. That tree *is* awful high, though. Maybe you're right. Let's leave it for now, and I'll ask her to come and take another look at it."

"No, let's finish up this foolishness and be done with it!" Kelly objected. "You men cut those roots and branches, and I'll go get a yoke of oxen to drag that tree out of the way."

"That'll be nothing but a waste of time," Grubbs pointed out. "We're on the wrong trail."

"Grubbs, that's enough!" Frank wheeled on the man and pointed at the white paint on the tree. "If this is the wrong trail, how did that get there?"

Grubbs shrugged. "Maybe a big sea gull flew over from the lake."

Willard and Jacobsen laughed, but Frank was not amused. Kelly started walking away. "I'll go get a yoke of oxen."

"Kelly, come back here!" Frank shouted. "I said we'll leave this tree for now, and that's what we're going to do!"

Kelly called back stubbornly that the tree should be removed, and Frank, struggling with his temper, insisted that it would remain. Jacobsen and Willard joined in the argument, while Grubbs sat down on a stump and watched.

The shouting match was ended by the sound of hoofbeats, and the men turned to look as Alexandra Woodling rode around a curve in the trail they had cut. She was wearing her usual riding breeches, knee boots, and black jacket and cap. Frank's daughter, wearing baggy trousers, followed her on a saddle horse, which looked like a pony compared to the sleek, muscular chestnut Alexandra was riding.

Alexandra waved a greeting as she controlled the spirited hunter, which fought against the bit. The young woman's serious expression, Frank knew, was partly due to her grief over the recent loss of her father; but it also indicated a strong personality. He suspected that Toby would have his hands full with this woman.

The four lumberjacks, who were not accustomed to the company of women—certainly not a young, exceptionally comely one like Alexandra, whose clothing did little to conceal her feminine curves—were virtually spellbound.

At last, following Frank's lead, they doffed their caps, all of them grinning like schoolboys. Reining up, Alexandra touched her riding crop to her cap.

"I can't tell you how grateful I am that you men are doing this for me," she praised them in her sweetly musical Southern tones.

"We're more than glad to, miss," Kelly blurted.

"That's right," Grubbs added, "even though this is the wrong trail."

"We was talking about this," Willard said, pointing to the fallen tree. "We think Frank is mixed up on the colors you used to mark things, miss. You want that tree cleared out of the way, don't you?"

Alexandra nimbly dismounted from the tall horse and tethered it to a sapling. The high-spirited animal stamped and snapped at her, but she pushed its head away as if she were dealing with a bothersome puppy. She stepped to the fallen tree, to gauge its height accurately.

"No, let's leave this, please. It's an excellent natural." She turned and counted her steps as she paced some twenty yards from the tree. "From this side, I'll begin the approach here. From the other side, the approach can be shorter, since it's slightly downhill."

Frank frowned. "Are you sure? That tree looks mighty high off the ground."

Alexandra stepped to her horse. "Yes, I'm positive. I'll show you. Lucy, dear, move your horse back so I won't frighten him."

Lucy guided her horse into the trees as Alexandra sprang lightly onto the saddle and rode back up the trail, disappearing around the curve. Frank and the lumberjacks backed away from the jump.

A moment later, hoofbeats sounded and the horse shot back into sight, leaning into the turn in a headlong run. Sod and leaves flew up from its pounding hooves, and Alexandra leaned forward in the saddle. At the approach, the horse lengthened its stride, its muscles bulging as it gathered itself. Then it leaped.

With legs folded under it, the horse soared over the fallen tree, landing in a run on the other side. Brush and saplings thrashed as Alexandra stopped and turned the animal. Then it thundered back down the trail and bounded over the tree from the other side.

As the horse landed, with Alexandra balanced lightly on the small saddle, the men burst into cheers and applause. Alexandra reined up, stroked the panting horse's neck, then touched her hat in acknowledgment. "Thank you. My horse likes that jump, and so do I. You men are making wonderful progress, and I appreciate it." She gave them a dazzling smile. "Well, Lucy and I had better get home. Thank you again."

The men waved as Alexandra and Lucy rode away. The short visit had altered the atmosphere in the same way that a sudden, cool breeze changes a sweltering summer afternoon into a pleasant, sunny day. The lumberjacks chatted cheerfully as they picked up their axes and walked around the fallen tree.

"Just how long a trail does Miss Alexandra want cleared, Frank?" Kelly asked.

"It joins another trail that loops back to where we started," Frank replied. "All told, it's about fifteen miles, with about ten left to go."

"That sounds fine to me," Kelly said, and Jacobsen and Willard nodded in agreement. "Anyway, this is a lot easier than felling oaks."

"It suits me, too," Grubbs pronounced, looking around. "You know, Frank, it could be that this is the right trail after all."

The first buds of spring lent a tinge of green to the trees lining a road outside Portland, Oregon. Eulalia Blake, an attractive, gray-haired woman of fifty-six, was looking absently out the carriage window, but the scenery was the last thing on her mind. Instead, her thoughts raced ahead to the carriage's destination, the horse ranch owned by her son, Toby Holt.

"I've heard so much about those horses," she said, "I should have long since gone to see them."

The other passenger, her husband, Major General Leland Blake, nodded as he puffed on his pipe. His white hair and tanned face gave him a distinguished look, fitting for the commander of the Army of the West, a post he had held for many years. He and Eulalia lived at Fort Vancouver, across the Columbia River from Portland, in a house provided by the government.

"When I saw Clara Hemmings last week," Eulalia continued, "she told me that hay was being shipped from California for them. Clover hay, the kind dairy farmers feed their cattle!"

"I'll bet that's costing a pretty penny," Lee observed. "Did Clara have anything new to say about her marriage plans? Toby is going to have to find someone else to keep house for him and look after Timmy and Janessa."

"Clara won't leave until Toby finds someone to replace her," Eulalia assured him. "That woman is a gem, and Toby's going to have a hard time finding someone to fill her shoes."

Lee murmured agreement, and Eulalia looked out the window again, lost in thought. The horses that had recently been delivered to her son's ranch had created a sensation when they arrived in Portland. They were thoroughbred hunters and show horses—finicky, expensive breeds that were rarely seen in the Northwest. They had even been accompanied by a handler, a man named Jonah Venable. But Eulalia was less concerned about the horses than she was about the reason for their presence.

Alexandra Woodling, who owned the horses and had raised and trained them, was a distant relative of Eulalia's from Kentucky. Months before, when Toby had gone there to settle some trouble at the Woodling horse farm, Eulalia began to suspect the existence of a budding romance between him and Alexandra. Since then, the girl's father had died, and Toby had taken Alexandra to his logging camp in Wisconsin, in order to help her recover from her grief.

At the same time, Toby had sent most of her horses to his ranch, which suggested to Eulalia more than a passing romance. For years, ever since her son's wife Clarissa had died, Eulalia had encouraged Toby to remarry, if only for the sake of his children, who needed a mother. But she had not expected him to fall in love with a teenage girl, who as far as Eulalia could tell had no qualifications whatsoever to care for children.

Indeed, Alexandra had grown up without any female tutelage, raised as she was by her widowed father. Her only apparent interest was horses, Eulalia thought, which certainly ill suited her for raising Toby's daughter, Janessa, who was about five years Alexandra's junior, and precocious and stubborn in the bargain. Trained by her mother in herbal medicine, Janessa planned to be a doctor. In addition to the instruction she received from her mentor, Eulalia's old friend Dr. Robert Martin, the girl needed guidance on how to be a lady. And as for Timmy . . . Eulalia sighed in frustration.

If circumstances had been different, Eulalia would have been extremely pleased with the budding romance. With a Bradford mother and a Kentucky aristocrat father, Alexandra had a lineage as impressive as her thoroughbreds'. But that was not Eulalia's overriding concern. While she felt deeply sympathetic toward Alexandra in her bereavement, Eulalia's top priority was the welfare of her grandchildren.

Suddenly a horse was beside the carriage, and its rider, none other than Janessa, leaned down and looked in the window. "Hello, Grandmama, Grandpapa."

Lee stuck his head out the window and called to the driver to stop. Janessa dismounted, tied her horse to the rear of the carriage, and joined her grandparents, explaining that she was on her way back from Dr. Martin's house.

Looking at Janessa, Eulalia felt a pang of nostalgia. Although the girl's mother had been a Cherokee Indian, the Holt family traits predominated in the child's face, and she bore a remarkable resemblance to Cindy, Eulalia's grown daughter. Tall for her age, Janessa had intelligent blue eyes, sandy brown hair, and delicate but determined features. Unlike Cindy, Janessa was not talkative, and Eulalia usually had to draw information out of her through tactful questioning. Timmy was always a good subject to start with.

The last time Eulalia had seen the boy, he was wildly excited about a velocipede that one of his schoolmates had acquired. A kind of bicycle with cranks directly on the front wheel, velocipedes weren't popular in Portland, where the streets were too rough for such an unstable conveyance. Timmy's friend was the only one in town who had one, as far as Eulalia knew, which worried her, because Timmy had a knack for getting himself into dangerous situations.

"Your brother seemed quite taken with his friend's velocipede the last time I spoke with him," she commented.

"Yes, ma'am. He still is."

"It's caused me no small concern, Janessa. Has he gone to the boy's house and ridden on it?"

"Oh, no, ma'am."

"I'm relieved to hear that. Has Clara forbidden him to go to the boy's house?"

"No, ma'am. The boy doesn't have it anymore."

"Oh, I see. Did his father sell it to someone else?"

"No, ma'am. His mother chopped it up with an ax."

Eulalia exchanged a surprised glance with Lee. "Why?"

"Because the boy fell and broke an arm while he was riding it. But Dr. Martin said he'll be all right."

"Well, I'm pleased to hear that." In truth, Eulalia was more relieved for her grandson than for his friend. "I hope the lesson wasn't lost on Timmy."

Janessa, however, did not confirm this last statement, and with a sigh, Eulalia dropped the subject and looked out the window as the ranch came into view. An impressive, rambling structure, part brick and part clapboard, it had expanded from a humble beginning as a log cabin that her first husband had built for her many years ago, when they came to Oregon with the original settlers. The saplings she planted in the yard back then had grown to large shade trees during the years she was bringing up Toby and Cindy.

Clara Hemmings, the attractive young widow who served as housekeeper, came out on the porch as the carriage drew up. Janessa jumped out and took her horse to the barn, and Lee and Eulalia accepted an invitation to come inside for coffee.

The couple seated themselves in the parlor, where Eulalia and Clara discussed the topic that lately had absorbed both of them—Alexandra Woodling.

"I realize your awkward position, Clara," Eulalia said, in reference to Clara's plans to remarry, "and I wish I could tell you more. But Toby's letters haven't mentioned what he intends to do."

"Considering that the young woman's father just died," Clara replied with her usual good sense, "any delay on your son's part is understandable. I'm more than happy to wait and see what happens. My oldest son, Clayton, is very interested in those new horses and has been helping Mr. Venable with them."

"I do hope he's careful. Janessa says those horses can be dangerous—"

The back door slammed, and Eulalia's grandson Timmy came running into the room. He was a tall, muscular boy of seven, with characteristic Holt blue eyes and sandy brown hair. He was wearing old clothes that were covered with grease and grime, and Eulalia kept him at arm's length as she kissed him affectionately.

As usual, Timmy was bursting with enthusiasm for the latest project he was working on, and he took Lee's hand and urged him to come look at his road locomotive. Eulalia's smile vanished. Toby had bought the huge steam-powered machine for the boy to tinker with, and even though it would probably never run, Eulalia had no doubt that it was dangerous.

Having finished their coffee, Eulalia and Lee followed Timmy out the back door. Eulalia immediately noticed two large, new barns among the outbuildings, while Lee exclaimed in admiration at what he saw in the corrals.

Alexandra's thoroughbreds were impossible to mistake for the ranch's customary quarter horses. Much larger and more muscular, they gleamed as they pranced about, their necks arched and their tails lashing. One in particular, a giant, jet-black stallion, caught Lee's eye. Temporarily forgetting the road locomotive, he went to the corral for a better look. He was joined by a wiry man of about sixty who was dressed as a stable groom. Eulalia assumed he was Jonah Venable.

Eulalia had heard that Venable had brought his lady friend to Portland with him—a widowed seamstress named Mabel Seeley—which wasn't exactly proper, since they weren't even engaged. It was also said that Mrs. Seeley supported a ne'er-do-well half brother by the name of Luther Bingham, who spent most of his time in Portland's taverns. Venable himself, however, looked respectable enough.

Eulalia's attention shifted to the horses. To her, they looked dangerously high-spirited. The stallion seemed almost wild, and indeed, as she watched, it suddenly charged the side of the corral where Lee and Venable were standing, causing Eulalia to gasp in fright. Snapping its bared teeth viciously, the animal darted away at the last second, kicking and plunging.

Timmy tugged at his grandmother's hand to get her to join the others at the corral, but the beast's display of temper made Eulalia hesitate. Lee beckoned her forward, however, and introduced her to Jonah Venable.

"I've never seen such a ferocious-looking horse," Eulalia said after shaking the man's hand.

Jonah chuckled. "Turco is just showing off, ma'am. He's lonely for Miss Alexandra."

"You mean Miss Woodling actually *rides* that stallion?"

Again Jonah seemed amused. "Ma'am, the horse ain't been foaled yet that she can't ride. I've spent most of my life around horses, but I've never seen man or woman who can handle them the way Miss Alexandra does. She was riding with a hunt club when she was twelve, and she won her first cross-country race that same year. And she's just as good in a show as in a race."

Eulalia had dozens of questions she wanted to ask, but a moment later they were joined by the ranch foreman, old Stalking Horse. Nearly seventy years old, Whip Holt's longtime Indian companion had been the foreman of the ranch for decades. With him was his ward, a strapping youth named White Elk, who would someday succeed him as foreman.

The men continued talking about the thoroughbreds, and Timmy pulled at Eulalia's hand, urging her to go look at his road locomotive. Not exactly eager to choose between the lesser of two evils, Eulalia followed him. They went into the barn where the machine was kept, and a slim man of medium height stood up from the bench where he had been sitting, his chin resting on his cane grip, apparently deep in thought. Calvin Rogers was a former hot-air balloonist who had been seriously injured in an unsuccessful ascent at the local county fair some two years before. He had been brought to the ranch, where he had become Timmy's constant companion and unofficial tutor.

He leaned on his cane as he tipped his hat in greeting. Eulalia inquired after his health, but her attention was riveted on the road locomotive, which was hard to ignore because of its sheer size. Designed as a replacement for dray horses, the gigantic, steam-driven machine had a fresh coat of paint and, to Eulalia's dismay, looked in good condition.

Her fears were somewhat eased, however, when Calvin began listing the problems with the machine, implying that it still needed considerable repairs. "And there's also something wrong with the steering," he concluded. "But it's fulfilling its purpose, because Timmy has learned a lot from it and enjoys working on it."

The boy's determined gaze confirmed Calvin's words, and as Lee and the other men came in, looking at the machine and talking about it, Eulalia, still feeling troubled, stepped back outside to have a look at the new barns. A quick inspection left her with the opinion that Alexandra's thoroughbreds lived in more comfort than did some of the residents of Portland.

She went to rejoin the men, who were now gathered near a new, smaller outbuilding with a sturdy-looking stone foundation. There was a padlock on the door, and as Stalking Horse produced a key from a cord around his neck, he explained with a smile why the building was kept locked.

"All our hands are honest," he said, his eyes twinkling, "but I don't see any point in tormenting them. According to Jonah, there are close to three hundred gallons of bourbon in the cellar under this building."

"That's right," Jonah confirmed. "Miss Alexandra's family has distilled its own spirits for three generations now."

"Indeed?" Eulalia's interjection was more an accusation than a question. "Well, why is it here?"

"That's what Toby wanted," Stalking Horse answered, unlocking the door. "The bourbon was shipped here, along with the furniture and everything else from Fair Oaks."

Reflecting that her son's arrangements for Alexandra indeed appeared permanent, Eulalia stepped into the building. The room was taken up by a still, with a narrow staircase descending against the foundation to the right. Jonah poured a splash of brownish liquor from a demijohn on a bench and handed it to Lee Blake.

Lee tasted it and raised his eyebrows in surprise. "That's remarkably smooth," he observed. He waved off another serving.

"It should be," Jonah said. "This here was made by Miss Alexandra's granddad. But there are people who think that Miss Alexandra's will be just as good, in time." Lifting the demijohn, he turned to Eulalia. "Could I offer you a nip, ma'am?"

"No, thank you," Eulalia replied crisply. "I don't drink whiskey." Having signaled Lee with her eyes that she was ready to leave, she followed him to the house to say good-bye to Janessa and Clara.

Later, as the carriage made its way back along the road to Portland, Eulalia was unusually subdued. She had visited the ranch in order to ease her anxieties on several counts, but she was coming away even more worried than before. It appeared that her grandchildren were going to be placed in the care of a madcap girl whose only interests and talents consisted of controlling unruly horses and making bourbon whiskey.

"Lee," she said, breaking the silence, "I don't want to jump to conclusions, but I'm concerned about how things seem to be working out."

"I know," Lee said sympathetically. "We don't have all the facts yet, however, and it would be typical of Toby simply to be assisting a young woman who needs his help."

Eulalia chose not to argue, but her common sense warned her that trouble lay ahead, and no amount of reassurance would convince her otherwise.

Late that same evening, Luther Bingham sat in a crowded, noisy waterfront tavern, at a table with half a dozen other men. As usual, he was penniless, but he had used his wits to get himself treated to enough drinks to create a euphoric glow within him. The others at the table were seamen and laborers—all of them, to Luther's mind, ignorant and oafish. By keeping them distracted with his tall tales and absenting himself from the table at strategic moments, he had shared several bottles of rum without buying a single drink.

Over the years, Luther had perfected the technique, but it never worked more than once or twice with the same group. Now, as a bottle made its rounds once again, he held his glass out to be refilled. It was, but a burly sailor across the table, whose face was scarred and disfigured, eyed him narrowly. "Say, you haven't bought a bottle yet, matey," he grumbled.

"Indeed, I haven't," Luther admitted readily. "I'll get the next one." He drained his glass and put it down, then acted surprised as he felt his pockets. "I must have left my wallet at home."

Several men glared at him. "That's a likely excuse," said the sailor.

Luther stood, a bit unsteadily, and summoned an offended expression. "Now, what sort of tone is that to take? I thought we were friends here, enjoying one another's company."

"The company is good," the man retorted, "but rum is always better. We've provided our share of both, and we expect you to do the same."

"I intend to," Luther said with conviction. "Do I look like a man who can't pay his own way? I'll go for my wallet and return directly."

His self-assurance, combined with the neat, expensive-looking suit his sister, Mabel, had made for him, eased the men's suspicions. They resumed their conversation as Luther unhurriedly left the tavern.

Walking along the street, he thought about going into another tavern but dismissed the idea. Portland, a bustling port city, was much better than Lexington had been for using his wits to get liquor; there were new faces in the Portland taverns each day. But in order to avoid trouble with the proprietors, he had to use judgment, which meant purchasing an occasional bottle when he could get money from his sister.

It was still early in the evening for him, and Luther was reluctant to leave the waterfront district, where the atmosphere was noisy and cheerful. At home, nothing but accusing looks from his sister awaited him, and he was in no mood for that. He decided to walk in the direction of the downtown area, although he had no specific destination in mind.

Soon the pleasant glow from the rum began to fade, and as always, Luther was assailed by guilt over his purposeless life. During such reflective moments, he had a vague desire to find some meaningful goal for himself, but he tried to avoid thinking about it. In fact, for the past five years, ever since the day his entire future had crumbled around him, Luther had tried to avoid thinking at all.

Back then, he had been a schoolteacher in the small town of Cedar Flats, Kentucky, and had been reasonably content with his life. But then he had met Melissa Thompson, a stunningly beautiful girl of sixteen with whom he fell desperately in love. Unfortunately, Melissa's father had been pressuring her to marry a friend of his, a middle-aged widower who owned a neighboring farm.

Melissa had been as opposed to the match as was Luther, and they made plans to elope. A few days beforehand, however, nature had taken its course, and as luck would have it, Melissa's father caught them expressing their passions in the barn. Luther had been quietly fired from his job, and Melissa had been forced to marry her next-door neighbor.

Rumors circulated widely about the reason why the young schoolteacher had been fired, making it impossible for Luther to find another teaching position—but that had meant nothing to him. Tortured by visions of his Melissa trapped in a loveless marriage with a man her father's age, he had found life almost unbearable. He returned to his half-sister's house in Lexington, took up drinking, and fell into an aimless existence.

At first, his experience in Cedar Flats had been too painful for him to talk about, and then other reasons arose that had prevented him from confiding in Mabel about it. She and Jonah Venable had urged him to find a job and sort himself out, and gradually their pleas turned into reproaches. Embittered and increasingly dependent on liquor, Luther had ignored them.

Now, as he walked along a quiet, dark street in the deserted business district, Luther thought about going home and trying to get some money from Mabel. He knew she was short herself, however, and he began reconsidering his decision not to go into another tavern. While caution would be necessary, and encountering former companions of the evening was always a danger, he longed to lose himself in the noisy conviviality of a public house.

Luther noticed he was across the street from Horace Biddle's general store. He had been in the store just the other day, to get something for Mabel, and had noticed a shelf behind the counter that was filled with bottles of liquor. A couple of bottles of good whiskey would make him more than welcome at the table he had left a short time before, and other bottles could be stashed away for future use.

Luther hesitated and looked at the store. While during the past five years he had done innumerable things that bordered on being illegal, he had never taken that final step of breaking the law. No one was around, however, and still somewhat befuddled by the rum he had drunk, Luther crossed the street to take a closer look at the store.

In the dark doorway, he was completely hidden from anyone who happened to look along the street. There was no padlock on the door, which meant that it was fastened on the inside with a bolt. Luther took out his pocketknife and slid the blade between the door and the jamb.

When the blade touched the bolt, he told himself he was simply seeing if he could open the door, as if it were an abstract exercise. He pressed down on the knife and slid it slowly toward him, to turn the rounded bolt. It turned, making a soft sound as the catch came out of its slot. He began working the blade side to side, edging the bolt out of the ring on the doorjamb.

In only a few seconds the door opened soundlessly on well-oiled hinges, and then Luther was inside the store.

His conscience spoke sternly, but the whiskey, only a few yards away, spoke louder.

He was walking softly down an aisle when he noticed light coming around a door at the rear of the store and heard a movement in the back room. At almost the same moment he bumped into a barrel of garden implements, which tumbled over with a deafening clatter. The door at the rear of the store flew open, revealing a man silhouetted in the light.

"Put up your hands or I'll shoot!" the man commanded.

Instinctively, Luther backed toward the door, but he tripped over a rake. As he stumbled, a pistol fired with a thunderous roar, and a bullet struck his shoulder and knocked him flat on his back. In panic, he leaped up and ran out the door.

After he had run a block, the heavy numbness in his shoulder turned into a throbbing, burning pain. He pressed a handkerchief to his shoulder and paused to catch his breath in a dark alley. Luther, completely sober, was appalled by what he had done. He also realized that he was seriously wounded and would inevitably be identified as the one who had broken into the store. His mouth went dry, and sweat beaded his brow.

The shame and remorse that swelled within him were as intense as the pain in his shoulder. Yet as much as he needed help, Luther knew he could not tell Mabel what he had done. That left only Jonah Venable. Jonah disliked him, of course, but Luther was sure that Mabel's friend would feel obliged to help. Clutching his shoulder, he hurried down a back street toward the road that led to the Holt ranch.

In a few minutes he had left the outskirts of the city behind and felt safe from pursuit. Being apprehended by the police was now the least of his worries. Blood was oozing down his left side and had already soaked his shirt to the waist, and he was becoming light-headed, stumbling frequently as he weaved down the rutted road. He fought the dizziness, but his legs were like rubber, and every step grew more difficult.

It seemed that hours had passed when Luther's knees

folded beneath him. He fell painfully on his shoulder but managed to crawl off the road and prop himself against a tree. Excruciating pain threatened to make him lose consciousness, but Luther fought it, and after a minute or two he summoned his strength, rose, and tried to get back to the road. He staggered away from the tree, going in the wrong direction as the world spun. Then the ground abruptly dropped away, and he slid down a steep bank. Darkness closed in on him.

IV

While riding to school the next morning, Janessa Holt was lost in thought about her brother. After her conversation with her grandmother the previous day, she had cornered Timmy and talked to him seriously and at length about velocipedes. With considerable difficulty, she persuaded him to abandon the idea of making one—an objective she had not mentioned to her grandmother.

Such a success with Timmy was rare indeed, and consequently Janessa was trying to think of a way to reward him. She recalled that he had talked about wanting to make friends with an inventor who lived on the outskirts of Portland, a man with the improbable name of Rufus Gooch. Calvin Rogers, however, had told her that such a friendship was unlikely, since inventors were secretive by nature, and Gooch was no exception.

Thoughts of how to approach Mr. Gooch were running through Janessa's mind when, by chance, she caught sight of what looked like a broad smear of blood on the bark of a birch tree bordering the road. Her first thought was that the blood was from an animal that had been wounded by a hunter, but she had never seen anyone hunting in the area. Recalling a terrifying experience two years earlier involving Timmy and a bear, Janessa looked around cautiously as she reined up. Calvin had driven by there only a few minutes earlier, taking Timmy and the Hemmings children to school, and she knew they would have returned to warn her if they had seen anything dangerous. And her horse was calm, which it would not be if it smelled a bear or other large animal.

Janessa dismounted and inspected the area around

the tree. A few yards away, brush at the edge of a dry gully was crushed down. Still cautious, she looped her horse's reins over a branch, advanced a few more steps, and peered down into the creek bed. Her heart suddenly pounding, she realized that the crumpled form lying there was Luther Bingham.

Janessa slid down the bank and rolled the man onto his back. At first she thought he was dead, for the left side of his coat was soaked with dried blood and his face was pallid; but a quick check revealed a faint pulse. After finding the wound and seeing that it had stopped bleeding, she scrambled back up the bank and jumped onto her horse.

At a headlong gallop, it took her only a few minutes to reach the ranch, where she found Jonah working in the corral. She shouted to him, explaining what she had found.

Once he had overcome his astonishment, Jonah wasted no time. He began hitching a team to a wagon while Janessa ran to get Stalking Horse and White Elk, who were with several other men at the smithy. "We need to get him to the hospital immediately," she said, after breathlessly filling them in. "Someone should ride ahead to Dr. Martin's house and tell him to meet us there. Jonah needs help hitching up the team, and we need a mattress or some hay in the wagon."

The foreman swiftly put her words into action. Janessa ran to the house to get bandage rolls, then, shouting to the men to hurry, galloped back along the road to the creek bed.

She was tying the last knots in a bandage around Luther's shoulder when she heard the wagon roll up. Jonah and Stalking Horse clambered down the bank, and with Janessa supervising, the two men picked Luther up, carefully carried him to the road, and laid him in the back of the wagon, where Janessa knelt next to him. She did her best to brace his shoulder during the bumpy ride to town.

The Portland Charity Hospital, where Janessa frequently worked, was an immense, barnlike clapboard building that had seen better days. Dr. Anton Wizneuski, who donated his time to serve as the institution's director,

would not arrive until late afternoon, and Janessa hoped
that Dr. Martin would be waiting for them.

Two volunteer orderlies, both elderly men, brought a
stretcher to help carry Luther inside, and to Janessa's
relief, Dr. Martin's buggy, with White Elk driving, pulled
up moments later. Dr. Robert Martin, at seventy-six years
of age, was thin and frail, but he still carried on a limited
practice, with Janessa as his unofficial assistant. A longtime
friend of the Holts, he was as determined as Janessa to see
that she one day became a medical doctor.

While Janessa helped the doctor out of the buggy,
she described Luther's condition. Dr. Martin frowned.
"The first thing is to get that bullet out of him. Do you
have anything important at school today?"

"Not this morning." Janessa did not mention that she
had a history test in the afternoon.

"Good. I'll write a note for your teacher."

Janessa and the doctor went straight to the surgery
room, where the orderlies had taken Luther. The room
smelled strongly of phenol, an acidic compound that Dr.
Martin and Dr. Wizneuski had found effective in prevent-
ing infection. A firm believer in the germ theory, Dr.
Martin insisted on working under the cleanest possible
conditions.

While the doctor donned a surgical apron and washed
his hands, Janessa checked Luther's heartbeat and pulse,
which were extremely weak. She then dabbed phenol
on and around the wound, and the doctor began probing
for the bullet.

During the hours since the shooting, Luther's injured
flesh had swollen, obscuring the path of the bullet. The
old doctor's hands were weak and trembled with age, and
after a few attempts with the probe, he gave up. "See if
you can find it, Janessa."

Janessa, who had already washed her hands, took up
the instrument, which had a porcelain tip, and eased it
into the wound. With her eyes closed, she felt for the path
of least resistance, working the long, slender rod deeper a
fraction of an inch at a time. Presently, she felt something
solid.

To an experienced hand, the porcelain tip of the

probe caused the instrument to have a different feel when touching different materials. Janessa had spent hours touching a probe to pieces of bone, metal, and other objects in order to learn to use the instrument. She now knew it was touching metal. "I've found it."

The doctor reached into a tray and picked up an extractor—a long, slender forceps with toothed jaws and a hole through its center so it would slide down a probe. He eased it into the bullet hole, following the probe, then opened the jaws. After pushing it a fraction of an inch deeper, he closed the jaws and pulled.

In a rush of blood the instruments slid out of the wound, and Janessa was relieved to see the lead slug clenched in the teeth of the extractor. She quickly applied a phenol-soaked compress, and the doctor went to a shelf to get bandage rolls. After they had bandaged the wound, the doctor checked Luther's pulse and heartbeat.

"I wish we had got to him a few hours ago," he said somberly. "He's lost too much blood to recover on his own."

Janessa was aware of a possible last resort in such instances, but its use sometimes simply hastened a patient's death. She waited to hear the doctor's verdict.

"There's nothing else we can do, then," he said at last, "except a blood transfer. Let's get cleaned up, and I'll have a word with Mr. Venable."

Out in the waiting room, Jonah had been joined by Mabel Seeley, as well as Horace Biddle and a policeman. Mabel was tearfully protesting that her brother would never break into a store.

"I ain't saying he did, ma'am," Biddle was comforting her. "All I know is that while I was inventorying my storeroom, I heard somebody in the front. When I went in there, it looked like he was raising a gun, so I shot him. He ran off, and I never did see who it was."

The policeman, who appeared accustomed to dealing with such cases, addressed Dr. Martin. "Did you get the bullet out, Doc?"

He nodded. "It's a forty-two caliber."

"Then that settles it," the policeman pronounced. "Mr. Biddle here is about the only one in town with a forty-two-caliber pistol. Do you want to charge him with breaking into your store, Horace?"

"Oh, no," Biddle replied quickly. "I'm just sorry this happened, and I sure hope he gets over it real soon, Mrs. Seeley."

The woman had paled visibly at the exchange between the doctor and the policeman, and tears filled her eyes as she turned to Jonah. "Luther has never been mixed up in anything like this before," she sobbed. "What on earth am I going to do with him, Jonah?"

Jonah put an arm around her, but before he could answer, the doctor spoke up. He described Luther's condition and the only course of treatment that offered any hope, then he explained the dangers involved. Jonah, Stalking Horse, and White Elk all promptly volunteered to give blood, but the doctor shook his head. "It's been my experience that taking a little blood from several people is much more dangerous than taking a moderate amount from one or two. I'll take a quart from two of you, and you can flip coins to see which two it will be."

Stalking Horse and White Elk won, and a few minutes later, in the surgery room, White Elk watched with wide eyes as Janessa, using a large, sterilized syringe, drew blood from Stalking Horse's forearm and injected it into a vein in Luther's arm. After this was repeated several times, the aged Indian got off the table, took a few cautious steps, and shook his head to dispel his dizziness. He wished White Elk good luck, then sat to watch.

When the doctor had finished, White Elk slid nimbly off the table, with no sign of dizziness. He patted a disgruntled-looking Stalking Horse on the shoulder and quipped, "I guess we've made him our blood brother, wouldn't you say?"

"That may be so," Dr. Martin put in sourly. "*If* he lives. But from what I've heard of young Luther here, being his blood brother isn't something to be especially proud of."

Luther was still unconscious when Janessa returned to school with the doctor's note. Over the past years, she had been working hard to make up for the formal education she had missed during early childhood. The medical college that the doctor wanted her to attend required an arts degree for entrance, and Janessa was hoping to qualify for enrollment in a liberal arts college by the time she was fifteen. Consequently, she tried to put Luther Bingham out of her mind and concentrate on her history test.

She was only partially successful; she kept thinking about the first peril of a blood transfer, which, when it did happen, always occurred within hours. For some reason, the patient's blood would begin clotting in the veins, resulting in death a short time later. When school finally let out, Janessa hurried back to the hospital. With great relief, she learned that Luther had survived the danger. Although he was still unconscious, his pulse and heartbeat were much stronger.

A second condition, taking longer to develop, was no less dangerous. It was a fever, which Dr. Martin believed was caused by germs on the equipment used in the transfer, and even phenol was less than totally effective in destroying germs. Janessa went home with these worries preying on her mind, but the next morning, when she stopped by the hospital before school, she found that Luther had regained consciousness and had only a slight fever, probably the result of his wound.

As soon as school was dismissed for the day, she returned to the hospital, where she encountered the director, Dr. Wizneuski, outside his office. A bald, heavyset man with a white beard and rimless glasses, Anton Wizneuski was a good friend of Janessa's and even allowed her to observe postmortem examinations. His habitual smile faded, however, when she asked him about Luther.

"His condition is excellent, all things considered," he said, showing her into his office, "but I wish I could say the same about his personality. The volunteer who brought lunch to him left the room crying. Luther was evidently very rude."

Janessa frowned.

"We already have enough trouble finding volunteers to work here," the doctor continued. "I talked to Luther, but it didn't seem to do much good. I'd gladly get rid of him, but he needs care and apparently doesn't have the money to pay for it. His sister came in to make a donation, but I took only a small amount from her. She clearly could not afford very much, no matter how generous her nature."

"Yes, I know about Mrs. Seeley," Janessa said. "Is it all right if I talk with Mr. Bingham, sir?"

"Certainly, Janessa. It might be a good idea to check his temperature again, in any case."

Janessa nodded and stepped to the cabinet where clinical thermometers were stored. A fairly recent invention that had replaced a large, clumsy apparatus, the new thermometers were expensive and fragile and were kept in felt-lined wooden boxes for protection. Janessa took one of the boxes and carried it carefully down the hall.

She paused outside Luther's room, for Jonah and Mabel were inside, and she did not want to interrupt their visit. Mabel sounded almost in tears.

"You've done a lot of foolish things, Luther," she was saying, "but this is the first time you've done anything criminal."

"Why are you surprised?" Luther muttered defensively. "You and Jonah have been telling me for years that it's the sort of thing I'd eventually end up doing."

"Stop that!" Mabel snapped, becoming angry. "I've done my best for you—far more than most sisters would do for a brother. You could at least try to explain yourself."

Luther's angry rejoinder was interrupted by Jonah. "Now, wait a minute. There's no sense in everybody getting hot and bothered and saying things they don't mean. We've had our problems, Luther, but I know that breaking into that store wasn't like you. Maybe you just had a few drinks too many. Was that it?"

The older man's attempt to keep the peace was futile. "No, I hadn't had enough," Luther sneered. "I broke into that store to get some whiskey."

"And you're not sorry for it, are you?" Mabel reproached him. "After all I've suffered because of you, Luther, this is too much. If you're going to be this way, then I'm through bothering with you."

"Good," Luther shot back. "It'll be a big relief not to have to listen to your complaining."

"Then you won't have to!" Mabel's voice broke on a

sob. Jonah tried to intercede again, but she cut him off. "No, Jonah, leave it be. I'm through with him until he straightens out. Luther, when you make something of yourself, you can come back to my house. Until then, you can forget I'm alive, because I intend to forget that I ever had a brother."

Before Luther could reply, the woman rushed out of the room, bursting into tears as she passed Janessa. Following her out, Jonah looked at Janessa and shrugged helplessly, then caught up with Mabel.

Janessa went into the room and was surprised when she saw a forlorn, grief-stricken expression on Luther's face. Then it was abruptly gone, replaced by a scowl. "Who are you?" he demanded.

"Janessa Holt, Dr. Martin's helper. I'm going to check your temperature, and you must be very careful with this thermometer."

"I know this dump is a charity hospital, but I didn't realize it was run by children."

Dumbfounded at the man's ingratitude, Janessa glared at him, rage swelling within her. She carefully removed the thermometer from its box, placed it on a table, then, holding the empty box by one end, stepped to his bed.

"Apologize for what you just said!" she ordered, taking Luther by surprise and soundly thumping his injured shoulder with the box. "Apologize!"

Howling in pain, Luther tried to twist away and fend off the box with his right hand, but Janessa was too fast for him. The box darted past his hand and rapped his shoulder again. "All right!" he finally shouted. "I'm sorry! I'm sorry! Are you crazy?"

"No. I'm sick of your acting like a spoiled brat. When that volunteer brought your lunch today, you said something that upset her. I suppose you think you're really courageous, hurting an old lady's feelings."

"She brought me a bowl of slop that a dog wouldn't eat," Luther grumbled, eyeing Janessa warily. "Why should I have to eat garbage like that?"

"Because," Janessa seethed through clenched teeth, "you're no better than anyone else here, and you are served exactly what the others eat. When you find a job and earn some money, you can go to a private hospital where the food will be more to your liking. Until then, you'll have to eat what others can afford to give you." For good measure, she knocked his shoulder again. "Understand?"

"Yes! Yes!" Luther exclaimed, shrinking away from her. "Yes, I understand!"

"Finding volunteers to work here is always a problem. The next time you see that woman, you must apologize to her. And when one of the volunteers does something for you, you must act grateful and be polite. Do you hear?"

Luther looked away and mumbled a grudging reply.

"Answer me properly and be polite," Janessa insisted, brandishing the box.

"I heard you," Luther growled, "and I'll do it."

Janessa lunged and prodded his shoulder once more. "That wasn't polite. I said to answer me properly and be polite."

His eyes wide with alarm, Luther grabbed his pillow to shield his shoulder. "All right! You win! I'm sorry for how I acted, miss. I promise I won't do anything to upset the volunteers." He bared his teeth in a quick, forced grin. "See? I'm smiling and being polite to you."

As Janessa went to the table for the thermometer, Luther gingerly touched his throbbing shoulder and looked at her with new respect. "You say you're Dr. Martin's helper? You help him with his patients?"

Janessa eyed him suspiciously. "In a few years, I plan to go to medical college." She walked back to the bed. "In the meantime, Dr. Martin lets me work with him and teaches me."

"I guess he hasn't gotten around to bedside manners yet," Luther attempted to joke.

The humor was lost on Janessa. "This thermometer goes in your mouth. It's very fragile, so don't close your teeth on it."

Luther obediently opened his mouth, and Janessa placed the end of the instrument under his tongue. After counting off the seconds in her mind, she removed the thermometer and looked at it.

"What is my temperature?"

"About two degrees above normal. In your case, that's very good."

Luther grunted. When Janessa put the thermometer away and started to leave, he called a question to her. "Do you have any books here?"

She turned back. "Not many, other than medical texts. Most of our patients can't read or write. I'll see what we have and ask one of the volunteers to bring you some."

Luther met her gaze squarely. "Thank you. I'll be polite when she does."

Janessa nodded and left.

Shifting to a more comfortable position, Luther winced in pain. Although he was resentful about what the girl had done to him, he was well aware of the humor of the situation, and his furtive smile became a quiet chuckle. Having people angry at him was anything but an unusual experience, and Luther had more than once faced up to and outwitted large, brutal men. But this fearless slip of a girl was the first one who had ever forced him to capitulate.

His amusement quickly faded, however, as he thought about what the girl had said about herself and how it compared to his own situation. Though barely more than a child, she was filling her days with useful activities leading to an admirable goal. More than ever, Luther regretted his lost, wasted years. And for the first time since his elopement with his dear Melissa had fallen through, he felt it might just be possible for him to do something useful and meaningful with his own life.

The sunlight on the rolling surface of Lake Michigan cast dancing spots of light into the wheelhouse of Albert Crowell's steam launch. The small but powerful vessel, which towed logs down the lake from Toby's logging camp in Wisconsin to his lumberyard in Chicago, was now making the return trip north, with Toby aboard. He had finished his business in Chicago and was eager to see Alexandra again.

While in the city, Toby had received some bad news, which now occupied his thoughts. Edward Blackstone, who had been partners with Toby and Rob Martin in the logging venture, had written to him from Oklahoma, where Edward and Rob now ran a cattle ranch. Edward's young wife, Tommie, had died of pneumonia over the winter. Having read that Edward was considering leaving the ranch to get away for a time, Toby had invited him to the logging camp.

The launch was now nearing the camp, and the long shoreline and broken cliffs gave way abruptly to dense forest, which extended inland for as far as the eye could see. The logging camp was in a clearing at the top of a steep bluff, from which a chute for logs reached down to a breakwater and a catch basin. Lumberjacks were at the top of the chute, tipping in huge logs that skidded down and raised towering spouts of water in the basin below.

Seeing the launch approaching, the lumberjacks started down the steep path to the shore, to help Crowell and his two-man crew hook up a tow of logs. Carrying his carpetbag and the box containing the present he had bought for Alexandra, Toby stepped to the rail.

The launch paused at the pier for Toby to leap ashore, and then its engine rumbled as Captain Crowell headed toward the catch basin, where the lumberjacks were hopping nimbly across the logs bobbing in the water. Toby waved good-bye and climbed the path to the camp.

Surrounded by evergreens and trees covered with bursting buds, the camp was a scene of rustic beauty. The homey, spacious log house where Frank Woods lived with his wife, Bettina, and her daughter, Lucy, was set back on one side of the clearing and flanked by four small cabins for visitors. Bettina's carefully tended flower beds added a springtime display of color.

On the opposite side of the clearing stood the log dormitory and dining hall for the lumberjacks. Beyond were stables and corrals for saddle horses and for the oxen that were used to drag logs through the forest to the camp. Nearby, Frank and several lumberjacks had built a small barn, corral, and jumping course for Alexandra's four thoroughbred hunters.

Seeing Alexandra and Lucy at the jumping course, Toby put down his bag and went to join them. Alexandra had undertaken to teach Lucy to ride the hunters and was

instructing the girl on how to fall. Consequently, Lucy
was sitting astride a saddle on the top rail of the corral,
and at a signal from Alexandra she kicked out of the
stirrups and threw herself off, landing in a pile of hay. As
she started to climb back up to the saddle, she saw Toby
approaching and excitedly grabbed Alexandra's hand and
pointed. Alexandra turned to him.

Slender and lovely in her riding clothes, she broke
into a smile and ran forward to greet him. Toby caught her
in his arms, kissed her, then held her back to look at her.
"Here, this is for you," he said, handing her the package.
"Did you miss me?"

"You mean you've been gone?" she said, her moist
eyes betraying her joking words. "And you're back a day
early. I hope that's because you couldn't stay away from
me."

"That's exactly why," he replied, watching as she
pulled the ribbon off the box.

"You don't have to bring me a present *every* time you
go somewhere. Of course, as long as it doesn't delay you
in getting back—" She broke off with a cry of delight as
she opened the box. "Toby, it's perfect!"

"I thought you'd like it."

"Like it? I adore it!" She held up the present, which
was a tooled-leather bridle with silver fittings that gleamed
in the sunlight as she turned it from side to side. A wide band
centered to fit between the horse's eyes bore a single silver
initial, A. "It's the most beautiful bridle I've ever seen."

"Then it's the one you should have." Toby felt intensely gratified, for the present had just the effect he had
intended; the grief that had saddened Alexandra's pretty
hazel eyes since her father's death was lost temporarily in
her pleasure over the bridle.

Lucy joined them to look at the bridle. As always, she
remained silent because of her severe stammer, so she
smiled in reply to Toby's greeting.

"I see that Alexandra has become your instructor,"
Toby commented.

Alexandra answered for her. "Lucy has determination, which is the most important quality of any student.
Have you had any news from Oregon, Toby?"

"Yes, a letter from Janessa. Your horses are all settled in and doing fine, as is Jonah."

"I hope they aren't interfering with things at your ranch."

Toby shook his head. "Janessa would have let me know. Is Frank about?"

Alexandra said he was out at a work camp and would be back by dinner, and Toby, not wanting to interrupt Lucy's lesson any more than he already had, excused himself so he could wash up and put his things in his cabin.

Toby was donning a clean shirt when he heard Frank's unmistakable kettledrum voice. Toby went around to the kitchen door of the Woods house.

Frank and the tall, attractive Bettina had been close friends of Toby's for many years. They greeted him warmly, but their smiles disappeared when he told them about Tommie Blackstone's death.

"That's terrible!" Bettina exclaimed. "She was such a sweet, kind woman—always so cheerful."

Toby and Frank sat at the kitchen table, and they talked about Tommie and Edward as Bettina poured cups of her strong, delicious coffee. A kettle of chicken and dumplings was simmering on the stove, and the aroma filling the kitchen reminded Toby that it had been several days since he had eaten one of Bettina's delicious meals.

A few minutes later, Alexandra and Lucy came in. Toby watched in concern as Frank darted a frowning glance at Lucy's trousers as she began setting the table, but a warning glare from Bettina made him keep silent. Toby hoped that Alexandra's influence on the girl was not creating a problem for the Woods family.

After dinner, as soon as the dishes were cleared and Lucy went to her room with Alexandra, who spent an hour or two each night tutoring the girl, Frank spoke his mind.

"I thought I had a girl, not a boy," he grumbled. "I mean no reflection on Alexandra, Toby, because it's up to her what she wears. But I think it looks improper on Lucy."

"Then you've found out why the Good Lord put a neck between your head and shoulders," Bettina put in tartly. "If you see something you don't like, you can turn your face the other way. For my part, I'm grateful to Alexandra for the time and trouble she's devoting to Lucy. Heaven knows the child needs a friend."

Frank reached out to pat his wife's hand. "I know, you're tired of me grousing about this, honey," he said. "And of course I'd like to see Lucy get over her stuttering as much as you would. Just give me time, and maybe I'll get used to seeing her in breeches."

Toby assured him he would, and privately he also hoped that Lucy's lessons would help distract Alexandra from her own grief. She kept it well hidden, even from him, but Toby knew what she was going through, and that she cried herself to sleep almost every night.

The following day was a Saturday, and the pace of work at the logging camp was more relaxed. After a big breakfast, Frank and Toby rode off to look at the new timberland Toby had leased. Alexandra, after cleaning out her horses' barn, began exercising each animal on the jumping course. Lucy watched with undivided attention.

By midmorning, lumberjacks were beginning to come in for the weekend from the nearer work camps. Some of the work camps were so distant that the men remained at them for weeks without returning to the logging camp, but the lumberjacks at the nearer camps always came in for the weekend. They milled about, relaxing, doing odd jobs, or tending their own garden plots behind the dining hall, while the cook conscripted some of them to prepare a firepit and spit a pig so that it could roast slowly through the afternoon and be ready for the Saturday evening festivities.

The previous year, in order to keep the men out of town and out of trouble, Toby had turned what had been an informal gathering into an evening of entertainment, complete with a feast and a cask of beer. There was no lack of talent: Several of the lumberjacks played instruments, four Welshmen among them formed a vocal quartet, and those who had no particular musical talent recited tall tales, presented skits or parts from plays, or even read poetry.

Alexandra was taking the last horse back to the corral

when Lucy worked up the nerve to stammer a question. Getting out the words was a struggle for the girl, but Alexandra quickly caught her meaning: Lucy wanted to know when she could ride one of the hunters.

"Anytime you wish," Alexandra replied. "But remember what I told you. Hunters aren't like saddle horses, and they're dangerous for inexperienced riders. They must be controlled constantly, and it frightens them to have a nervous rider. When they get frightened, they might bolt or start rearing up. Do you still want to try?"

The girl nodded eagerly, and Alexandra led her back to the course. Alexandra had her walk around it and take down all except the bottom bar on the obstacles. Lucy asked several questions, each a struggle, but Alexandra listened patiently and answered every one, making certain the girl understood what to do.

At last Alexandra helped Lucy mount. Perched high on the horse as it pranced about, Lucy looked terrified. The horse, sensing its rider's uncertainty, became increasingly nervous, but Alexandra held the bridle, trying to calm the animal and get it started around the course.

At Lucy's nod, Alexandra released the bridle and hoped for the best. Lucy clung to the saddle at first, barely managing to hold the horse to a canter. Clearing the low bar on the first obstacle was hardly more than a high step for the hunter, but Lucy lost her stirrups and almost fell off. Alexandra shouted instructions and encouragement, and after the first round of the course, Lucy was better balanced and released her tight grip on the saddle.

When the girl gained more confidence, the horse sensed it and, becoming less nervous, settled down to a steady pace. Alexandra sat on the top rail of the fence, calling tips to Lucy on how to correct her posture in the saddle. Hearing someone behind her, Alexandra turned and saw Bettina.

"How is she doing?"

"Quite well," Alexandra replied. "Simply staying on a hunter is an achievement for an inexperienced rider. Lucy is a determined girl."

"Yes, she is." Bettina exchanged a wave with her daughter as the girl rode past. "I'm sure the reason she's so set on learning to ride is she wants to copy you in everything, Alexandra. I'm grateful you spend the time on her."

"It's no trouble, Bettina, truly. I like Lucy."

Bettina smiled wistfully. "Like most parents, I want more for my child than I've had. Lucy's a bright girl, and heaven knows what she could do if only she could get over her stuttering."

"Stuttering is something I know very little about," Alexandra admitted. "But I have heard about children who stammered and eventually outgrew it."

"So have I." Bettina sighed and waved to Lucy again. "In any event, I'm very grateful to you, dear."

After telling Alexandra that lunch would soon be ready, Bettina returned to the house. Watching Lucy, Alexandra thought about the conversation. She wished she could help the girl overcome her speech impediment, but she had no idea of how to go about it. She also feared that the stammering could be made worse by calling attention to it.

When the girl showed signs of tiring, Alexandra climbed down from the fence. She helped Lucy dismount, and they led the horse to the corral and unsaddled it. Happy and excited, Lucy stammered incoherently as she tried to express her feelings. Alexandra smiled and affectionately slung an arm around the girl's shoulders as they walked to the house.

The Saturday night entertainment drew people from small farms in the surrounding area, who were always made welcome with the warm hospitality characteristic of this logging camp. In the afternoon, Alexandra changed into a dress to help Bettina and Lucy, while the remainder of the lumberjacks filtered in from the work camps and Toby and Frank returned.

An appetizing aroma rose from the pig roasting over the fire pit, and the lumberjacks, eager to eat, set up trestle tables and benches in front of the makeshift stage and hung up strings of lanterns. At sunset the Guthries and the Raffertys, good friends of Toby's, arrived from the backwoods brewery where they lived and worked. They had a cask of beer in their wagon.

Fred Guthrie, a former tavern owner who was almost as big a man as Frank Woods, climbed down from the wagon on his wooden leg and helped his German wife, Ursula, down. Paddy Rafferty, the brewery's jack-of-all-trades, did the same for his wife, Colleen, while their redheaded children spilled from the back.

Ursula clucked in resignation when Toby, greeting the guests with Alexandra, asked about Ursula's daughter, Maida. Maida, who had recently gotten married, was the brewery's master brewer, and she was so dedicated to her work that she rarely left the premises.

While Ursula and Toby talked, a fiddle player on stage struck up a tune, and the lumberjacks lit the lanterns. The cook, assisted by Lucy, served up the food on platters, and Toby and his friends joined the line.

For the first hour, everyone concentrated on eating, and the lumberjacks did justice to the delicious food. It was a boisterous gathering, and all present seemed to forget their troubles in the merry, carefree atmosphere. The musicians played lively tunes, and afterward a lumberjack with a booming voice took the stage to recite a dramatic poem. The Welsh quartet followed with "The Men of Harlech," a rousing song about an ancient battle in Wales.

Paddy Rafferty was next, and with the fiddler accompanying him, he sang a popular but sad Irish ballad, one that Alexandra's father had often sung or hummed while he worked. As the audience grew hushed and listened raptly, Alexandra felt her control slipping. She quietly left the gathering and went to her cabin.

Alone, she sat down on the bench beside her door and buried her face in her hands. After a while, there was a movement in the darkness, and Lucy appeared and sat down next to her. The girl took out a handkerchief and silently dabbed at Alexandra's tears. Alexandra, deeply touched, held the girl close and wept.

V

The gardeners working in the flower beds flanking the drive leading up to the front entrance of Grevenhof doffed their caps and bowed to the passing carriage with more than their usual attention and curiosity when Henry Blake returned after his long absence. In his eagerness to see Gisela and their son, Henry barely noticed.

The butler, normally a stolid fellow, looked uncharacteristically nervous as he took Henry's cap and told him that the baroness awaited him upstairs. Henry noted absently that the entryway seemed somewhat bare, but he dismissed the thought and ascended the stairs two at a time.

It was not until he opened the door to the sitting room that he knew something was wrong. Seated on the couch, Gisela was as bewitchingly lovely as always, but she looked wan. His first thought, which sent a chill of fear through him, was that she had suffered an attack of her recurring illness.

He rushed to her and took her into his arms. "Gisela, you've been ill again, haven't you? Why didn't you send me a telegram? Perhaps I could have returned a day or two sooner."

She lifted a hand and caressed his face. "No, I haven't been ill, Heinrich."

"But I can see that you have," he insisted, knowing she was always reluctant to admit that she wasn't perfectly well. "Why do you say that you haven't? You should have let me know."

"Heinrich," she repeated curtly, "I have not been ill.

70

Perhaps my appetite has been poor, and I haven't been sleeping well. That is all."

Her haughty, striking beauty, as Henry was well aware, could be intimidating as well as alluring. Her blue eyes, which usually betrayed her unqualified devotion to him, were now cold with the harsh glare that she customarily turned on the world. Her hand was still resting on his face, and Henry could feel the fingernails on his skin.

"Gisela, what is wrong?"

"Wrong?" she echoed in a tightly controlled voice. She looked away and pushed at her hair. "Wrong, Heinrich? Should something be wrong?"

Suddenly recalling how the gardeners and the butler had acted, Henry glanced around the room. Every ornament and other small object was gone. He immediately knew what had happened to them. "Gisela, are you angry about something?"

"Angry?" She shrugged. "Should I be angry?"

"I can *see* you are angry. Please tell me why."

Gisela reached to adjust the lapel on his uniform. Then, suddenly, she seized it and jerked him closer. "I have found out about Adela Ronsard!" she hissed in his face. "Now that we are married, I am like an old shoe to be cast aside while you consort with strumpets! Did you think you could keep her hidden from me? Do you think I am a fool?"

A moment passed, their noses an inch apart. Henry, controlling his temper, pulled her hand off his lapel and put it on her lap. "You know better than to act that way with me," he said quietly. "If you have something to say to me, say it in a normal tone."

Her lips trembling and tears welling in her eyes, Gisela turned away. She drew in a deep breath. "I apologize," she said in a tense but still angry voice. "Please forgive me. I have found out about Adela Ronsard. Now please tell me all about your affair with her."

"I know of no one named Adela Ronsard."

Gisela shook her head unbelievingly. "You must be truthful with me, Heinrich. I may be angry for a short time, but I love you, and I will forgive you. I promise that

the woman will come to no harm . . . no physical harm.
But you must tell me everything."

"Gisela," he repeated impatiently, "I know of no one
named Adela Ronsard."

Gisela frowned skeptically. "This is not a rumor I
have heard or a tale someone told me. The woman herself
is here in this house. She was brought here, seeking you,
and will speak to no one but you. How do you explain
that?"

"How can I explain something I know nothing about?
I know only that I've never heard that name until a
moment ago."

Her eyes still narrow with suspicion, Gisela went to
the bell pull beside the window and tugged on it. The
butler, who obviously had been waiting in the hall, appeared an instant later. "Fetch the nurse," Gisela ordered.

The butler bowed and withdrew, and Henry looked
at Gisela in perplexity. "The nurse? What does she have
to do with this?"

"Fräulein Ronsard proved to have a talent for pacify-
ing the baby and keeping him quiet," Gisela explained
stiffly. "And I thought she should do something for her
keep, since she eats like a horse. One would never know
it, though."

Gaining weight was a sore point with Gisela, and the
jealousy in her tone did not escape Henry. A minute later
the butler reappeared with a young woman, then quickly
left without waiting for further instructions.

Henry scrutinized the woman, who was strikingly
beautiful, with large, dark eyes, olive skin, and black hair.
She was in a maid's smock and had her left arm in a sling,
which was puzzling—but Henry's overall impression was
that Gisela had good grounds for feeling jealous.

The woman bobbed a curtsy. "Are you Captain Blake,
sir?" Her German had a heavy French accent.

"You've never even *seen* him before?" Gisela exploded.
"Why didn't you tell me that?"

Adela's apprehension showed that she was more than
familiar with Gisela's temper, but she was spirited and
lifted her chin as she replied; "Because I could speak only
with the captain, Madam Baroness."

"Then please do," Henry encouraged. "I am Captain Blake. Kindly state your business with me, fräulein, and let's put an end to this."

"Yes, sir." She glanced nervously at Gisela, as if reluctant to speak in her presence, but Henry assured her that he kept no secrets from the baroness. "Well, first, sir," Adela began, "I must ask if you are familiar with Hermann Bluecher."

Henry frowned. "Yes, I am. He is the head of internal security for German military intelligence."

"Until a short time ago," Adela continued, "I lived in Berlin, where I was—I was a courtesan. Herr Bluecher was one of my clients. While in his house, I read certain papers that contained information of vital importance to Germany, as well as to you, sir. He tried to have you killed, and he intends to do so again. Herr Bluecher is also plotting to have Chancellor Bismarck and General Fremmel assassinated."

Henry stared at the woman in mute astonishment. Gisela glanced at him, her own surprise mixed with dismay as she sat back on the couch. Henry pulled up a chair and told Adela to sit down.

Her story about Bluecher's intentions to have him killed confirmed Henry's long-held suspicions, and as he questioned Adela, everything she told him seemed to make sense, as unbelievable as it might have sounded to Gisela. And the attempt on Adela's own life was conclusive evidence. Someone had gone to great lengths to silence her.

Unfortunately, she was unable to remember many details of Bluecher's papers. Several names had been mentioned, she recalled, but other than Bismarck, Fremmel, and Henry himself, the only one she could remember was Kurt Gessell. The name meant nothing to Henry.

At Henry's urging, Adela related how she had fled from Berlin. "When I reached Grevenburg, a man was waiting for me." She pointed to her sling. "He did this, and another bullet grazed the side of my neck. I hope he thinks I am dead."

"I see no reason to believe otherwise," Gisela said to Henry. "Other than the servants and Dr. MacAlister, only the stationmaster and his wife know she was brought here, and I told him that I wanted the matter kept quiet."

"Good," Henry said. "Fräulein Ronsard, I may question you again later. In the meantime, you must not leave the house."

"Oh, I won't, sir," Adela assured him, standing up. "I am still in danger and have no desire to leave. And I am grateful to the baroness for extending to me the protection of her home."

Gisela nodded graciously. "It is my pleasure," she said. "If I have been sharp with you, I apologize. Within a day or two, I will talk with you about an appropriate wage for attending to the captain's son."

When the young woman was gone, Gisela looked at Henry. "And so," she said, her eyes cold with anger, "Hermann Bluecher was the one who tried to have you killed. I can easily arrange to have him ruined, or worse. I—"

"No," Henry cut her off quickly. "This has nothing to do with you, Gisela. You must disregard what you have just heard. I will attend to it."

Gisela looked unconvinced, but she recognized the finality in his voice. "What do you propose to do?"

"I'll have to notify Washington first," Henry said, "but then I'll contact General Fremmel. Bluecher would find out about it if I went to the general's office, but the fact that he is Richard's father-in-law simplifies matters. I'll have Richard arrange to have the general meet me privately."

Gisela moved close to him. "That means you'll soon leave again, and you just got here. The weeks you have been gone seemed like years to me, loved one. But we'll have a day or two together, won't we?"

Henry smiled. Readily forgiving her for his initial cold welcome, he embraced her as he had been longing to do for weeks. He sought her lips, and she responded with her usual zeal, pulling his hand to her breasts. Their kisses and caresses swiftly became urgent, and Henry gathered her up in his arms and carried her to her bedroom.

Three days later, Henry was sitting in the drawing

room of a modest brick residence in the city of Kassel, not far from the headquarters of the Twelfth Dragoon Brigade. Major Richard Koehler, Gisela's nephew, was wistfully casting a sidelong glance at the new maid as she carried in a tray of drinks and then left. General Hans Fremmel, Richard's father-in-law, was standing across the room, engaged in conversation with his daughter, Ulrica.

"I enjoy married life, Heinrich," Richard confided to his friend in a low voice. "It places a certain limit on one's activities, but it has compensations—" He fell silent and busied himself pouring glasses of cognac as his father-in-law occupied a seat near them. Every inch a Prussian general, Hans Fremmel was a large, rigidly military man, and his immaculate uniform tunic was taut over his bulging chest and stomach. His scalp gleamed through a bristle of gray hair. He had craggy, flushed features, with a prominent, veined nose and a deep saber scar on one cheek.

Ulrica, a stout, cheerful young woman, stood behind his chair. She had married Richard only a few weeks before and was blissfully happy.

Noting the general's cool glance at his civilian clothes, Henry decided to start the discussion. "Because of the nature of the information I have for you, sir, I thought it best not to wear my uniform. It always draws attention, which I wished to avoid."

Fremmel grumbled a reply and turned to his daughter. "Would you please excuse us, my dear?"

Ulrica withdrew, and Henry related what Adela Ronsard had told him.

Richard's expression reflected astonishment and alarm, but the general merely listened and occasionally grunted. He was a stern, humorless disciplinarian whom some thought dull, but Henry knew that the general had a keen mind.

"Do you think the woman is telling the truth?" Richard exclaimed when Henry had finished. "Her story seems unbelievable!"

"I am sure that she believed she was telling the truth," Henry replied. "And I suspect what she said was indeed accurate, for the general appears willing enough to accept it. She herself became a target after she escaped from Berlin, and Bluecher knew that Grevenhof was a likely haven for her. How else could she have known where I lived?"

Fremmel nodded. "For many years, Herr Bluecher has been ignoring the limits of his authority. He is a wealthy man and has been using his personal wealth to recruit private agents—who as often as not undermine the policies of the government. One of my first decisions as head of intelligence was to replace him."

"He must have found out about your plans," Henry observed.

"Undoubtedly." Fremmel looked pained. "I discussed the decision only with the Chancellor himself, which means Bluecher must have an informant in Prince Bismarck's office. It should not surprise me, for Bluecher has any number of politicians and industrialists in his pocket. It is precisely because of the undue influence he wields that the Chancellor and I must act cautiously in removing him from his position."

"This may be your opportunity," Henry suggested. "Regardless of how much influence he has, no one will support him if this is made public."

Fremmel was silent a long moment. "Besides you, who else knows about this, Captain Blake?"

"The baroness," Henry replied. "Her discretion can be trusted absolutely. I also notified my superiors in Washington, where the information will be held in strictest confidence. No one else knows. Fräulein Ronsard is staying in seclusion at Grevenhof."

"Good," Fremmel approved. "With caution, it will be possible to keep Herr Bluecher unaware that his plans are known. Unfortunately, as you now know, I can't be certain whom to trust, even in my own office. In view of that, I would like to recruit your assistance, Captain Blake. Will you be able to work with me on this?"

Henry smiled. "My superiors in Washington have already ordered me to place myself at your disposal, sir."

"Excellent. Now, this Kurt Gessell you spoke of—" The general shifted his bulk in his chair. "He is a Saxon, from a wealthy, politically prominent family. When he was voted out of the Reichstag a few years ago, he moved to Bern, Switzerland. He's an agitator who has caused us trouble before." Fremmel asked Henry several questions, and they agreed that the plot was evidently still in the talking stages, which gave them time to plan a counteraction and obtain evidence against Bluecher.

The safety of Bismarck was the first priority, however, and General Fremmel would take no chances in this regard. The duty of providing the Chancellor's personal guard was periodically rotated among army units, and the present unit was due to be replaced within the month.

"Tomorrow I'll arrange to have the duty assigned to a company of dragoons," Fremmel said. It will appear to be a normal action and will not make Bluecher suspicious. You will be placed in command of that company, Major Koehler."

Richard stood. "That will be an honor, sir. The moment I am relieved of my present command, I will leave for Berlin."

"I have a means of obtaining information from Bern," Henry offered. "Colonel Andrew Brentwood, our military attaché there, is a friend of mine. If Gessell is recruiting men or buying arms, Andrew might be able to find out about it."

"Then contact him, by all means," Fremmel agreed. "We need a source of information in Bern, and it would be unwise of me to trust my agents at present."

As the three men discussed the implications of the plot, they were keenly aware of the importance of the responsibility that had been thrust upon them. Over the past years, through a delicate balancing of policies and agreements among European and neighboring nations, Bismarck had helped to create a period of peace for the region.

"If he were assassinated," Fremmel concluded gloomily, "I fear war would result. We three are soldiers, and each of us stands ready to fight for his nation. But no one regrets war more than soldiers, for we realize what it entails."

Henry and Richard nodded in somber agreement,

and in that vein the conversation continued late into the night.

After arriving in Paris on an evening train, Cindy Kerr was up before daybreak the next morning, eager to see the city. Gilbert Paige had rooms in an apartment hotel on the Île Saint-Louis, one of the two islands in the Seine at the heart of Paris. A well-maintained seventeenth century stone building, the hotel filled one end of a small cobblestone square off the Quai d'Orléans, the street along the south side of the island.

Cindy paused outside the hotel, trying to decide which way to go. Only delivery wagons and street cleaners were moving about at the early hour, and it seemed she had the vast city almost to herself. In front of her the Seine was covered in mist, and just beyond the opposite embankment lay the fabled Latin Quarter. Cindy set off toward the nearby bridge.

The trees along the quay were decked out with spring blossoms, and a vagrant breeze sent petals drifting down as she hurried along the sidewalk in her eagerness to see everything. Once across the river, Cindy turned onto the Boulevard Saint-Germain, which appeared unchanged from medieval times. Everywhere she looked she saw a subject for a sketch. The architecture was like nothing she had ever beheld, ranging from elaborate, monumental Gothic stone structures to quaint, fascinating old houses tucked back into alleys and courts. As the sun's first rays appeared, the cafés and streets came to life, and aromas of brewing coffee and baking bread were everywhere. Cindy passed the famous Sorbonne and wandered through a warren of narrow, winding alleyways somewhere off the Boulevard Saint-Michel, realizing after a time that she was lost.

She stopped at a corner and was wondering which way to turn when a man stepped up to her and lifted his hat.

"Excuse me," he said in French, "but you appear to be unfamiliar with this district. May I help you?"

He was tall, handsome, and well built, and appeared to be slightly younger than she. Cindy's French was easily good enough to ask directions, and she decided to admit the truth.

"Yes, sir, I am lost. Could you please tell me how to get to Île Saint-Louis?"

The man's smile became wide. "Ah, you are English! I always enjoy talking with our English visitors. My name is Pierre Charcot."

"I am American, sir," Cindy corrected, not liking to be teased about her accent. She did not reciprocate by telling the stranger her own name.

"I beg your pardon! I enjoy talking with Americans even more," Charcot said, unperturbed. "And you wish to go to Île Saint-Louis? Very well, I will escort you there. Let us go this way—"

He offered his arm, intending to lead her toward a narrow alley, but Cindy stood fast. The young man exuded charm and sophistication and appeared trustworthy enough, but appearances could be deceiving, Cindy knew. She certainly wasn't going to allow any amorous Frenchman to get *her* into a deserted alley.

"That isn't the way I came," she said.

"It is a shortcut." He gently took hold of her arm. "Come, it will require much less time for us to reach the—"

"No, thank you." Cindy disengaged his hand. "I have plenty of time, and if you are in a hurry, sir, it would be better for you to proceed about your business. I can easily ask someone else for directions."

"Are you frightened of me?" he asked with exaggerated surprise.

"Not in the least." Cindy attempted a bland smile. "I am perfectly capable of defending myself, sir, so there is no reason for me to be frightened. But I am sure that I am taking up too much of your time, so I will bid you good day."

"Wait, please," he pleaded as she started off in the other direction. "I was only joking with you, certainly not ridiculing you for the caution that a beautiful young woman must exercise in a strange city. Let me call you a carriage, and I will have it take you to Île Saint-Louis."

"I would rather walk. But if you would point out the

route to the Boulevard Saint-Michel, I will find my way back from there."

"It is in that direction," he said, gesturing along a street. "But you could become lost again. Please permit me to escort you."

The street he indicated was narrow, but there were people about, so Cindy capitulated gracefully. As Charcot led her onward, he told her about himself, and Cindy felt more relaxed in his company. He was a sculptor, he said, and occasionally lectured to art classes at the Sorbonne, where he had been going when he encountered her.

A few minutes later, they were on a corner of the Boulevard Saint-Michel, and Cindy immediately recognized her surroundings. She thanked him for his assistance and said she hoped she hadn't made him late.

"If I am," he answered with a Gallic shrug, "the students will enjoy the respite. Farewell, mademoiselle, and I earnestly hope that we shall meet again."

By the time Cindy got back to the hotel, she had been gone for almost two hours, and without having told Paige she was leaving. She exchanged greetings with the concierge, a gruff, middle-aged woman who was sweeping out the entry, and hurried up the stairs. Paige, to her dismay, opened his door as soon as her footsteps sounded in the hall.

Slim and of medium stature and with a smooth, un-lined face, Gilbert Paige looked almost youthful, even though he was in his fifties and had snowy white hair. A well-known American artist, he had generously taken on Cindy as a protégée the previous year, and she wanted to be of as little trouble to him as possible.

Cindy was ravenously hungry after her walk, and to her delight Paige had laid out a breakfast of fruit, cheese, hot brioches with butter and preserves, and cups of strong, aromatic coffee. While they were eating, they discussed going to see the woman who Cindy hoped would take her on as a pupil.

It was, Cindy knew, a slender hope. Madame Kirovna, a Russian émigré and the owner of an art gallery, had been a world-renowned etcher before arthritis in her hands had brought her career to an end. While she would be the most qualified teacher Cindy could find, the woman had never taken on an apprentice, apparently because she had neither the temperament nor the inclination to teach.

After breakfast, Cindy fetched the portfolio of etchings she had assembled to show Madame Kirovna and went downstairs with Paige, who had arranged to have a carriage waiting for them.

During the drive across the city, in the opposite direction from which Cindy had walked, Paige pointed out interesting sights and tried to make small talk. Cindy was too worried to enjoy the ride.

It was midmorning when the carriage reached the gallery, which was just off the Rue du Faubourg Saint-Honoré. The small, tree-lined street seemed completely given over to fashionable clothiers, elegant restaurants, and art galleries. Cindy stepped out of the carriage and set her chin firmly as she followed Paige into the Kirovna Gallery.

Obviously a prosperous business, the gallery occupied the entire lower floor of a new-looking stone building. Elegantly dressed customers glided about and chatted in the exhibit room, while salesclerks stood by helpfully. Paige led Cindy through a door at the rear of the room.

A small, gray-headed woman, shriveled with age and wearing a stark black dress, was standing at a high desk, poring over a ledger with a frown. Her wrinkled face reflected a stubborn, dour disposition, and she wore woolen gloves on her gnarled hands.

To Cindy's relief, the woman's frown disappeared when she saw Paige, and she greeted him pleasantly, in French with a marked Russian accent. "So you have returned for the season?"

"Indeed I have, Anna, and with a friend. This is Cindy Kerr, and she has some etchings to show you."

Not bothering with a greeting, the old woman motioned for Cindy to put her portfolio on the desk and told her to open it. Trying to conceal her nervousness, Cindy did as instructed, then watched as Madame Kirovna shuffled through the etchings and looked at them for what seemed like minutes before she said anything. "You need improvement" was her blunt verdict, "but you are a good etcher."

"Thank you, madame," Cindy said.

"Thank your talent, not me," the old woman retorted. "I merely stated a fact. Very well, I will display your work. But I will set the prices for it and choose the locations in the gallery, and you must not display your work elsewhere. Do you agree?"

"Actually, we had something else in mind," Paige interposed. "Cindy would like to work under your guidance."

"Impossible." The old woman shook her head almost violently. "I am a gallery owner, not a teacher. You know that, Gilbert, and you know I have never taught etching. Why would you make such a suggestion?"

"Because of Mrs. Kerr's talent," Paige replied, picking out one of the etchings. "I would never insult you by bringing an ordinary apprentice to you, Anna. Mrs. Kerr learned the craft only last winter, and look at the work she is already doing."

"Last winter?" The old woman reappraised the etching Paige handed her. "Well, perhaps she will be a master etcher. But she will have to work with someone else. I am not a teacher."

"Yes, I know that," Paige persisted, "but we hoped you might make an exception."

"Never." The old woman began looking through the etchings again. "I agree that she has much talent, but she needs to work with someone to perfect her craft." She pointed to a faintly lighter area on one etching. "What is this?"

"It's where I corrected the plate," Cindy answered.

The old woman made a disgruntled sound. "What did you use? A sledgehammer? When making a correction, you must always place the plate on a firm surface and use the mallet gently, to avoid bending the plate." She put the etching aside and looked at another one. "But I cannot teach you, young lady. I am not a teacher, and I would not know how to begin."

"We could begin by being friends," Cindy said impulsively. "I would like to be your friend, and I would like you to be mine."

The old woman looked up, her dark, wary eyes suddenly wistful. She was a lonely person, Cindy realized, far from her homeland—and with a personality like hers, she probably had few friends.

She stubbornly shook her head again. "I have no time." She opened the door to the exhibit room. "Look at my salesclerks. They are all silly girls searching for husbands, and I must watch them constantly. Attending to my gallery takes all my time."

"I could help you manage the gallery," Cindy offered. "In fact, I would enjoy it. I've kept accounts for my brother's ranch, and this couldn't be much different. I could learn what to do very quickly."

Madame Kirovna mumbled something in Russian; apparently she was annoyed at herself because she was wavering. She turned vehemently on Paige. "Why did you do this to me? You know that I do not teach!"

Paige broke into a smile. "Yes, but I can see that you want to work with her, Anna. There's no disgrace in changing one's mind."

The old woman turned back to Cindy. "We will try it for a time," she declared crossly. "Prepare yourself to work harder than you ever have, because that is what you will do here. I have a spare room in my apartment. I'll have the maid prepare it for you." She shook her head as Cindy began thanking her profusely. "Save your thanks, young lady. And leave the etchings here. I want to look at them while you are fetching your belongings."

Cindy exchanged smiles with Paige as they walked out of the gallery. If her first morning in Paris was any indication of the future, she reflected happily, she had a busy and rewarding stay ahead of her.

The *Beluga* was off the coast of Brazil when a clamor erupted on deck early one morning. Marjorie awoke to voices bellowing and what sounded like tin plates and cups clattering in a riotous din. She quickly dressed and was just about to leave her cabin when someone pounded on her door.

"All landlubbers on deck!" a gruff voice shouted. "All

landlubbers must present themselves to King Neptune's court!"

Realizing what was happening, Marjorie drew in a deep breath and steeled herself. She had read accounts of the initiation ceremonies new sailors had to endure when crossing the equator for the first time; and for the first time she had a twinge of regret over insisting that she be given no special consideration during the voyage.

Outside her cabin she found two sailors dressed in rags and wearing mops for beards waiting in the passageway. They seized her courteously but gleefully and rushed her up the companionway to the deck, where they paused to tie her hands loosely behind her back before shouting to their shipmates that they had discovered a landlubber.

The deck was a pandemonium, with sailors running about in tattered, outlandish garb and banging cups against plates. Ned Baylor, wearing a makeshift crown and sailcloth cloak and holding what looked like a real trident, sat enthroned on a cask in the midst of them. Beside him, an older sailor named Morton was seated on a smaller cask. He was wearing a bulky canvas apron and a mop wig.

Baylor shook his trident at Marjorie as the two sailors presented her before the throne. "I am King Neptune, lord of the depths," he intoned in a suitably deep baritone voice, then motioned toward Morton. "And this is Queen Amphitrite. Sailors, put that landlubber with the others."

The cabin boy and a half dozen other victims were in a line at the rail, their hands also tied. The two sailors positioned Marjorie next to David Cornell, who exchanged a wry smile with her. Captain Tench, Marjorie noticed, was watching the proceedings from the quarterdeck with undisguised amusement, while Horatio Cade, at the rail opposite, was gazing sourly into the distance, taking no part in the levity.

A sailor draped in canvas and with paper and pencil in hand stepped along the line. He introduced himself as the judge of King Neptune's court and demanded that the sailors and Marjorie state their names so he could make a list of them. When that was finished, he presented the list to Baylor, who glanced at it, thumped his trident on the deck, and motioned for silence. "Ahoy, the master of the ship!" he called to the quarterdeck. Everyone's attention turned to the captain.

Tench became suddenly serious. "Aye, what is it, King Neptune?"

"King Neptune and his court would like to drink a toast and wish you fair winds and a speedy voyage, Captain! But we don't have anything to drink!"

The crew signified their agreement with another chorus of cup-clattering.

"Aye, very well, King Neptune," Tench conceded once the noise died down. He went to the deck shelter that housed the pantry and the galley and called through the door. "Cook, fetch two bottles of rum for King Neptune and his court!"

Evidently the order had been expected, for the words were hardly out of his mouth before the two bottles were handed out. A cheer rose, and the sailors quickly lined up with their cups.

When the toasts and both bottles were finished, Baylor again pounded his trident on the deck. "King Neptune and his court have been treated well," he proclaimed. "Accordingly, this vessel is guaranteed fair winds and a speedy voyage—"

"Not yet it ain't," Morton interrupted in a falsetto voice. "I smell landlubbers aboard."

In response to that announcement, the sailors clattered their utensils and shouted.

"Aye, so do I," Baylor agreed, sniffing the wind. "I almost forgot about them. Judge, who is the first landlubber for the court to try?"

The canvas-robed sailor consulted his list and called out a name. During the voyage, Marjorie had had plenty of opportunities to observe the sailors' rough-and-ready sense of humor. Inured to the perils of their occupation, they frequently played tricks on one another that struck her as dangerous. As Baylor and the others discussed aloud what to do with the young sailor, Marjorie thought all the suggestions sounded more harsh than amusing.

They finally decided to give the first victim a bath, in order to wash the stench of land off him. The young man was pulled from the line, and a rope was passed under his arms and secured behind him. With no further ado, several sailors hoisted him over their heads, rushed to the rail, and threw him overboard. After a few seconds he was hauled back to the deck, coughing and spluttering. As his hands were untied, the judge called out the next name, that of the cabin boy.

After a discussion that focused mostly on the victim's youth, Baylor announced a decision. "Seeing as how he's only a baby, then," he called out, "we'll put a diaper on him."

The cabin boy squealed and struggled as the sailors began undressing him, and Marjorie averted her eyes. When he was stripped, the sailors put a canvas diaper on him and poured a bucket of seawater into it for good measure. To hilarious cheers, the judge called out the next offender.

He was sentenced to have his hair cut off, which was done roughly with a pair of tin shears. The next victim, known for his vanity, was sentenced to have his hair caulked, and he howled in dismay as tar was smeared on his wavy blond locks.

Watching with mounting anxiety, Marjorie wondered what was in store for her. She felt reasonably certain the captain would intervene if the sailors started to cut her hair or smear tar on it.

Or, she quickly added to herself, if they attempted to undress her and put a sailcloth diaper on her. That was the fate of the next sailor, who was almost as young as the cabin boy, and as Marjorie again averted her eyes, she noticed Cade looking at her from the quarterdeck. The man's expression reflected satisfaction over her plight—which made her all the more determined to face stoically whatever happened.

The next to last victim, David Cornell, had a fair complexion and virtually no beard, so he was sentenced to be shaved with a dull harpoon—a painful process that he endured without a whimper. Marjorie was now the only one left at the rail, and when the judge announced her name, Baylor looked at her with exaggerated astonishment. "What was that name, Judge?"

The judge stepped closer to the throne and stood on tiptoe. "Marjorie White!"

Baylor winced. "That's what I thought you said. It's an odd name for a sailor, I must admit." After stroking his mop beard, he got up, walked over to Marjorie, and closely examined her chin. "Mr. White doesn't have much of a beard, does he? In fact, he doesn't have any beard at all!"

"No, but he makes up for it in hair," the judge returned. "In fact, Mr. White has more hair than any sailor I've ever seen."

Baylor nodded soberly. "If his hair was any longer, Mr. White would be tripping over it, wouldn't he?"

Morton, who had joined him, bent over and scrutinized Marjorie's dress. After slowly straightening up, he surveyed her torso from a few inches away. "King Neptune," he said, "do you know what I think?"

"What do you think, my queen?"

"I think that Mr. White is a woman!"

The onlookers exploded into bedlam, leaping about and whooping and wailing at the tops of their voices. On the quarterdeck, the captain looked vastly amused, while even Cade smiled somewhat grudgingly.

"Throw her over the side!" Morton shrieked. "She'll bring bad luck to the ship! Toss her over the rail!"

"No, wait!" Baylor bellowed, stopping the sailors who approached Marjorie. "She'll bring bad luck to my kingdom!"

Before Marjorie knew what was happening, someone had tied a thick blindfold over her eyes. Unable to see a thing and with her hands still tied behind her, she felt extremely uneasy as the uproar around her continued.

"We've wished fair winds and a speedy voyage for the ship!" Morton squealed. "How can that happen with bad luck aboard?"

"It can't!" Baylor shouted back. "But I don't want the bad luck sent down to *my* kingdom!"

"Then at least get her off the ship while we decide what to do!" Morton demanded. "Hang her over the side!"

"Aye, that's a good idea, my queen. Look alive there,

mates! Bend a line around the bad luck and pass it through a block! Hang her over the side and get her off the ship!"

Marjorie felt a wide rope threaded under her arms, and it grew taut as a pulley overhead squeaked. She was lifted off the deck, and with a sickening sensation she felt herself sway sideways as she was hoisted higher. Panic seized her as she felt herself being lowered. The voices and clatter of cups against plates were now high above and to one side, and she prayed to hear Captain Tench's voice announcing that that was enough. But the noise and the debate continued, and Marjorie, thinking of Cade, struggled to control her panic.

Then Baylor's voice abruptly changed, losing its joking tone and becoming serious. "Quiet! Be quiet, men! Who rigged that block?"

The noise abruptly ceased, and Morton called out anxiously, abandoning his falsetto voice. "Haul her back up to the deck—hurry!"

"No, no, belay that!" Baylor roared. "The line might break when it passes through the block! You there! Get aloft and get a grip on that line. Starboard watch, get the gig over the side! On the double!"

A sailor yelped, and Marjorie felt a sudden jerk on the rope and almost shouted out as she felt her feet and legs dip into the waves. Numb with terror and knowing she would sink like a stone with her hands tied, she was still determined to deny Cade the satisfaction of hearing her scream in fear.

Abruptly the blindfold was snatched from her eyes. She was hanging perhaps twelve inches over the deck, with her feet in a tub of seawater, and the sailor who had jerked the blindfold off was standing in front of her with a wide grin. All his companions were perched along the mainsail yard high above the deck.

As she looked around in bewilderment, realizing what had happened, the crew burst into howls of laughter. For an instant, embarrassed rage swelled within her, but she quickly controlled it and even forced herself to utter a thin laugh.

The men scrambled down from the yard, lifted her legs from the tub, and lowered her to the deck. Captain

Tench joined the group, and the sailor who had acted as judge handed out certificates to all the victims, attesting that they were sailors in good standing. Captain Tench personally handed Marjorie her certificate and congratulated her for being such a good sport.

"I've seen that trick played on more than a few," he said, "but you're the first I can recall who didn't end up squalling to the heavens."

Baylor, Morton, and several of the sailors crowded around to concur, and Cade, to Marjorie's secret satisfaction, was looking on. His thin face was expressionless, but there was a gleam of something like respect in his eyes.

The gathering broke up, with everyone in jolly spirits, and the shipboard routine was resumed. Marjorie started toward her cabin to put away her certificate and change into dry clothes, and Cade, as if to spite her, waited for her to pass him, then began bellowing at the young sailors and ordering them into the uppermost part of the rigging. Marjorie's self-satisfaction immediately vanished, and her extreme dislike for the cruel first mate returned with renewed force.

VI

Down at the lake, the whistle on the steam launch hooted, signaling that a visitor was aboard. Alexandra, perched on a fence rail while watching Lucy ride one of the hunters, beckoned the girl toward the corral. Toby, Frank, and Bettina were already heading down the path to greet the visitor, and after Alexandra helped Lucy unsaddle the horse, they walked toward the pier. From what Toby had told her, Alexandra knew right away that the visitor could be none other than Edward Blackstone.

Tall and handsome, the Englishman was wearing an impeccably tailored suit, while his steady eyes and the firm line of his jaw revealed that he was anything but a dandy. Alexandra knew that he had recently lost his wife, whom he loved deeply, and she could fully sympathize with him.

She walked out onto the pier with Lucy, and Toby introduced her to Edward. The Englishman took her hand and commented that he shared her interest in fine horses. "Then we'll have to go riding together," Alexandra offered. "Frank has made an excellent cross-country course through the woods."

"I said interest, not skill," Edward pointed out. "From what Toby tells me, I might not be able to keep pace with you. But I enjoy a good steeplechase, and I accept the invitation." He turned to Lucy with a smile. "My word, look how you've grown! It's good to see you again, Lucy."

The girl smiled shyly. Edward was either distracted by his recent misfortune or had forgotten that Lucy stuttered, for he went on to question her: "Let's see, you must be thirteen now, aren't you? Or fourteen? Which is it?"

Her face flushing, Lucy shook her head helplessly. Still failing to understand her silence, or interpreting it as shyness, Edward chucked her playfully under the chin. "Cat got your tongue? I won't let you get away without talking to me. Now, how old are you, my dear?"

Lucy turned crimson and glanced around beseechingly. Frank and Bettina exchanged an uncomfortable glance, and Alexandra was about to say something when Toby put a hand on his friend's shoulder. "Edward, it's undoubtedly slipped your mind that Lucy sometimes has a bit of trouble talking."

"Good Lord!" Edward exclaimed. "How stupid of me to forget! Lucy, my dear, please forgive me—"

But the girl burst into tears and raced off the pier and up the path. Edward tried in vain to call her back, then began apologizing profusely to Frank and Bettina. The couple brushed it aside, but Edward was obviously distressed and angry at himself.

Alexandra, watching Lucy disappear up the path, came to the decision that the present state of affairs was intolerable and that something had to be done. "Bettina, I'll go find her," she said, then excused herself and started up the path.

She found Lucy sitting beside a stall in the barn where the hunters were kept. Her face buried in her arms, the girl was weeping uncontrollably. Alexandra sat beside her, put her arms around Lucy, and talked to her quietly. It took a long time to calm her, and when Alexandra mentioned going to dinner, Lucy shook her head furiously.

"Lucy," Alexandra pleaded, "Mr. Blackstone is as embarrassed as you are, if not more. He'll feel twice as bad if you don't come to dinner. And you'll have to face him sooner or later because he's staying here, isn't he? Come on, let's go."

The girl finally relented, and as they walked toward the house, Alexandra broached the possibility that she could work together with Lucy to try to overcome her stuttering.

Lucy looked apprehensive and shook her head vigorously.

"Try not to worry, Lucy. We'll just give it a try, and if our efforts make you unhappy, we'll stop immediately. In the meantime, you must show Mr. Blackstone that you forgive him, all right?"

Lucy wiped her tear-stained cheeks as she nodded.

In the kitchen the three men were sitting at the table and talking while Bettina minded the stove. Lucy smiled wanly and let Edward apologize, then busied herself helping with the meal. Bettina looked to Alexandra in grateful acknowledgment.

Edward had been telling Toby and Frank about the ranch in Oklahoma that he and his friend, Rob Martin, had bought. He continued on the subject during dinner, explaining what they had been doing. Tick fever, a highly contagious, lethal disease among cattle, was rampant all over the Southwest. Longhorns were immune to it, but they were small, thin cattle. Edward and Rob had been trying to crossbreed them with other cattle, to create larger animals that were immune to the deadly disease. Unfortunately, the experiment was not successful.

"We tried to keep our Herefords separated from the longhorns as much as possible," Edward explained, "but somehow the tick fever got among them. We've lost about a third of them."

Toby grimaced. "That's too bad, Edward. But I hope you'll stick with it. The country needs a breed of large beef cattle that's immune to tick fever."

"It certainly does," Edward agreed. "And we're far from out of business yet." He helped himself to more of Bettina's rich stew. "In any event, time will tell how it works out. Rob assured me he can manage alone for a while."

"You know that this place is your home for as long as you like, Edward," Frank said. "We're pleased to have you here."

Toby had already expressed the same sentiments, and Edward was characteristically agreeable. "For the next few days, at least, Frank, I'd like to have a good ax and plenty of trees to cut down."

There was general laughter around the table, and Toby assured Edward that his wish would be easy to fulfill; but Toby knew that Edward's desire for hard physical labor was due to his need to work out his anger and grief with strong swings of the ax.

When Edward asked Toby about his future plans, the mood at the table quickly changed, for Toby's response was completely unexpected.

"Two days ago," Toby explained, "a telegram for me arrived in Chicago. Captain Crowell brought it, and I read it before dinner. It was from an official in the Interior Department. I expect I'll have a letter or a visitor in the next few days that will clarify what it's all about."

Toby looked at Alexandra in mute apology for not having had a chance to tell her sooner and in private. But her sole concern now was the probability that Toby would leave. Her love for him was the only thing that had sustained her during the past difficult months, and she dreaded the prospect of being parted from him again.

The next morning, however, Alexandra's thoughts were temporarily distracted from Toby, for Lucy had agreed to her first speech lesson. They saddled horses and rode along the shoreline trail until they came to a place where the bluff had eroded into a gradual bank. There they rode down to the shore and dismounted.

When the horses were tethered, Alexandra gathered up about a dozen small pebbles and washed them in the lake. In her rhetoric classes at school in Kentucky, she explained, the students had read about Demosthenes, a famous Greek orator who had practiced speaking with his mouth filled with pebbles. Demosthenes, Alexandra confidently added, had suffered from a severe stammer—a dubious assertion, but since the story struck her as mythical in any case, she didn't see any harm in embellishing it to good purpose.

Willing to try anything, Lucy eagerly took the pebbles and put them in her mouth. Meanwhile, Alexandra produced a small book from her jacket pocket, and after cautioning Lucy to be careful not to choke on the pebbles, she opened to a dog-eared page.

The book was Alexandra's favorite volume of poetry, and the poem she chose was Alfred, Lord Tennyson's

"The Charge of the Light Brigade." She handed the book to Lucy, sat on a driftwood log, and told the girl to read aloud.

The immediate results were, at best, inconclusive. Afraid of choking, Lucy faltered over every syllable, and her voice was so muffled by the pebbles that Alexandra was unable to discern whether or not she was stammering. Nevertheless, Alexandra smiled, nodded encouragement, and told the girl to begin again when she had finally reached the end of the poem.

An hour passed, with Lucy reading the poem over and over in a droning monotone, and Alexandra still had no idea if the procedure would ever help the girl. But the shoreline was a pleasant spot, the day was bright and clear, and Alexandra enjoyed the warm sun and the beauty of the scenery.

Her contentment abruptly faded when she spotted an unfamiliar vessel steaming toward the camp. The realization that the vessel was carrying a visitor who would call Toby away forced everything else from her thoughts.

She stood and told Lucy they would continue the lessons the next day. The girl spit the pebbles out and immediately stammered a question, asking Alexandra if she thought the method was working. Her thoughts still on the vessel, Alexandra gave her an absent smile and spoke encouragingly.

When they returned to the camp, they saw Toby conferring with a stranger outside Frank's office. The man was wearing dark, conservative clothes, and the empty left sleeve of his coat was folded up.

Alexandra joined them, and Toby introduced the visitor as Colonel Frank Bolton from Washington. Alexandra's fears were confirmed.

"I'll have to go away for a time," Toby explained. "It might be for as long as a few months. Will you be all right?"

Alexandra knew that this was the price of her love for the man she admired above all others. His first duty was to his nation, and if she wanted their relationship to thrive, she knew she could not stand in his way. "Of course," she replied, forcing a bright smile. "I'll help you pack your things, Toby."

At thirty-seven years of age, Colonel Andrew Brentwood had lived through pitched battles, Indian fights, desert campaigns, and about everything the army had to offer a soldier, but he considered none so unenjoyable as diplomatic receptions.

So far, Andrew's duties in Bern, a quaint medieval city nestled in the Swiss Alps, had been undemanding and even pleasant. Indeed, except for the unusual message he had received from his colleague Henry Blake, his days had passed uneventfully. In response to Henry's request, Andrew had made discreet inquiries among his few acquaintances in the city, but as yet he had come up with no information about suspicious activities among the city's German exiles.

The matter was far from Andrew's thoughts at present, however, as he waited in the reception line in the grand ballroom of the Dutch embassy. The American ambassador, Howard Ely, and Mrs. Ely were in front of him. Wearing his formal dress uniform, Andrew admired the display of finery all about him. The reception was in honor of Duke Rudolf von Hofstetten, whom Andrew knew next to nothing about and who was not even present yet, according to Martha Ely. The ambassador's wife, a formidable, outgoing woman, was speaking to Andrew in a low voice, identifying the various important people present, and Andrew was doing his best to absorb the information.

"Rudolf von Hofstetten," she was saying about the absent guest of honor, "is actually only the titular head of the Hofstetten family. The *real* leader is his uncle, a count named von Lautzenberg, who is a minister at the court in Vienna. He and the duke are both related to the Hapsburgs, of course, as Howard probably told you. The duke's wife, Lydia—you'll meet her shortly, since she's greeting the guests—is from the Rumanian nobility. It's rumored that their marriage was arranged in order to provide the duke an heir. Von Hofstetten, as anyone who has met him will tell you, cares more for his art collection than for anything else—even his lovely wife."

Andrew was about to ask a question about the duke's relation to the Hapsburgs, the illustrious and powerful ruling family of the Austro-Hungarian Empire, but Mrs. Ely was not finished.

"They haven't had any children yet, though. The duchess is quite young, in her early twenties, and very attractive. He's forty-odd and rather unprepossessing. They have a box at the opera—I've seen them there a few times. They usually arrive late—"

A rising murmur from the guests diverted Mrs. Ely's attention. "There he is now," she informed Andrew.

The duke had emerged from a side door, and Andrew reflected that Mrs. Ely's description of the man as unprepossessing had been an understatement. Frail and sickly looking, with pallid, soft features and almost no chin, he appeared to be the result of too many generations of marriages between cousins.

Evidently he was also petulant and ill-mannered, for instead of joining his wife and his host in the reception line, he wandered off and began examining the paintings on the walls. His rude conduct caused some confusion and embarrassment, especially for the Dutch ambassador, who trailed after him as he peered at the paintings through a lorgnette and criticized them in a thin, high-pitched voice.

The duchess smoothed over the interruption and continued greeting the guests as though nothing untoward had happened. The line had advanced enough for Andrew to get a good look at her, and he reflected that Martha Ely's description of the duke's wife had also been an understatement.

Lydia von Hofstetten was breathtakingly beautiful, with soft blue eyes and blond hair. She was easily the most striking woman present, and her dignified composure in the face of her husband's boorish behavior added to her stature in Andrew's eyes. In contrast to the other women, who were dressed in colorful, elaborate gowns with long trains, plunging necklines, and bare shoulders, she was wearing a modest ivory silk evening dress with long sleeves and a lacy collar. Andrew thought it suited her perfectly.

He was admiring her at his leisure when, to his

surprise, her gaze moved down the line and rested on him.

Their eyes met and held for a few seconds; then with a slight flush rising to her cheeks, Lydia looked away. Andrew felt numb, for the undeniable force of attraction he experienced for this complete stranger had been totally unexpected.

A few minutes later, the Elys were introduced, and Andrew was next in line. The protocol officer glanced down at a list. "Colonel Andrew Jackson Brentwood," the man said. "Military attaché at the embassy of the United States."

Lydia's slender fingers were a feathery touch against his palm, and her delicate perfume wafted around him as Andrew bowed over her hand. Avoiding a repetition of what had happened before, Lydia kept her gaze fixed on a point to one side of his face. "I see that you are the namesake of a famous American, Colonel Brentwood," she said in Rumanian-accented English, her voice pure music to Andrew. "Do you model your life after his?"

"My aspirations aren't as high as his were, Your Grace," Andrew replied. "But I try to live by the same principles he did."

"Considering your age and rank, it seems your aspirations hardly kept pace with your success. Thank you for joining us, and I hope you enjoy the occasion."

"It has already afforded unsurpassed pleasure, Your Grace."

Her smile almost became more than polite, and her eyes met his for the briefest instant before she greeted the next guest. Andrew moved off, took a glass of champagne from a passing waiter, and joined Martha and Howard Ely, who were discussing the duke's rude behavior. The duke was still inspecting the paintings, occasionally dabbing at his lips and forehead with a handkerchief as he lectured his host.

Lydia von Hofstetten eventually joined a group of people across the room, and when the Elys started talking to a British couple, Andrew, almost without thinking about what he was doing, wandered in her direction.

Their eyes met again. Instead of acknowledging him,

Lydia blushed and moved away, and Andrew realized she was avoiding him. His few seconds near her had been like a moment of basking in the sun after an eternity of darkness and freezing cold, but Andrew realized it had to end with that. After all, she was a married woman and a member of a ruling family of Europe, and he was a simple soldier.

Nevertheless, Andrew could hardly prevent himself from glancing in her direction every so often, and once he caught her gazing at him.

It was more than an hour later, while he was engaged in a desultory conversation with a member of the French embassy, when he noticed that Lydia and her husband were moving toward the door with the Dutch ambassador, making their farewells. Despondent, Andrew felt he had discovered a priceless treasure, only to have it snatched from his grasp.

Yet even as he watched, the duke suddenly stopped and peered nearsightedly across the room at him, or at someone behind him. The polite smiles of those in the duke's party faded while the man fumbled for his lorgnette and then held it to his eyes. He started walking briskly toward Andrew.

All conversation in the room became hushed as the duke halted in front of Andrew and inspected the insignia on his uniform. "You are an American army officer?" he asked.

"Yes, Your Grace," Andrew replied. "I am Colonel—"

"Come with me!" the duke interrupted.

"I beg your pardon?"

"Come with me!" von Hofstetten repeated, taking Andrew's arm. His petulant frown changed to the first smile Andrew had seen on the wan face, and he tugged on Andrew's arm. "Please," he added.

Their voices were loud in the silence that had settled over the room. People were craning their necks and looking on in surprise and perplexity that matched Andrew's. Howard Ely, catching Andrew's eye, motioned frantically for him to do as the man asked.

As Andrew walked toward the door with the duke, he glanced at Lydia, who followed slightly behind. She appeared disconcerted, yet at the same time, he realized, her lovely blue eyes were shining with amusement. He was whisked into the duke's carriage outside and was moving away from the embassy before he found out the reason behind the strange, urgent invitation. The duke, sitting across from him, explained that he had an etching of a military scene he wanted to question Andrew about and that he was delighted to have found an American army officer. Glancing again at Lydia, who sat next to her husband, Andrew reflected that the duke's delight could not possibly compare with his own.

A short time later, the carriage drew to a halt in the courtyard of a stately, stone-built town residence. The duke quickly climbed out and hurried inside, leaving Andrew to help Lydia. Without hesitating, the duchess gathered up the hem of her gown and put her arm through his as Andrew assisted her up the steps.

Inside, von Hofstetten beckoned them to hurry across the entry hall. Lydia paused to give instructions to the butler who took their coats, while Andrew followed the duke into a vast room cluttered with paintings leaning against the walls and tables piled high with stacks of prints. The duke leafed through a stack and, finding what he wanted, handed it to Andrew.

"This arrived yesterday from my agent in Paris," he said. "It is an etching by a new artist, and the execution is magnificent. Unfortunately, the subject matter confuses me. These are American soldiers, are they not? But the ones they are fighting are not your Western Indians, or at least do not appear to be."

At first Andrew was as mystified as he was surprised. The etching depicted a cavalry charge, and the officer leading the troops looked exactly like Reed Kerr. A glance at the signature in a bottom corner made everything clear. Andrew had learned from one of his mother's letters that Cindy Holt Kerr was studying art in Paris, and the signature was "C. Kerr."

Andrew explained to the duke about the comancheros. "This group," he said, "was led by a man called Calusa Jim. Here they had attacked a supply train traveling from Fort Yuma to Fort Peck, in the Arizona Territory. The artist, Cindy Kerr, was being escorted by the supply train, and her husband, this man, was killed in the battle."

His eyes wide with astonishment, von Hofstetten clutched his handkerchief to his brow. "You know the artist?" he exclaimed.

"I know her very well indeed. Her family and mine have been friends for years. Her brother is one of my closest friends. Cindy is now studying in Paris with a Russian woman—a Madame Kirovna, I believe."

"Madame Kirovna!" the duke gasped. "She is a supreme master! The artist is associated with *her*? You must tell me all about it! I want to know everything about the artist!" Apparently overwrought, the duke swayed on his feet, and Andrew reached out to support him. Lydia, who had been standing behind them, came to his assistance, and she called to the butler, who had just appeared with a tray laid out with a decanter and tiny glasses. The butler helped her ease the duke into a chair beside the fire.

"There, Your Grace," she said. "You must calm yourself. Colonel Brentwood, please sit down."

The duke was panting and wiping his face with his handkerchief. Lydia dismissed the butler and filled the small glasses from the decanter, and the duke drained his in a single gulp. She refilled it, handed Andrew a glass, then sat down.

The drink, a sweet, thick apricot liqueur, seemed to restore von Hofstetten's strength, for he asked to hear more about Cindy. He listened in fascination as Andrew told him about Cindy's background, and his politely worded questions were in stark contrast to his earlier rudeness.

Out of kindness, Andrew tried to include Lydia in the conversation, but the duke seemed completely unaware of her presence or of Andrew's interest in her. Lydia herself grew less reserved, as if no longer keeping Andrew at a distance.

A door suddenly opened, and a tall, somberly clad man stepped into the room. After a moment of awkward silence, Lydia introduced him as Emil Villach, the duke's private secretary. About fifty years old and with sharp, saturnine features, Villach was wearing a dark suit that struck Andrew as extremely elegant for a private secretary. His bearing and gaze were also not those of an employee. Andrew noted that the duke was eying him with ill-concealed dislike.

Villach appeared dissatisfied by Lydia's terse introduction. "I presume the colonel was a guest at tonight's reception?" he prompted.

"Yes," Lydia answered, then explained why Andrew had been invited to the house.

"A friend of the artist—that is most fortunate indeed," Villach said without enthusiasm, the suspicion gone from his narrow eyes. He bowed almost imperceptibly. "It was a pleasure to meet you, Colonel Brentwood. Your Grace, please forgive my interruption."

The duke's only reply was an annoyed grunt as Villach withdrew. Lydia refilled the glasses, and Andrew soon forgot about the intrusion as von Hofstetten questioned him about the fate of Cindy's husband. The fact that Reed Kerr had died in the charge was of no particular interest to him, but Lydia was appalled. Clearly of a romantic disposition, she was nearly moved to tears by the tragic tale.

It was growing late, and the duke looked haggard with fatigue. When Lydia mentioned the hour, Andrew quickly volunteered a suggestion: "We could discuss this further at your convenience, Your Grace. Also, I could write to Cindy to learn if more of her etchings are available."

"Yes, please do." The duke heaved himself from his chair with his remaining energy and warmly grasped Andrew's hand. "I would be most grateful to you, Colonel Brentwood. Now, if you will excuse me—" The butler stepped in, and the duke leaned on his arm as they left the room.

Left alone, Andrew and Lydia at first did not know what to say. The silence stretched out, and the blush on Lydia's delicate features grew deeper by the second. Andrew, to spare her further embarrassment, moved to the door and held it open for her.

In the entry hall, she found her voice as she retrieved Andrew's hat and cloak.

"I will summon the carriage to take you home, Colonel Brentwood," she offered quietly.

"Thank you, Your Grace, but I live only a short distance away and will benefit from the walk."

At the door he bowed over her hand, but as he straightened, she squeezed his fingers gently and, for the first time, favored him with a smile. Andrew, not expecting such a gesture, was absolutely spellbound.

All the way home, he kept telling himself that Lydia was a married woman. Yet the joy he felt in his heart could not be subdued. He lay in bed sleepless for hours, looking up into the darkness and thinking of her.

The next morning, the events of the night before seemed almost like a dream, but Andrew had concrete evidence of their reality when he reached his office. Ambassador Ely had come to the embassy earlier than usual and was waiting to ask him what had transpired when he accompanied the duke home.

Andrew's brief recounting of the events was greeted with delight. Regardless of what Ely himself felt about the man, Rudolf von Hofstetten was a member of the ruling family in Vienna, which made a friendship with him a diplomatic coup. Ely was dismayed, however, when he found that Andrew had been contemplating merely writing to Cindy. "Surely you could make a trip to Paris, couldn't you, Andrew? Your duties aren't all that pressing, and your expenses would be paid, of course."

"Yes, I suppose I could go there, sir. I would have to cancel a few appointments, but nothing urgent."

"Good," Ely said. "Check with me personally the minute you get back."

Thus, the next morning Andrew was packing a bag in his apartment, with the intention of catching the early train for Paris. He was just leaving for the station when, to his surprise, Duke Rudolf's private secretary, Emil Villach, pulled up in a carriage. Villach had found out what was happening, for he asked Andrew what train he was leaving on, then offered to drive him to the station.

The man lifted a hand when Andrew started to demur. "Please," he said, "it is a very small thing to do, Colonel Brentwood. I am grateful for your efforts on His

Grace's behalf, and the least I can do is make those efforts less burdensome."

Andrew accepted the short ride to the station, and Villach said hardly another word. It wasn't until Andrew had boarded his train that he recalled something Martha Ely had said: Rudolf von Hofstetten was only the titular head of the family; the real leader was his uncle, Count von Lautzenberg.

All at once the situation became clear to Andrew: Villach worked for the count, not for the duke. He had the nominal title of private secretary, but in actuality he was the duke's *keeper*, responsible to the count for ensuring that von Hofstetten did nothing to embarrass the family.

Apparently, a quick exchange of telegrams had taken place between Bern and Vienna early that morning, with the count giving his blessing to a friendship between the duke and an American army colonel. But that failed to explain everything, and as Andrew stared out the window at the passing Swiss countryside, he could not shake the uneasy feeling that there were aspects to the situation he knew nothing at all about.

When the *Beluga* began battling its way around Cape Horn in the teeth of a raging gale, Marjorie finally understood the first officer's purpose in making the young sailors clamber about in the rigging.

The storm canvas had to be constantly adjusted to take advantage of every change in the wind, and the weary deckhands had no respite. They climbed aloft again and again, with the rigging encrusted with ice from the freezing rain and snow. Yet the young sailors for whom Marjorie had feared were now expert hands, in no more danger of falling than the older and more experienced men.

During the gray, stormy second day that the ship was working its way around the Cape, Marjorie became increasingly aware of another sound above the howling of the wind and the groaning of the ship's hull as it tossed on the waves. Because the fierce pounding of the waves had opened leaks in the hull, the bilge pumps were working nonstop with a rhythmic, knocking noise. Both watches were exhausted from fighting the storm, and Marjorie,

who could not lend a hand aloft, felt obliged at least to
help with the pumps.

As she emerged on deck for the first time in nearly
thirty-six hours, the icy wind and spray almost took her
breath away. Waves were breaking over the bow, and
Marjorie waited for the water to subside, then grasped the
storm lifeline firmly and started forward. She had taken
only a few steps when another wave broke across the deck
and almost swept her off her feet, soaking her to the waist
through her oilskins. Clinging to the lifeline, she struggled
on.

The pumps, situated next to the mainmast, were op-
erated by two large, wheeled cranks, a sailor at each one.
Marjorie grabbed the arm of the nearer sailor. "I'll take
over now!" she shouted over the wind.

The man, his eyes dull and his lips blue with cold,
looked at her doubtfully. "Are you sure you can do it,
ma'am?"

"If you'll get out of the way!"

He untied his safety line and fastened it around her
waist, and she gripped the wooden handle and began
turning the heavy wheel.

A few minutes later, Cade came along the lifeline and
halted beside her. His dour face was as unreadable as
always, and without saying a word he checked her safety
line, tied an extra knot in it, then gripped the lifeline
again and went on about his business.

After a time, Marjorie stopped shivering from the icy
wind and the freezing seawater surging around her. She
had become numb. She was dimly aware that her arms
and back ached from turning the heavy wheel, but presently that pain, too, faded into numbness.

Her sense of time disappeared, and it seemed there
was nothing in her mind but her dogged determination to
keep the wheel turning. When Cade was at her side again,
with a sailor to relieve her, Marjorie was surprised to
realize that darkness was falling and she had been at the
pump most of the day.

Her legs were weak, and Cade wrapped an arm around
her waist and helped her to the companionway. She stiffly
descended the ladder and went into the officers' mess,

which was dimly illuminated by a lantern swinging wildly from the ceiling. Tench and Baylor were asleep on the floor, and wet blankets were scattered about. A plate of cheese and ship's biscuits was on the table, and Marjorie ate a few bites, then felt her way to her cabin. She pulled off her oilskins, and, not bothering to undress, she huddled in her bunk with a blanket pulled around her.

A change in the motion of the ship woke her some hours later. She could hear Cade bellowing orders on deck. Marjorie threw off her blanket, donned her soaked oilskins, and tiredly felt her way back down the dark passageway.

When she emerged on deck, she immediately noticed that the storm had lessened. Listening closely to the orders Cade was roaring, she also realized that the wind had changed direction, for hands were being sent aloft to set more sail to take advantage of it.

The danger of being swept overboard was still acute, especially in the darkness, and Marjorie cautiously advanced along the lifeline. When she reached the pumps, she shouted to the sailor, transferred the safety line, and recommenced turning the crank. The rough wooden handle pained her blistered hands, and all her aches and pains returned with renewed intensity, but presently she became numb and lost her sense of time again.

Gray, bleak dawn broke over the ship and the tossing sea, and Marjorie realized that some of the sails had been ripped to shreds and were streaming out from the yards, while others had gaping tears in them. But most of them were bulging tautly, speeding the ship into the vast Pacific, with Cape Horn falling rapidly behind.

At midmorning, a sailor took Marjorie's place, and she returned to her cabin, collapsed on her bunk as before, and immediately fell asleep.

When she woke, the ship's motion had moderated. After washing and changing into dry, clean clothes, she went on deck to see the late afternoon sun shining through clouds. Realizing she was famished, and smelling an appetizing aroma issuing from the galley, Marjorie went below to the officers' mess, where Tench, Cade, and Baylor were seated in their accustomed places, waiting for their first hot meal in days. She gratefully accepted the captain's invitation to join them.

Baylor and Captain Tench were ebullient over the unusually quick, easy passage around the Cape, and even Horatio Cade was grudgingly cheerful. The captain complimented Marjorie on her fortitude at the pumps. "You've certainly earned your sailor's certificate," he said, "as well as the crew's unbounded admiration."

"I did little enough to deserve it," Marjorie replied. "But I did learn something during the past days." She turned to the first mate. "Mr. Cade, I grievously wronged you the first day we were at sea. I accused you of putting the young sailors at risk, but now I know that you were training them to be able to handle danger. Contrary to what I said, you do have a sincere concern for those young men, which proves to me that beneath your hard exterior beats a heart of purest gold. I hope you will find it in that heart to forgive what I said."

Cade's leathery face had turned crimson, and he glared at Marjorie in speechless discomfiture. Baylor, with some difficulty, concealed his amusement, but Captain Tench fairly beamed. "Come, Mr. Cade," he said, chuckling, "why are you so vexed? That's as pretty a speech as I've ever heard. In return, you might relent from accusing her of bringing bad luck to the ship. She obviously hasn't, and you'll have to admit it."

"I'll admit it, then," Cade growled. "But that's all I'll admit." He was saved further embarrassment by the appearance of the cabin boy with the meal—thick slices of broiled salt pork with potatoes and lentils. While Cade and Tench ate, they discussed repairs that would have to be made and the course they would steer across the Pacific.

"Winds and weather permitting, we'll head straight for the south of New Zealand," the captain decided. "The hunting should be good there this time of year."

"We can expect to keep a full crew, then," Cade offered with his accustomed gloom. "When we put in for fresh water, it won't be at some port town where the men will get drunk, make trouble, and end up in jail."

"That's true," the captain agreed. "The west coast of

South Island isn't exactly the liveliest place on earth for a run ashore."

Te Pomore, a Maori village chief of the primitive Tuhoe tribe, picked his way across a densely forested valley near the west coast of New Zealand's South Island. His people, loaded down with heavy bundles, straggled behind him in a long line. The chief walked slowly, for the women and children were weary, and many of the warriors were yet recovering from wounds.

A few weeks before, Te Pomore and his tribesmen had clashed with the mighty Ngatitoa tribe of North Island and been defeated. The Ngatitoas were fierce enemies, and to avoid capture and enslavement, Te Pomore and his people had fled across the narrow strait to South Island. After looting storehouses on a few isolated farms, they had begun the long march southward into the untracked wilderness along the west coast, in search of a suitable site for a new village.

The forest had been nearly impenetrable in places, and the climate here was colder than on North Island, making the trek arduous. It appeared to Te Pomore, however, that the journey was now near an end and had been well worth the hardships.

On every side the chief saw trails made by wild pigs, as well as an abundance of edible plants. And just ahead, toward one side of the valley, was a knoll that would be easy to defend. Although clashes with other tribes or with white settlers were unlikely in this remote place, the chief was wary of being pursued by farmers they had looted. In time, a palisade wall could be built atop the knoll to turn it into an impregnable fortress.

Behind him, the chief heard others expressing the same thoughts. He led the villagers to the top of the knoll, and for the first time in weeks, their conversation was cheerful as they looked around. Te Pomore called his two chieftains to one side, and they agreed that a perfect place for a village had been found.

"There is a stream," one of them said, pointing toward the center of the valley. "We shall have a good source of water."

"And the coast is but a short march away," the other chieftain added. "We shall have a good supply of shellfish and other food from the sea during seasons when edible plants are scarce."

Te Pomore needed no further counsel. "Have the people build fires and start working on shelters," he directed. "I will follow the creek and look at the coastline."

The chieftains walked away, shouting orders, and Te Pomore picked out two warriors and set off down the valley. Without the villagers to slow them, the three men covered the miles rapidly, and when the ocean finally came into view, Te Pomore was well pleased.

The creek emptied into a sheltered bay, and the beach nearby was littered with barrel staves and the remains of a broken boat. There were places where fires had been built. The warriors realized that ships had been coming to the bay and sending boats ashore to fill water casks in the creek.

"We can keep a boy on watch here," one of the warriors suggested excitedly, "and when a ship comes, we could seize it."

Te Pomore was thinking the same thing. "Yes, a ship would yield us rope, tools, and many other treasures." Reflecting on the fate his own tribe had narrowly escaped, he broke into a wide grin. "We could make slaves of the crew, for this is a place from which they could not escape. And if they refused to work"—he rubbed his empty belly meaningfully—"we could have a feast of long pig, as in the days of our grandfathers."

The two warriors, not certain if he was joking, looked at him searchingly. Then, deciding he was not, they, too, grinned in hungry anticipation.

VII

Carriages were crowded along the curb in front of the Kirovna Gallery, and the display room was filled with customers when Andrew Brentwood went inside. After a moment he spotted Cindy at a high desk near the back of the room.

With her sandy blond hair, blue eyes, and unmistakable Holt features, Cindy struck Andrew as somehow essentially American, and as he crossed the room toward her, he observed by the way the shop girls addressed her that she had quickly worked her way into a position of authority—also characteristic of a Holt.

When Cindy saw him, she exclaimed in delight. "Andy!" She hurried from behind her table and hugged him. "I can hardly believe it's you! But you're stationed in Bern, aren't you?"

Andrew took her hand, intending to express his condolences over Reed's death, but then changed his mind. It was evident Cindy had put her grief behind her, for he had never seen her look more radiant. For an instant, Cindy, too, hesitated, apparently having the same doubts about mentioning Andrew's wife, who had died since the last time Cindy had seen him. Andrew smiled, released her hand, and asked her how she liked Paris.

"I love it!" Cindy paused to nod to a customer and tell him in French that she would be with him shortly. "I only wish I had more hours in the day to enjoy it. As you can see, I'm working hard—but not too hard. And excuse me if I look a little tired. It's because I went to a friend's birthday party last night and was up till all hours. But what brings you to Paris? Are you here on official business?"

"I guess you could say that." Andrew glanced over his shoulder at the customers and clerks. "You're busy now. Could we get together for dinner? Or if you're tired, we could wait till tomorrow to talk."

"Absolutely not. Besides, tired or not, I'm always ready to go out on the town as soon as the sun sets. Do you have a room yet?"

"No, I came directly here from the station."

Cindy went to her desk and scribbled a note on a piece of paper. "There's a good, reasonable hotel right down the street." She handed him the note. "All our out-of-town customers stay there. It's the Chaillot—just give that to the desk clerk. The gallery closes at six, and I live upstairs. Shall I expect you at seven?"

She walked him out to the street, and by the time Andrew had installed himself at the Chaillot and unpacked and changed, it was almost seven. Cindy, who had changed into a stylish blue muslin dress, took him upstairs to introduce him to Madame Kirovna, and then they left.

Outside, she explained that the aged woman suffered from arthritis, but Janessa had sent a concoction of herbs that had been remarkably effective in relieving the condition. "She can even work on her etchings now, and she finished a couple just this week, both of them absolutely superb."

They went to a restaurant on the fashionable Champs-Élysées. Once inside, Andrew saw that Cindy had made herself completely at home in Paris. The maître d'hôtel greeted her by name and led them to a choice table, and the waiter also addressed her by name.

During the meal, which featured a bouillabaisse, a spicy fish stew, Andrew recounted the unusual circumstances behind his visit to Paris. Cindy, flattered by the duke's interest, responded with characteristic generosity. After explaining that the etching in the duke's collection was one of a set of five, she told Andrew that she would assemble a complete set for him. "And collectors have been eagerly awaiting the new works by Madame Kirovna, so I'll get him copies of those. I'm sure she won't object."

"Neither will the duke," Andrew added as an understatement. "I'll pay for them, of course, and he can reimburse me—"

"No, I won't hear of it," Cindy interrupted. "Besides, they sell for enormous sums, far above what I consider their true value. So for personal friends we can afford to give them away."

"Then business is good?"

"Almost too good," Cindy said with a laugh. "And all Madame Kirovna has to do is select the right artists to display, and she has a genius for that. Of course, in the art trade, making too much money is considered gauche, so it's also a little embarrassing for her."

The waiter brought another bottle of wine, and after they had finished the meal, Cindy suddenly asked Andrew if he had seen or heard from Henry Blake.

The subject was touchy, because a major upheaval had occurred in the Holt and Blake families when Henry had broken his engagement with Cindy. It had happened years before, but Andrew knew there were still raw feelings about it. Uncertain of Cindy's attitude, he replied cautiously that he had.

"I'm certain he's doing well, of course," Cindy said wistfully, "because I heard he's a captain, while most of his classmates are still second lieutenants. But I often wonder if he's happy. He still lives with that baroness, doesn't he?"

"Yes. They have a child now, a son."

Cindy laughed—a bit nervously, Andrew thought. "A child out of wedlock?" she asked. "He'll certainly get a chiding from Toby the next time they meet."

"Without a doubt." He strongly suspected that Henry and the baroness were married by now, if only for the sake of their child. But he was uncomfortable discussing the subject with Cindy and was grateful when the conversation was interrupted by a young, well-dressed man who approached the table. Cindy greeted him warmly and introduced him as Pierre Charcot, a sculptor and a friend of hers. Andrew asked him to join them and called to the waiter to bring another wineglass.

"I see that you are out again tonight," Charcot teased Cindy. "I am sure that others who were at the party last night are in bed early, but you have the energy of ten people."

"You're also out tonight, aren't you, Pierre?" Cindy needled.

"Only because I was hungry," the man replied. "I've had my dinner, and if I don't go to bed soon, I'll fall asleep in my chair."

Listening to the conversation and observing Charcot, who seemed a bit jealous of him, Andrew concluded that the young man was in love with Cindy. But it was equally clear that she viewed Charcot only as a friend.

Cindy changed the subject, saying she wanted Andrew to visit the studio where Charcot worked and see the project currently in progress. The Frenchman readily agreed. "Don't say another word, Pierre," Cindy said quickly. "I want it to be a surprise. Andy, what time did you say you planned to leave tomorrow?"

"At three."

"That will give us plenty of time," she said. "I'll ask Madame Kirovna to look after the gallery. We'll all have lunch together and go to Pierre's studio at one."

The next morning, after a leisurely carriage drive around the city to see the sights, Andrew arrived at the art gallery shortly before noon. Cindy, who had already wrapped the etchings protectively, gave the driver the address of a sidewalk café in Montmartre, which offered a panoramic view of the city. Lunch was cold poached chicken, salad, and fruit, with white wine, and Charcot and Cindy, both evidently well-known in the district that was the cultural center of Paris, exchanged greetings with numerous passersby. During the meal, she and Charcot talked about the city's notable artists, who included Degas, Manet, and Renoir.

After lunch the three of them took a carriage down from the heights of Montmartre toward the Seine. The studio where Charcot worked was on a narrow street near the river, and when Andrew saw the name of the proprietor on the door, he immediately knew what was in store.

The name, Frédéric Auguste Bartholdi, had been in all the newspapers, for he was the master sculptor responsible for the monumental statue called Liberty, being built as a gift to the United States. Andrew had seen artists' conceptions of the statue, but they paled in comparison to the model that he beheld as he walked through the door.

The master sculptor himself came in while Charcot was explaining to Andrew how the full-size statue was being made. A slim, studious, and quiet-spoken man of forty, Bartholdi was delighted by the visit of an American army officer. Andrew expressed his gratitude for what the sculptor was doing.

"It is an honor for me to do this, Colonel Brentwood," Bartholdi said. "I have an opportunity to glorify liberty and to symbolize the friendship between our two great nations."

The sculptor took Andrew's elbow and led him to another, smaller model, this of the statue's right hand. "The centennial of your country will be celebrated soon, and I hope to have the torch and the right hand ready for exhibition in Philadelphia."

Bartholdi's studio was only a short distance from the railroad station, and as Andrew took his leave, waving to Charcot and Cindy, he reflected that his trip to Paris had been far more successful and enjoyable than his most optimistic expectations. Not only had he obtained more than he had come for, but he had also been able to see the model of the Statue of Liberty, and, most important, he had found Cindy in good spirits and clearly recovered from her recent tragedy.

Rudolf von Hofstetten's excited reaction to the etchings was alarming. It was midafternoon of the following day when Andrew stood in the duke's cluttered study, watching the man leaf through the prints.

Lydia was also there, to Andrew's delight. She was even more lovely, he thought, than the first time he had seen her. She was wearing a simple white muslin lawn suit, which seemed to heighten by contrast the rosiness of her cheeks.

The duke was plying his handkerchief and spluttering, searching for superlatives to express his gratitude. Once again, to Andrew's alarm, the man's enthusiasm proved to be too much, and he swayed on his feet, his features turning as white as Lydia's dress. She took his elbow to steady him. "Are you ill, Your Grace?" she asked. "Is it one of your headaches?"

Clutching his forehead and wincing in pain, he nodded. "Ring for the butler," he murmured. "Colonel Brentwood, I must once again apologize for this indisposition."

"There is no need to apologize," Andrew said, moving to support the man as Lydia rang the bell.

The butler appeared at once. "I will look forward to seeing you tomorrow evening, then," von Hofstetten called back weakly as the butler took his arm and helped him to the door. "Order refreshments for our good friend and entertain him," he directed Lydia.

The door closed. Andrew's gaze met Lydia's. "I can't help but feel somewhat responsible for this. Will he be all right?"

"Yes, by tomorrow, probably," she replied. "This often happens when he becomes very angry or excited. He is not a strong man." A touch of amusement transformed her features. "I've been commanded to entertain you. Would you like to go out to the gardens?"

"If you go with me," Andrew said, stepping ahead of her to open the door. He was somewhat disconcerted to see Emil Villach crossing the entry hall toward them; the man's expression revealed little, however, as he greeted Andrew. While Lydia gave instructions to a servant, Villach spoke with Andrew about the duke's sudden illnesses. "Alas, they are very frequent. I am sure His Grace wished to talk with you at length, Colonel Brentwood."

"His Grace has invited the colonel to dinner tomorrow evening," Lydia put in as she rejoined Andrew. Her tone indicated she was dutifully informing Villach of the invitation rather than making a passing remark, thus confirming Andrew's conclusions about the Austrian's position in the household.

"Excellent," Villach commented woodenly.

He left, and Lydia escorted Andrew out into the warm spring sunshine. A high stone wall enclosed the garden and provided privacy. The flower beds were ablaze with color, and the snowcapped Alps loomed high, making for spectacular surroundings. Lydia and Andrew walked along the flagstone path to a lawn table and chairs in a leafy bower. The servant appeared, put a tray on the table, and left.

Lydia filled the two tiny, stemmed glasses with a purplish liqueur from the decanter, and Andrew lifted his glass in a silent toast and took a sip. The potent drink combined the flavors of lemon, citron, spices, and honey, and Andrew, unfamiliar with it, asked Lydia what it was called.

"It is made in the Loire Valley," she replied vaguely. "Your friend Cindy Kerr and the tragic fate of her husband have been much on my mind, Andrew. Is she well and happy in Paris?"

Noticing Lydia had used his first name, Andrew hesitated a moment, then described Cindy's position at the art gallery. "She's made a new life for herself, and I've never seen her happier." He caught her gaze and held it. "What did you do while I was in Paris, Lydia?"

She started to toss off a light reply, then stopped when she saw Andrew's expression. "I thought about us," she admitted quietly, looking away as her face reddened. "I resolved that when you returned, I would find a way to end this . . . improper attraction. But the moment I saw you, my resolve vanished." She looked truly miserable. "We both have our responsibilities, Andrew. We should look to them instead of to each other."

"Of course we have our responsibilities," he agreed, "but I don't see how they are involved in this."

"Then you are ignoring the obvious. I am a married woman."

Andrew knew that what he was about to say was unfair, but he could not stop himself. "Married to whom? A title? A ghost of a husband who doesn't care a whit for you? If what is between us were only a frivolous attraction, it would be another matter entirely, but this feeling I have for you is strong and very real—more real, perhaps, than your marriage."

Lydia could not answer him, and she chose instead to change the subject and refill their glasses. "I have a great interest in aboriginal peoples," she said. "Did you find the Indians of your West interesting?"

Andrew nodded resignedly and began telling her about his experiences. Simply to be in Lydia's company was enjoyable, and the time seemed to fly past until Andrew had to take his leave.

The next day, Andrew met with Ambassador Ely to relate the results of his trip to Paris, and in the evening he returned to the von Hofstetten residence.

Dinner was a sedate affair, served in a small dining room. The duke ate sparingly, having only soup and a few vegetables, while Andrew and Lydia did justice to course after course. The duke repeatedly expressed his deep gratitude for the etchings and his desire to purchase more whenever they became available, but otherwise he fell into long silences, which Lydia gracefully filled.

"The season at the opera house will end soon," she said. "Rudolf and I will attend the closing night, of course. As sponsors of the company, we could hardly miss it."

The duke did not appear pleased. "I wanted nothing to do with that," he grumbled. "Lydia constantly gets me involved in activities that waste my time." He suddenly looked at Andrew with renewed interest. "Did you say you were going, Colonel Brentwood?"

Andrew was momentarily taken aback. "I—I hadn't considered it seriously, Your Grace."

"You might like it—and you could escort the duchess. You would have a better seat in our box than in the audience, and my carriage would be at your disposal, of course."

"I would be honored," Andrew started to answer. "That is, if the duchess—"

"Good! It's settled, then." The duke was beaming.

"My pleasure, Your Grace." Andrew wasn't sure how else to reply.

Lydia, seemingly as surprised as Andrew, glanced between him and her husband but did not object; Andrew even thought he detected a smile.

Later, when it was time for Andrew to leave, the duke took him aside and commented on how pleasant the evening had been. "By the way," he added, his tone one of confirming something that was understood, "you will dine with us tomorrow, won't you, Colonel Brentwood?"

Andrew did not refuse.

The following evening, and then the next, were much the same, except that the duke regarded Andrew ever more favorably. Andrew consequently learned more about the duke and Lydia, such as the startling fact that they had seen each other for the first time on their wedding day. It soon became clear that the duke expected Andrew to provide Lydia with companionship. Since the older man was interested only in his art collection, he viewed her company as an intrusion, and the more Andrew occupied her attention, the happier the duke was.

On the Saturday after he returned from Paris, Andrew took Lydia on an afternoon outing to the heights above Bern, and the next day he escorted her to a garden party organized to raise funds for an orphanage. When they were alone, he occasionally took her hand, but Lydia was so ruled by her conscience that he refrained from pressing his attentions on her.

When Andrew escorted Lydia to the opera, it was late in the evening when they returned. Andrew kissed Lydia in the carriage, and she did not object. The house was quiet and dark, with everyone but the butler retired for the night. Lydia dismissed him and, taking a decanter and glasses, bade Andrew to follow her to her sitting room upstairs, where she had a book she wanted him to see.

The volume turned out to be a collection of lithographs of American Indian scenes, and Lydia, taking a seat beside Andrew on the couch, asked him to tell her whatever he could about the Indians represented. She poured him a glass of the same potent, purplish drink they always had. Andrew took a sip and asked her what it was called. "It is made in the Loire Valley," she answered.

"Yes, you told me that before. But what is it called?"

Lydia met and held his gaze. "Parfait Amour."

"No wonder it tastes so good."

Lydia let the book fall closed as Andrew kissed her. At first she remained passive, but Andrew, sensing a change in her, kissed her more passionately, and Lydia relaxed in his arms in complete surrender.

When Andrew started to gather her up in his arms, she pulled away and quickly got up and went into her bedroom. Andrew heard clothes rustling, and a minute later she called to him softly. With eager steps he went to her.

Toby Holt paused in the back door of the ranch house to take in the spectacular beauty of the New Mexican sunrise. A grass fire somewhere in the vast reaches of the Llano Estacado, the Staked Plain east of the Pecos River, left a hint of smoke on the horizon, turning the sunrise into a burst of crimson light. Copses of trees and knots of browsing cattle scattered over fertile grasslands made a peaceful panorama, but several mounds of earth, where dead animals had recently been buried, were a jarring sight.

Toby stepped back into the kitchen and put down the pail of milk he was carrying. The room was spacious and homey, but dust and disorder revealed the lack of a woman's care during the past weeks. On the stove a coffeepot was boiling furiously, and a pan of biscuit dough on the table had finished rising. Toby moved the coffeepot to one side, put the biscuits in the oven, and emptied the pail of milk into a pitcher.

A moment later, heavy boots thumped against the floor, and a man emerged from the hallway. Bill Hawkins, a muscular, grizzled man of forty and the owner of the ranch, buttoned his shirt as he greeted Toby. "You're up early, Tom," he remarked.

Knowing that his name might be recognized and wanting to proceed as carefully as possible with his investigation, Toby had introduced himself to his host as Tom Miller. "I like to get a head start on the day," Toby replied, taking a slab of bacon from the food safe. "I hope you don't mind my making breakfast."

Hawkins chuckled as he stepped to the sink. "Certainly not, especially after that supper you fixed up last night. You can do all the cooking you want." Working the pump, he looked out the window. "Reckon it's going to be another warm, clear one." After washing his face, he sat down at the table. "I'd sure like to offer you a permanent job, but with the shape those comancheros left me in, I'm just barely scraping along."

Toby sliced the bacon and laid the strips in a hot frying pan. "That's all right. I think I'll ride west and see what I can find around the Rio Grande."

"From the looks of you," Hawkins commented, "you look more like a lawman or ranch owner than a drifter. Well, one thing is sure—you're more'n handy enough at cooking to get a job doing that."

"I like to eat," Toby said. "When you shift for yourself, you have to learn to cook." Toby removed the bacon from the pan and waited for a reply. His choice of words had been deliberate, meant to get the man to talk about the comanchero attack. Hawkins had said little about it, for the experience was painful to him, and the only information Toby had obtained was what he had been able to see for himself.

For a moment, it looked as though the man would talk about it, but as he sipped the coffee Toby had poured, Hawkins noticed the pitcher on the side of the stove. "Where'd you get that milk?" he asked when he saw Toby grin. "You mean you milked one of those range cows?"

"Sure did," Toby acknowledged ruefully, rubbing a shin that was sore from a kick he had been unable to avoid. "I sneaked up on her while it was still dark and she was asleep. But it didn't take her long to wake up and figure out I wasn't her calf."

Hawkins whistled in wonder. "You're lucky you're alive! You can't milk a range cow!"

"Then tell me where I got that milk," Toby retorted. "Old bossy and I had a tussle, but I got enough milk from her to make gravy."

Hawkins howled with laughter, and Toby turned back to his cooking, browning flour in the bacon grease and then stirring in milk to make gravy. He would have to wait for another opportunity to inquire discreetly about the comancheros. Except for a brief meeting in Santa Fe with Governor Mills and Colonel Hamilton, Toby had been searching for information ever since he had arrived in New Mexico. It was obviously impossible for a lone man to deal directly with scores of bandits, which left only stealth. But to employ stealth required information, and the comancheros left precious few witnesses behind.

After a meal of biscuits, bacon, and gravy, however, Toby had another opportunity to glean information. Hawkins patted his comfortably full stomach. "That's the best food I've had since—" The man's voice suddenly broke, and he looked away. "Since the comancheros took Sarah away," he finished in a quiet voice.

This time Toby pursued the subject. "When did it happen, Bill?"

"About three weeks ago," the man muttered.

"How did it happen?"

Hawkins was silent for a moment, then, as if relieved to talk about it at last, he related the entire story: He had been up the river, searching for stray cattle, and had heard gunfire at the ranch house. Some thirty minutes passed before he got back, and by then the comancheros were gone. There was no sign of his wife, and the comancheros had taken his horses. His own horse was exhausted from the ride back, so he was unable to follow the raiders' trail.

Toby noted that the attack fitted the pattern of other attacks. The comancheros seemed to know all about their targets, including the best times for a surprise attack. But the source of that knowledge remained a mystery to Toby.

He started to ask Hawkins if any drifters had visited the ranch before the attack, but the man talked without pause, his voice hollow with despair. "All I want is to get my Sarah back. All I want is to get her back." The man burst into tears and turned away in embarrassment. "I wasn't good enough to her. I didn't do enough for her, and now I'll never have another chance."

"Don't torture yourself, Bill," Toby soothed, trying to comfort him.

"I could have done a lot more for her." Hawkins controlled his tears and wiped his face with his sleeve. "A peddler came here selling buttons, lace, and that sort of thing. Sarah only bought a few trinkets, but I told her we didn't have the money for foolishness. If I had it to do over, I'd buy everything that peddler had and give it to her."

Toby frowned. "When was the peddler here?"

"Oh, I don't know," Hawkins replied indifferently. "A

week or two before the attack, I suppose. I was out working with my stock and never saw him."

"Did your wife mention his name or what he looked like?"

Hawkins's eyes narrowed. "Why do you want to know?"

Toby answered with a shrug, then changed the subject, saying it was time for him to leave. After packing his belongings, he went out to the barn, and Hawkins helped him saddle his horse.

As Toby buckled on his spurs, Hawkins grew thoughtful again. "The worst part is the not knowing," he said, looking into the distance. "Not knowing what kind of torments she's suffering, or even if she's alive or dead."

"I wish there was something I could do," Toby said offering his hand.

Hawkins shook it. "If you're ever back this way, stop in. You'll always have a bed and a meal here."

Toby thanked him, then mounted and rode away. Glancing back, he saw Hawkins trudging toward his house, his face buried in his hands.

Many times in the past, Toby had come into conflict with those who lived outside the law. But never before had he been more determined to put an end to the misery perpetrated by criminals. His own sister, Cindy, had lost her husband at the hands of the comancheros, and that alone had been enough to steel Toby's determination. As he rode toward the west, he vowed anew to bring the comancheros to justice, even if it took him the rest of his life.

Leaving the fertile valley of the Pecos far behind, Toby rode through sandy, scrub-covered hills that seemed barely touched by the spring rains. Dead volcanoes lifted their barren cones against the sky amid expanses of volcanic tuff that had been carved into labyrinthine gullies by centuries of wind and rain. Giant mesas, their variegated layers sculpted by erosion, rose with proportions so colossal that, in comparison, Toby and his horse seemed but a tiny mote crossing the landscape.

That night, Toby made camp in a sheltered ravine, and by the next afternoon he saw the Manzano Mountains in the distance, gradually resolving from a dark shadow on the horizon to pink and dun terraces of foothills lifting to dark, forested peaks. Ahead, where the rolling terrain fell away into a flatland, small lakes gleamed in the sunlight. The water had begun to recede from its spring level, leaving behind a thick crust of salt.

For millennia, Indians had trekked across vast distances to gather salt at these lakes. Toby rode along a shoreline, his horse tramping through the salt, which encrusted rotted grass baskets, broken scoops, and other debris that had been left behind over the centuries. Here and there he saw broken lances made for casting with a spear thrower, a weapon that antedated the bow and arrow.

A group of fifteen Indians, mostly women, was on the side of the lake nearest the mountains. In the traditional fashion, they had scooped up damp salt and formed it into balls the size of a man's fist, leaving them to dry in the sun. As Toby approached, the Indians were gathering up the balls in grass baskets and preparing to return to their temporary camp in the mountains. He lifted a hand in greeting.

An aged patriarch, carrying his share of the salt, was the apparent leader of the group. Toby dismounted to speak with him. "I'm going up in the mountains to get water," he explained. "You and your people can put your salt on my horse, and I will walk to your camp with you."

The old man weighed the offer, then took a small piece of turquoise from a deerskin pouch and silently held it up. Toby smiled and shook his head. "No, I don't want any payment."

Grinning, the Indian motioned to the others. They hung their grass baskets across his saddle, and Toby led the horse and talked to the old Indian as they walked toward the mountains. The Indian explained in surprisingly good English that they were Mescalero Apaches, from the reservation far to the south.

"Yes, I know where it is," Toby told him. "I was near there a week ago, and it's a very long distance to come for salt. It surprises me that you can't get salt from your Indian agent."

"That is salt for food," the old man scoffed. "This is the salt we have always used for drying winter venison and for ceremonies."

"I understand that," Toby said. "But why don't you have young men to help you?"

"We had two young men," the Indian said in disgust, "but they left. They were troublemakers who never worked, so the chief sent them with me. But on the way here, they left." He motioned toward the south. "Perhaps they went to join the bad ones."

Toby realized that the old man was referring to the comancheros. He knew that the group was made up in part by renegade Indians.

The path leading into the foothills grew steeper, and at last they came to the place where the Indians had set up camp beside a spring in a small clearing. Two women and an old man were at the camp, and the women were mending clothes beside a fire. Toby noticed several spools of thread that looked new and a distinctly new package of needles. He addressed the old man while the others unloaded the salt from his horse. "Forgive me my curiosity, but where did the women get their needles and thread?"

"From a white man who sells such things," the old man replied. "He came to our village during the last full moon."

"Did he talk with the two young men who left to join the bad ones?"

"Yes, he did—and with others. He said he knew how the young men could get their own good guns, whiskey, money, and other things. But few listened to him because they thought he was a bad man and a troublemaker, as I did."

"Do you know his name?"

The old man turned and spoke in his own language to the women, but they shook their heads. Toby then asked if the peddler had mentioned where he intended to go after leaving the Apache village. The Indian conveyed the question to the women, and one of them answered Toby directly.

"Acoma," she said.

The town was west of the Rio Grande, a substantial

journey away, and Toby did not wish to waste time. He bade the Indians farewell, mounted his horse, and rode down the path. At the foot of the slope, he turned west.

The next day, Toby reached the Rio Grande, which was still in its spring flood. The lush river valley had evidently been visited by the comancheros, for stock was corralled and under guard, and the people working the fields had firearms within reach. In many places, brush had been cut back from the old, tile-roofed farmhouses to give a clear field of fire. Warrens of adobe pueblos, with their tiny windows and jutting ceiling poles, were scattered along the river, and Toby noticed guards posted on the flat roofs.

Isleta, a short distance south of Albuquerque, was a well-known pueblo that had been ancient when the Spanish had entered the region. Its main structure, a huge, rambling building, reached four stories in some places. Here, too, sheep and cattle were corralled under guard, and other guards patrolled the perimeter of the pueblo.

Not pausing at Albuquerque, Toby took a ferry across the river and continued west, camping that night in an arroyo beside the narrow trail. At midday the next day he reached a brush-dotted plain and saw Acoma in the distance. Although he had never visited the town, Toby had heard and read about it. Acoma was, by legend, one of the oldest continuously occupied settlements on the North American continent.

In a region where the history of other communities had often ended violently in fire, terror, and bloodshed, the reason for Acoma's long existence was easy to see. It sat atop a sandstone mesa with sheer four-hundred-foot sides that rose abruptly from the plain. Centuries before the Navajos, Apaches, and Comanches had migrated into the region, a band of Indians had laboriously cut a path up one wall of the mesa and established a village. When the more warlike tribes had arrived, their assaults had been easily repelled. Only the Spanish, with their gunpowder and cannon, had been successful in attacking the town, but Acoma had survived and recovered.

At the foot of the mesa, cotton, corn, beans, and

squash were grown, and Indian laborers in the fields watched Toby curiously as he passed. The path up the side of the mesa was much too steep and narrow for riding, so Toby dismounted and led his animal, which puffed with the effort.

At the top, a dozen Indians who had been watching him shook their heads when Toby started to talk. One young man said in English that the chief would speak with him, and a moment later, a wizened man with white hair appeared, and the others moved out of his path.

With the young Indian translating, the aged chief asked Toby his business at Acoma. "I am a traveler, and I wish to rest," Toby replied, deciding to wait until later to ask about the peddler. "I will pay for food and water for me and my horse."

The chief listened to the translation, then stared into Toby's eyes for a long, silent moment.

"You are a good, honest man," the young Indian translated. "You and your horse will have food and water, and you will not pay."

One of the Indians took Toby's horse, and Toby followed the young man up a pole ladder onto a flat roof, then through a trapdoor and down another ladder, which led into a vast, windowless chamber. The dim room, illuminated by a fire in the center, one torch to the side, and daylight filtering through the smokehole in the ceiling, was the town kiva, the Indian told Toby. It was where the men held meetings, and conducted ceremonies, and withdrew for a quiet retreat at other times.

Against one wall was a fire-blackened stone altar, with ceremonial masks and drums placed around it. A few men were lounging on a stone bench in a far corner, talking quietly. The Indian with Toby explained his presence to them, and the men nodded amiably.

Toby observed that the kiva seemed to be the repository for the long history of Acoma. Much of the wall surfaces were covered by a mural in wide bands, and the pigments in the older sections were dusty and faded. Unlike the symbolic designs of some Indian pictographs, the figures and scenes were rendered with primitive but realistic accuracy. The notably good and bad growing seasons through the ages were represented, along with severe storms and other natural events. Toby gazed with awe at a portion high above the floor, which appeared to depict the story of the attack by the Spanish. Nearby, an artist was working by torchlight, dipping his brushes in earthenware pots of pigment and painting with painstaking care.

Looking over the man's shoulder, Toby saw that the figures were those of a white man on a horse leading a mule. Toby asked the painter about them, with the translator's assistance. The answer did not surprise him.

"He was a peddler who sold buttons, needles, and other things," the young man translated, then added, on his own, "But he was a troublemaker. He talked to the young men and told them they would get guns, money, and whiskey if they went to join the bad ones."

"Did any of the men leave?" Toby asked.

The Indian's eyes gleamed with amusement. "One of the young men's fathers told the white man to return down the path whence he came, or he would show him the fast way down. He left."

Toby smiled in appreciation of the story. "Do you know the peddler's name?"

"Mosely," the Indian replied without hesitation. "Alvin Mosely."

Toby repeated the name to himself, satisfied with what he had learned and knowing now what had to be done. He turned his attention back to the artist's rendering and watched the portrait take shape before his eyes. He would not forget the face of Alvin Mosely.

VIII

The muted sounds of conversation, coughing, and babies crying carried from the waiting room of the Portland Charity Hospital into the examination room. Janessa Holt was cleaning and putting away medical instruments, and Luther Bingham was helping her.

Almost recovered from his gunshot wound, Luther had undergone a dramatic transformation in the past weeks. His grudging respect for Janessa had changed to admiration, and that, together with the knowledge of how his life had been saved by a blood transfusion, had at once humbled and inspired him. His cynical attitude was a thing of the past, and he now worked full time at the hospital as an unpaid volunteer.

Dr. Martin, sitting at a desk in a corner, was making notes on the last patient. "Go ahead and call in the next one, Luther. I'll be finished here in a minute."

Luther checked his list, then opened the door. "Mr. Latham," he announced.

Chauncey Latham strode in and greeted the doctor breezily. With a tall, athletic build, curly blond hair that was the envy of the women, and chiseled features, Latham had long been considered Portland's handsomest bachelor, and in his prime he had been said to possess looks that would do credit to a statue of a Greek god. But now he was on the downhill side of life, with his formerly trim waist bulging into a paunch and his aquiline nose marked with broken blood vessels. His famous locks were now covered with a hat, which he did not remove.

"I don't want you to think I'm a charity patient, Doctor," Latham declared right away. "I went to Dr.

Wizneuski's surgery and found it closed, so I went to your house and was told to come here. I'll be glad to pay."

"Anton took a vacation," Dr. Martin replied. "Sit down, and I'll be with you in a minute."

Latham, who was a bit nearsighted but refused to wear eyeglasses, moved to a chair and squinted in the direction of Janessa, who was standing by a cabinet in the corner. "Why, Miss Holt," he exclaimed expansively, "how on earth could I have failed to notice you! My deepest apologies, my dear young lady. It's such a pleasure to see you again. I must say that you look very pretty today, as you always do."

Janessa, wearing a wrinkled duster and her hair needing combing, took the remarks for what they were. Chauncey Latham was the lothario of Portland and greeted all females in the same fashion, regardless of how they looked or whether they were six, sixteen, or sixty.

The old doctor stood and stepped toward the patient. "Well, what happened to you?" he inquired, staring at the hat. "Did some husband break a fence rail over your head?"

"No, nothing like that." Latham slipped the hat off. "I ordered some hair restorer from an advertisement I saw in a magazine, and it seems to have made my head sore."

The doctor winced as he inspected the red, blistered skin under the thinning hair. "Good heavens! Why did you continue to use it?"

Latham looked crestfallen. "I thought it might be working. True, it stung a little, but I didn't mind. I thought it was correcting my condition. There's no reason, after all, why I should be losing my hair."

"No reason!" The doctor snorted. "Whether you want to admit it or not, you're getting older, Mr. Latham. It happens to everyone, and many men your age are as bald as onions." He peered closely again at the scalp. "We'll get sepsis here if we aren't careful." He turned to Janessa. "Mix an ounce of phenol into one of those jars of burn ointment, if you would, Janessa."

Latham gingerly fingered the top of his head. "You don't think this will make me lose more of my hair, do you?"

Dr. Martin shrugged indifferently. "You can always buy a wig."

"I haven't been able to find one that matches my hair." Latham cleared his throat and glanced toward Janessa. "Uh . . . there's something else I'd like to ask you about, Dr. Martin. Something private."

Without waiting for the doctor to ask her, Janessa gathered up the ingredients for the salve, beckoned Luther to come with her, and stepped into the adjacent supply room. She closed the door, and Latham's voice was a soft murmur as he asked the doctor a question.

"I don't know," the doctor replied in a normal tone. "You might try eating raw oysters or swallowing a raw egg in beer every day. I've heard those help, but I don't have any personal knowledge about it, and I don't consider that a situation for professional medical treatment."

"And you don't know of anything else I could do?"

"Yes, I do!" The doctor's tone was irate. "You can grow up and act your age! If there's a woman who'll have you, you can marry her and settle down instead of trying to pester everyone in a skirt in Oregon!"

Luther suppressed a chuckle, while Janessa, fully aware of the subject under discussion, remained unsmiling as she mixed the salve. When she had finished, she picked up the jar and went back into the examining room.

An irrepressible man, Latham pocketed the salve and continued chattering amiably, while Dr. Martin listened in annoyance. Luther was attempting to escort the man politely to the door when Latham said something that caught Janessa's attention.

"You say Mr. Gooch has a toothache?" she asked.

"He certainly does, my dear young lady." Latham changed to his confidential tone. "I saw him in Horace Biddle's store this morning, buying some medicine for it, and all I could get out of him was a grunt—which isn't unusual, I suppose. He's an odd one, all right."

"There are different ways for people to be odd," the doctor said pointedly. "I'll send you a bill."

Finally taking the hint, Latham donned his hat with care and gallantly bade Janessa farewell.

"I'd like to go see Mr. Gooch," Janessa said when he

was gone. "If I can get him to come in and have that toothache seen to, he might be willing to do me a favor."

"Rufus Gooch?" The doctor looked up from his desk. "I wouldn't recommend that. The man's a nitwit, and it wouldn't be safe for you. Anyway, what favor could he possibly do you?"

"Actually it's for Timmy," Janessa confided. "His latest passion is velocipedes, and I was afraid he might hurt himself, so I got him to promise not to try to build one. I'd like to do something for him in return. He wants to make friends with Mr. Gooch and look around in his workshop, and maybe I can help. Mr. Gooch shouts at people and makes threats, but from what I've heard, he's never harmed anyone."

Both Dr. Martin and Luther looked surprised, for Janessa rarely spoke more than a few words at a time. "Your interest in your brother is commendable," the doctor said. "But I don't think it's wise for you to go alone to visit Gooch."

"I could escort her," Luther volunteered. "There are only a few more patients in the waiting room, and it's still early in the day."

Dr. Martin sighed in resignation. "Rufus Gooch," he said, shaking his head. "I hope you know what you're getting yourself into."

Late in the afternoon, Luther drove Janessa across town in Dr. Martin's buggy. They talked mostly about work at the hospital, until they drew near to Gooch's house. "It's good of you to go to so much trouble for your brother," Luther said. "Timmy is lucky to have you for a sister, just as I'm lucky to have Mabel."

"Are you getting along all right?"

"Better than we have for years. She's relieved I'm working again, even if it isn't for pay. Of course," he added dryly, "it's not entirely a philanthropical endeavor. If I work hard and prove myself, Dr. Martin might give me a recommendation to a medical school. But I suppose you've already figured that out."

"He's never mentioned it to me," Janessa answered truthfully. "But I think he'll give you a recommendation."

They had passed a row of shabby warehouses, and the road, which was now no more than two muddy ruts, paralleled the river through a boggy, overgrown wasteland. Just ahead, on top of a scrubby knoll, was a high plank fence surrounding a ramshackle cluster of buildings. It was the domain of Rufus Gooch, the eccentric Portland inventor.

Curious mechanical noises issued from behind the fence as the buggy pulled to a stop. Luther helped Janessa down, then rapped loudly on the gate. After a minute it was jerked open.

Towering over Luther and Janessa, the rail-thin Rufus Gooch stood glaring at them. He had a wild tangle of gray-streaked hair, and his thick brows, beard, and mustache nearly obscured his face, save for his nose and bulging, bloodshot eyes. His clothes were soiled and wrinkled.

He interrupted when Janessa tried to introduce herself. "I know who you are," he snapped. "You're the only girl in Portland I've seen with a cigarette in her mouth. What do you want?"

Janessa ignored the reference to her smoking, which she knew was a minor scandal in Portland. "Mr. Chauncey Latham was at the hospital today," she began, "and he said that you have a toothache. I thought I would come to see if something could be done for it."

"Why?"

"I thought you might let my brother, Timmy, look around in your workshops."

"*What?*" Gooch's bloodshot eyes widened. "Let that boy nose around in my work? Not on your life, young lady!"

"Let's not be hasty, please," Luther soothed. "Miss Holt didn't mean to leave the impression that this is strictly a *quid pro quo* situation. As I'm sure you're aware, Mr. Gooch, she works with Dr. Martin and devotes many hours to helping the ill. Her offer to you is made in the same generous spirit, together with the hope that a lasting amicable relationship may result."

Gooch looked as if he couldn't believe what he was hearing. "I like her way of talking better than yours," he said at last. "At least she speaks her mind. But I'm not going to let any boy prowl around my—"

"I heard you the first time," Janessa interrupted. She pointed to an empty wooden crate that had been discarded beside the gate. "Sit down there and let me have a look at that tooth."

Gooch harrumphed but obediently sat and allowed Janessa to peer into his mouth. "The second premolar on your lower right side," she pronounced. "A cavity of moderate size." She stepped back. "Well, you have very good teeth for your age. And I believe that tooth can be saved if you don't wait too long."

"I've been taking Dr. Armbrewster's Toothache Remedy," Gooch said, standing. "But if I do go and see a doctor—and I'm not saying I will—I'll pay for it cash in hand. I don't intend to let any boy nose around in my workshops."

"You don't have to keep telling me that!" Janessa tried to control her temper. "That remedy you're taking has a lot of opium in it. It'll stop the pain for a while, but if you take enough of it, you'll have a craving for it the rest of your life. And you shouldn't take it and work around machines."

Gooch snorted. Obviously he didn't like to be lectured. "I don't need you to tell me about my work. And I'm not going to have any boy poking around in my workshops!"

Reddening, Janessa grabbed Luther's elbow and pulled him back to the buggy. "If you want to work around machines when you're half-drugged, then suit yourself," she called back. "But don't come to me and Dr. Martin when you get your hair and beard caught in something and pulled off. Let's go, Luther."

"I trust you will have a good day, sir," Luther said, tipping his hat. But all he received in return was a sour grunt, before Gooch slammed the gate shut behind him.

After church the next morning, Janessa went to the hospital. Sunday was always a slow day, and only one patient was in the waiting room. Sitting on a bench made for people of average height, Rufus Gooch looked vaguely like a grasshopper. His bony knees were almost even with his chin, and his lanky arms rested on his thighs.

"I've come to see the doctor about my tooth," he grumbled, "but I'll pay for it cash in hand. I'm not going to have any boy prowling around in my shops and spying on what I'm doing."

"I believe you mentioned that in passing yesterday." Janessa held open the door to the examination room. "Come in, then. The doctor should be here directly."

Gooch went into the examination room and sat down, and Janessa ignored him and busied herself preparing the dental instruments. Luther came in a few minutes later and was surprised to see Gooch. Then Dr. Martin arrived. The doctor looked at the tooth and agreed it could be saved, and Luther went into the adjacent room and brought out the drill machine.

Mounted on wheels and powered by a crank, the machine consisted of a set of gears that drove a sheathed cable, and Gooch scrutinized it suspiciously. The doctor fitted a reflector on his forehead and selected a tiny drill bit to go on the end of the cable, while Janessa filled a medicine dropper with tincture of opium. She placed drops of the liquid onto the tooth, and the doctor nodded to Luther, who began turning the crank.

The drill bit whined, and Gooch groaned and stiffened, clutching the arms of the chair and working his long legs. Luther was attempting to suppress a smile, while Dr. Martin scolded the patient to take it like a man. After a few more minutes, during which Gooch continued to squirm and moan, the doctor finished.

"There, that looks pretty clean to me. What do you think, Janessa?"

"I still see a small spot in the back," she answered after a brief examination. "It could cause trouble later."

"Yes, you're right." Dr. Martin handed her the reflector. "You clean that out, and I'll get the gold wire."

The whine of the drill and Gooch's groans again filled the room as the doctor opened the safe in the corner and took out a spool of gold wire. When Janessa had finished, he used tiny punches and a mallet to form the soft wire into a solid mass, which he drove into every corner of

Gooch's cavity. Janessa used a scraper to shape the surface of the gold to the proper contours, and the doctor inspected her work and voiced his approval.

"That tooth will be sore for a while," he warned Gooch as the man rose from the chair, "but you'll be fine in three or four days. We'll send you a bill."

"I'll pay as soon as I get it," Gooch mumbled, rubbing his jaw. "I don't want to be obliged for anything, and I certainly don't want—"

Janessa interrupted him before he could finish. "No one's going to snoop around your confounded workshop! And as for being obliged, I'd be greatly obliged if you would forget I mentioned it!"

Gooch muttered something under his breath and went out. The doctor sat down at the desk. "I know you wanted your brother to see Mr. Gooch's workshops, my dear," he said mildly, "but don't you think you were a bit sharp with the man?"

Luther was grinning as he trundled the drill machine back to the supply room, and Janessa glared at him. She was about to tell the doctor what had happened, but deciding that any explanation would be too difficult, she apologized instead and gathered up the instruments.

In the following days, Janessa put Rufus Gooch from her mind. She settled back into her routine of school and going to the hospital for a few hours afterward to assist Dr. Martin.

As one of the more mature girls at school, Janessa often helped the teachers with the other students, and after lunch one day, she was asked to maintain order in a class of younger pupils while they studied. It was the Thursday after her last encounter with Gooch, and she was behind the desk at the head of the class when the quiet was shattered by a frightened squeal from a girl near the window.

The panic spread across the room in an instant, and Janessa turned and saw that Rufus Gooch was standing outside, looking through an open window. She picked up a ruler and rapped it against the desk until silence settled once again, although the children kept glancing nervously toward Gooch. He stuck his head through the window. "My tooth stopped hurting yesterday," he told her.

"That's what Dr. Martin told you would happen, isn't it?" she retorted.

Gooch beckoned for her to come to the window, which she did. "Can that brother of yours come to my place on Saturday? That aeronaut who looks after him can bring him."

"I'll tell him," Janessa said brusquely. "Thank you."

"You're welcome." Gooch strode off.

When Janessa saw her brother that evening, she decided that the good news could keep until Saturday. Otherwise, she knew, Timmy would get excited and badger her with questions. She did tell Calvin Rogers, however, and he expressed astonishment at what she had accomplished.

Not until she was ready to leave for the hospital early Saturday did Janessa speak to Timmy about Gooch, and then she warned the boy to behave himself and stay with Calvin. When she returned to the ranch late in the afternoon, Calvin and Timmy were still gone, so she sat in the kitchen and had a cup of coffee with Clara Hemmings. A short time later, the wagon rumbled to a stop outside.

The door flew open and Timmy burst in, his face flushed and his eyes wide with excitement. "Janessa, Mr. Gooch showed me all his workshops! He has all sorts of machines and things he's working on! He even has an engine that runs on petroleum!"

"I'm glad you enjoyed yourself," Janessa said, smiling.

"He also has a refrigeration machine, and I saw how it works! And he has tools for making gears and other parts, and he showed me how they work, and he said he might let me come back again sometime!"

"I hope you were polite and thanked him properly."

Timmy nodded as he caught his breath.

"That's good. Now go get ready for dinner, because it's—"

"But the best part was just before I left, Janessa! Come and look at what he gave me! It's in the wagon!"

Janessa let her brother pull her outside, where Calvin was standing beside the wagon, inspecting what Gooch had given Timmy. Janessa's satisfaction with the success of the boy's visit to Gooch suddenly changed to shocked disbelief.

"A velocipede," she said numbly.

"Well, not exactly," Calvin explained. "Properly speaking, it's called a bicycle, because the wheels are the same size and it has a chain drive. Mr. Gooch bought it to experiment with, then decided it wasn't worth the trouble. So he gave it to Timmy."

Janessa listened numbly, trying to figure out what she had done wrong.

"I said I wouldn't try to make one, Janessa," Timmy reminded her. "But we were talking about the kind with a big wheel and a little one, and this is a different kind, and I didn't make it. So it's all right for me to keep it, isn't it?"

"I suppose so." Janessa was still staring at the two-wheeled contraption. "Put it away and get ready for dinner, Timmy."

The boy and Calvin climbed into the wagon, and Janessa went back inside. She sat down at the table and lit a cigarette. Clara, stirring a pot on the stove, glanced over her shoulder. "Is something wrong, dear?"

"I feel like I tried to bandage a scratch on someone's finger and broke his arm instead," Janessa admitted.

"Whatever do you mean, my dear?"

Janessa recounted the story, but Clara's reaction, when she had finished, was little consolation. "My, my," the woman commented, "I can imagine what your grandmother will say."

Janessa ground out her cigarette and wondered what she had done to deserve such a fate.

Modestly holding the bedclothes to herself, Lydia von Hofstetten nestled against Andrew Brentwood, who was sitting on the side of the bed, pulling on his boots.

"I am so happy, fate itself must be jealous," she whispered, as Andrew put an arm around her and kissed her on the neck. "Perhaps it *is* jealous, and some dire penalty awaits us. Perhaps Herr Villach will find out about us."

Andrew gently stroked her cheek, then stood and began buttoning his coat. "We'll have to be cautious."

"I hope that will be sufficient. Herr Villach is a very shrewd man. He seems to know everything."

"No one knows everything."

"Perhaps not." Lydia's tone was less than certain. "I never told you, but a few weeks ago, three Germans visited the duke and attempted to involve him in a plot against the German government. Of course His Grace didn't realize what was afoot, but Herr Villach did and forestalled it."

Andrew immediately thought of the letter he had received from Henry Blake. So far, Andrew had been unable to glean any information of value concerning the German exile community, but Lydia's remarks seemed to point to precisely what Henry was looking for. "This happened a few weeks ago?"

With no further prompting, Lydia recounted the entire incident: Three Germans had called unannounced on the duke, ostensibly to present him with a painting. They had wanted him to meet with a friend of theirs to discuss the use of one of the Hofstetten estates near the German-Austrian border, and they stressed that the matter must remain private. The duke, interested only in the painting, agreed to meet with the men's friend. The three struck Lydia as disreputable, and no sooner had she thought of warning Villach than he suddenly appeared.

"He questioned them," she said, "then returned the painting, ordered them out of the house, and warned them not to come back. The duke was furious, naturally."

"Naturally," Andrew echoed absently. "Do you recall the men's names?"

"The one who did most of the talking was called Fischer, but I don't remember the other two. They were dressed like clerks. The 'friend' Fischer mentioned was Kurt Gessell. I remember the name because it sounded familiar. Why are you interested in this, Andy?"

Andrew ran his fingers through his hair to smooth it. "Just curious. I thought they might be smugglers. But I've heard the name Gessell, too. If I'm not mistaken, he's quite wealthy and lives in a chateau near the city. What made you think they were involved in a plot against the German government?"

"That was Herr Villach's phrase." Lydia dismissed the subject. "Will I see you tomorrow, Andy?"

"Of course, my darling." He bent to kiss her tenderly. It was past time for him to leave, and as he had done on several other occasions—although he was still not quite used to it—he simply went through the sitting room to the hall, walked down the darkened stairway and across the entry, and let himself out the front door. The servants had long since gone to bed, and in any case, the duke himself had instructed them that the American was free to come and go as he pleased. Still, Andrew felt guilty over what he was doing, especially since he had developed a genuine liking for Lydia's husband.

The church bells in the city were chiming two o'clock as he walked through the dark, deserted streets back to his apartment. Before going to bed, he wrote down what Lydia had told him while it was still fresh in his mind.

Six hours later, before most of the embassy staff arrived for work, Andrew had already written out, encoded, and dispatched a telegram to the attaché in Berlin, with instructions to deliver the text of the message to Captain Henry Blake at Grevenhof by fast courier.

Thirty-six hours later, when Andrew was returning home from the embassy at the end of the day, a tall, muscular workman carrying a canvas tool bag blocked his path. Andrew started to step around the man, but the fellow purposely moved in front of him again. Annoyed, Andrew looked at the smudged, unshaven features under the grimy cap, only to realize he was facing Henry Blake.

By the time he had recovered from his astonishment, Henry was walking away, taking long strides. Andrew followed and found himself hurrying. Henry turned onto a side street, and Andrew reached the corner just in time to see him disappear into an alley. Andrew followed, but when he reached the alley, Henry was nowhere in sight.

"Over here." Standing in the shadow of a doorway, Henry glanced toward one end of the alley, then the other. He spoke quietly and rapidly: "There is a haberdashery on the corner five blocks north of your apartment. Can you meet me on that corner at midnight?"

"Yes, of course." Andrew started to say more, but Henry was suddenly gone, striding back toward the street. Andrew waited a minute, then retraced his steps, not quite knowing what to think. When he and Henry had been stationed in France, in an observer detachment that Andrew had commanded, their relationship had been typical for a junior and a senior officer. But then Andrew had rushed home when his father had taken ill, and Henry assumed command. Thanks partly to information picked up from Gisela von Kirchberg, Henry had since enjoyed one success after another, and except for a six-month stint back in the United States, he had been stationed in Europe ever since. Andrew had visited him once, to arrange financial help for his mother's shipping business in Independence, and he had been astonished and impressed by the change in his friend. It was completely understandable why Henry was now the youngest captain in the army. Walking back to his apartment, Andrew wondered what kind of life Henry now led.

At midnight, under the cover of darkness and with the streets silent and empty, Henry was more relaxed and greeted Andrew warmly. The two men spoke for a while of family and friends, although Andrew, considerate of Henry's sensitivities, avoided the subject of Cindy. He did explain his strange relationship with the von Hofstettens, admitting he was in love with Lydia. He recounted in detail everything she had told him about the duke's three visitors and their apparent connection to Kurt Gessell. Henry did not react, other than to ask a few questions about Gessell, which Andrew could not answer, and inquire about which taverns were frequented by the city's German exiles.

Before they parted, Henry surprised Andrew by mentioning that he had heard of the von Hofstettens and had met the Countess von Lautzenberg. The count, he added meaningfully, had a reputation as a formidable man—implying that Andrew had best watch his step. Then, again to Andrew's surprise, Henry asked about Cindy, explaining that he had learned of her present circumstances in letters from mutual friends. Andrew told Henry about his visit to Paris, and although Henry's reaction was again hard to read, Andrew sensed that his friend seemed relieved that Cindy was happy. The two men then shook hands warmly and parted, the entire conversation having lasted little more than ten minutes.

The next day, Andrew had reason to wonder whether Henry's veiled warning about Count von Lautzenberg had been prophetic. He was in his office shortly after noon when Emil Villach suddenly appeared. The secretary's manner was even stiffer than usual, his eyes lifeless as he bowed. "Count von Lautzenberg has arrived to visit with His Grace," he announced. "The count wishes to speak with you, sir."

Andrew's heart jumped, for he immediately assumed that Lydia and he had been found out. "Would he like to see me this evening?"

"No, sir. Now, please."

The peremptory tone, belying the polite words, would have brought a heated rejoinder from Andrew under other circumstances, but as it was, he wanted to learn the worst and get it over with as soon as possible. Without further comment, he got up, retrieved his hat, and followed Villach outside to the von Hofstetten carriage.

During the drive to the residence, Villach maintained a stiff silence. Andrew, himself in no mood to talk, followed the man inside and along the hall to a drawing room.

The day was warm, but a fire blazed in the fireplace. The count, a small, shriveled man who looked to be in his eighties, sat near the hearth with a blanket around him. He bore no resemblance to his nephew the duke, and even though his body was deteriorated with age, his eyes were clear and alert, and he had the proud, rigid bearing of a man used to wielding authority.

Lydia was sitting on a couch at one side of the room, her hands clenched tightly in her lap and her face flushed with shame. Seeing her distress, Andrew was seized with rage. He barely had the self-control to bow perfunctorily as Villach introduced him.

The count's lips twitched in a smile, and his voice was

a hoarse whisper. "I perceive," he said in impeccable English, "that I have excited the colonel's sense of chivalry. Please accept my assurances, Colonel Brentwood, that I have caused Her Grace no more disquiet than absolutely necessary."

"I do not consider Her Grace's feelings to be a proper subject for levity, sir," Andrew retorted stiffly.

The count shrugged and pointed to a chair. "Be that as it may, sit down and let us talk."

"No, sir!" Andrew snapped angrily. "With due consideration to your rank, position, and age, I am dissatisfied by your attitude."

The count's eyes narrowed with responding anger. "Young man," he shot back, "I am the minister of internal affairs for the Austro-Hungarian Empire. I have no difficulty in putting to rest the demands for independence of howling mobs in the numerous and dissimilar dominions ruled by Vienna, so I can certainly deal with you." He turned his glare toward Lydia. "Your Grace, have you been offended?"

Lydia cleared her throat nervously. "No, I have not been offended."

"You see?" He turned back to Andrew. "This is not a battlefield, and the solution we seek is more in the nature of the intellect than a cavalry charge. Now kindly sit down, Colonel, and let us converse in a civilized manner."

Lydia, her eyes pleading, silently begged Andrew to cooperate. He sat, and the count's anger abruptly cooled.

"I was led to believe," the count began, "that you were a man of intelligence and judgment, Colonel Brentwood. Your conduct thus far scarcely bears that out." He glanced at Lydia. "But perhaps we should attribute your rash behavior to the intensity of your tender feelings for Her Grace and a consequent eagerness to defend her."

"I hold Her Grace in the highest esteem, sir," Andrew said cautiously.

"And why should you not?" The count sounded almost jovial. "She is a lovely young woman, and you are a handsome young man, so nothing could be more natural. It is clear that she feels the same, and her husband also holds you in high regard. When I talked with my nephew, I found that he views you as a close friend."

"That is a view I am honored to share, sir," Andrew said truthfully.

The count seemed to weigh the reply. "You actually like the duke, don't you?"

"Yes, I do, sir." Andrew was not sure where the conversation was leading.

The aged man wheezed with laughter. "Good! I want the duke to be happy, and your friendship will undoubtedly contribute to that. Don't you agree?"

"I hope that will be the case."

"And I also want Her Grace to be happy," the count continued, his amusement fading and his eyes once again becoming cold. "Unfortunately, her happiness, as well as that of the duke, must be subordinated to the general welfare of the family they head. They are relatives of the Hapsburgs, and their personal affairs must be beyond reproach. Do you understand?"

Andrew nodded, waiting for the blow to fall.

"As a family friend," the count went on, "you have been escorting Her Grace to the opera, to social affairs, and on weekend outings. I consider that entirely within the bounds of propriety." He hesitated, fixing Andrew with a piercing gaze. "If there have been any improper intimacies between the two of you, they have occurred only in private, because your conduct in public has been beyond reproach. That is to continue without fail. Do you thoroughly understand that, Colonel Brentwood?"

The tacit approval of his affair with Lydia took Andrew by surprise. He glanced at Lydia, who looked similarly astonished. "Yes, I understand completely."

The count put his blanket aside and feebly rose from his chair, Villach quickly moving to assist him. Andrew stood.

"I am a man of the world," the count concluded, leaning on Villach's arm as they moved toward the door. "I can accept human nature, and I ask only that you exercise proper discretion. Please join us for dinner at the usual time this evening, Colonel Brentwood."

Andrew bowed in acknowledgment. As the door closed,

he turned to Lydia. She was still speechless, her eyes wide with disbelief. He stepped to the couch and sat beside her, taking her into his arms. "I wonder how they found out."

Lydia leaned against him, burying her face in his shoulder. "Count von Lautzenberg and Herr Villach know everything, Andy. We were fools to think that we could hide it from them."

"But the count doesn't care!" Andrew could hardly conceal his delight. "The worries that have been plaguing us are finished!"

"For the moment," Lydia warned. "But I am so ashamed! That wicked old man knows what we have been doing. I have never been so embarrassed!"

Andrew smiled and held her closer. Her modesty only made him love her all the more. For now, he was beside himself with joy, and even though a whisper of doubt rose briefly in his mind, reminding him that the situation was indeed too good to be true, he was willing to ignore it for as long as Lydia remained his.

IX

The rigging on the *Beluga* was dark with fresh soot from the tryworks as the whaler approached the west coast of New Zealand's South Island. The blubber of six whales had been rendered down into oil in the past week, and Captain Tench was making landfall to refill the fresh-water casks. Marjorie stood on the quarterdeck and gazed at the rugged coastline ahead.

At the rail Baylor was scanning the shore with the captain's telescope, while Tench and Cade stood nearby. "It appears to be a snug harbor," the second mate asserted. "And it's certainly quiet enough."

"So is a cocked pistol just before it fires," Cade observed. "I'd best take a boat in first and look it over."

"Be my guest, Mr. Cade," the captain said. "I've put in here before, as I've said, and I've never laid eyes on a Maori. But better safe than sorry."

Marjorie would have liked to go in the boat, but she knew it was useless even to ask. She had succeeded in gaining the first mate's goodwill—if the term could be applied to him—but one upshot was that he now took great pains to make sure she was not subjected to any undue danger—as if the voyage itself was not dangerous enough. Consequently, she had to wait until Cade had made a circuit of the bay in one of the whaleboats before the ship finally came to anchor and she was allowed to join one of the shore parties.

It was winter south of the equator, but the day was pleasantly mild, and the low waves in the bay sparkled in bright sunlight as Marjorie sat in the bow of the boat, her equipment cases under her feet. The scene all around was

144

spectacular. The forest came right up to the edge of the pristine white beach, and the vegetation was entirely different from anything Marjorie had ever seen. Varieties of ferns ranging from tiny shoots to masses of huge, spreading branches crowded beneath trees draped by what an older sailor told her were liana vines. The weird, melodic calls of the forest birds could be heard over the water, and off to her left a half-dozen penguins gamboled on rocks near the water's edge. In the distance, tiers of dark, hazy mountains reached to towering, snowcapped peaks.

Baylor was in charge of the sailors who were filling the casks in the creek that flowed into the bay. He had the men stop working and pose for Marjorie, but when she had finished and was walking away with her camera, he cautioned her to stay within sight of the beach.

Marjorie waved in acknowledgment, although she had no intention of leaving the beach. Nearby, the cook and cabin boy were collecting baskets of wild celery, which grew in profusion among the ferns, and Marjorie paused to take their picture.

At a distance from the creek, she set up her camera to photograph the penguins and an expanse of the bay. She had just started back when a mark in the sand at the edge of the trees caught her eye.

It looked unmistakably like a human footprint. Leaves and twigs that had fallen from the trees made it impossible for her to see other footprints, if any. Feeling uneasy, Marjorie hurried back toward the creek.

Baylor was unconcerned when she told him what she had seen. "Assuming it is a footprint," he said, "it could have been made by the cook or the cabin boy. They were down that way."

"It's too large for the cabin boy," Marjorie told him. "I suppose the cook could have made it, but he wears shoes, and it looks more like a footprint of someone who was barefoot."

"I'm sure it's nothing for us to be worried about." Baylor turned to shout orders to the men, and Marjorie, still feeling ill at ease, dropped the subject.

Later, back on the ship, she took advantage of the new supply of fresh water to develop her backlog of plates.

Her work absorbed her, and she forgot all about the footprint she had seen on the beach. It was near sunset when she finished, put her cabin back in order, and joined the officers for dinner.

The crisp wild celery was a welcome addition to the menu, for the stores of fresh vegetables had long since been consumed. The cook stuck his head in to accept the captain's compliments, as well as to get permission to go fishing at the entrance to the bay the following day.

"Aye, but leave some fish for the penguins," Tench quipped. Even as she laughed, however, Marjorie found her attention straying to the cook's footwear. Unlike the other sailors, who went barefoot almost all the time, the cook always wore shoes.

"It's probably nothing to be worried about," Tench said when Marjorie told him her suspicions. "We could stand out to sea, I suppose, but both wind and tide are against us. Also, I've told the men they'll have a day or two of rest here, and I'd hate to summon them on deck."

"The men will follow orders, sir," Cade put in bluntly. "If you want to stand out to sea, we'll weigh anchor within ten minutes."

The captain shook his head. "No, Mr. Cade. Just post an anchor watch."

Feeling more secure, Marjorie retired at her usual hour and woke well before dawn. She got out of bed, lit her lamp, and began dressing, for she wanted to take full advantage of the day ashore. She was lacing her shoes when she heard something splash in the water, the sound loud in the early morning quiet. She sat still and listened, and icy fear gripped her as she heard scores of bare feet running across the deck. A man called out in alarm, and his shout triggered a chorus of bloodcurdling whoops, followed by gunshots. In a matter of seconds, Marjorie heard sailors shouting and swarming out of the forecastle. A battle apparently was raging on deck.

Marjorie glanced around for something she could use as a weapon, but suddenly the cabin door was jerked open, and she jumped up in terror, being confronted by a figure that looked more like an apparition than a human being. Naked to the waist and brandishing a wicked-looking club, the man was tall and muscular, with broad shoulders and a chest marked with scars.

Most fearsome, however, was his face. Covered with black ridges of spiraling tattoos, it had a hideously ferocious appearance, and as Marjorie shrank back instinctively, the man bared his teeth, muttered something in his language, and grabbed for her. Marjorie dodged and again looked around for a weapon, but the heavy club moved with astonishing speed, tapping her head only in warning but still nearly knocking her unconscious. She reeled and almost collapsed as the warrior gripped her arm and dragged her to the companionway.

On the deck the battle was over. The crew, many of them wounded, had been herded to the rail, as dozens of tattooed warriors, armed with hatchets, clubs, and old muskets, whooped and leaped about triumphantly. On the distant beach, women and children were shouting impatiently as warriors paddled dugout canoes back to the shore to bring the others out to the whaler.

The warrior shoved Marjorie against the rail beside Captain Tench and walked away. All three officers were wounded, Cade the worst, for he was unable to stand and seemed only semiconscious. Tench had an arm wound, and Baylor was holding a handkerchief over a gash on his forehead. Marjorie started to speak, but Tench motioned her to be silent. Three Maoris, the tallest of them the chief from the way he acted, were walking along the line of prisoners, apparently discussing their fate.

When they reached Marjorie, the chief eyed her in evident disgust. He pinched her slender arm, then said something to his companions, who laughed with him uproariously. Still laughing, they moved down the line.

Moments later, Marjorie found out that some of the Maoris spoke English. She had started to whisper a question to Baylor, but a warrior stepped over to her. "No talk!" he bellowed in her face.

Marjorie fell silent and watched with mounting apprehension as the Maori women and children climbed on deck. The fate of the ship soon became obvious, for the women immediately set about cutting down the rigging, carrying items up from below, and even prying loose

metal fittings. Marjorie felt a helpless despair as she watched
the stout ship that had been her home during the past
months being dismantled. If she and the others could
manage an escape, transportation would be a problem.

The warriors had broken open the holds and were
struggling to lift out the casks of whale oil. The chief
shouted and pointed, and his men who could speak English ordered the sailors to help carry things out of the
hold. One warrior singled out the crewmen who were
badly wounded and made them lower one of the whaleboats and climb down into it. Several of the crew gently
lowered Cade over the side.

The warrior approached Marjorie and turned and
shouted a question to the chief, who motioned that she
was to climb down to the boat. Marjorie obeyed, and as
the boat was rowed ashore, escorted by a canoeload of
heavily armed Maoris, she wondered whether she and the
wounded sailors were to be massacred.

Once they were ashore, however, her fears were
relieved, at least for the present. Four warriors escorted
them into the forest, following the course of the creek. A
sailor who was wounded in the leg found it difficult to
keep up, and Marjorie came to his aid, wrapping his arm
over her shoulder while she supported him by the waist.
Cade was carried by two of the sailors. Baylor, walking in
front of her and also helping another man, replied to her
whispered question that they were probably being taken
to the Maori village. Marjorie recalled that the cook and
the cabin boy had intended to go fishing, and her hopes
rose considerably when Baylor informed her that they had
indeed left before the attack and perhaps would bring
back help.

A warrior shouted at them to stop talking, but it was
hardly necessary, for already Marjorie was breathless from
the steep uphill climb and the exertion of helping the
wounded man. After what seemed at least an hour, the
dense foliage opened out in a wide valley with a knoll in
the near distance. Atop the knoll were two dozen thatched
huts, plus a larger wooden structure, presumably a meetinghouse, rising in the center.

The villagers who had remained behind—most of them

older and less excitable—stared curiously as Marjorie and the others were led up the slope, past the huts, and to the clearing in front of the meetinghouse, where they were ordered to sit on the ground. Marjorie did what she could to make Cade comfortable, but that was precious little.

About two hours later, a large party of warriors, women, and children, plus the rest of the crew from the ship, filed into the village, nearly all of them laden with articles from the ship. They deposited their loads on the ground and immediately left, and quiet settled once again.

It was midafternoon when the Maoris returned with another load. The cabins had been thoroughly looted, and Marjorie could see her crates of supplies and her equipment cases among the belongings being piled in the clearing. The chief, apparently deciding that enough had been done for the day, ordered the uninjured crewmen to sit with Marjorie and the other prisoners.

The villagers were remarkably disciplined. All were excited, but they refrained from touching anything in the huge pile of plunder as the chief and the two men who were always with him examined it. The chief seemed enthralled by a pistol that had been among the ship's arms, for he stopped everything to load it, then shouted something to his warriors.

To Marjorie's surprise, they seized one of the other Maoris, who appeared to be a worker rather than a warrior, for he carried no weapons. She watched in horror as the man was dragged up to the chief, who casually lifted the pistol and shot him dead. A roar of exultant whoops rose from the onlookers.

"He must have been a captive from another village," Baylor whispered to her amid the bedlam. "Captives are regarded as slaves, their lives already forfeit, and they can be killed at any time."

The chief, apparently satisfied, stuck the smoking pistol in his belt and resumed examining the booty, turning his attention to the harpoons, lances, flensing irons, and various whaling tools that were always kept razor-sharp. One of the chieftains with him began rummaging through the personal items taken from the cabins, and Marjorie, though still half-numb with terror from having

witnessed the execution, suddenly was on her feet, her
fear overcome by another reaction that was automatic. The
chieftain had picked up a carton of photographic plates,
and before he could open it, Marjorie was halfway to him.
Baylor and Captain Tench were too late as they tried to
stop her.

"Don't open that, you fool!" she shouted, marching
up to the man. She grabbed the carton from him, put a
hand against his chest, and shoved him away. "If you open
it, you'll ruin the plates!"

The man gaped at her in disbelief, and the chief and
the other headman scowled in anger and astonishment.
The crowd of villagers fell silent.

Realizing what she had done, Marjorie froze in panic.
Then, forcing a smile, she hastily opened an equipment
case and took out a stereopticon viewer and a slide. By the
time she had the slide in the viewer, the chief had overcome his surprise and was reloading his new pistol, clearly
intending to repeat the previous demonstration.

"Here, look at this," Marjorie said, offering him the
viewer. "Don't you want to see this? Take a look. Right
through these lenses."

The chief's tattooed face glanced up from the pistol,
and with curiosity temporarily overcoming his anger, he
took the viewer in hand and looked. As Marjorie had
suspected, photography was a novelty to the villagers, and
the chief exclaimed in amazement as he beheld the three-
dimensional image.

The two chieftains jostled each other to take turns
looking, their awe matching that of the chief. Marjorie
removed other slide prints from the case and put them
into the viewer one by one, then beckoned to a warrior
who spoke English. With his help, she explained to the
chief that she could photograph him.

The chief eagerly accepted the offer, and as he began
primping, Marjorie quickly set up a camera. While she
worked, she explained that all her equipment and supplies
must be kept in a safe, dark place, or their power would
be destroyed. She photographed the chief, who posed
regally, and when she was finished, he shouted orders to
his warriors.

The crewmen were herded away, deeper into the village, but Marjorie was allowed to remain in the clearing, to point out her equipment and whatever she would need to make photographs. She took the opportunity to include the medicine chest, plus a few other items that might prove useful.

Marjorie accompanied the four warriors who carried the cases and crates into the large, round hut where the sailors had been taken. The warriors brusquely ordered the sailors to move aside and piled Marjorie's things against the low wall, then left. Several guards were posted outside the door.

Captain Tench and Baylor were delighted when they saw the medicine chest, and Cade, who was now fully conscious, expressed his gratitude. Every captive was pleased that Marjorie had interested the chief in her photographs, for while their own fate was still unknown, she had at least opened a means of communication and a common ground of interest with the hostile tribe.

Late in the day, women brought food and water to the hut, and Marjorie asked for and received sheets of canvas with which to fashion a darkroom and give herself privacy, plus buckets of water to use in developing her plates. When darkness fell, she lit her red lamp behind the canvas and went to work.

When it was time to expose the photographic paper to light, her only good source of illumination was the fire in the middle of the hut, which produced a dull, muddy print. Still, the chief was delighted with it the next morning, and he assigned a warrior who spoke English, a man named Katoa, to be Marjorie's escort and personal translator. Through Katoa, the chief explained that he wanted the ship photographed, so when a party of villagers left for the bay, Marjorie and Katoa accompanied them. Compared with some of the other warriors, Katoa seemed amiable enough, but he was totally lacking in civilization's gentlemanly conventions, and he strolled along carrying only his war club while Marjorie struggled with her equipment cases.

When she saw the *Beluga*, Marjorie almost cried. Most of the rigging had been taken down and several of the spars removed. Maoris were swarming over the ship, unfastening everything they could and loading whatever wouldn't float into the whaleboats. Marjorie exposed two plates, then trudged back up the steep path, Katoa following.

When she returned to the hut, Captain Tench informed her that in her absence the chief had given a speech to the crewmen and ordered them to construct a palisade wall around the village. Through an interpreter, he had also explained that once the wall was built, they would be marched north and ransomed in exchange for food, weapons, and other articles. Tench had already divided the crew into work parties, and they were to begin their task as soon as the rest of the warriors returned from the bay.

Baylor added that the wall was no doubt meant as a defensive measure that might well be necessary once the ransom demand was made. The Maoris customarily fortified their villages strongly, he said, and the wall might take months to build.

"I suppose they're in no hurry," Tench added dryly.

"They obviously don't know that the cook and cabin boy escaped," Marjorie said in a low voice. "But even if they do make it to a settlement, it will probably do us little good. An army could search this wilderness for months without finding this village."

"My words exactly." Cade, who was still too weak to walk, was sitting nearby, propped against the wall. "Rescuers could track them here from the ship," he added, "but it'll probably be scuttled and the footprints covered long before the cook and cabin boy can bring help."

Marjorie described how rapidly the Maoris were dismantling the *Beluga*. "They'll be finished in two or three days. It appears the best we can hope for is to be ransomed after months of captivity."

"During which," Baylor said grimly, "we'll be under constant threat of death. We're captives, which means we can be killed at any time."

The conversation ended on that somber note, for Katoa called for Marjorie, saying the chief wanted his wife and children photographed.

* * *

The next morning the chief announced his satisfaction with the prints of the ship and his family, then relayed through Katoa a long list of things he wanted photographed. When Marjorie had heard him out, she was thankful that she had an abundance of supplies.

She soon discovered, however, that it was necessary to watch her equipment cases because the Maori children, who were naturally inquisitive and intrigued by the cameras, followed her everywhere. Eventually the novelty wore off, and they shifted their attention to the work parties of sailors, but one boy continued to follow her. A thin, grubby, silent lad of about ten, he seemed to be constantly underfoot, no matter how often she shooed him away, and after dusk he even trailed her to the hut, where he sat just inside the door and watched her and the others.

When Marjorie woke on the third morning of her captivity, the boy was sleeping soundly beside her on her canvas mat. She chased him away, but he reappeared behind her when she took the previous day's batch of prints to the chief. That morning, the chief demanded more photographs of the ship, leading Marjorie to believe that the *Beluga* would soon be sunk.

When the boy stayed close to her heels on the steep path to the bay, Marjorie, who was irritable from the unending tension and having to lug the heavy equipment cases by herself, finally complained about the child's constant presence to Katoa. He abruptly seized the boy by the nape of the neck and hefted his war club.

"Wait!" Marjorie shouted. "What are you going to do to him?"

"He slave," Katoa answered. "He trouble, I kill."

"Well, he isn't that much trouble." Marjorie held out one of her cases. "Here, he can carry my tripod for me."

The boy eagerly grabbed the piece of equipment the moment Katoa released him. His name, Katoa said, was Hari. Marjorie was soon impressed by the lad's intelligence, for at the bay Hari helped her set up the tripod, knowing exactly what to do from having watched her, then put it away neatly when the photograph of the ship had been made. That evening, Marjorie sent him for water to develop the plates, and by the next morning, when she again awoke with the boy curled up near her, she resigned herself to the fact that, like it or not, she had been adopted by Hari.

That afternoon Marjorie was at the bay again to photograph the *Beluga*, now little more than an empty shell and three bare masts. As she had expected but still dreaded to witness, the Maoris towed the hulk to the deepest part of the bay, where they burned and sank it.

Two days later, Marjorie and the others were restricted to their hut and ordered to extinguish their fire, while the rest of the village was ominously quiet. The captives speculated that the cook and the cabin boy had guided a ship with a search party to the bay.

Unfortunately, Marjorie and Cade's earlier conclusion that no search of the wilderness would be attempted appeared correct, because the next day activity in the village returned to normal. The crewmen resumed their work on the palisade, and Marjorie was ordered to take more photographs. It seemed that the chief wanted pictures of everything, and Marjorie had to limit herself to four or five plates a day, so that she would not run out of supplies. Nevertheless, each day she used at least one of her plates to record the villagers going about their routine activities, or some other scene she found interesting. It occurred to her that her celebrated pictures of the Great Chicago Fire were of less intrinsic value than those she was now making, for a detailed photographic account of captivity in the Maoris' compound would create not only a national but also a worldwide sensation. Still, Marjorie wondered if her photographs would ever be seen by anyone other than the chief and his friends. In her blacker moments, she would think about her husband and wonder if she would ever see him again.

Her doubts intensified when two sailors, faced with months of hard labor in captivity, decided to escape. The Maoris chased them down and brought them back, both dead. That same evening, Marjorie was horrified to learn that the Maori women were making an earthen oven, intending to roast the bodies and eat them.

*   *   *

The man across the table from Henry Blake was talking, but his voice was almost lost in the loud, drunken laughter and conversation in the rowdy tavern. A dark, dingy place that reeked of stale tobacco smoke and spilled liquor, the Spielkeller was one of the taverns Andrew Brentwood had told Henry about.

The fellow in Henry's company had been among the three who visited the von Hofstetten home with a painting for the duke. A braggart named Bauer, he worked as a carriage driver, and he was relating a tale of how he had cheated some Swiss who had hired him.

Slumping in his chair and leaning on an elbow to act as drunk as Bauer actually was, Henry listened absently and waited for him to finish. Posing as a Prussian named Kauptmann who was disillusioned with the German government, Henry had tracked the three down, quickly identified Bauer as the easiest one to pump for information, and spent the past few days winning his confidence.

It had been well worth the effort. Bauer had already boasted that there would be changes in the German government, and on one occasion he even boasted that the changes would come about because there would be a new chancellor. He had also divulged a connection between Fischer, the leader of the three, and Kurt Gessell, the man who had been mentioned in the papers Adela Ronsard had read.

Bauer finally finished his long anecdote and laughed gleefully. Henry picked up his beer stein and took a small sip. "You are very shrewd, Franz."

"I know my way about." Bauer hefted his own stein, gulped noisily, and wiped his mouth with the back of a hand. "But you, Kauptmann, are also very intelligent. I saw that in you the very first time we met, and I know it even better now."

Henry shook his head morosely. "No, an intelligent man would not have as many enemies in his homeland as I have."

Bauer banged his stein down. "Nonsense! That is the proof of your intelligence. No good man could live happily in Germany now." He winked and nodded wisely, then took another deep drink. "But as I told you, that will change, and you will be able to go home again."

"My father is very ill," Henry said. "I'm afraid he will die before I see him again. I wish I could go home now."

"After the first week in August," Bauer began, "you'll be able to—" He halted with his stein almost to his lips. He was suddenly sober, as if thinking about what he had said. "Please don't tell Herr Fischer and my other friend I told you that."

Henry sipped his beer. "If it's a confidence, of course I won't. But I hope it is true, for my father's sake."

Bauer put down his stein and rubbed his face with his hands. "I must leave now. It's getting late, and I have to be at work early tomorrow."

"That's too bad. By the way, what has Fischer been doing lately? It's been a day or two since I've seen him."

"He's been busy." Bauer stood up unsteadily. "I'm to meet him tomorrow evening at the Reiff Kurhaus, but if you're there, please don't mention what I said."

"I have already forgotten it."

The man weaved toward the door. A few minutes later, Henry left the noisy tavern and went directly to his lodgings. The following day, he walked about the city and idled away the hours until evening. A little after seven, he went to the Reiff Kurhaus, a far more genteel establishment than the Spielkeller. Pausing near the door, he spotted the three Germans at a corner table, talking quietly with a fourth man. Henry immediately turned and went back out, hoping he had not been seen.

The previous year, while posing as an arms merchant and tracking down the men involved in a plot against the king of Spain, Henry had met the fourth man at the table—Josef Mueller. At the time, it had appeared that Mueller was an agent working for someone whose identity Henry had never been able to learn.

Now it appeared that Mueller was also involved in the plot against Bismarck. But whatever the man's business, Henry reflected, it was certain that Mueller would immediately recognize him. He hurried to his lodgings and began packing his belongings in preparation to leave on the next train to Germany.

Alexandra's routine at the Wisconsin logging camp

was interrupted by the unexpected arrival of Marjorie White's husband. A tanned, well-built man in a dark business suit and western boots and hat, Ted Taylor had tried to smile genuinely as he was introduced, but Alexandra could tell he was troubled.

Ted had come by train from Nevada, where he worked as a security agent for a mining company. He had hoped to find Toby at the lumberyard office in Chicago, but when Dieter Schumann had been politely but firmly evasive as to his employer's whereabouts, Ted wasted no time and hopped a train north to the camp, certain that Frank Woods could provide more specific information. Only a week earlier, Ted had received a telegram from the shipping company that owned the *Beluga*, informing him that the whaler and its crew had been lost off the coast of New Zealand, apparently seized by a band of Maoris. The information had been conveyed by ship, undersea cable, and telegraph halfway around the world, from the American consul general in Wellington, New Zealand, and Ted was now on his way to Maine, to take passage on a steam freighter owned by the same company that owned the *Beluga*. The steamer was to depart in a week's time for Wellington, via Cape Town and Sydney, and Ted hoped to enlist Toby's aid in tracking down Marjorie and the whaler's crew.

Unfortunately, Frank and Alexandra had been of as little help as Dieter, since all they were able to do was confirm that Toby couldn't possibly help Ted at present. Edward Blackstone, however, jumped at the opportunity to make himself useful—especially since he was an old friend of Marjorie's—and he and Ted left for Chicago the following morning on Captain Crowell's launch.

Alexandra almost wished she could go, but she knew she had to remain at the camp and wait for Toby. This morning, as she had done nearly every day for the past several weeks, she sat on the beach and listened to Lucy recite "The Charge of the Light Brigade" with her mouth filled with pebbles. Alexandra had almost given up on the idea as crazy, but surprisingly, Lucy was finally beginning to make real progress.

By now, of course, the girl had memorized the poem,

and with only three or four pebbles in her mouth, she could recite it almost without hesitating. Alexandra felt sure that the pebbles only gave Lucy something other than her stammer to worry about, for when the girl was alone with Alexandra or had her mind on something that absorbed her, she hardly stammered at all. Self-confidence was all she needed, Alexandra concluded.

Suppressing a yawn as she sat on her driftwood log, Alexandra gave her pupil an encouraging smile. Working with Lucy kept her mind off her father's death and her loneliness for Toby, but she had made the mistake of choosing her favorite poem, which Lucy murdered by reciting in a lifeless monotone that robbed the words of any meaning.

Having endured the flat recitation countless times, Alexandra decided to say something before Lucy began again. "Honey," she ventured, "couldn't you give it a bit more feeling? If those cavalrymen had charged the way you recite, the poem wouldn't have been written."

The girl spit the pebbles out into her hand and looked at Alexandra in surprise. "It . . . really happened?"

"Of course! It was during the Crimean War, in 1854, and the charge was near a place called Balaklava. The Earl of Cardigan led a brigade of British light cavalry against hundreds of Russian cannons. It was one of the most famous charges ever!"

"I didn't know it was . . . true," Lucy said in wonder.

"Listen." Alexandra stood up and began reciting the poem, gesturing and speaking the lines with all the emotion that the story created within her. Always quick to copy Alexandra in everything, Lucy shared her excitement and mouthed the lines with her. When Alexandra finished, she asked Lucy to recite the poem.

The girl did, clenching her fists as her voice rang with an intensity Alexandra did not realize she possessed. Not until the last line did her voice fade as she realized what she had done. Alexandra stood there, grinning broadly. With the pebbles still in her hand, Lucy had recited the entire poem without stammering.

"Do it again," Alexandra ordered.

But the inspiration seemed to have passed.

" 'H-Half a l-league, half a l-l-l—' "

"Close your eyes," Alexandra interrupted. "Concentrate on the battlefield. Imagine the shells bursting among the cavalrymen charging with drawn sabers. Visualize men and horses falling everywhere, but then the survivors reaching the artillery positions, slashing right and left, and the gunners fleeing in terror. Think of that, Lucy!"

The girl closed her eyes and concentrated, then began reciting with hardly a stammer. On the second stanza, she opened her eyes, and her voice was ringing with emotion again. With only an occasional hitch, she went through the rest of the poem, and when she finished, Alexandra threw her arms around Lucy in gleeful triumph.

Alexandra sat back down, and Lucy recited the poem again in the same fashion. Later, as they rode back to the logging camp, Alexandra conversed casually, and Lucy spoke with little trouble.

Alexandra had planned nothing more than to have Lucy demonstrate her newfound confidence to her parents, but suddenly a better idea occurred to her, something that would be more dramatic and would give Lucy absolute self-assurance—*if* she could go through with it. The girl was doubtful when Alexandra described the plan, but she gamely agreed to try. When they reached the camp, they put the horses into the corral and went to the house, where Lucy remained as closemouthed as ever. But there was a gleam in her eyes whenever Alexandra looked at her.

The following day was Saturday, and as the lumberjacks filtered in from the work camps and the cook prepared the food to accompany the evening's entertainment, Lucy grew increasingly agitated. To keep her distracted, Alexandra took Lucy out on the hunters, but what she depended on most to get the girl through the evening was the determination that she saw in Lucy's eyes.

At sunset the wagon from the Oberg brewery arrived, along with a few other people who lived in the area. The food was dished up, and a fiddler took the stage. Alexandra sat with Lucy at a trestle table near the front. She grew worried as she noticed that Lucy lacked her normal appetite. When the dinner was ending and the fiddler stopped playing, Alexandra climbed the stage.

"Are you going to sing for us, Miss Woodling?" a man called.

"No, that doesn't happen to be one of my talents." Alexandra, feeling a bit nervous herself, saw no reason to delay. "Tonight, you have a rare treat in store. I wish to announce that you will now hear a recitation by Miss Lucy Woods of 'The Charge of the Light Brigade.' Come on up, Lucy."

An excruciating silence fell, and everyone's attention turned to the girl as she got up from the table and took the stage. From the anxious looks on the faces, not a person in the audience was unaware of Lucy's severe speech impediment.

Alexandra moved to one side, to provide moral support, and Lucy cleared her throat and composed herself. After an agonizingly long pause she began, making a bad start and stammering. Wisely, however, she stopped, drew in a deep breath and closed her eyes, then started over.

> Half a league, half a league,
> Half a league onward,
> All in the valley of Death
> Rode the six hundred.

The first few lines were delivered with nerve-racking deliberation, but by the second stanza, Lucy became caught up in the poem. Opening her eyes, she recited with growing conviction, as she had at the lakeshore, gesturing with clenched fists and her voice ringing out. A few of the lumberjacks apparently liked the poem as much as Alexandra did, for they whooped in appreciation when Lucy lifted an arm and raised her voice on the particularly stirring lines:

> Storm'd at with shot and shell,
> Boldly they rode and well,
> Into the jaws of Death,
> Into the mouth of Hell . . .

The men's reaction, to Alexandra's surprise, seemed to instill Lucy with even greater vigor, and by the time she came to the last stanza, the entire gathering was exploding into applause and cheers.

> When can their glory fade?
> O the wild charge they made!
> All the world wonder'd.
> Honour the charge they made!
> Honour the Light Brigade,
> Noble six hundred!

She had finished, and the only people silent in the crowd were Frank, who was looking on in stunned disbelief, and Bettina, who was weeping with joy. Finally overcoming his temporary paralysis, Frank went up to the stage and lifted Lucy down, hugging her, and Bettina sobbed as she kissed the girl. Everyone crowded around, complimenting Lucy, and when she replied to their questions, she stammered occasionally, but no more than any excited child might.

Spotting Alexandra, who was still on the stage, Bettina went through the crowd to her. Tears streaming down her cheeks, she hugged the younger woman. "I can't tell you how grateful we are. How did you manage it?"

"I'm not quite sure myself," Alexandra admitted. "But it had something to do with a Greek and some pebbles."

"With *what*?"

"I'll explain later," Alexandra promised with a smile. "But somehow or other we succeeded, and for now that's all that matters."

"Yes, it is." Bettina turned and looked at her daughter. People were still crowding around Lucy, who was talking and blushing happily. The evening of entertainment had been temporarily disrupted, but no one appeared to mind in the least.

X

Henry Blake wasted no time in reporting what he had learned in Switzerland. The evening after he arrived in Berlin, Richard Koehler arranged for him to meet General Fremmel, whose reaction to Henry's information was guarded satisfaction. The first week in August—the schedule Bauer had let slip—was precisely when Chancellor Bismarck was due to arrive in Bad Kissingen to take the waters, and only a handful of government officials knew of the timing of the visit this far in advance—one being Hermann Bluecher.

To Henry's consternation, however, Fremmel informed him the following day that Bismarck refused to change his plans, despite the obvious threat. The Chancellor had made it clear that he wanted the conspirators caught red-handed at the scene, so that both they and Bluecher could be made examples of. Bismarck agreed that reasonable safeguards should be taken, but calling off the trip was out of the question. Consequently, Henry and Fremmel had little to do but wait until the end of July, when the plotters would likely proceed to Bad Kissingen.

When Henry arrived back at Grevenhof, Gisela rushed into his arms at the front door, as though he had been gone for years instead of weeks. The news she had for him, however, was less than welcome.

"We won't be completely to ourselves quite yet, loved one, because a man arrived here yesterday to see you. He is an American, John Lawrence. I am afraid he is a newspaper reporter, but he insists that his business with you is personal."

Henry recognized the name immediately. The previous year, at the request of his friend Clifford Anderson in the State Department, Henry had helped arrange Lawrence's release from a German prison, where the headstrong young journalist had been cooling his heels after overeagerly pursuing a story and being mistaken for a spy. Anderson had informed Henry that Lawrence intended to thank him personally, although Henry would just as gladly have forgotten the entire matter.

"He speaks passable German," Gisela went on. "I put him in an upstairs guest room, with orders to stay away from my offices, but he has spent most of his time in the back gardens. Adela is there now with little Peter, and Lawrence no doubt is with her. Not surprisingly, he finds her attractive."

"I hope Adela is being discreet."

Gisela assured him on that point. "She is as trustworthy as any of my employees, and more closemouthed than most. If you wish to talk with him now, I'll return to my work."

"I don't want to, but I suppose I'd better." Henry kissed her. "I'll hear him out, then see him on his way."

He followed a terrace that led around the east wing to the formal gardens at the rear of the house, where carefully pruned hedges and meticulously cultivated flower beds were arranged geometrically around fountains and classical statuary. Henry found Lawrence sitting on a stone bench next to Adela, who was holding the baby and keeping him amused with toys.

Wearing a neat, stylish suit, Lawrence was a handsome man in his late twenties, and he stood to greet Henry. Although he had the brash manner of a reporter, he seemed less abrasive than many in his profession and was genuinely charming as he thanked Henry for arranging his release from prison.

After hearing Lawrence out, Henry took the baby from Adela and held him high, playing. But little Peter was fretful and began crying lustily. Adela explained it was time for his nap, and Henry handed him back. Peter abruptly stopped crying, and Adela took him inside.

Lawrence laughed when Henry asked if his accommodations were satisfactory. "Magnificently luxurious would be a better description, and the cuisine is superb. Even so, I feel like a pariah. I understand why the baroness would wish to keep her business affairs private, but why does the nurse refuse even to tell me her name?"

"Perhaps she values her privacy," Henry answered with a smile. Clearly Lawrence was smitten.

The journalist brought up the subject of his sister, the famous New York actress Valerie Lawrence, whom Henry had met while arranging John's release. "She has a very high opinion of you, Captain Blake, which is unusual, given her radical views. She told me to send her love and gratitude. Those were her exact words. She said she's feeling much better these days—whatever that means."

Henry knew exactly what it meant, for he had persuaded Valerie, after some spirited resistance on her part, to give up opium smoking. Evidently she had not told her brother about the episode. John talked on, describing the success of his sister's latest musical play, then abruptly changed the subject and told Henry that he had been in Independence, Missouri, the previous year when a cholera epidemic was raging there. While covering the story for his newspaper in New York, he had met Janessa Holt and Dr. Robert Martin, who were there to help the local doctors deal with the epidemic.

"I never did understand why," Lawrence continued, "but when I mentioned your name in Miss Holt's presence, she grew quite livid."

Henry had no intention of telling Lawrence about his broken engagement with Janessa's aunt. "It's a family matter" was his blunt reply. "But I can understand Janessa's feelings, and I hold no ill will toward her. She's a remarkable young lady."

"Indeed she is," Lawrence agreed. "She and that old doctor set up a clinic in a warehouse and had a better recovery rate than any hospital in the city. But the doctor cheated me out of the best story I found in Independence. With that girl's help, he apparently cured a man of a disease that is supposed to be incurable, but I couldn't turn in the story without incurring his wrath. He actually threatened to have me horsewhipped, tarred and feathered, and run out of town!"

As Lawrence talked on, Henry fondly recalled the old doctor and other friends he had known in Portland. Only when Lawrence mentioned what had been wrong with the patient did Henry's attention snap back to the present. "What did you say?" he interrupted.

"Perityphlitic abscess," Lawrence repeated.

Henry could hardly believe what he was hearing. It was the same disease that afflicted Gisela, threatening her with a slow and painful death should she have another attack. During the past years, that danger had been a constant worry for Henry; indeed, at times it seemed more of a burden for him than for Gisela, who was inclined to be indifferent about her health. "You say that Dr. Martin cured him? Are you certain?"

"I interviewed the patient and learned all the particulars from him," Lawrence replied, puzzled by Henry's sudden interest. "His name's Simon Whiting. He lives in Independence."

"What sort of cure did the doctor use?"

"It was a surgical procedure—an abdominal operation." Lawrence frowned in remembered frustration. "And there was the *real* story, Captain Blake. Dr. Martin didn't have another doctor assisting him. He was helped by that girl, Janessa Holt. I know that for a fact."

Henry was more interested in the details of the surgical procedure, a subject he had delved into more than once while interrogating doctors about Gisela's condition. They had heard of similar operations, but the patients had all died of severe internal inflammation as a result of opening the abdomen. "How did Dr. Martin prevent infection?"

Lawrence shrugged. "That gets into things I couldn't find out. The doctor refused to talk about it. But I suspect phenol is involved. I could smell it a hundred yards from that warehouse."

"But you're absolutely certain a surgical procedure was used?"

"I'm positive. I saw the scar on Simon's stomach." He

pulled back his coat and traced a line on his abdomen. "It's about this long."

Lawrence's curiosity had been aroused by Henry's questions, and it took some doing for Henry to get him to drop the subject. After inviting Lawrence to join Gisela and him for dinner, Henry excused himself and went to find Dr. MacAlister, Grevenhof's household physician. The short, feisty Scotsman was in his drawing room, reading.

"Yes, I've heard of such instances before," MacAlister said when Henry had finished. "But that doesn't change my recommendation. I can assure you that the doctor who performed that procedure would recommend it only as a last resort. Phenol is used to prevent infection, as Mr. Lawrence indicated, but it isn't always fully effective. The risks outweigh the benefits."

"Don't you think it might be prudent to write to Dr. Martin and ask him about his procedures? I'm personally acquainted with him, and I'm sure he would give us all the facts."

"That wouldn't be of any use to me," MacAlister stubbornly persisted, "because I would never risk such an operation. He may have had a fluke success with it, but I consider it a death warrant." The doctor leaned forward confidingly. "Why torment yourself with this, Captain Blake? It's been a long time since the baroness has been troubled with her illness. That remission could very well continue into her old age."

It was true that a considerable period of time had passed since Gisela had suffered an attack, but Henry nonetheless felt frustrated and disappointed as he left the doctor's quarters. For a few minutes, he had thought it possible that Gisela might be cured and the threat of her illness eliminated. Now that worry would continue to haunt him.

As he lurched out of bed and reached for his robe, Hermann Bluecher fumed with discontent. For the first time, he regretted having ordered someone killed. He wished he had captured Adela Ronsard and kept her in one of his basement cells, because in comparison with her, every other prostitute who had been brought to his house had been stupid and unskilled.

The woman on the bed sat up, smiling idiotically. "Did I please you, sir?"

His dissatisfaction suddenly mounting into rage, Bluecher gripped the woman by the throat. Her smile turned to a terrified expression, and she screamed, but his fingers dug deeper, and her scream faded into a gagging sound. She fought to twist away, then flailed at him helplessly. She thrashed about and tugged at his hand, her eyes bulging and her mouth opening wide.

Then Bluecher changed his mind. The satisfaction of killing her, he decided, was not worth the trouble of disposing of the body. With a grunt of disgust, he thrust her into the pillows, then turned away, shrugged into his robe, and pushed his feet into his slippers. The woman had rolled off the bed and was cowering on the floor, gasping for air and weeping in terror. Ignoring her, Bluecher walked out the door.

The butler awaited instructions at the foot of the stairs. "Bring a repast to my study," Bluecher ordered. "Send that woman back, and pay her nothing. Make certain she is never brought here again."

Bluecher brushed past him and went into his study. He lowered himself into the oversize chair behind his desk and surveyed the papers before him. All of them concerned the assassination of Bismarck—although as a precaution they were in code. A few weeks before, Bluecher had made a crucial decision on how to proceed with the plan, and now it appeared that he had chosen the right course of action.

The decision had involved risk, for he had sent his own agent to Switzerland, thus establishing a direct link to himself. Before he sent the man, however, it had appeared that Gessell and his flunkies would fail due to sheer incompetence.

Intending to strike across the Austrian border, Gessell had sent his underlings to contact Duke Rudolf von Hofstetten, which, Bluecher thought, had been unnecessary and stupid. There was no need for Gessell and his

men to leave Switzerland until the time came to carry out
the plan, and they should have known that involving a
relative of the Hapsburgs was only asking for trouble.

Living apart from his men, Gessell had failed to control them adequately or to enforce discipline. The three
had been drinking too much, talking too much, and seeing
too many people. There had been no methodical approach
to the plan, no organized, logical schedule of preparations.
Now all that was changed.

Bluecher shuffled through the papers, searching for
the report from Josef Mueller. In addition to being his
most reliable agent, Mueller was efficient. He had clamped
tight controls over Gessell's men, clearly defined the
necessary preparations, and set up a schedule for their
completion.

The butler came in with a tray of cream puffs and a
tankard of cocoa, put them on the desk, and went back
out. Bluecher pushed one of the light pastries into his
mouth and savored the taste as he chewed, custard filling
oozing down his robe. He washed it down with a deep
gulp of cocoa, then pushed another cream puff into his
mouth. As he ate, he thumbed through a report from
Mueller, which he enjoyed almost as much as the pastries.

The memorandum covered each subject thoroughly
and included a complete list of the conspirators' acquaintances. Each name had been checked to make certain that
none had official connections.

Only one name remained unaccounted for. For a
time, Bauer had been drinking with an exiled Prussian
named Kauptmann. Mueller had searched Bern diligently
for the man but had been unable to locate him. Bluecher
stopped eating and sucked his teeth as he reread the
sentences about Kauptmann.

It probably meant nothing, Bluecher reflected. Yet it
worried him.

Toby Holt rode down the main street of the dusty
mining town of Silver City, and what he saw pleased him
immensely: A notion dealer's pack mule was among the
horses tied to a hitching rail in front of a saloon. After

weeks of patient tracking, Toby had finally caught up with Alvin Mosely.

Silver City, in the foothills of the Pinos Altos Mountains, was a crowded cluster of raw-timbered buildings and dirt streets edged by boardwalks. It was quiet during the early afternoon siesta hour, with no one moving about. Unshaven and dressed in trailworn clothes that were suitable for his role as a drifter, Toby reined up in front of the saloon and dismounted.

Two of the horses at the hitching rail were painfully thin, he noted, their flanks and sides raw where they had been spurred savagely. Inside, Toby identified Mosely right away; the short, pudgy peddler was wearing a suit and a hat and was seated at the far end of the bar, sandwiched uncomfortably between two other men, apparently locals and the only other customers. From their looks, the two were bullies and, Toby guessed, the owners of the mistreated horses outside. For amusement, they were taunting Mosely.

"You sell the ladies needles," one of them sneered at Mosely as Toby stepped to the bar. "I have some holes in my drawers, so maybe you'd like to sew them up for me."

The two guffawed while Mosely stared at his drink. The bartender, who appeared from the back room to serve Toby, tried to calm the bullies. "Now why don't you fellers just drink your liquor and let everybody else do the same?"

"Why don't you shut up?" one of the bullies snarled back.

The bartender, obviously no match for the troublemakers, frowned worriedly and looked at Toby. "What'll it be, mister?"

Although he felt no personal obligation to protect Mosely, Toby realized he had arrived at an opportune moment for the success of his mission. And his instinctive dislike for bullies made it easier for him to do what he had to. "I'll have whiskey," he replied, dropping a coin on the bar. Then he raised his voice: "And I want some quiet in here while I drink it."

The two bullies turned in surprise. They were hefty

men, feeling the effects of their liquor. "Why don't you make us be quiet, then?" one challenged.

Toby moved toward the men, who, forgetting Mosely, immediately knotted their fists and rushed to meet him. Toby dodged a punch toward his face from the nearer opponent and doubled the man over with a hard right to his midsection, then deftly ducked as the other man took a wild swing at his face. Toby reached up, grabbed the man's sleeve, yanked him off balance, then gripped a handful of hair and slammed his forehead against the edge of the bar. The man yelped in pain and slumped to the floor.

The first man straightened and charged with flailing fists. Toby weaved and fended off blows, took a punch in the stomach, and waited for an opening. When the man dropped his guard, Toby jabbed him in the chin with a sharp right. Staggered and dazed, the bully lowered his hands and left himself wide open. Toby's right connected again, this time to the side of the jaw, and the man collapsed to the floor beside his companion. Gripping the men's collars, Toby dragged them to the door and heaved them out onto the boardwalk.

"I sure appreciate that, mister," the bartender said gratefully when Toby returned to the bar. "Those two were nothing but trouble from the minute they walked in."

"The reason I did that," Toby replied gruffly, "is that I wanted some quiet while I have a drink. Now it's quiet, but I'm still waiting for my whiskey."

The bartender hastily reached for a bottle, put a glass in front of Toby, filled it to the rim, then produced a cigar from under the bar. He pushed Toby's coin back. "This is on the house."

"Thanks." Toby pocketed the coin, and the bartender struck a match and held it out. Toby puffed on the cigar, and the man retreated to the other end of the bar to talk to Mosely. The two of them conversed in low tones, glancing at Toby and speculating as to who he was.

When Toby's glass was empty, the bartender returned and offered to refill it. "It's still on the house."

"Thanks," Toby repeated. "I'm not exactly loaded down with money."

"Then let me buy you a drink as well," Mosely offered. "Better still, I'll buy a bottle, and we can sit at a table to drink it."

Toby tried to appear nonchalant as he accepted the offer. At the table he removed his hat, and Mosely eyed the scar on Toby's temple but said nothing. After filling their glasses, the peddler introduced himself.

"Miller is my name," Toby responded tersely. "Tom Miller."

"I take it you're not from around here," Mosely said, "or I would have heard of you before."

Toby glared at him. "Why do you want to know where I'm from?"

"Uh—just making conversation." Mosely gulped his drink. "There's no harm in people talking about where they're from."

"Maybe not for some," Toby muttered.

"Yes, I see what you mean." Mosely's tone became confidential. "So you had a little trouble somewhere. That's not so unusual. But you can trust me, Tom."

"I can't trust anyone." Toby suspiciously eyed the bartender after draining the shot of whiskey.

"Well, maybe you've just been running with the wrong kind of men," Mosely suggested in a lowered voice, pouring Toby another shot. "I hope we have a chance to get to know each other, because you'll find that you can trust me. I travel around and meet a lot of people. I know how a man like you, who's maybe had a brush or two with the law, can make plenty of money."

Toby eyed Mosely for a long moment, and the two of them seemed to come to a silent understanding, as if both admitting they were criminals. "If you know of a bank or something that's an easy mark," Toby confided, "I'll do the job and cut you in. But it has to be something I can do by myself."

"Actually, I had in mind introducing you to some people," Mosely said, lifting a hand as Toby started to object. "These are people you can trust, Tom. None of

them could go to a lawman to collect a reward, and the
leader could use a man like you."

"How big is the gang, and what do they do?"

Mosely hesitated warily, then spoke in an even softer
voice. "It's very big, and they do most anything that's
worth the trouble. You'd fit right in, believe me."

"If it's already a big gang, why would they want me?"

"Because you're a good man on your own, from what
I've seen. A few are like you, but most will turn tail and
run if they're not together. The boss is always looking for
men who'll put some backbone into the others. He'll be
glad to have you there."

"You're talking about comancheros, aren't you?"

Mosely looked uneasy. "What if I am? I'm not *saying*
I am. But what would you say if I was?"

Toby took a drink and smiled without humor. "I'd say
you were right when you told me I'd fit in. I've thought
about joining the comancheros, but it's hard to find them."

"It sure is." Mosely flashed Toby a conspiratorial
grin. "Can you meet me here in about—say, ten days?"

Concealing his excitement, Toby replied that he would.
Before leaving a short while later, Mosely warned him not
to do anything in the meantime that would draw attention,
and Toby agreed to lie low in the mountains until the ten
days were up. A few minutes after Mosely had ridden off,
Toby left.

Four days later, during early afternoon, Toby arrived
in Santa Fe. After going to a hotel to change clothes and
make himself presentable, he walked to the Palace of the
Governors. Patrick Mills greeted him warmly and sent for
Colonel Hamilton, who arrived only a few minutes later.
The two officials listened intently as Toby related what he
had done.

"So you're all set up to infiltrate them," Hamilton
summed up. "That's an extraordinary achievement."

Toby was more cautious. "It's only a first step, Wayne.
I still have a long way to go."

"It's also a very dangerous step," Mills warned. "You're
going to have to exercise the greatest caution."

Hamilton agreed, then raised the question Toby knew

was coming: "Since we last met with you, Pat and I have given considerable thought to luring the comancheros across the border, but we haven't come up with a viable scheme. Do you have a plan in mind?"

"No, I don't," Toby admitted. "Even assuming I *can* lure the comancheros across the border, you'll have to know when and where to have a cavalry troop waiting."

As the three men discussed several alternatives, Toby concluded that only one good possibility existed. At the crucial moment, he would have to find some means of leaving the comancheros for a day or two. If he were gone longer, Calusa Jim might suspect a trap and change his plans.

"Unless I'm mistaken," Toby said, "Calusa Jim's hideout has to be fairly close to the border, or else Mosely would've needed more time to get back to me in Silver City. Why can't we post a man somewhere in the southernmost part of the territory, where I could contact him overnight? He would have to be in disguise, of course, and be an excellent horseman, to get a message to the nearest army outpost in very little time."

There was no immediate reply from the others. Hamilton stood and paced the room while he considered. "Assuming you could get away from the camp, that's an excellent suggestion. And I know just the man to be your contact. He's a second lieutenant who reported here only a few days ago, so he's not well-known in the territory. He's a fine horseman, and I was planning to assign him to a cavalry troop. I'll have him sent for immediately so you can talk to him, Toby."

While they waited for the governor's secretary to summon the lieutenant from the garrison, Mills told Toby that the comanchero raids had declined sharply in the past weeks, probably because of the heavy cavalry patrols and the fact that many of the farmsteads in the territory had become like small forts. The governor considered the threat as serious as ever, and he planned to cancel the annual fiesta at Albuquerque. Such a large gathering would be too difficult for the cavalry to protect, and people traveling to and from the popular event would be easy targets for the comancheros.

When the lieutenant arrived a few minutes later, Toby stood and, to the others' surprise, greeted him by name. Lieutenant Walter Stafford, a handsome Southerner in his early twenties, had been Henry Blake's second-in-command at a weapons procurement detachment in Connecticut, where Toby had met him briefly the previous year.

Once the assignment was explained to him, Stafford was eager to accept, and Toby felt optimistic for the first time in days as he sat with the others and completed the strategy. Surely the choice of Walter Stafford had been a favorable omen, and if the coming weeks were to bring success, he knew he would need all the good luck he could get.

XI

Little more than a week after leaving Santa Fe, Toby was with Alvin Mosely in the Chihuahuan desert south of the border. Their destination, a barren mountain in the distance, was almost due south of Mesilla, the town where Walter Stafford would be waiting; but covering the rolling, sandy hills between the border and here had already taken more than a day, and Toby felt growing doubts as to whether he would be able to contact Stafford.

As they rode closer to the mountain, Toby noticed that Mosely was becoming increasingly nervous. The day was only moderately warm, but Mosely was sweating profusely, and he talked without letup about how difficult it was to find suitable places for the comancheros to raid. After a few minutes, Toby realized the man was rehearsing what he was going to say to Calusa Jim.

Using the curt tone he had adopted back in Silver City, Toby interrupted the chatter. "Are you telling me I'm wasting my time coming down here? If all I'm going to do is sit around, I could have done that someplace more comfortable."

"No, no, you're not wasting your time," Mosely quickly assured him. "I'm certain things will change pretty soon."

Toby paid close attention to the terrain as they entered the foothills. Mosely guided them through a brushy depression, and when they emerged at the other end, they were at the entrance of a narrow ravine. Two comancheros were pointing rifles at them.

The two outlaws were grimy and ragged but heavily armed with good weapons—Winchester rifles and Colt pistols, Toby observed. The man on the left waved a signal to guards farther back, then lowered his rifle, though it was still pointed in Toby's general direction.

Mosely reined up. "Howdy, McSween," he said. "Are Calusa Jim and all the others inside?"

"Gonzales ain't," the man replied. "He got into a fight with Camargo, and now he ain't with us no more. Who's this?"

"Miller, the new man that Calusa Jim told me to bring down. Miller, this is McSween and Garcia."

Hard stares were exchanged, then McSween turned back to Mosely. "Camargo said he'll lift your scalp if you don't find us someplace to raid."

"That's Camargo," Mosely said, laughing weakly. "He sure likes to joke."

McSween gave a wolfish grin. "Yeah, Camargo thought it was really funny when he stuck a knife into Gonzales's belly, and so did I. Both of us laughed for the rest of the day."

Mosely paled visibly and rode on, and Toby followed him into the narrow ravine. Rocks clattered under the horses' hooves, and when Toby looked up, he could see guards on the edge of the steep, high walls. Even in pitch darkness, a sudden dash out of the hideout to safety would be next to impossible. If his purpose was discovered, he was doomed.

About a hundred yards on, the ravine opened out into a wide, rock-and-scrub-covered valley surrounded by sheer cliffs. Numerous cooking fires were scattered about, with some seventy-five comancheros sitting or dozing beside them among a litter of saddles, blankets, and other belongings. A score of ragged, forlorn-looking Mexican and American women moved about doing chores. Toby guessed that the more attractive women had been sold as prostitutes. A hundred or so horses were picketed off to the right, and on the opposite side of the valley was a solitary tent, which Mosely approached.

As Toby watched, a bearded giant of a man stepped through the canvas flap. Toby's gaze was immediately drawn to the steel hook at the man's right side, and he had to struggle to hide his feelings. Calusa Jim's missing right hand was a souvenir of the aborted ambush in which

Toby's own brother-in-law had been killed. Toby resisted a strong impulse to shoot the man on the spot.

Calusa Jim was wearing a French officer's tunic, and after Mosely had made the introductions, the comanchero leader nodded toward a table under the tent awning. Toby and Mosely sat opposite Calusa Jim, who rapped his hook loudly against the table.

The summons brought a Mexican woman hurrying from the tent with an earthenware pitcher and gourd cups in her hands. She looked younger and more attractive than the other women in camp, but it was obvious that she had been mistreated. Her pretty face was swollen and bruised, and she moved with the flinching hesitance of a dog that is used to being beaten. She filled the cups with pulque, a strong, sour beverage made from the juice of agave plants, then put the pitcher on the table and disappeared back into the tent.

Ignoring Toby, Calusa Jim began questioning Mosely in a heavy French accent about the settlements he had visited north of the border. Mosely's answers evidently were not satisfactory, for Calusa Jim was growing increasingly upset. "Did you not find anything at all? Every town and ranch in the territory cannot be fortified! I think you have just been sitting around up there doing nothing, then lying to me."

"I'm not lying!" Mosely's face was flushed, and his voice quavered. "There were cavalry patrols everywhere I went, and just about every ranch has guard dogs or a lookout. You want me to find you some *safe* places to raid, don't you? Well, I'm doing my best! You can get mad all you want to, but I can't find what's not there!"

"Stop sniveling, Mosely." Calusa Jim spat in the dirt in disgust. "All right. Go east of the Rio Grande this time. Look around the Rio Penasco and see if you can find anything there. Don't waste any time."

Mosely heeded his dismissal without delay, and the outlaw leader turned his cold gaze on Toby, as if trying to fathom what kind of man he was by staring him down. Toby looked back without flinching, and at length Calusa Jim began questioning him.

The questions were few, and Toby lied without compunction, saying he was wanted on a bank-robbery charge in Idaho. Seemingly satisfied, Calusa Jim told him there were two firm rules to observe in the hideout:

"The first is that no one leaves without my permission. By and large, that means we leave only as a group. Mosely is the only one who comes and goes. Understand?"

"I understand," Toby replied evenly.

"The second is that trouble between the men is settled with knives or fists, never guns. The sound of a gunshot carries for a long distance out here in the desert, and sometimes people pass close to this mountain. So no gunplay in the hideout. Understand?"

"I understand."

"All right. Go find yourself a place to settle down."

Toby left the table and went to his horse. Mosely was already leaving, riding toward the ravine and leading his pack mule. Toby walked his horse across the valley to picket it with the others, and as he glanced around, he found it easy to believe that fights there were common. The men spread out before him clearly were rabble to whom a dog-eat-dog existence was natural.

Indeed, his first trouble came even sooner than he expected. After picketing his horse, Toby carried his saddle and other belongings to an empty area beside a fire. As he made himself comfortable, a burly, long-haired man beside an adjacent fire stood and moved closer, eyeing the Winchester in Toby's saddle scabbard.

"That rifle is better than mine," the man stated matter-of-factly. "You can have mine, and I'll take yours."

Toby stood with deliberate slowness, but when the man took a step toward his saddle, Toby swung his fist with lightning speed. Expecting a fight but not the swift reaction, the man grunted and doubled over when the punch slammed into his stomach, but he immediately butted Toby with his head. Bracing himself, Toby took the impact on his midsection and at the same time swung his hands down and clapped the man's ears with his palms.

Bellowing in pain and clutching his head, the man staggered backward. Toby followed him, hitting him twice in the face. The second blow knocked him flat. The fight was over, as far as Toby was concerned, but he knew that ending it without inflicting punishment would be interpreted as weakness, so he kicked the man in the ribs. As the fellow rolled away, Toby followed to kick him again.

The man struggled up to his hands and knees and scuttled away. Toby walked slowly back to his place beside the fire, aware that many of the comancheros had scarcely bothered to look at the fight. Calusa Jim was still sitting at the table in front of his tent, however, and he had witnessed everything.

Another man, sitting beside a fire a dozen or so yards away, had also watched closely, as though weighing Toby's strengths and weaknesses. A swarthy, muscular half-breed with knife scars on his face and neck, he waved over another fellow, who bent to whisper something to him. A little later, Toby heard the scar-faced man addressed as Camargo.

The evening meal, prepared by the women, consisted of tortillas, chili, and pitchers of pulque. After he had finished eating, Toby leaned back against his saddle with a cup of foul-tasting coffee. He noticed that the guards at the ravine had been changed. The one Mosely had talked with, McSween, was standing by the food kettles and was conversing quietly with Camargo.

A few minutes later, McSween swaggered over to where Toby was resting against his saddle. "Hey, you're in my place!" he snarled.

"Then find another one," Toby replied without moving.

McSween shifted his weight to kick, but Toby, fully prepared for the move, shot out a leg and twisted himself around quickly, hooking a spur behind McSween's left knee. The man lost his balance and stumbled, windmilling his arms. Toby sprang to his feet and readied himself.

McSween was big but cautious. He climbed to his feet with fists clenched and approached slowly, looking for an opening. He feinted twice, and Toby lowered his guard intentionally, waiting for the man to put his weight behind a blow. It came almost immediately. McSween lunged and swung his right fist.

Toby dodged the blow, gripped the extended arm, and pulled the man off balance. As he stumbled forward,

Toby hit him in the stomach, knocking the wind out of him. With his opponent momentarily helpless, Toby rained rights and lefts into his face until the man collapsed to the ground.

McSween quickly regained his feet and, moving to a safe distance, wiped his bloody nose and mouth. He glared over his shoulder as he walked off.

Toby could see that the man was only retreating, not defeated. He would make trouble again. Sitting back down, Toby noticed that more people were watching him this time. And both Calusa Jim and Camargo were staring in his direction.

Not long after sunset, the men lay down to sleep, and the camp became quiet. Toby spread his bedroll and pulled a blanket over him, and as the fire at his feet burned down, he fell asleep. But as always in places where danger was present, his slumber was shallow and restless.

When a boot crunched softly nearby, he woke immediately. Someone was leaning over him, silhouetted against the stars, and Toby rolled to one side as a knife flashed down and dug into the ground where he had been lying.

The assailant tried to flee, but Toby grasped one of the man's boots and held on to it. Lifting himself to his knees, he twisted and raised the foot, and the man crashed heavily to the ground, dropping the knife. Toby pounced on him, and in the dim light he could see it was McSween. The man put up a good fight, but raging fury had seized Toby, and ignoring blows, he pounded the prone form into semiconsciousness, then climbed to his feet and kicked the man until McSween begged him to stop.

Still angry, Toby stepped to the fire and threw a pile of branches onto it, then stood in the light of the jumping flames and looked around. All the comancheros in sight were sitting up, watching. "All right, does anyone else want to fight me?" he shouted. "If anyone else here thinks he can whip me, then let him step right over and try it!"

No one accepted the challenge. At Calusa Jim's tent, a cigar glowed in the dark as the leader observed what was happening. Toby knew that Camargo was also watching, biding his time. Toby stepped back to his bedroll, lay down, and pulled the blanket over himself.

At dawn he rolled up his bedroll and heated water to wash. The lazy, slovenly comancheros were late risers, and sunrise came and passed, while most of them were still lying in their blankets. The camp women moved about, feeding the horses and making coffee and tostadas, and Calusa Jim washed and dressed under the awning in front of his tent. The young woman who had served him the previous day held a towel ready and then brushed his tunic after he put it on.

When the men finally started getting up, Toby noticed that many had only tequila or pulque and a cigarette for breakfast. The languorous activity was abruptly interrupted when one of the women screamed and dropped a coffeepot. A large rattlesnake had crawled from under a rock near her, and it coiled and sounded its warning.

The men laughed uproariously, and several of them picked up rocks to kill the snake. Camargo stopped them. "No, don't kill it!" he shouted. "Compadres, we have a real bad hombre among us—at least he thinks he's bad, judging from how he was bellowing like a bull last night. I'll bet he can kill that rattler with nothing more than his bare hands!"

More shrill laughter greeted his words, and everyone looked at Toby to see how he would respond. Like a pack of curs, they were always ready to turn on anyone or anything, and they closed in from all sides as Toby approached Camargo and the snake. Calusa Jim left his breakfast on the table and walked over.

Years before, Toby's father, the famed wagonmaster Whip Holt, had shown him how to kill a poisonous snake with his hands. It was a wilderness skill that could come in handy in some circumstances, such as when confronted by a snake that had to be killed silently because an enemy was nearby. But it was perilous and required lightning reflexes to avoid being bitten.

The men fell silent. The snake was a diamondback, almost five feet long and as thick as a man's wrist, and its rattle made a steady, ominous chatter. Camargo had a wide grin on his unshaven face.

"I guess if I can kill that snake with my hands," Toby challenged, "then you should be able to do the same with another, Camargo."

The men, eager for more cruel amusement, looked at Camargo for his reaction. Calusa Jim suddenly spoke up: "That's right. If Miller kills that one with his hands, then Camargo will show us if he can do the same. There are plenty of rattlers in this valley."

Camargo's smile faded, then returned. He was confident that Toby would be unable to kill the snake with his hands. "That's right, Miller. If you do it, I can."

"Everybody get back and give me room, then." Toby turned his attention to the snake, and the men formed a ragged circle, those in the rear craning their necks to watch.

Toby stepped forward cautiously and stopped when he was about six feet from the snake. Leaning over, he moved his left hand in a slow, smooth arc, while closely watching the snake's reaction. The large, flat head bobbed menacingly, but Toby knew that before the diamondback struck, the rattles would fall silent and the head would move back even farther. Inching closer, he passed his hand in another arc, but still the snake did not gather itself to strike. Toby moved nearer still, and his hand had reached the middle of the third arc when the deadly chatter stopped.

The head jerked back, and Toby swept his left hand away as the rattler disappeared into a brown blur of movement, its fangs barely missing his outstretched fingers. In the instant that the rattler's body was fully extended, Toby darted out his other hand, seized the tail, and without hesitating or interrupting the motion swung the rattler around his head to keep it from coiling again, then rapidly snapped it twice like a whip to break its back.

The snake was squirming in its death throes as Toby tossed it at Camargo's feet. The man leaped back in fright and astonishment, and the others were silent for a moment, equally astounded. Then they began whooping and laughing, and Calusa Jim shouted over the uproar, "All right, find another snake! It's Camargo's turn!"

As quick to turn on Camargo as they had on Toby,

the men howled gleefully and spread out to search under rocks. Camargo's face was ashen, and his eyes revealed fear as well as hatred as he glared at Toby. Two men found snakes at the same time and flipped them along the ground with long sticks toward Camargo.

One snake was as large as the one Toby had killed, the other only half the size. Toby expected Camargo to choose the wrong one, and he did, picking the smaller of the two, which would be faster and more unpredictable. The men killed the other one with rocks, then formed a circle around Camargo and the remaining snake.

It was over within seconds. Camargo tried to do the same as Toby but ended up with the snake's fangs sunk into the base of his thumb. The other comancheros roared with laughter at the man's frantic, terror-stricken movements as he shook the snake loose.

The snake finally fell to the ground, and the comancheros pounded it with rocks. A few women gathered around Camargo to treat the snake bite, and the Mexican gritted his teeth and cursed as one of them cut open one of the fang punctures to suck out the venom.

"All right, the fun is over," Calusa Jim announced. "You'll be sick for a few days, Camargo, but you will probably live. And maybe you will learn not to bite off more than you can chew. Miller, go to my tent. We must have a talk."

Toby wasn't exactly sure what Calusa Jim had in mind, but he was certain that he had made a deadly enemy of Camargo. He would have to be on guard at all times against a knife in the back.

The young woman emerged from the tent to fill a gourd cup with coffee for Toby as he sat alone at the table outside. She glanced at him timidly, then looked again in surprise, as if reading something in his eyes. "Gracias," he said as she put the coffee in front of him.

"You are welcome," she replied in English.

"What is your name, and how did you come to be here?"

"I am Juanita Zuniga," she said softly. "I was a lady's maid at Casa Robles. Then one night they came—" Her voice breaking on a sob, she retreated into the tent.

Feeling intense pity for her, Toby recalled what he had heard about the raid at Casa Robles, a large ranch near the Rio Grande: It had happened months before, one of the first times the comancheros had struck in New Mexico. Everyone was thought to have been killed—men, women, and children massacred in a frenzy of slaughter in revenge for the spirited defense the *rancheros* had put up. But one young maid from the household still lived.

While he waited for Calusa Jim, Toby wondered how he could possibly lure the comancheros into an ambush, if he himself remained for all intents a prisoner. And worse still, if some target to raid was soon identified, that would be his virtual death warrant. He would be obliged to try to stop Calusa Jim, and when he did that, the others would never let him live.

In the harbor at Cape Town, where the waters of the Atlantic and the Indian Ocean blended, Ted Taylor stood with Edward Blackstone on the quarterdeck of the steamship *John S. Carver*, watching cargo being unloaded into a lighter. The ship was anchored in the outer harbor, and in the distance, against the backdrop of the spectacular Table Mountain, the city spread back on terraced hills from the teeming waterfront.

The *Carver*'s captain, a tall, blue-uniformed Yankee named Harvey Spencer, was standing at the rail amidships, watching the cargo being unloaded. After shouting a string of orders, he climbed the steps back to the quarterdeck. "It's proceeding well, Mr. Taylor. We'll stand out to sea again before sunset."

"I'm pleased to hear that, Captain."

Ted was indeed grateful, for he knew that Spencer was doing all he could to speed the voyage; the man had even informed Ted that he intended to make the call at Sydney a brief one, then lay over a few days in Wellington in the event he could be of help. At the same time, it required all of Ted's self-control to conceal his impatience. Back in Maine, he had bought extra weapons in case he obtained information about Marjorie's whereabouts, and he had been studying maps of New Zealand's South Island. Now it was simply a matter of waiting, but the days seemed endless.

Edward called their attention to a small boat in the distance, with a man at the oars and a single passenger. "They appear to be headed our way," he said.

As the boat drew nearer, the passenger, a plump, middle-aged man in a wrinkled suit, stood up in the stern and lifted his hat with a flourish. "Have I the honor and good fortune of addressing the master of this fine vessel?" he called in an Irish brogue.

"I'm Harvey Spencer, the captain. Who might you be?"

"Edgar Dooley of the Honorable East India Company," the man replied as the boat drew alongside. "It's my great, grand pleasure to meet you, sir, and I earnestly hope you're disposed to help one who is in need. Unless I misunderstood what passes for English in the harbormaster's office, you're bound for Sydney. I urgently need passage there, and I'll pay in gold."

"I'm very sorry, but I can't help you, Mr. Dooley. I have only one passenger cabin, and these two gentlemen are sharing it."

Dooley, whose nose and cheeks looked red from too much drink, frowned in consternation. "Captain Spencer," he pleaded, "fate has often placed me in surroundings from which swine would flee in disgust. A hammock in your crew's quarters would be sheer luxury to me. If you'll but grant me that, eternal gratitude and a full cabin fee in gold will be yours."

The captain seemed amused and shook his head, but Dooley, undeterred, asked if some nook elsewhere on the ship could be found for him. Ted, feeling sorry for the man, exchanged a glance with Edward, who seemed to read his mind and nodded in reply.

Ted addressed the captain. "If you've no objection, Captain Spencer," he suggested quietly, "Edward and I can make room for him in our cabin."

The captain, wanting to let the man aboard, needed no further urging, and when the good news was relayed, Dooley was profuse and long-winded in his thanks, falling silent only long enough to puff his way up the ladder a crewman put over the side.

"God bless you, sir!" he exclaimed as he reached the

deck. "And you gentlemen as well. Your kindness to a traveler in distress is in the true spirit of the Samaritan on the road to Jericho." He shook hands all around, and as the sailors finished loading the cargo and the captain prepared to get under way, Dooley explained his background to Ted and Edward. He said he was an accountant, a traveling auditor for the East India Company, and was constantly on the go between the shore stations the company maintained for its vessels in every port in the region.

He had traveled in Africa and the Orient for thirty years, and as he talked it became evident that he had considerable knowledge of this part of the world. When Edward asked him why he was in such a hurry to get to Sydney, he explained that he had missed an earlier ship on which he had booked passage.

"Frankly, I was in my cups, and my memory of what happened from last Tuesday until this afternoon is unclear. In fact, if a kind lady of the town hadn't awakened me this afternoon, I wouldn't have known that this ship was in port. You see, I was in deep repose under the bushes in her back garden, but how I came to be there I cannot say." He winced as he rubbed his ribs. "She could have been more gentle with her broom, but she sent me on my way to catch this ship, so I'm grateful enough."

Edward chuckled at the tale, but his next comment was more than half-serious. "Under such circumstances, it's a wonder you've kept your position as long as you have."

"You'd not say that if you knew what my position entails," Dooley responded, eyeing him. "My employers can't find anyone else willing to venture into some of the pestholes where they send me."

That evening, when the voyage had resumed and Ted, Edward, and Dooley joined the officers for supper, the accountant regaled them all with anecdotes gathered from his years of traveling. Some of the tales were hardly believable, but truthful or not, they were entertaining.

Not everything in life was a joke to Dooley, however, and after the meal, when the subject of Edward's ranch came up and Edward explained the problems associated with tick fever, Dooley proposed a possible solution:

"You need some Brahma cattle from India, Mr. Blackstone. They thrive on roadside weeds and water from the filthiest ditches you can imagine. Insects of all sorts swarm over them, disease abounds around them, yet the only things they die from are injury and old age."

Edward frowned thoughtfully. "I have an uncle in the army there, in Calcutta. I've exchanged a few letters with him over the years, and he mentioned that the native cattle were incredibly hardy. They're also considered to be holy by the Hindus. That would make it difficult to get them out of the country."

"Aye, there's the rub, as they say." Dooley was silent for a long moment. "But difficult does not mean impossible."

Later, in the passenger cabin, Dooley, after making himself comfortable on a pallet on the floor, related a humorous story about how he had once ended up in Trincomalee, in Ceylon, when he was supposed to be in Karachi. Edward's mind was evidently elsewhere, however, for he offered only a perfunctory laugh and again brought up Brahma cattle.

"The trouble is," he said, as if the subject had never been dropped, "they aren't the same species as European cattle, if I remember my zoology. Brahma cattle are actually zebus, *Bos indicus*, while ours are *Bos taurus*. So the question is, can they interbreed to produce the strain of beef cattle that Rob and I want? Or will the offspring be mules, themselves sterile? I don't know if anyone's ever tried it. . . . I don't think so. It would be an interesting experiment."

Edward yawned deeply, and eventually, after both he and Dooley had fallen asleep, Ted got up and, as he did on most nights, quietly dressed and left the cabin.

The waves hissed alongside the hull as he stood by the rail and glumly stared out over the dark ocean. Edgar Dooley had been a welcome diversion for a short time, but Ted's thoughts, especially at night, reverted without fail to Marjorie. He prayed that she was still alive.

On the third day after the *Carver* had left Cape Town, the lookout spotted sails to the north—a large vessel following a smaller one downwind. At first they were both specks on the horizon, and Ted and Edward paid scant attention to them, for numerous other ships had been sighted in the past days. But as the vessels drew nearer, heading south in front of the steamer, Dooley went to the rail and stared at them intently.

The captain, standing near the helm, noticed his interest. "That larger vessel is a dhow, Mr. Dooley. But as you have no doubt observed, her rigging is different from that on most dhows."

Dooley nodded. "I've seen that sort of rig along the east coast of Africa and once off the Gulf of Aden, but never this far south. It happens to be a favorite of Madagascar pirates."

The captain, in sudden concern, stepped to the rail with his telescope. "By God, you're right! She's bristling with cannon, and that sloop she's chasing is an East India Company vessel, with her flag upside down in distress." He lowered the telescope and stood there tight-lipped, as if wondering what to do.

Ted could readily understand Spencer's quandary. As captain of a merchant vessel, he was responsible to the owners for any damage to his ship or injury to the crew, and the dhow was heavily armed. Ted asked to borrow the telescope and peered through it. "The tiller on that ship is in the open," he observed. "If we get close enough, Edward and I could use a couple of my Winchesters and keep everyone away from it. I don't know about the range of their cannon."

Spencer looked through the telescope again. "They can't bring most of them to bear if we stay well astern. I may end up losing my job, but I'll be damned if I'll ignore a distress signal. How close do you need to be?"

"I've never tried to shoot at anything from the deck of a ship, but—three or four hundred yards should be close enough."

Spencer stepped to the edge of the quarterdeck and called to the first officer. "Mr. Soames, break out the swivel gun from the hold and clear the deck for hostile action. That dhow off our port bow is a pirate vessel, and the sloop is flying a distress signal."

As the mate shouted orders, Ted, Edward, and Dooley

went below for the Winchesters. Dooley, having recovered his usual cheerful attitude, laughed and shook his head when Ted asked him if he was a good shot.

"I've never fired a gun in my life, so I can't rightly say, Mr. Taylor. But I can pass the ammunition well enough."

By the time they had returned to the deck and taken positions in the bow, the pirate ship was some three or four miles away and appeared to be within easy cannon shot of the sloop it was chasing. Captain Spencer was closing rapidly but keeping the faster and more maneuverable steamship to the dhow's starboard quarter, out of the angle of her gunports.

A few minutes later, Soames and four sailors struggled to the bow with the heavy swivel gun. A small cannon that fired a seven-pound ball, the swivel was lifted and clamped to the rail, and no sooner was it in place than puffs of gunpowder smoke rose from the front of the dhow as it fired a bow chaser at the fleeing sloop. Smoke eddied from the sloop as it responded with a stern cannon, and seconds later the dull thuds of the reports carried across the distance.

The sailors hurriedly loaded the swivel. "They'll fire on us with their own swivels any minute," Soames predicted. "But it takes a lucky shot to do any damage with a small gun."

His words proved accurate, for a short while later a shot splashed into the water off to one side as a puff of smoke rose near the stern of the dhow. The pirate swivel fired twice more, but Soames waited patiently, carefully adjusting the angle of his own gun. Then, when the distance had closed to nearly a thousand yards, he gave the order to fire.

Smoke belched from the cannon as it roared and leaped against its mount. A second later, a stanchion and a length of the dhow's midships rail turned into flying fragments of wood, and the *Carver*'s sailors cheered. Captain Spencer shouted from the quarterdeck over their voices, "Good shooting, Mr. Soames!"

The first officer made no reply, intent as he was on reloading the gun. The dhow had begun turning to bring its main battery to bear on the *Carver*, and Captain Spencer, anticipating the maneuver, ordered a quick change of course to minimize the target he offered.

As the dhow and the steamer turned, the sloop also began changing course, so as not to be separated from the steamer. Soames closely observed the sailors on the dhow, then spoke to Ted. "She's coming up sharp on the edge of the wind, Mr. Taylor. If you can get her helmsman when I give the word, she'll probably come aback of the wind and lose a good part of her rigging."

Ted nodded, willing to give it his best try, although the dhow was still some five hundred yards away, on the edge of accurate range, even if he had been on land. As it was, the steamer was running close to full speed, its deck heaving as its bow slammed through the waves. Ted nodded to Edward, and they readied themselves.

The dhow's swivel fired again, along with several of her side cannon, but the shots fell wide, and when the distance had closed perhaps another fifty yards, Soames responded with the *Carver's* swivel, then directed Ted and Edward to open fire. The helmsman and other crewmen on the pirate vessel were now clearly visible, and using high elevation, Ted and Edward began to empty the magazines on both Winchesters.

After a few seconds, Soames and the sailors paused in their reloading and whooped in glee. "You got him!" Soames shouted. "Now just keep the others away!"

Sure enough, Ted saw other men running toward the tiller, which had swung to one side. He fired again, and when his hammer dropped on an empty chamber, Dooley handed him a loaded rifle, then another to Edward. Two pirates were already lying wounded in the stern, and a third was cut down just as he started to grasp the tiller's handle.

With the dhow turning out of control, Soames muttered oaths and moved his hands as if to push the bow on around. The pirate vessel slowed, and its sails became slack as the wind touched them on the edge. Then they began filling and bulging backward.

"She's aback!" Soames and some of the swivel's crew were yelling exultantly, and the captain and the other deckhands cheered as they watched what was happening.

The nautical term was meaningless to Ted, until he saw the dramatic result. The dhow's sails were now taking the full force of the wind on their forward side, and the spars and topmasts, which were not properly trimmed and braced to withstand the abrupt change, snapped off and tumbled down in a tangle of canvas and rope.

Some of the wreckage dragged in the water, immobilizing the vessel. Yet as he watched, Ted noticed pirates moving around some of the dhow's cannon, for the *Carver* had swung full into their sights. He and Edward again opened fire, and the men began scattering, and another round from the *Carver*'s swivel sent the remaining pirates scurrying for cover.

The *Carver* slowed, approaching cautiously, while Ted and Edward kept up an accurate fire on anything that moved on the crippled vessel. When they were within fifty yards and no sign of life was visible, Captain Spencer ordered a boat lowered with an armed boarding party. Ted took a place in the bow as Edward and the crew of the swivel covered them from the *Carver*'s bow.

The East India Company sloop stood off nearby, and its master hailed the American steamer, relaying his and his crew's heartfelt thanks. They also lowered a boat with a boarding party, and from opposite quarters the two small boats approached the dhow.

The sloop's master himself led the British boarding party, which was heavily armed and looked bent on revenge. They boarded simultaneously with the *Carver*'s party, but at first all that was in evidence on the wreckage-strewn deck of the dhow were a few bodies. A noise in the forecastle soon revealed the hiding place of the rest of the crew.

Waving the others to take cover, Ted ordered the pirates to surrender, and when there was no reaction, he opened fire at the door. A chorus of terrified shouting came from inside, and when he stopped firing, the door opened. A dozen men came out, their hands over their heads, and the sailors immediately seized and bound them. A thorough search of the rest of the vessel turned up nothing more. When Captain Spencer came aboard, the sloop's master, a Scot named Arbogast, greeted him warmly and offered to take charge of the prisoners.

"We're en route to Perth," he said, "and I can turn them over to the authorities there. They'll get a fair trial, though I scarcely think they deserve one."

"That sounds fine to me," Spencer agreed. "And as far as this hulk goes, I have no use for it."

"Good. It'll be my pleasure to burn and scuttle her." Arbogast shouted orders to his men, then turned back to Spencer. "Still and all, she was almost the end of us. I'll never be able to thank you enough, sir."

"We're more than glad we were able to help, Captain. And most of the credit goes to Mr. Taylor and his friend, and my first mate. They're the ones who did the shooting."

"And a fine bit of marksmanship it was!" Arbogast pumped Ted's hand, then Soames's. "My galley isn't the best, as you gentlemen may imagine, but I'd be more than glad to host you to the best dinner we can manage. That's the least I can do."

Spencer glanced at Ted before he answered. "We appreciate the invitation, sir, but we've a schedule to keep. If we ever meet in port, however, I'll be glad to let you buy the first drink."

"I'll keep my eye out for the *Carver*, then," Arbogast promised, "and my purse ready."

After handshakes all around, Captain Spencer's crew returned in their boats, and the *Carver* steamed away, resuming its course. Edward, Dooley, and the crewmen looked back at the thick smoke rising from the pirate vessel, but Ted Taylor gazed in the opposite direction, his thoughts racing thousands of miles ahead to New Zealand.

XII

It had been three days since Lydia's doctor confirmed that she was pregnant, and Andrew, still overcome by the news and tortured with self-recrimination, was waiting for the other shoe to drop. Emil Villach, Lydia had frantically insisted over and over, would soon find out about the doctor's visit and her condition. She had no doubt on that point.

It was because of his mixed apprehension and joy—after all, Lydia was pregnant with *his* child, Andrew kept reminding himself—that he was unable to concentrate on his work at the embassy. He had no idea how the old Count von Lautzenberg would react to the news, and Andrew's sense of foreboding became acute when, one morning at work, a clerk handed him a letter postmarked Vienna and embellished with the colorful Hapsburg coat of arms.

As it turned out, however, the letter was from the Ministry of War and was an invitation for him to be an official observer at maneuvers scheduled for the following month. Andrew couldn't have been more surprised.

He immediately took the letter upstairs to show to the ambassador, who was equally astonished. The Austro-Hungarian Empire, because of its varied ethnic composition and aggressive military tradition, was one of the few European states that conducted frequent war exercises. But the Vienna government had always been secretive about its military capability and never allowed outsiders to view the maneuvers.

"Washington will be amazed," Ely declared, glancing up from the letter. "We must notify the State and War departments at once."

"Yes, sir. I'll see to it this minute." For the rest of the day, however, Andrew remained vaguely troubled, and that evening, when he told Lydia about the invitation, she was just as perplexed as he.

At work the next morning, Andrew found that the reaction from the War Department to his message had been as prompt as expected. A telegram instructed him to accept immediately, then set forth paragraph after paragraph of questions the department wanted answered about the Austro-Hungarian Army. Ely enthusiastically assured him that a commendation, possibly even a promotion, would result from the invitation.

Andrew went through the motions and prepared himself for the assignment, yet he could not shake the feeling that the invitation was too good to be true. Lydia was absolutely certain that Villach and Count von Lautzenberg knew of her condition, and Andrew wondered whether the following weeks would bring, instead of a promotion, the end of his army career.

The possibility that Alvin Mosely would find a suitable target for the comancheros to raid had remained a constant worry for Toby, and consequently he felt vastly relieved when he saw the man riding into the valley with a frightened, hangdog look that could only mean he had bad news for the outlaw leader.

The comancheros around the fires concluded the same, and discontented grumbling rose among them as they eyed Mosely. Calusa Jim emerged from his tent, and Mosely gestured apologetically as he tried to explain. The tall man bellowed in rage and, lifting his right arm, threatened the quailing Mosely with the gleaming hook.

If it had been someone besides Mosely, Toby might have felt a twinge of sympathy; instead, he watched with ironic satisfaction as the man suffered a tiny measure of the terror he had brought upon others. Besides, Toby knew it would be suicide for him to intervene; the men around him had no scruples about taking a human life, and they would enjoy taking his.

Toby was only slightly surprised when Calusa Jim, apparently getting an answer he didn't like, knocked Mosely sprawling and bent over him, pressing the tip of the hook against the man's nose. The comancheros craned their necks to watch, and some even stood to get a better view. Calusa Jim was asking questions in a voice that sounded like a snarling animal, and Mosely whimpered barely audible replies.

Then the moment of peril passed. The outlaw leader straightened and moved back, and the comancheros muttered in disappointment. Calusa Jim dismissed Mosely in disgust, then shouted and beckoned to Toby.

After Toby's first few days in camp, Calusa Jim had frequently talked with him, sometimes for hours at a time. Impressed with how Toby had handled himself, the outlaw leader used him as a sounding board for ideas and tried to impress him in return, boasting about his exploits and his plans. It had given Toby an opportunity to size the man up and find out how difficult it would be to deceive him. Toby concluded that it would be very difficult indeed but he thought of a plan that just might work.

As Toby sat at the table with Calusa Jim, who was still breathing heavily from his encounter with Mosely, Juanita came out with a pitcher of pulque. The pity Toby felt for the young woman could place both of them in peril, but her eyes wisely avoided his as she poured the beverage and hurried back to the tent. Calusa Jim took a deep drink. "I guess you heard, Miller. That worthless fool Mosely didn't find any likely targets."

"Yes, I heard."

"I am going to have to take this bunch out of here and do something, or they will start getting hard for me to handle. Tomorrow we will head south and find a town to take over for a few days so the men can work off steam. You don't like sitting around here any more than the others, do you?"

"No." Toby forced himself to drink some of the sour-tasting pulque as he formulated his answer. "But I also don't see any sense in wasting time on some dirt-poor town. It's been a good while since you've raided up north, hasn't it? If you play your cards right, you might be able to get the army to pull in those patrols."

Calusa Jim looked interested. "How?"

"By bluffing a raid on the Mexican army garrison at Chihuahua, then pulling out after giving a good show. The commander there would make the most of it and spread the word that he'd bravely driven off the comancheros, and it wouldn't take long for the news to reach Santa Fe. They would conclude that you've moved deep into Mexico and that you're low on ammunition."

"Why would they think I am low on ammunition?"

"Why else would you attack a garrison? In any event, the cavalry up north has been spending seven days a week, fourteen hours a day in the saddle, as heavily as they've been patrolling. They're probably looking for an excuse to stop."

"Yes, you might be right." Calusa Jim glanced across the camp. "I could send that hyena Mosely up there and check to see if they've stopped. And when they do, the people at some of those ranches will be breathing a lot easier, too." He grinned evilly. "But not for long. We would come right in on Mosely's tail and raid as many as we could hit in a day or two."

"That's right—but Mosely should check both east and west of the Rio Grande. You'd want to make certain the patrols hadn't just moved."

Calusa Jim frowned. "You are right, Miller. But it would take him two weeks or longer to check the entire area."

"Then send two men." Toby brushed past the point quickly. "But I believe you could do more than raid a few ranches. If you waited for a while, things would get really quiet up there, and you could raid the Albuquerque fiesta. That would be a target worth the time and trouble."

Calusa Jim guffawed and slapped the table. "The Albuquerque fiesta! Miller, you are a bold one!" The smile faded. "Unfortunately, the governor has canceled the fiesta. Did you not hear about that while you were there?"

"I heard that he was *thinking* about it," Toby corrected the man. "And I also heard that a lot of people were angry about it. If he thinks you're far down into Mexico and low on ammunition, he won't cancel it." He lowered his voice confidentially, making an appeal to the man's sizable ego. "Whoever made a raid like that would go down in history."

Calusa Jim became reflective. "You are right about that, Miller. No one has ever made such a raid! We could come out of there with forty or fifty women and more loot than we could carry. People all over the United States would be talking about Calusa Jim. Newspaper reporters would want to interview me."

Sipping from his cup, Toby listened and occasionally nodded as the outlaw leader convinced himself to go forward with the bold plan. Calusa Jim was doing such an excellent job, Toby decided, it would be unwise for him to press the idea any further at present.

During much of the rest of the day, Calusa Jim sat at the table in front of his tent, lost in thought, and after the evening meal, he again called Toby over.

Evidently the man had been trying to resolve the problems involved in getting the comancheros to Albuquerque without being detected. The obstacles were formidable, for the only convenient route was the road up the Rio Grande Valley, through the territory's most densely settled area. Using his hook, the outlaw leader drew a rough map in the dirt and explained his reservations.

Toby suggested leaving the hideout three or four days before the fiesta and crossing the Rio Grande south of Las Cruces. "It's mostly open country there," he pointed out, "so we shouldn't have any trouble crossing the river unseen. That would put us in the desert along the foothills of the San Andres Mountains, and no one lives in that area. We could travel slowly and save the horses, then be up west of Socorro by the day before the fiesta."

Calusa Jim's reaction was precisely what Toby expected. "Yes, that part is easy, my friend. But what about the ranches along the river north of Socorro? We couldn't get past them without being seen."

"Perhaps not. But I believe we could do it without worrying anyone. We could wait until dark to move out, and if you could keep the men quiet and in a double file, people would think we're a cavalry troop."

Again Calusa Jim burst out laughing at the audacity of Toby's plan. "I like that, Miller! People thinking we are cavalry! But that would put us into Albuquerque during daylight, would it not?"

"No. Before dawn we could hide in the mountains just east of town. By nightfall the fiesta would be in full swing. Then we could ride out and attack."

Calusa Jim stroked his bristly chin. "Maybe it would also be a good idea to cut the telegraph lines to Las Cruces."

Again Toby had anticipated the suggestion. "That might alert the army forts down there. But yes, we should cut them before we leave, or we might have cavalry waiting for us. Also, I think it would be best to leave the horses on the outskirts of town. That many horses going through the streets to the main square will draw a lot of attention."

Calusa Jim darkened. "We are dead if we lose our horses."

"You could leave enough men behind to guard them. Even if no cavalry is around, we'll still be in the middle of a large town, where most of the people can get to guns within a few minutes. We want to be as quiet as possible, right up to the moment we attack."

Calusa Jim clearly was intrigued by the plan, for he started asking questions about the layout of Albuquerque. At Calusa Jim's request, he drew on the ground a map of the city's main streets and squares, describing the quickest routes into town. Having covered the points essential to his own scheme, Toby refrained from making further suggestions, to avoid arousing suspicion.

It was dark by the time Toby returned to his place beside the fire. Nearby, three comancheros were snoring loudly, but sleep evaded Toby. He lay there and looked up at the stars, haunted by the fear that he had spoiled his plan by seeming too helpful and too ready with suggestions. Finally he fell into a restless slumber, prepared to wake instantly at any movement or sound.

The next morning, after breakfast, Calusa Jim walked over to Toby.

"I am still thinking about what we discussed last night," he said. "In the meantime, we will stage the raid on the Chihuahua garrison. It is a long, hot ride down there, and we will need plenty of spare horses, so I will use only half the men."

Toby shrugged. "Like I said, by the time the garrison commander makes his report, the number of attackers will have doubled anyway."

Calusa Jim eyed Toby for a long moment, then he abruptly turned, lifted an arm, and pointed down the middle of the encampment. "Everyone on this side of my arm," he shouted, "get saddled up. The rest of you stay put."

The men who were to remain behind complained loudly, while the others eagerly gathered up their saddles and weapons and made for the horses. Watching them, Toby wondered if he would be told to stay in camp. If so, he might have an opportunity during Calusa Jim's absence to slip away to Mesilla and inform Walter Stafford about his plan.

But Toby's thoughts were interrupted as the outlaw leader again shouted to his men, "Hold on!"

All faces turned in his direction.

"Everyone gather around! There's something I've got to do before anyone leaves."

Their curiosity piqued, the comancheros quickly collected around Toby and Calusa Jim. With scores of sweaty, unshaven faces staring at him from all sides, Toby felt extremely uneasy. Silence descended as Calusa Jim seized Toby's left arm, gripping it tightly by the wrist, then raised the shining hook and held it out for all to see.

The comancheros stood frozen in anticipation as Calusa Jim held Toby's arm in an iron grip, as if daring him to defend himself. Long seconds passed, each like an eternity to Toby. His right hand hovered near his pistol. If he was to die now, he would not go alone.

Abruptly Calusa Jim brought the sharpened point of the hook against the skin of Toby's forearm, just below the rolled-up sleeve. The metal pressed down, breaking through skin.

"Does that hurt, Miller?" Calusa Jim asked.

Toby thought the man's expression verged on madness. He could feel his heart pounding against his ribs as he returned the outlaw leader's stare. "I believe I'll live through it." He was still ready to draw his pistol.

Calusa Jim chuckled, slowly pressing deeper, until

blood welled copiously from the puncture wound. "I don't believe in oaths sworn to God, and I don't think much more of oaths on a mother's grave, because few of my men care anything about their mothers. But I do believe in oaths that a man swears on his own blood, on his own life. Do you understand, Miller?"

"I suppose so," Toby responded. "But what does that have to do with me?"

"I want you to swear an oath on your own blood." Calusa Jim removed the hook and held it out so that Toby could see the red drops falling to the dust at his feet. "An oath of loyalty to me and my men." The outlaw grinned wickedly. "You don't have to do it, but you'll never leave here if you don't. Now repeat after me. 'I, Tom Miller, hereby swear on my own blood . . .'"

Toby hesitated only an instant. He had no compunction about lying to Calusa Jim or about swearing an oath under an assumed name.

"I, Tom Miller, hereby swear on my own blood . . ."

"'. . . that I will always be loyal to Calusa Jim and his men,'" the outlaw leader continued, "'and will never betray them in any way.'"

Toby repeated the words.

Calusa Jim released Toby's wrist, pulled out a red neckerchief, and tossed it to him. "Here, wrap that around it. When the cut stops bleeding, you can wear that around your neck as your badge of rank." He turned to the comancheros and spoke loudly. "I have decided to appoint Miller my lieutenant. As long as he wears that red neckerchief, an order from him is the same as an order from me. Understand?"

The men muttered an unenthusiastic acknowledgment, and Calusa Jim dismissed them, then turned back to Toby. "You get saddled up too, Miller."

Toby revealed no reaction as he finished wrapping the neckerchief around his arm. "What about you? You coming along?"

"Not this time. I want you to lead the men."

Toby looked up in genuine surprise.

"Yes, that's right," Calusa Jim continued. "This is your opportunity to prove yourself. Do you not like the idea, Miller?"

"It's just fine with me." As Toby moved to gather up his gear, he reflected that he had succeeded almost too well in his masquerade. After all, qualifying as a comanchero leader was not exactly his idea of success in life.

He also noticed that Camargo was among those going on the raid, which promised trouble. Lieutenant or not, he had not the slightest doubt that the Mexican was still biding his time, awaiting an opportunity to get even.

It was uncomfortably cold in New Zealand, and Ted Taylor had his collar turned up against the biting wind as he walked down a street in Wellington, the colony's capital. His meetings with the American consul and the colony's military and civil authorities had produced no results, although everyone had expressed sympathy for his predicament and admitted there was no firm evidence that the *Beluga*'s crew was not still alive. The cook and the cabin boy had long ago shipped back to the United States, and Ted, despite his bitter frustration, kept reverting to the incongruous thought that, wherever Marjorie was, he hoped that she had been able to take her winter coat with her.

Situated at the southern extremity of North Island, Wellington was a thriving, attractive town on an extensive, well-sheltered bay. As he turned a corner and the harbor came into view, Ted saw the *John S. Carver* tied up to a wharf in the distance. To gain precious time, he and Edward Blackstone had left the steamer unloading back in Sydney and came ahead of her to New Zealand on a mail clipper. The *Carver* had caught up with them yesterday, and Ted now had only a few days before Captain Spencer would be obliged to set off on his return trip.

After turning another corner, Ted found himself at his destination, a waterfront tavern where he had been told he could locate a backwoods guide named John Atkinson. He stepped inside the noisy, smoke-filled taproom and soon spotted a man fitting the description that had been given him.

About forty years old and wearing durable workclothes and heavy boots, the squat, muscular man standing at the bar had features that revealed he was half Maori. He shook hands readily when Ted introduced himself, and the two sat down at a table.

"So you're the one whose wife was on that whaler captured by the Maoris. I heard you were asking around."

"A surveying company official gave me your name," Ted explained. "He said you knew South Island better than anyone in Wellington and might have some ideas about what I could do."

"I might." Atkinson eyed him appraisingly. "Frankly, I'm not surprised that the government and the military couldn't help you. All they know is North Island, because this is where most of the people live and where most all of the trouble with the Maoris has occurred. South Island's a different story, now. A good part of it's uninhabited. Pure wilderness."

"Yes, everyone seemed surprised the ship was captured there," Ted replied. "They said that parties of Maoris go there to mine stone along the coast, and some of them might have captured the ship."

"Greenstone." Atkinson shook his head. "Mining parties are usually small. From what I heard of the cabin boy's account, that whaler was taken by a large, well-armed party, perhaps an entire village. That got me to thinking: Around that time, a Tuhoe village on this island got into a fracas with the Ngatitoa tribe, and the Tuhoes were driven out. Seems they crossed the strait to South Island. There were some unexplained raids on farms there, not far from the strait."

Atkinson's conclusion seemed logical to Ted. "I've been told that searching down there would be a waste of time. But do you—an experienced wilderness guide—think you might be able to find my wife and the others?"

Atkinson again shook his head. "I doubt it. Mind, I've worked as a guide for the army, and I've tracked down villages that were very remote and well hidden. But searching that wilderness could take years."

Ted was about to say something else, but the man cut him off. "I have a friend who lives on South Island—a farmer, Sam Willey. Sam might be able to help. He's one of the victims of those raids."

Determined to hire both men if at all possible, Ted asked Atkinson what he was doing at present, and the man replied that he had just returned from several weeks in the bush, collecting a substance called kauri gum. "It's a resin that seeps out of kauri trees and falls off in lumps," he explained, "and it's used for making varnish and other things. The ground around old kauri trees is full of it, and it brings a good price. But it's hard, dirty work." He smiled ruefully. "If you have in mind enlisting my help, I can take a vacation from gum gathering."

Ted held out his hand. "I'd like to hire you as a guide, Mr. Atkinson, and go with you to talk with your friend. If he has any ideas about where Marjorie might be, I'd like to hire him as well. I want you to know that I'm a lawman of no little success and experience. If we run into trouble, I feel confident I'll be able to handle it. I intend to rescue my wife."

The New Zealander shook the offered hand. "I don't want to take your money for nothing," he said. "So first let's find us a boat ride and talk with Sam."

"We can set out within three or four hours," Harvey Spencer said when Ted and Atkinson found him in his hotel. "My cargo should be unloaded by then, and I have steam up. If you have a good notion as to where to find your wife, I reckon I can stretch my stay in these waters for a week to ten days."

Atkinson agreed to make use of whatever time Spencer could give them, and by early the next morning, after a calm passage across Cook Strait and around Cape Stephens, the *Carver* came to anchor in Tasman Bay, where a breathtaking vista of white beaches and verdant hills stretched in both directions from the small settlement called Motueka. Atkinson was rowed ashore in the ship's boat to fetch Willey from his farm in the nearby mountains.

Ted grew anxious as the hours passed. Sea gulls wheeled overhead, and people on shore stared in curiosity at the *Carver*. Finally, Atkinson reappeared on the beach with another man and was rowed back to the ship.

A few years older than Atkinson, Sam Willey had the look of a man who spent most of his life outdoors. After the introductions were made, they all assembled in the captain's day cabin, where Spencer unrolled a chart of South Island on the table.

Ted pointed to the bay where he had been told the *Beluga* disappeared. Willey agreed with Atkinson that the Maoris who had attacked the whaler were probably the Tuhoe villagers who had been dríven off North Island. "They came ashore right here," he said, indicating an arm of land a few miles from where the *Carver* was anchored. "Then they set out to the south, looting storehouses and stealing a few sheep along the way. I lost four sheep myself from one of my back pastures."

"Then the tribe disappeared?" Ted inquired.

"No, not entirely" was Willey's unexpected answer. "A few weeks later, an Arawa chieftain I know came by my farm. He and a half-dozen others had been digging greenstone and were on their way back to North Island. He told me he had seen the Tuhoes." He pointed to a spot on the map well inland of the north coast. "From what he said, they must have been about here. And that's the last I heard of them."

Atkinson pointed to a place a few miles inland from where the whaler had been attacked. "When I was a boy, my dad and I camped in a valley somewhere around here. It was overrun with pigs."

"Yes, I've heard of the place." Willey bent to scrutinize the area on the map. "It was toward the end of our warm weather when the Tuhoes left North Island. They would want to find a good location for their village and build shelters before cold set in. Judging from how long it took them to get to where the Arawas saw them, they would have reached that valley about the time the weather changed."

"And they wouldn't want to go much farther south," Atkinson added. "It gets cold down at the other end of the island." He tapped the map with a finger. "Sam, I say that that valley is our best bet."

"I believe it is, too."

"How long would it take to find out?" Ted asked, feeling a bit of hope for the first time.

"Five or six days," Willey replied after some thought. "In this steamer, we can be there tomorrow, but we can't just anchor in the bay and go straight to the valley. If they are there, they'll have sentries posted. We'll be wanting to take them by surprise, and the only way to do that is to anchor in a bay to the north and head overland. That's rough terrain, so it'll take two or three days to reach the valley."

"That's no problem for me," Spencer declared. "I can spend another five or six days here."

Ted hoped he was making the right decision. "Very well, I'd like to hire you gentlemen to go down there."

"I'm ready to go," Willey said without hesitation. "John told me you have some new Winchester rifles, and we'd each like to have one in lieu of, if it's worth it to you."

Ted quickly agreed.

"Looks like we have the makings of a small army, then." Spencer grinned. "In case you don't know it, Ted, nearly every man in my crew has volunteered to help with the rescue. I have some extra weapons we can take, to hand out among the whaler's crew, if they're still alive and we can fight our way through to them."

"We won't be needing an army, I hope," Willey put in. "The Arawas said the Tuhoes weren't well armed— although they will have plundered the arms chest on the *Beluga*."

"Then let's be on our way." Spencer strode out of the cabin and called to the first officer to prepare to weigh anchor, and minutes later the *Carver* was steaming out of the bay.

By midafternoon they had left Cook Strait behind and were in the open waters of the Pacific, west of South Island. The day ended in a brief, winter sunset and twilight, and the *Carver* continued steaming southwest at full speed through the night. Just before dawn, Captain Spencer changed course to the south and slowed, cautiously approaching the rugged coastline.

It was dawn when they entered a bay north of where the whaler had been attacked, and by the time the sun had risen, the *Carver* was anchored and the men were mustered on deck, as Ted and the first mate, Soames, passed out weapons. Captain Spencer and five of the crew remained behind while the ship's boats shuttled the remainder of the men ashore. Counting Ted, Edward, Atkinson, and Willey, the rescue party was twenty-two strong.

Ted had seen rough terrain while working in the Rockies, but nothing to compare with the New Zealand wilderness. They were faced with a series of sharp peaks and steep valleys, and every inch was covered with dense foliage interlaced by liana vines, which made progress excruciatingly slow. Atkinson and Willey fought their way on a zigzag path uphill, and Ted and the others struggled along behind them.

While many of the crewmen grew quickly exhausted, Ted, in his eagerness to reach the valley and find out if it was the right place, had boundless energy and was intensely regretful when darkness forced them to stop. The night was damp and cold, and as he wrapped himself in a blanket, Ted again found himself wondering whether Marjorie had her winter coat with her.

The next day, not long after they had set off, Ted's spirits soared when Atkinson called a halt and showed him a rotted sandal, a fragment of a basket, and other debris that had been discarded months before. The two New Zealanders had apparently found the Tuhoes' earlier trail, and they now followed it southwestward.

By nightfall they were only a few miles from their objective, and early the next morning Atkinson and Willey turned off the overgrown trail to approach the valley from the east. At midmorning they emerged from dense foliage onto a rocky ledge overlooking the valley, and Ted could see a Maori village on a distant knoll.

Kneeling in the brush as the others were directed to remain under cover, Ted hastily opened the *Carver*'s telescope, which Captain Spencer had insisted he take along. After scanning the village a few seconds, he sagged with relief. "There she is! It's Marjorie!" he exclaimed in a tense but controlled voice. Then, to the others' puzzlement, he actually grinned at what he saw. A captive in circumstances that most people would have thought intimidating, Marjorie looked perfectly normal: She was busily photographing a group of villagers in front of a large building. Shaking his head, Ted grinned in spite of himself.

Ted also noticed with satisfaction that she had on her winter coat. He handed the telescope to Edward and pointed out Marjorie. Edward muttered in amazement. "Except for that hulking fellow near her, she could be on any street in America. She certainly doesn't look frightened." Edward scanned the rest of the encampment. "That's a formidable-looking wall they've built. And if I'm not mistaken, I think I see some of the sailors working on the firing platforms, off to the right." He handed the telescope to Atkinson.

"Aye, that's a right pretty wall. I reckon it's kept the crewmen busy. But it won't cause us any trouble."

Edward and Ted exchanged a doubting look.

"He's right," Willey confirmed. "Maori villages always have an escape tunnel to use if the walls are breached. John and I will go down there after dark and find it. It's probably in the brush on the side toward the creek."

"The other side looks better to me," Atkinson decided, still peering through the telescope. "I'd say the exit is in those rocks to the left."

Willey shook his head and grabbed the telescope. The two men argued the point, finally wagering a shilling. By the time Ted got the telescope back, Marjorie had disappeared. He studied the village's streets and defenses, trying to memorize the layout. It wasn't until dusk that he saw Marjorie again, going with the crewmen into one of the huts in the village.

Full darkness fell, and after the rescue party had eaten their rations, Atkinson and Willey quietly left. When they returned, more than two hours later, a grinning Atkinson was holding up a shiny shilling; the exit from the escape tunnel was in the rocks, as he had predicted. He, Willey, and the others settled down to sleep, but Ted remained wide awake. Well before dawn, they all had something to eat, and then, leaving everything behind but the weapons, they followed Atkinson and Willey down the mountain and toward the village.

The darkness was still thick, and Ted was barely able to see the two New Zealanders as they moved quietly through the foliage ahead of him. About an hour later, the village wall loomed in the near distance, a darker shadow surmounting the silhouetted knoll. At the tunnel entrance,

Ted whispered to Atkinson and Willey that he wanted to go through first, and they moved aside for him.

The tunnel was pitch dark and claustrophobically small, and Ted's shoulders brushed the sides as he crawled ahead, feeling his way. At length he emerged inside the village wall. He saw the dark shape of a hut a few yards away, and he moved toward it in a crouch. The other men followed him a few at a time, then gathered silently around him behind the hut.

Marjorie shivered in the cold of dawn as she tied back her hair and pulled on her coat. Stepping from behind the canvas screen that bounded her quarters, she saw Tench and Cade sitting up beside the fire, along with the slave boy Hari. The rest of the men were still sleeping.

She was about to say good morning when a gunshot sounded, echoing in the forest silence. Tench and Cade immediately sprang up and hurried to the door, while the other men began sitting up from their sleeping mats. Outside the hut, the Maori guards exchanged alarmed shouts.

"Hold your tongues!" Cade barked when the awakening crewmen broke into a babble of excited conversation. "Be quiet and listen!"

The men fell silent, their voices replaced by the sound of Maoris shouting angrily. The commotion came from across the village, but it was moving closer. Suddenly several pistols and muskets fired, followed a few seconds later by a disciplined fusillade from rifles, more than a dozen firing simultaneously.

"It must be the army!" Baylor exclaimed. "They must have found out where we are!"

Everyone listened in suspense as the sound of the battle grew louder. Outside, warriors were running past, toward the scene of the action. As the men crowded toward the door, the two Maori guards stepped inside, brandishing their spears and clubs and shouting threateningly. A few of the sailors stepped back, then suddenly Cade and David Cornell leaped from opposite directions at one of the guards.

The other guard raised his club to help his companion, but several other sailors were on him in an instant, and both the Maoris went down under a swarm of men, who seized their weapons. Others crowded to the door and looked cautiously out.

Marjorie caught Hari's arm and held him back as he went to join the men. "No, you stay with me," she said firmly. "Danger! Do you understand?"

The boy, who had learned a good deal of English, remained reluctantly at her side. The men at the door abruptly scattered and crouched in panic as bullets flew through the thatched walls of the hut, and Marjorie pulled Hari down beside her on one of the mats.

Despite the confusion, Marjorie realized that the battle taking place outside was one of modern weapons against great numbers of poorly armed warriors. When several more bullets flew through the hut, one striking the canvas partition, she suddenly became concerned about her photographic plates, which were stacked in wooden crates in her sleeping area. She crawled toward the canvas enclosure, dragging Hari with her.

She was hurriedly moving the top crates to the floor when the men at the door burst into shouts and cheers, apparently having spotted their rescuers. Marjorie kept moving the crates and ordered the distracted Hari to help her.

The battle drew nearer, and Marjorie could hear barefoot warriors retreating. The crewmen were charging outside, into the clearing in front of the hut. Curiosity finally got the better of her. Holding Hari's hand, she went to the door, and when she looked out, she was amazed to see not British uniforms, but what looked to be American sailors, and Edward Blackstone among them. Someone shouted her name, and Marjorie's heart leaped as she saw Ted rushing toward her.

He paused only long enough to smile reassuringly. Then he handed a pistol to Horatio Cade, and both men moved off, into the thick of the battle.

Marjorie stood there with tears in her eyes and waved back to a smiling Edward, who somehow managed to look dapper while holding a pistol and a bloodstained sword, a rifle slung over his shoulder. He, too, ran on after the warriors, and Marjorie saw him give the rifle to one of the *Beluga*'s crewmen. Many of the sailors were whooping and rushing ahead in their eagerness for revenge.

The men disappeared around a group of huts, and heavy gunfire erupted a moment later. Apparently the warriors were making a stand near the meetinghouse, and Marjorie, wanting to assure herself that Ted was all right, started with Hari through the village.

Staying close to the huts at one side, Marjorie crouched low to the ground and motioned Hari down, for bullets were flying in their direction. The clearing came into view, and Marjorie saw that the bulk of the Maoris were taking shelter in and around the meetinghouse. In the distance the main gate was standing open, and a few warriors were herding the women and children through it.

The rescue party was drawn up just ahead, across from the meetinghouse, and Marjorie gasped as she saw Ted suddenly dash out into the clearing, toward the fire that was always kept burning there. Bullets kicked up dirt around his feet, but he reached the fire and, without slowing, snatched up a long, burning branch and hurled it up at the meetinghouse's thatched roof. It scattered embers as Ted ran back to rejoin the men.

Seconds later, flames started leaping up, and thick smoke boiled from the damp thatch. The morning breeze fanned the flames, which spread rapidly, and soon the fire was licking at the eaves of the neighboring huts. A few Maori defenders broke and ran toward the gate, but most bravely stood their ground.

A sailor leaped out, intending to throw another firebrand at the huts, but instead of running in a rapid zigzag as Ted had, he made straight for the fire, and a bullet knocked one of his legs from under him. Ted and another man ran out to get him, and spears heaved from the meetinghouse clattered around them as they dragged the man to safety.

There had been no need for another firebrand, for the heat and smoke were rapidly becoming intolerable for the warriors. Dozens retreated toward the gate, and as several more of the defenders fell from the rescuers' gunfire, the last Maoris broke and ran. Marjorie saw the chief among them.

A sailor from the *Beluga* dashed out and began shooting at the fleeing Maoris, but Ted shouted at him to stop. The man wheeled around angrily. "Mister, you don't know what they did to us!"

"That's no reason for us to slaughter them!" Ted retorted, stepping forward and lowering his Winchester. "The battle's over, and we won. Let them go!"

Not everyone agreed with Ted, and there was more grumbling, but to Marjorie's relief the shooting stopped. Edward and the others walked out into the open, and Marjorie released Hari's hand and went toward Ted.

Too late, she noticed the chief turn back at the gate, lift his pistol, and fire. She shouted a warning, as did others, but the bullet struck Ted, who staggered and fell. Edward and four or five others had weapons shouldered in an instant, and a fusillade knocked the chief back against the gatepost, where he slid to the ground.

Marjorie ran to Ted and forced her way through the men gathering around. She fell to her knees beside him, her disbelief giving way to panic as she saw the pallor of his features and the hole in his coat near his heart. His total self-assurance in the face of danger had always made him seem indestructible.

Smiling, he lifted a hand to her lapel and tried to say something about her coat, but the effort made him cough and brought a stain of red to his lips. His smile fading, his hand fell away, and his eyes gazed up at her sightlessly.

Marjorie clutched at him and collapsed, sobbing.

XIII

Toby looked at the comancheros mounted to his right and left in the ravine and reflected that his missions for the government had occasionally placed him in the most extraordinary circumstances. Certainly he had never imagined he would be involved in anything as bizarre as leading a band of comancheros in a mock attack on a Mexican army garrison.

Most of the comancheros were now spread out in a line abreast, as Toby had ordered, but a half dozen were clustered together, talking. "Get back into line down there!" he shouted. "We don't have all day!"

"Listen to *el capitán*," Camargo sneered. The half-breed was only a few yards away, where Toby could keep an eye on him. "Now we are supposed to play soldiers."

"Shut up and do as you're told!" Toby snarled. "You know what you'll get if I have any more trouble out of you!"

Several of the comancheros snickered, for Camargo's face was already swollen and blotched from the beating Toby had given him two nights before. Falling silent, Camargo glared at the men who were laughing.

The past days had been a frustrating ordeal for Toby. The red neckerchief he now wore, his supposed badge of rank, meant nothing to the comancheros. They were the most ill-disciplined assemblage of fighters he had ever seen. The Indians were the best of a bad lot, for most of them were simply surly, lazy, and slow to obey orders. The remainder could be controlled only by threat of force, and Camargo had been the worst until two nights before. Since then, they all had been somewhat more disciplined, but not much.

The comancheros were finally sorted out into a rough line, and Toby ordered them forward at a walk. They moved up the sandy incline, and at the top Toby commanded them to halt. They were now overlooking a vast, scrubby valley, across which, some three hundred yards away, sat the Chihuahua garrison and the town beyond. As Toby had expected, the sight of the long line of comancheros immediately created a reaction in the garrison.

Soldiers raced about behind the low parapets and in the quadrangle, and a moment later an officer appeared, looking through binoculars. A bugle blew, sounding the alert.

Toby pulled his rifle from its scabbard and fired into the air. "All right, let's get down in the dry wash!" he shouted. "And keep your gunfire high. We don't want them chasing after us!"

The comancheros fired pistols and rifles into the air, shrieking and whooping as they rode forward in a ragged wave. The dry wash ahead was deep and wide, offering ample protection from small-arms fire, and Toby had seen no artillery or Gatling guns in the garrison during his reconnaissance.

Answering gunfire erupted from the parapets as the comancheros reached the dry wash. After Toby had the outlaws picket the horses, he ordered the men to spread out and continue firing. As they obeyed him in no particular hurry, Toby saw that his fears about getting Mexican soldiers killed had been unfounded.

Most of the comancheros congregated in small groups under the edge of the dry wash, where they passed around bottles and fired weapons into the air. The Mexican soldiers, for their part, seemed to have no great desire to unduly provoke the enemy, for only an occasional bullet was aimed low enough to kick up dust on the ground ahead.

Finding a comfortable place, Toby sat down to wait, intending to let sufficient time pass to make the attack look credible. When the gunfire became too sporadic, he shouted at the men, and it increased again. Responding rifle fire issued from the garrison.

The walls of the dry wash were irregular, with deep

niches carved by raging torrents during flash floods. Some fifteen minutes after the mock attack had begun, a furtive movement in a recess where Camargo had taken cover caught Toby's eye. As he watched, Camargo suddenly stepped out and leveled a pistol at him.

Toby rolled to one side and reached for his Colt. Camargo fired, and the bullet slammed into the dirt where Toby had been sitting. Still rolling, Toby thumbed back the hammer on his pistol and in a blur of motion aimed and fired. Camargo was still aiming his pistol when the bullet ripped through his heart, killing him instantly.

The pistol shots were drowned in the other gunfire, and the exchange happened so fast that none of the other comancheros saw it. When the nearest group—four Mexicans—looked over, all they saw was Toby with his pistol in hand, standing over Camargo's body at the bottom of the wash.

Toby rolled the body over with his toe, then holstered his pistol and looked at the four astonished comancheros, who were gaping at him. "I said to keep firing! *Pronto!*" he barked at them.

The men evidently thought he had killed Camargo for wandering about instead of firing his gun, because one of them, who was holding a whiskey bottle, dropped it, hastily snatched up his rifle, and fired rapidly into the air. The bottle, completely forgotten, slid down the bank, its liquor gurgling from it. The four kept glancing at Toby apprehensively, firing their guns into the air and then reloading as quickly as they could.

Toby was almost amused by the men's stupid misunderstanding. But as he went back to where he had been sitting, he reminded himself that these men were savage killers who might easily turn on him, as Camargo had tried to do.

After another hour of gunfire, Toby ended the charade. He assembled the comancheros and had them mount, then galloped after them along the dry wash until they were a mile from the garrison. He would have led the column, but after the incident with Camargo, he had no intention of inviting a bullet in the back. Eventually he had them turn north, cutting back over rocky ground so as not to leave a trail in the unlikely event the garrison commander sent soldiers to see which way they had gone.

At length the ragged column arrived back at the canyon where spare horses, food, and other supplies had been left under guard. Apparently word had spread about Camargo, for no one voiced objections when Toby immediately ordered them to saddle up the fresh horses to continue the long ride back to the hideout.

When they were ready to leave, Toby assembled the men; during the ride south, he had barely restrained them from ravaging the towns they passed, and as long as the men were under his control, Toby was determined to keep them from harming others. He told them about Calusa Jim's plan for a large raid.

"Part of the strategy," he continued, "is for everyone to think we're far south of the border. If we're spotted on our way back to the hideout, it will ruin the raid. So we're going to stick to the mountains and deserts, keeping completely away from towns and ranches."

"You won't get any argument from me," one of the Mexicans spoke up. "You're worse than Calusa Jim, killing Camargo just because he stopped shooting his gun."

"Just follow orders, and you won't have any trouble," Toby said. "Camargo got what was coming to him. All right, let's go."

During the ride back, Toby thought again about his own plans to wipe out the comancheros. One factor working greatly in his favor was Calusa Jim's ignorance of anything beyond his own sphere of action. Toby doubted that news of a comanchero attack on the Chihuahua garrison would cause any great sensation in Santa Fe, and he knew it would take more than that to stop the cavalry patrols. Calusa Jim, however, had accepted Toby's claim without reservation, which was all that mattered.

At the same time, the man was slyly suspicious of everything and everyone. That was an obstacle to the most crucial part of Toby's scheme, which was contacting Stafford in Mesilla. If the outlaw leader prevented Toby from leaving the hideout, the cavalry patrols would continue and the plan would fail.

Worse still, Calusa Jim might go ahead with Toby's

idea without giving him a chance to get away, meaning
Toby would be responsible for what could be a disaster in
Albuquerque. That possibility concerned him greatly as he
rode north through the night, leading the comancheros
back to their den.

They arrived at the hideout four days later. The guards
at the ravine entrance watched sullenly as Toby rode past,
leading the column of sweaty horses and weary, dusty
men. In the camp the comancheros who had remained
behind gathered around to talk to the men who had gone
with Toby.

Mosely was there, Toby noticed, and Calusa Jim was
sitting at the table in front of his tent, watching the
activity and puffing on a cigar. After tethering and unsad-
dling his horse, Toby walked over to him.

Calusa Jim motioned with his hook for Toby to sit. "I
see that one man is missing," he remarked.

"Camargo." Toby shrugged in genuine unconcern.
"The men think I killed him for disobeying orders, but it
was because he tried to kill me."

Calusa Jim chuckled. "Let them think what they please.
I knew that only one of you would come back, and I
figured it would be you. What happened in Chihuahua?"

Juanita Zuniga appeared with the inevitable pitcher of
pulque as Toby detailed the events. Behind Calusa Jim's
back, Juanita smiled at Toby, but her pretty face quickly
became expressionless again as she stepped around the
table. Calusa Jim seemed not even to notice her as he
listened to Toby's brief account of the attack.

The outlaw leader puffed on his cigar in silence for
some time after Toby had finished. "So if what you expect
to happen does in fact happen, the cavalry patrols should
stop soon. How soon?"

"About two or three days. Four at the very most, I'd
guess. It won't take long for news of the latest comanchero
attack to reach Santa Fe."

"We will have to check to make sure they stop."
Calusa Jim eyed Toby closely, as if to gauge his reaction to
the next statements. "And as you said, we will have to
check on both sides of the Rio Grande, just to make

certain. I can send Mosely to take a look on the east side, and maybe I will go to the west myself and leave you in charge here."

Toby tried to display indifference that he did not feel. "It's up to you, but I can't control these men the way you can." He pointed to the gleaming steel hook. "You would also be taking a big chance, because everyone up there is looking for a man with a hook."

"That is true." Calusa Jim still scrutinized Toby with hooded eyes. "Maybe you would like to go up there and check the west side yourself, Miller."

"I wouldn't mind," Toby replied evenly. "I could use a hot bath, a steak dinner, and a drink of good liquor. I'm not crazy about this pulque."

Calusa Jim did not look amused. "Do you have an idea about going anywhere else? Maybe as far as Santa Fe, to see somebody there? You know where the hideout is, and there is a price on my head."

"You're not the only one with a price on his head," Toby replied. "And even if I was stupid enough to get myself arrested, what would I tell them? That you're here in Mexico? If the cavalry could cross the border, they would have done so already. What are you worried about?"

Calusa Jim weighed Toby's answer, then took a drink of pulque. "A man with as many enemies as I have must be careful, Miller. All right, you check for patrols west of the Rio Grande. I want you and Mosely to come back as soon as the cavalry patrols stop. If they don't stop within five days, come on back, and we will figure out something else."

Toby took a drink from his cup to hide any trace of the satisfaction that swelled within him. Calusa Jim shouted to Mosely, and the fawning peddler hurried over to receive his orders.

The next morning, Toby and Mosely left at the same time and split up outside the hideout, as Calusa Jim had directed. With plenty of time for what he had to do, Toby didn't push his horse, and at nightfall he camped near the border. The following morning, he rode on into Mesilla to find Lieutenant Stafford.

When Toby had first arrived in New Mexico, it had

been necessary for him to make an effort to look like a drifter, but no longer. As he rode down the main street of town, he was still bearded and dusty from his long ride to Chihuahua, and he felt almost at home as he went into the run-down saloon where he had agreed to meet Stafford. Toby had to stifle a laugh when he saw the young lieutenant, who had made a sincere attempt to look like a drifter but still carried himself as the gentleman and West Point graduate he was under the beard and grimy clothes.

Others were in the saloon, so Stafford and Toby merely exchanged a nod. Stafford finished his beer and meandered out, and after a quick drink Toby also left. He spotted the lieutenant across the street and followed him up the outside staircase of a cheap hotel. Stafford was waiting in the doorway of his room on the third story.

The Southerner was astonished and then amused when Toby related what he had done. "You mean you led the comancheros against the Mexican garrison at Chihuahua?"

"The men thought it was a lark," Toby admitted wryly. "I've been in some odd situations, but never one like that. I did manage to keep innocent people from being hurt, and everything worked out as I planned. Do you have pencil and paper?"

Stafford fetched writing implements from a table and looked on in growing excitement as Toby drew a rough map of Albuquerque and explained what he wanted done.

"It'll work like a charm!" the young man exclaimed when Toby had finished. "It'll be a perfect trap, and we'll get every one of them!"

"Well, they might not do exactly what we want," Toby cautioned. "If I've learned one thing, it's to leave latitude for the unexpected when making plans. So when you talk with Colonel Hamilton, make certain that some extra men are placed so they can be deployed where necessary."

"Yes, sir!" Stafford jotted down a note for himself. "And I'll make it a point to talk personally to every soldier about that red neckerchief," he added, referring to an important point of Toby's plan. "You know, Mr. Holt, when I was brought in on this, I had serious doubts that one man would be able to do anything about those devils. Now I realize that I couldn't have been more wrong."

Toby laughed good-naturedly at the compliment. "I had some luck, Lieutenant Stafford, which certainly helped. In any event, we haven't bagged our quarry yet."

"No, but I'm sure we will." Stafford folded the paper and put it in his pocket. "The first thing for me to do is get those cavalry patrols stopped, so I'd better be moving on."

"I suggest you go to the post at Las Cruces and telegraph Colonel Hamilton from there. Then you can ride on to Santa Fe and take care of the details."

While Stafford moved about the room and gathered up his things, Toby stepped to the window and gazed out. "I hope we can soon put an end to this sorry mess. I've found out that the comancheros have been selling kidnapped women."

"Selling . . . women?" Stafford turned to Toby in dismay. "You mean selling them to—?"

"To bordellos." Toby's expression was grim. "Yes, and I won't consider this matter closed until I can do something for them, too. But first we must make certain that those comancheros never harm anyone again."

As Cindy Kerr and Pierre Charcot sat down to lunch at an outdoor café in Montmartre, the atmosphere between them was strained. At dinner the previous evening, Pierre had asked Cindy to marry him, and she had refused. She had candidly stated that it was pointless for him to think of her in romantic terms, although she was pleased to have him as a friend.

It now occurred to her that she had been too blunt. Pierre tried to hide his feelings, but it was clear that he was deeply hurt, even though Cindy had never meant to mislead him. Out of consideration for his friendship, she had agreed to meet him for lunch, although now she was not sure it was a good idea. They both attempted to fill the tense silences with falsely hearty conversation, mostly about the menu and passersby.

Trying to think of something else to say, Cindy asked Pierre about his work. His smile was starting to wear thin, and she avoided his gaze as he made a lame reply. By pure chance, a discarded newspaper on the table next to him caught her eye, and Cindy's heart almost stopped when she saw the headline on one article.

With great self-control, she forced herself to wait until Pierre had finished talking, then gestured toward the newspaper. "Would you hand me that, please, Pierre?"

He reached for it and glanced at the headlines as he passed it to her. "You sound upset," he said. "What could be so important that—"

"Please, Pierre." She quickly scanned the article about a whaling crew and a woman who had been rescued in New Zealand. Marjorie's name was in the lead paragraph. "It's Marjorie White, the photographist," she explained. "She's a friend of mine, and . . ." Swiftly scanning the story, Cindy gasped in dismay when she read of Ted Taylor's death. "Oh, how horrible!"

"What is it, Cindy?"

Feeling sick at heart, she handed him the paper. "Marjorie was so happy," she said. "She had been looking forward to that voyage for so long. Her heart must be broken."

"Yes, this is very sad," Pierre agreed when he had read the account. "What an amazing adventure it must have been, but with a tragic ending." He paused, and Cindy could see he was thinking about Reed's death and how that had affected her. "Do not feel bad, Cindy. Your friend will soon be back in her country, it says here. Once she is with her family, they will be of comfort to her."

"That's just it. Marjorie doesn't have a family. She has no close relatives. Someone should meet her when she arrives in Maine, but I'm in no position to leave Paris right now. I have obligations to others."

Pierre was quick to fasten onto the words. "What others?"

"Madame Kirovna, mostly. She depends on me to help her manage the gallery."

The answer seemed to disappoint him. The waiter brought their lunch, but Cindy could not eat. After watching her listlessly toying with her food, Pierre made a suggestion.

"Why can Madame Kirovna not manage the gallery on her own, as she did before you arrived?"

"It would be impossible." Cindy pushed away her plate. "She is busy with her etching, and the business in the gallery has increased greatly."

"As a result of your efforts," Pierre added. He leaned forward and took her hand. "You know I don't want you to leave Paris for even a day, Cindy, but I would rather you did what you think you should. Madame Kirovna will have to give up time from her etchings, but she can manage without you. Of that I have no doubt, because she is, as you Americans say, a tough old bird."

Cindy smiled weakly, touched by Pierre's sentiments. And perhaps he was right, she thought. If she did go to Maine, she could probably use Gilbert Paige's house, which would provide a peaceful, private refuge for Marjorie. The more Cindy thought about the idea, the more she liked it.

"I'm sure he wouldn't mind," Pierre said when she told him what she was considering. "After all, he is your close friend." He hesitated, then smiled wistfully. "And while you are gone, maybe you will miss me and have a change of heart." He lifted a hand as Cindy started to reply. "No, say nothing now. Two refusals in as many days would be too much for me to bear."

Cindy took the newspaper with her when she left the restaurant. She found Madame Kirovna in her cluttered workshop at the rear of the gallery.

"Yes, you've told me about her," the old woman said after reading the article. She handed back the paper. "So you intend to go back to the United States to spend time with her?"

Cindy was taken aback. "I—I didn't say that, Madame Kirovna. I am considering it, but I realize it could cause problems. That's why I wanted to discuss it with you."

"What sort of problems?"

"Well, with the gallery. I wouldn't feel right leaving you here with so much work to do."

"Bah! The work can wait." The old woman gave Cindy one of her rare smiles. "Your sense of responsibility is admirable, my dear, especially in one so young. But if you need to go, you should go."

"You mean you don't mind? I—"

"Don't *mind*? Of course I mind! It will be more work, and I will miss your company, but as long as I know you will be coming back—"

"Of course I'll come back." Cindy hugged the old woman. "I'll be back, as soon as possible, I promise."

On a Sunday after church, Eulalia Blake paid a visit to the Holt ranch. While her husband toured the pastures with Stalking Horse, Eulalia sat in the kitchen, where Clara Hemmings and Janessa were preparing the noon meal. The women were discussing the recent tragedy in New Zealand, and since both Eulalia and Clara had lost husbands, they knew the grief that Marjorie was suffering. Eulalia was about to express the opinion that it was fortunate Marjorie didn't have any children, when a metallic crash and a yelp of pain caused her to exclaim in alarm and hurry to the window. She could see Timmy sprawled in the barnyard, his new bicycle on top of him. Waving to her, Timmy grinned meekly and picked himself up.

"Is that what has taken you so long, Timmy?" Clara said in exasperation as he came in the door. "You could have walked to the house in half the time."

"I thought Grandmama might want to see my bicycle," he explained excitedly. "Don't you want to see my bicycle, Grandmama?"

"No, not right now, my dear," Eulalia replied tightly. "I must leave for home in a few minutes. And about that bicycle—I've been meaning to talk to you."

Timmy knew what was coming, and he glanced at his sister, who purposely ignored him. He forced himself to listen patiently to his grandmother's warnings about being careful. She was interrupted when Lee returned, and a little later the two of them left in the carriage. Clara told Timmy that dinner was almost ready and to put his bicycle back in the barn, and he did as instructed.

Because the ground in the barnyard was rutted, he pushed the bicycle instead of riding it. Balancing his weight on the seat, he had found, was difficult enough, but when one of the steel wheels hit a rock or a rut, it was impossible to keep from tumbling over. And, unfortunately, the road to Portland was just as bad as the barnyard. He had found a few smooth stretches, where he had learned to balance himself with confidence, but they were all too short for him to build up adequate speed. Calvin Rogers had not viewed that as a particular disadvantage and had expressed the opinion that speed itself was not important. But Timmy wanted to find out how fast the bicycle could go.

Until that very morning, he had searched in vain for a long, smooth stretch of road. On the way to the new church in town, he had spied the perfect place, a straight, unrutted stretch on a steep hill.

The fact that there was no brake on the bicycle did not concern Timmy because he was certain he could figure out some way to stop himself at the bottom. He was willing to accept a certain amount of risk, as long as the bicycle did not get broken, and in any case there would be little or no traffic on a Sunday.

He went back into the house, and as he ate, he planned the exact place where he would start the ride and tried to imagine how fast he would go.

Janessa's voice broke into his thoughts. "Are you up to something, Timmy?"

"No! All I'm doing is eating." He could never figure out how his sister could virtually read his mind. "You can see that, can't you?"

"I can see you're thinking about something. And when you're thinking about something, that usually means trouble."

Clara came to Timmy's defense. "Now, Janessa, the boy is behaving himself perfectly."

Janessa continued eyeing him suspiciously, while Timmy, grateful for his narrow escape, turned his attention to his food with renewed vigor.

Dinner seemed to last forever, but finally it was over, and Janessa left to join Dr. Martin at the hospital. Timmy ran to the barn, got his bicycle, and set out for town. He was able to ride down some stretches of the road, but in many places he had to walk. A farmer passing in a wagon called out jokingly, telling him to get a pony.

Finally reaching his destination, Timmy looked down

the hill in glee. The road was completely empty of traffic,
and nothing was moving anywhere, except for a few children playing with a ball about halfway down. Just to be
safe, Timmy shouted to the children, motioning them to
one side. Then he pushed and hopped onto his bicycle,
gripping the handlebars tightly. It weaved as he pedaled
and gained his balance, then straightened out as the hill
grew steeper.

The bicycle picked up speed so quickly that Timmy
no longer had to pedal. Standing on the pedals to absorb
the bumps, he was tense with excitement as the bicycle
bounced over the uneven spots and continued accelerating.

The road became steeper still, and his shirt and hair
whipped back in the wind as he picked up more speed.
The children watching were jumping around and cheer-
ing, urging him to go faster. Their excitement drew the
attention of a family sitting on its front porch, and a
woman called out for him to be careful, while a young man
stepped to the railing to laugh and shout encouragement.
The bicycle hit an unexpected rut and, without warning,
became airborne. Timmy's instant of panic changed to
exhilaration as the bicycle slammed back down on its
wheels, still under control.

Other people came out to watch, and the road rang
with cheers and laughter. Leaning over the handlebars,
Timmy shot past the children, delirious with joy in his
moment of glory. Then, at an intersection near the bottom, he saw a farm dray starting across the road in front of
him.

The team was plodding along, pulling a heavy load,
and Timmy recognized the driver, old Isaiah Hogg. Over
his own shouting and the wind keening past his ears,
Timmy could hear the children screaming and people
bellowing at Hogg, who was hard of hearing. Oblivious to
the uproar, the old man stared straight ahead.

Something finally drew his attention, and he slowly
turned his head. But it was too late. He gaped wide-eyed
at Timmy speeding toward him on the bicycle, then snapped
the reins and shouted at the team. The jaded horses
walked a bit faster, drawing the wagon to the center of the
road.

Timmy was unable to turn, and he steeled himself for the collision, thankful at least that the dray was low and sideless and he could probably land atop it. But then, aghast, he saw what was in the dray.

In the treatment room at the charity hospital, Janessa held out a steel basin for Dr. Martin, who dropped a buckshot pellet into it. She handed him a swab dripping with diluted phenol, which he applied to the place where he had extracted the pellet. Then he began rooting out another pellet with a pair of tweezers.

"Ouch!" Chauncey Latham's handsome face was crimson. He was lying prone on the table, with his shirt gathered up to his waist and his trousers down around his knees. He had already had at least a dozen of the lead pellets removed, but he appeared more distressed by Janessa's presence than by the pain. "Whatever happened to Mr. Bingham, Doc?" he asked.

"Luther is at medical school in Chicago," the doctor replied, working the tweezers. "I know you don't like Janessa to be here, and I don't like it either. It goes against an agreement I made with her father for her to treat only women and children. But this being Sunday, she was the only capable assistant available."

"This has been a truly mortifying experience in every way," Latham observed, wincing as the doctor probed deeper. "I've been waiting here for hours, you know."

"And you couldn't even sit down." The doctor clucked his tongue. "Well, I was at church, and so was Janessa, which meant that those who lead less righteous lives had to wait. It's unfortunate this happened when Dr. Wizneuski was out of town, and you were forced to wait for me, but it could have been worse, Mr. Latham. If Bud Hensley had used a rifle, it would have been all over except for your funeral."

"There would also have been a murder trial," Latham grumbled. "As it is, I'm considering whether or not to bring charges against Hensley for assault with a deadly weapon."

The doctor dropped another pellet into the basin. "You can bring charges, of course, but I don't think they'd go far. After all, he did find you with his wife in the bushes in his own backyard. I don't think I'd go to court with a case like that."

"I wasn't in his backyard," Latham objected. "I was in a field that happens to be behind his house, and I was attending to the call of nature."

"Is that so?" The doctor did not pause in his work. "Well, I've noticed that you don't have any holes in the tail of your shirt, and one of your socks is wrong side out. Did you have to take off all your clothes to answer nature's call?"

Latham muttered under his breath, then fell silent as the doctor removed the remainder of the pellets and disinfected the wounds.

Latham had left, and Janessa was cleaning up when an orderly stuck his head in and told her that Isaiah Hogg was outside in the waiting room, wanting to see her about her brother. Janessa dropped what she was doing and hurried out of the room.

The aged, bearded Hogg, who was holding his ragged hat, touched his forehead in greeting. "Howdy, Miss Holt," he said in the loud voice of those with impaired hearing. "Your brother run into my wagon with his bicycle machine."

"Is he injured?" Janessa asked in concern.

The old man cupped a hand behind an ear, then shook his head in perplexity. "No, he's not in here. He's outside, by my wagon."

Deciding it would be quicker to go see for herself than try to find out from the old man, Janessa ran to the front door. Hogg followed her, and Dr. Martin was close behind.

Outside, Janessa stopped on the step. Timmy had no broken bones or serious injuries, she could see at a glance, but that was about all she could see.

A crowd had followed from the scene of the accident, but they were keeping their distance from Timmy and the wagon as they looked on.

"I was hauling away the compost pile at Murphy's Stable," Hogg boomed in explanation. "The boy landed right in the middle of it. It's all my fault, Miss Holt. Like my wife says, I shouldn't have been working on the Sabbath."

Timmy was standing beside the dray, and he was covered from head to toe with glistening black manure. Unlike Dr. Martin, who was chuckling at the sight, Janessa was unamused. "Are you all right?"

The boy nodded, but it was obvious he did not want to open his mouth. "Go around to the standpipe behind the hospital," she ordered. "I'll hook up a hose and wash you off."

The boy did as he was told, and Janessa turned back to Hogg. "Where's his bicycle?" she asked.

The old man again looked perplexed. "He didn't have one, far as I know. Where would he get an icicle this time of year?"

"His machine!" Janessa shouted. "What happened to it?"

"Oh, I have it right here." Hogg went to the dray. "What there is left of it, anyway. It got busted up pretty bad."

The old man stepped onto the low bed and threw down parts of the bicycle, and Janessa surveyed the manure-encrusted wreckage in satisfaction.

The old man shook his head apologetically as he stepped back down. "There's all that was left of it, Miss Holt. Like I told you, it got busted up pretty bad."

"I'm glad it's broken, Mr. Hogg."

"I'm sad too," the old man replied. "But there was nothing I could do. By the time I seen the boy, it was too late. Do you want me to carry them pieces around back, so you can put a hose on them? And if I was you, I'd put a hose on that boy, too."

Janessa started to answer, then merely nodded vigorously in reply.

XIV

The hoofbeats of the comancheros' horses were loud on the narrow, dark road approaching Albuquerque, as a double line of close to eighty men rode at a trot behind Toby and Calusa Jim. The outlaw leader was nervous, and he looked closely at each shuttered, silent building they passed. "I don't see a sign of life, Miller," he growled. "You would think there would be some lights and people."

"Not on the first night of the fiesta," Toby assured him. "Everyone will be there, having a good time. I can hear the music now."

Calusa Jim cocked his ear, and even over the hoofbeats, the strains of lively music carried from the city's main plaza. But he was still suspicious and continued looking around. A large church with a walled courtyard loomed up out of the darkness, and Toby pointed to it. "That courtyard would be a good place to leave the horses. We're close enough to town now."

Calusa Jim reined up and halted the column of riders. "It looks to me like we still have distance to go," he said. "We would be a long time getting there and back on foot."

"No, it isn't that far." Toby tried to appear nonchalant and fingered the red kerchief he was wearing around his neck. "But suit yourself."

The man's crafty eyes gleamed in the moonlight as he scrutinized the church and the adjacent buildings. "There are no lights here, either. All the priests would not be at the fiesta, would they?"

"How should I know?" Toby was getting impatient with the man's wariness. "I'm no more a priest than you are. I guess they could go if they wanted to."

"Maybe so. But I don't like the looks of this. Everything is too quiet."

"Then let's get out of here," Toby suggested with an indifference he did not feel. "I don't see how anyone could know that we're within miles, but if you think they're onto us, then let's turn around right now."

Toby waited tensely as Calusa Jim made up his mind. He knew that the man had instincts that matched his cunning, or he would not have eluded capture or death so many times before. Those instincts had been alerted by the unnatural quiet of the area cleared by the cavalry so no innocent bystanders would be endangered.

"I guess I'm just jumpy," Calusa Jim finally decided. "It makes sense that everyone would be at the fiesta, and maybe the priests, too. All right, we leave the horses here."

Toby rode through the wide courtyard gate with him, and the others followed. The men dismounted, and Calusa Jim picked out a half dozen to guard the horses and make certain no one left the church buildings. He and Toby then set out along the street, leading the remainder of the comancheros.

During the next few minutes, Toby listened anxiously for gunshots from behind—a dire possibility if soldiers were waiting in the church, as he expected. But everything remained silent until, when they were a good distance away, several of the horses whinnied shrilly.

Calusa Jim stopped so suddenly that one of the comancheros bumped into him. The outlaw leader snarled an oath and slashed with his hook, but the man alertly ducked. "What was that?"

"Our horses must be sensing the tension among the men who stayed behind," Toby suggested, not knowing what else to say.

The outlaw leader looked at him narrowly, and another tense moment for Toby passed before Calusa Jim turned and they continued along the street.

There were no more sounds from the church, and Toby guessed that the escape route for the comancheros had been successfully closed, with the guards overpowered and the horses now being watched by soldiers. The

plan seemed to be working perfectly so far, but it was not
yet completed.

Ahead, a blaze of light from the main square silhouetted the rooftops, and the dance music was loud, punctu-
ated by whoops of revelry. Whatever uneasiness Calusa
Jim and the other comancheros had felt was now lost in
their savage eagerness to reach their quarry. Approaching
the square lined with shuttered buildings on a dark street,
the comancheros began running, all impatient to be first.
With their spurs jangling and heavy boots thumping, they
held their weapons ready and cocked. Brutal grins spread
across their rugged faces, and a few outlaws began laughing in anticipation.

Toby winced in regret when he saw a vendor's wagon
piled with goods near the end of the street. Apparently it
had been left there to make the scene appear more natural, but it would also provide cover for comancheros who
were smart enough to use it.

Toby and the first of the comancheros rushed past the
wagon and into the square, and suddenly the music and
whooping stopped. At the opposite end of the plaza, the
musicians and young men providing the whoops and shouts
dived for cover, disappearing within seconds into door-
ways. At the same time, the street behind abruptly was
flooded with light from carbide lamps on the roofs, and a
squad of blue-coated soldiers wheeled a Gatling gun into
position at the far corner.

From a rooftop, Colonel Hamilton shouted through a
megaphone: "You are surrounded! *Son mis prisioneros!*
Drop your weapons and put up your hands!"

The scene erupted into pandemonium. Panic-stricken
comancheros toward the rear of the group wheeled around
and opened fire, but one short burst from the Gatling gun
was enough to discourage them. Others raced into the
square as more carbide lamps flared to life on the rooftops.
A few comancheros fired wildly, immediately provoking
awesome retaliation as soldiers concealed on the roofs
fired in thunderous unison.

The outlaw leader, with his animal instincts for self-
preservation, reacted faster and with better judgment than
most. At the first sign of a trap, he raced for the vendor's

wagon and slid under it. Toby attempted to follow, but he was caught in the confused press of men trying to run every which way.

A dozen comancheros made another attempt to charge the Gatling gun, and again the soldiers fired a short warning burst, which this time failed to stop them. Consequently the soldiers reopened fire with a steady, battering roar, the stream of lead ripping into the comancheros and cutting them down with gruesome efficiency.

Toby's red neckerchief was protecting him from rifle fire, but the bullets from the Gatling gun had no eyes. As they whined past him, he dropped to the street, then started crawling toward the wagon. Comancheros stumbled over him as they darted about, and several fell wounded. Hamilton was still shouting into the megaphone for them to surrender, but it had no effect on the outlaws, who were reacting with the blind panic of trapped rats.

More of them fired at the soldiers on the roofs, bringing the same swift, deadly retaliation as before. A young Mexican collapsed to his knees a few yards from Toby, more bullets penetrating his body even as he knelt there. Somehow, through the sheer bedlam surrounding him, Toby got to a spot where he could see the wagon clearly.

A comanchero who was ducking to slide under it suddenly stumbled and rolled on the ground in agony, clutching his chest. Calusa Jim was killing his own men, not wanting them to draw gunfire to him. Another comanchero staggered back from the wagon, shot by his leader, and Toby, using the body as a shield, cocked his pistol and aimed it.

Just as Toby lined his sights on Calusa Jim, the man scrambled from under the wagon, sprinted across an open stretch, and leaped with a crash through a shop display window that had been too big to shutter. Hoping the soldiers would see his neckerchief, Toby jumped up, dashed to the window, and vaulted through the jagged hole, landing in a clutter of sandals and shoes behind an overturned table. In the glare from outside, he saw a shadowy form pause at a doorway near the rear of the store.

Another comanchero crashed through the window behind Toby, obviously intending to escape, too. Outside, the gunfire from the rooftops had abruptly increased. The soldiers, having been warned not to aim near the man with the red neckerchief, had purposely withheld their fire while Toby raced across the square, but now everyone remaining in the square was fair game. The chatter of gunfire recommenced.

Calusa Jim aimed his pistol at Toby. "I know now what happened, Miller! You tricked us into a trap, but I'll get even with you!"

Toby drew his pistol and ducked behind the overturned table as Calusa Jim's gun discharged with an ear-splitting roar. The comanchero beside Toby, also hearing what his leader had said, swung his rifle, but Toby shot him first, from no more than a foot away. In the smoke and confusion, Calusa Jim disappeared through the back door.

Toby could hear objects clatter and tumble over in the storeroom as the outlaw leader bulled his way through it. Toby ran down the aisle and into the backroom, which was pitch dark, but a rear door was ajar. Stumbling over the shop's inventory and supplies, he ran out to the alley.

A bullet slammed into the door as Toby ducked outside. Calusa Jim, crouching at the far end of the alley, fired again as Toby snapped off a shot. Both of them missed, and the outlaw leader disappeared around the corner. Toby ran after him and slid to a stop at the corner, peering into the darkness, ready to fire.

The narrow street was lined with stables and storerooms belonging to the businesses on the main square. Nothing moved, but Toby suspected that Calusa Jim might be waiting in a doorway with his pistol cocked. Toby slowly started down the street.

A horse burst from a stable, twenty yards ahead. Calusa Jim was riding bareback and leaning low. He fired wildly at Toby, who ducked aside, aimed, and fired. But his target had been too small, and the night had been too dark for his aim to be true. In any case, he told himself, he knew where Calusa Jim was going. Toby started back toward the plaza, replacing the spent bullets in his pistol.

The gunfire had ceased, and when Toby went back through the store, he saw that the soldiers had the situation well in hand. He shouted through the window to alert them of his presence, then unlatched the door and emerged into the lighted square. Soldiers were dragging dead comancheros into a row under the glare of the carbide lamps, while those who had been wounded or had surrendered were being shackled or led away.

Colonel Hamilton hurried up to congratulate him, but the man's smile faded when he noted Toby's expression. "What's wrong?"

"Calusa Jim got away." Toby pulled off his neckerchief and wiped his powder-stained face. "This won't be ended until we get him because he'll just recruit more men. Unless I'm mistaken, he's on his way back to his hideout, so I'll go there and deal with him."

"Are you sure, Toby? He might go somewhere else."

"No, I don't think so, Colonel. It's very secure, and he left a couple of men guarding it. He knows you can't chase him into Mexico, and he wouldn't be worried about just one man."

Walter Stafford, transformed back from the drifter who had met Toby in Mesilla, stepped forward. "There'll be two men," he said. "I'm going with you."

Toby shook his head. "I'm going to Mexico, Walter. You know you can't come along."

Stafford was undeterred. "I have my civilian clothes with me, and I can change and be ready in a few minutes." He came to attention and addressed Hamilton formally. "I request a leave of absence, sir."

"Granted," the colonel promptly replied.

Toby could not help but smile. "I guess I have no choice, then." He slapped Walter on the back. "Go get changed, then, and meet me at that church where the horses are. We'll pick out some spares to lead so we can make good time. Colonel, I'd like the rest of those horses taken to Las Cruces, if you would, because I'm going to need them."

Hamilton hesitated a moment, then, deciding not to question Toby's motives, told him that an escort would leave with the horses the next day.

Dawn was touching the sky in the east as Toby and

his young companion, both armed with rifles, crept up to the entrance of the comancheros' hideout. Under cover of darkness the previous night, they had ridden the last few miles to the opposite end of the mountain, where they had rested for several hours. Hobbling the horses, they had set out on foot for the ravine well before dawn.

Peering around a boulder, Toby saw no one in the brush that concealed the narrow opening, but he was certain that a guard was nearby. His own choice would have been to place one man at the entrance and the second farther back in the brushy ravine, and he suspected that Calusa Jim would do the same.

Crouching low and choosing each step with care to avoid making a sound, Toby moved around the boulder toward the mouth of the ravine. Darkness lingered between the high walls of the narrow cleft, and Toby glanced back to see Walter Stafford following, rifle at the ready.

Toby had taken a few more steps when he heard a cough not far ahead. He froze and listened closely. A moment later, the guard evidently shifted to a more comfortable position, for Toby heard boots scrape against rock. He estimated the man was just around the curve, only yards away. Moving twigs and rocks from his path, Toby inched forward.

At last he spotted the guard, through the screen of brush. The man was perhaps fifteen feet away, leaning against the wall of the ravine and holding a rifle at the ready.

Toby was tempted to rush him, but the distance was too great, and the guard would surely be able to get off a shot, which would alert the other guard and Calusa Jim. Toby was trying to think of a way to get closer without being detected when the man put his rifle under his arm and took out a bag of tobacco to roll a cigarette.

Toby laid his rifle down gently, slid his pistol from its holster, and gripped it by the barrel. He waited until the man was holding the lighted match in cupped hands, then sprang forward. The man dropped the match, and the cigarette fell from his lips as he tried to grip his rifle, but Toby had covered the distance rapidly and slammed the pistol butt down on the man's head, knocking him to the ground before he could get his finger on the trigger.

Walter rushed in behind Toby. Without having to be told what to do, he ripped off the guard's shirt and belt and used them to gag and bind the man. Toby hid the man's rifle and retrieved his own, then moved on along the ravine.

By now it was full daylight, and Toby peered cautiously around every bend in the twisting chasm, hoping to catch the other guard by surprise. The man was more alert than his fellow, however, for at the next curve Toby ducked back just as a rifle fired with an echoing blast.

Toby knew that Calusa Jim had now been warned. Of more immediate concern, however, he and Walter had to get past the second guard, who was in a protected position behind a boulder near the wall of the ravine.

"I could try rushing him," Walter suggested. "You could cover me and make him keep down."

Toby shook his head. He looked around, then stepped back along the ravine to a clump of dried brush, where he broke off a long branch with a fork at its tip. He trimmed it with his knife in a few quick strokes, then, to Walter's puzzlement, began probing under rocks with it.

Only a minute or so later Toby was rewarded with the angry buzz of a disturbed rattlesnake, which he dragged from under the rock with the stick. Almost four feet long and still lethargic from the chill of the night, the reptile moved sluggishly as Toby pinned its head to the ground with the fork, then gripped it firmly just behind the stick.

The thick, heavy snake became wide awake as Toby carried it back to where Walter was waiting. Rattling furiously, it coiled its supple, powerful body around Toby's forearm and squeezed tightly, trying to free its head. Toby unwrapped it, signaled Walter to ready his rifle, then leaned out and heaved the snake over the boulder where the guard was hiding.

Shrieking in fright as the snake landed on him, the guard instinctively leaped out into the open, and the frightened snake slithered away under a boulder. Realizing his mistake, the man started to lift his rifle, but Walter's weapon was already shouldered and aimed. "Don't try it," the lieutenant warned.

The guard hesitated, as if to surrender, and Toby knew what was running through his mind. At best, a noose awaited him for the crimes he had committed, so he had nothing to lose. As the outlaw started pulling the hammer back, intending to shoot from the hip, Walter fired. At such close range, the bullet killed the man instantly. Toby and Walter hurried onward.

Near the last curve, Toby moved warily, knowing that Calusa Jim could be aiming a rifle toward the mouth of the ravine. The canyon opened into view, and Toby could see the now-dead fires where the comancheros had left many of their belongings. Near one of the fires, a knot of frightened camp women huddled together, wondering what was happening.

More of the canyon came into view, until Toby could see Calusa Jim's tent. The outlaw leader was beside it, holding Juanita Zuniga in front of him. The tip of his hook was at her throat, and a pistol was in his left hand. Seeing Toby, he laughed harshly. "I've been waiting for you, Miller! I thought the guards would hold you up longer than they did, but I knew you would be here."

"My name isn't Miller," Toby replied. "It's Toby Holt."

Calusa Jim seemed to stiffen, but then he laughed again. "Well, I will have to admit that you fooled me, Holt. But I vowed that I would get even with you, and I will."

"I'm ready to give you a chance, then. Turn the woman loose, and we'll settle this in any way you choose."

"Turn her loose?" Calusa Jim's amused howl echoed through the canyon. "I will turn her loose, Holt, just as soon as I rip out her throat."

"The woman's done nothing to you. There's no point in harming her."

"Oh, but there is a point. I want you to see her blood gushing down her, Holt."

Toby quickly tried to think of a way to rescue Juanita. Calusa Jim was much taller than his hostage, and although the range was long, his head and shoulders made a good target. But even if Toby got off a lucky shot, the hook would stab into Juanita's throat as the man fell.

The impasse was ended in a way that took both Toby and Calusa Jim by surprise. Juanita, moving with a speed and strength that her previous submission had given no hint of, suddenly gripped the deadly hook with both hands, jerked it away from her throat, and threw herself to the ground.

Toby had a clear shot, and he did not hesitate. Before Calusa Jim could aim his pistol to kill the woman or duck for cover behind the tent, Toby fired, hitting him in the shoulder. In his fury the outlaw leader still got off a shot, but his bullet struck a rock, and a well-aimed shot by Walter Stafford, almost simultaneous with Toby's second shot, reeled Calusa Jim back and spun him around.

Toby quickly recocked his rifle and took careful aim, but Calusa Jim had lost his balance and sprawled heavily on his stomach. His torso suddenly became rigid, his feet thrashing as he shrieked a cry that was something between a human scream and the howl of a wild animal. It was the most hideous sound Toby had ever heard.

Dropping his pistol, the man struggled to his knees and opened his mouth wordlessly. He had fallen on his own hook, which was stuck deep in his throat, and blood spurted down the military tunic. He tried to utter the weird cry once more, a shocked, angry rejection of death, but it could barely be heard, and he toppled and fell on his back, his limbs twitching, then motionless.

Juanita ran to Toby as he walked toward the tent. "I knew you weren't one of them," she said, clutching him and sobbing with relief. "I knew you were different, that you would rescue me."

"I couldn't have helped if you hadn't done what you did." As he held her, Toby stared down at the outlaw leader's lifeless body. "It's a fitting end for a man like him." Toby gestured for Walter to assist Juanita. The other women were rushing forward, some of them crying, too.

Toby turned and scanned all sides of the canyon. "I know you're here, Mosely!" he shouted. "So show yourself. If I have to root you out, you'll wish I hadn't!"

The man emerged, trembling, from behind boulders near where the spare horses were picketed. He walked forward with his hands over his head. Toby kept his rifle trained on him.

"I heard you tell Calusa Jim who you really are, Mr. Holt," Mosely said as he approached, "and I've heard of you plenty of times. I know you're a man who respects the law, and you're witness to the fact that I've never personally harmed anyone."

Toby ignored the man's effrontery. "All I want to hear from you right now, Mosely, is where are those women who were captured and sold to bordellos? And you'd better tell the truth."

Mosely hesitated. "If I get clemency for cooperating, I'll tell you everything. But if it isn't going to do me any good, why should I talk?"

Toby was in no mood to negotiate. "On our way to Santa Fe, we'll pass places where men are still wondering what happened to their wives and daughters. Would you rather be questioned by them?"

Mosely blanched and stepped back. "All right. But remember, I'm being cooperative. They're all at one place. I took them to a dealer in Nogales. Apodaca, his name was. He owns a place on the outskirts of Mexico City. The Casita de Extasis."

Toby looked with disgust at the peddler, then called to Walter Stafford. "Tie him up, Walter."

The lieutenant searched Mosely and then bound him. Juanita, who had been talking with the other women, came up to Toby. "These women would like to know what you want them to do."

"I want them to return to their families. And that goes for you, too, Juanita. All of you can take whatever you like from around the fires and help yourselves to the horses over there."

The women, exclaiming in delight, quickly scattered to rummage through the things around the fires. Juanita did not go with them. "I want nothing from here," she said, "and I have no family or place to go. They were all killed."

"In that case," Toby replied promptly, "you can come

with Walter and me. We're taking Mosely back to Santa Fe. I don't want to stop to buy supplies, so gather up what you can."

A little later, they all rode out of the canyon, and Toby and Walter stopped to tie the still-unconscious guard over the back of one of the spare horses. At the mouth of the ravine, all the Mexican women were profuse in their thanks, and Toby waved to them as they rode off to the south.

The fact that all the women who had been sold to a brothel were in a single place would make their rescue less complicated, Toby reflected, but Mexico City was still a long distance away. In addition, he was certain he would meet with resistance in trying to free them, and even with Walter's help it would be a daunting task.

When they camped that night, not far from the Rio Grande, Toby questioned Mosely about the Casita de Extasis. Situated on the road north of the capital city, the establishment catered to a wealthy clientele, and if what Mosely said was true, it was well guarded at all times, both to keep the women from escaping and to discourage bandits who might be tempted to rob the rich patrons.

The men whose wives and daughters had been kidnapped were an obvious source for volunteers, but Toby was reluctant to ask their help, knowing he would have a hard time restraining them. The next day, after the party had crossed the border and was on the road to Santa Fe, Toby discussed the problem with Walter. The lieutenant shared Toby's reservations.

"I agree that the husbands and loved ones will be out for blood. No one can blame them, of course, but they're liable to kill every man in the place."

"And have army patrols searching for us all the way back," Toby added. "But I can't do this job alone."

Walter looked thoughtful, then brightened. "I have the perfect solution," he said.

"What's that?"

"Army volunteers. While I was getting ready to come down here with you, any number of men asked me if they could change into civilian clothes and come along. They resent not being able to cross the border to stop raids here, and a quiet word in the garrison at Santa Fe about what you intend to do would bring a stampede of volunteers."

Toby acknowledged that it was a good idea, but he had strong misgivings about taking what amounted to an army patrol deep into Mexico. So far he had completed his mission with signal success, and he was reluctant to end it by creating problems for the government.

They reached Santa Fe in good time, and Toby, ignoring Mosely's bitter protests, handed him and the hideout's guard over to the jailers in charge of the other comancheros. With no urging from Toby, Governor Mills offered Juanita Zuniga the hospitality of his home until permanent arrangements could be made for her, and later, at a meeting with Colonel Hamilton present, he also put forward a suggestion as to how to gain the release of the women who had been captured by the comancheros.

Toby frowned when he heard the suggestion, which was to proceed through normal diplomatic channels. Both he and Hamilton objected strongly, citing a variety of reasons. Apodaca, the owner of the bordello, undoubtedly wielded enough political influence at least to delay any action, and in the meantime, a mob of furious husbands and fathers would find out what was happening and go charging into Mexico, creating a multitude of problems. Most importantly, the innocent women had suffered enough, and to prolong their captivity and sexual exploitation was, in Toby's opinion, inhuman.

When Colonel Hamilton, who had already spoken to Lieutenant Stafford, made a pointed reference to "other possible solutions," the governor set his jaw in obvious displeasure, but he had the sense to know that he had little choice in the matter. Getting up to leave the room, he directed Toby and the soldiers to discuss it in private.

With the colonel's blessing, Stafford had already talked with several of the soldiers, and the arrangements were quickly concluded. Two days after arriving in Santa Fe, Toby set out for Las Cruces to get the horses that had been taken from the comancheros and to continue on southward into Mexico. With him were fourteen cavalrymen commanded by Walter Stafford and a sergeant named Lyons.

Even in civilian clothes, the men were unmistakably military as they rode in two neat, orderly columns. But Toby voiced no objections because he knew that for the perilous mission that lay ahead, these were the best possible men.

As his train rolled into the outskirts of Vienna, Andrew Brentwood gazed in regret at the scenic skyline of church spires, domes, and slate roofs. Two weeks before, while passing through Vienna en route to the Carpathian Mountains, where the Austro-Hungarian army maneuvers had been held, he had been fascinated by his glimpse of the elegant, ancient city and had wanted to stop, but he had not had the time. And now, with Ambassador Ely eagerly awaiting his return, he once again would have time enough only to change trains. In his bags were the answers to nearly all the questions Washington had posed, as well as a wealth of other information, and Ely would never understand a delay.

As soon as Andrew stepped off the train, however, a well-dressed, middle-aged man spotted his uniform, approached him, and introduced himself as a representative of Count von Lautzenberg at the Ministry of Internal Affairs. "The count apologizes for any inconvenience that it may cause you," the man pronounced summarily in a heavy accent, "but he would like to talk with you at once, Colonel Brentwood."

The man's attitude left no room for a refusal, and Andrew told himself that Ambassador Ely would simply have to wait. In any case, Andrew had puzzled for weeks over the lack of reaction from the count concerning Lydia's pregnancy, as well as the unexpected invitation to observe the maneuvers. Whatever was going to happen, Andrew wanted only to get it over with as soon as possible.

Ironically, he found himself too preoccupied to enjoy the sights of the city as he rode in a state carriage to a grandiose government building. The count's representative, as uncommunicative as a stone, led him to an opulent baroque anteroom, where a private secretary immediately went through a door and reappeared, holding it open for Andrew.

Count von Lautzenberg's private office was lavishly furnished, but overwhelming everything else were, on one wall, portraits of the emperor and empress, and on another, a huge map of the empire.

The count, in an oversize chair behind an immense table, nodded in response to Andrew's bow. "Please forgive me for not standing," he said in a soft voice, "but I must plead age and infirmity, which require me to conserve my strength."

"I understand," Andrew replied shortly.

"Sit down." The count pointed to a chair beside a window.

Andrew did as he was told, and the count commenced the interview by asking him if he had found the maneuvers informative.

"Yes, to say the least, sir. I presume that I have you to thank for the invitation."

"Yes, I did arrange it, and I was pleased to do so." The count smiled enigmatically. "You are a friend of a family that values its friends, Colonel Brentwood. I trust that you left Her Grace in good health and spirits?"

His failure to include the duke spoke volumes, but Andrew maintained his self-control and replied that both von Hofstettens had been well. The questioning moved on to innocuous subjects, and Andrew, who was still waiting for the ax to fall, was nonetheless taken by surprise when it did.

"By the way, when you escort the duchess on outings and other amusements," the count said, jumping back to the subject, "you must make certain she never overtires herself and is careful about her health. I'm sure that you do, but I mention it only because now that she and the duke are in the fortunate position of expecting an heir, we must be doubly cautious about Her Grace's health."

The matter-of-fact reference to Lydia's pregnancy took Andrew aback, but after only an instant of confusion, everything became sickeningly clear to him. The whole scheme was so obvious that he could hardly believe he had not thought of it before. The count wanted an heir to the ducal title, and Andrew had unwittingly obliged him.

Andrew felt like a naïve fool, but most of all he was

gripped by indignation. "We both know," he said, standing up defiantly, "that the duke had nothing whatsoever to do with Her Grace's present condition."

The count stiffened, his predatory eyes gleaming. "Young man," he rasped in his hoarse whisper, "the most infuriating thing about dealing with you is that, despite your intelligence, you are given to puerile, senseless outbursts."

"But it's true!" Andrew insisted hotly.

"What is truth?" the count snarled. "It is what people collectively believe, which can easily be manipulated. If people believe the child to be a von Hofstetten, then it will be!"

"It will not! I absolutely reject such an absurd notion!"

The count dismissed the subject with an impatient wave. "If you must act like a schoolboy, then I shall deal with you accordingly and explain the punishment you may incur. It is within my power to have you cashiered from your army. It is also within my power to have a bill of divorcement enacted and to return Her Grace to her family in dishonor. If you persist in this attitude or make a comment like that again, then I shall do so. Do you understand, Colonel Brentwood?"

The anger had completely left the man's voice, making the threat all the more ruthless. Andrew knew the count could and would do precisely what he had threatened. Andrew controlled his own anger.

"I take your silence as assent," the count continued, suddenly cordial. "And now that we understand each other, there is no cause for us to be unpleasant. After all, everyone involved in this matter has more than ample reason to be content, if not perfectly happy. The child, a von Hofstetten, will be born in the best circumstances. You and the duchess will still have the liberty to enjoy your affection for each other. And both the duke and I will have what we want—an heir for the family." He picked up a small bell and rang it. "Let us have refreshments while we discuss other things, Colonel Brentwood."

The secretary appeared with glasses and a decanter, and the count mentioned that the Austro-Hungarian Army would have more maneuvers during the coming autumn and that he would look forward to having Andrew observe them again.

Still in a turmoil, Andrew scarcely heard what was being said. Beyond the fact that he had been cold-bloodedly manipulated, the child born to Lydia would be a Brentwood. It would be a grandchild of Samuel Brentwood, who had devoted his life to building a nation. Andrew wanted the child born of his and Lydia's love to know its heritage, yet that appeared impossible. He seemed to be trapped by circumstances he was unable to change.

Only after taking a sip from the glass that the secretary had left him did Andrew realize what was in it. It was the same sweet, purplish liqueur that he and Lydia often shared during their private, special moments. That the count knew about it was yet another demonstration of his limitless knowledge and power.

The old man's piercing eyes reflected the satisfaction of victory as he stared wordlessly at his guest, and Andrew put the glass down, unable to drink its contents.

XV

The famous spa and resort city of Bad Kissingen was crowded with summer tourists, and the platform in front of the railroad station was shoulder-to-shoulder with onlookers awaiting the arrival of Chancellor Bismarck, the most important man in Germany. At the edge of the crowd, Henry Blake, inconspicuous in a dark business suit, scanned the roofs of nearby buildings and the faces on the platform.

Just down the track, a freight train was chugging into the switching yards, and a thrill of expectation rippled through the crowd. People began shouting and pointing. At the rear of the train, just visible because of the curve of the tracks, was a private railcar, its doors emblazoned with Chancellor Bismarck's coat of arms. Henry ignored the train and continued watching the crowd and the roofs.

Bismarck traditionally vacationed at Bad Kissingen, and for several years now he had arrived in this same manner, with his private railcar pulled by a freight. The car was customarily parked on this sidetrack, and the Chancellor would greet well-wishers, then proceed by carriage to his vacation house in the forested hills outside town.

This year, however, Bismarck was not on the train—a fact of which the tourists were unaware. Weeks ago, Henry had pointed out to General Fremmel that it was an invitation to disaster for the Chancellor to follow the same routine again this year, and consequently Fremmel had persuaded Bismarck to take the precaution of leaving the train before it reached the city. A troop of dragoons, under the command of Major Richard Koehler, had already escorted Bismarck without incident to his vacation house.

The train stopped, and a brakeman stepped along the tracks to throw a switch so the private car could be backed onto the siding. Henry searched for faces he would recognize from Bern, while taking note of anyone who was not sharing in the general excitement. He saw nothing suspicious, however. The locomotive's engine had just puffed into reverse when a thunderous clap rang out, causing the earth to shake and sending a heavy concussion through the air. The private car had exploded into a mass of flying debris, and windows in the station showered glass onto the platform. People screamed and darted every which way in panic, and some who had been injured by the glass or debris staggered about. Policemen charged from the station and ran toward the sidetrack.

Henry waited until the police had passed, then, seeing no one suspicious lurking about, he walked into the station, edged his way through the frantic crowds in the waiting room, and went out to the street, where a uniformed dragoon was struggling to control two horses. Henry took the reins of one of the horses, mounted up, and rode with the man at a gallop away from the station.

At the outskirts of the city, the street became a narrow country lane, and Henry and the dragoon turned off onto the road to the Chancellor's vacation house. In the distance a troop of dragoons was approaching at a run, and Henry recognized Richard Koehler leading the cluster of horsemen in their gleaming, spiked helmets and bright uniforms.

When Richard saw Henry, he reined up, and the others stopped at his command. Richard's tanned, handsome face was pale and drawn as he took off his helmet and wiped his brow with a handkerchief.

"What's wrong, Richard?" Henry asked as he drew near. "You look ill."

"I thought you were on that train!" Richard's anxiety quickly changed to annoyance. "But obviously you weren't. When I heard that explosion, I thought—" He put his helmet back on. "Well, I jumped to the wrong conclusion."

"It was only a mine under the tracks," Henry said

with a shrug. He pulled up to ride beside his friend as Richard turned back toward the house.

"Oh, is that all?" Richard smiled thinly. "I was concerned, of course, that if you were injured, there would be no one left to keep the baroness content. My aunt is difficult enough as it is."

Henry chuckled appreciatively, then described what had happened at the station while Richard listened intently. "Undoubtedly," he said when Henry had finished, "our troubles have only begun. Other attacks could come at any time."

Henry agreed. "Once they realize the Chancellor is still alive, there's no question about that. We'll have to remain on guard constantly until we find the conspirators and deal with them."

A few minutes later, the forest road emerged into a meadow, at the rear of which stood Bismarck's vacation house. A large, two-story stone structure, it was surrounded by dragoon guards, but the distance from the edge of the meadow to the house was well within rifle range, Henry noted. Worse still, behind the house rose a steep, wooded hillside with scattered outcroppings of rock, several of which offered perfect cover for would-be assassins.

General Fremmel was waiting in the entry. Henry dismounted and began to explain to him what had happened, when a door opened and the Chancellor himself, in his shirt-sleeves, came down the hall toward them.

Henry and the other two men stood at attention. Approaching sixty, Bismarck was a tall, heavy man with craggy features that were splotched with broken veins. Even though he had a paunch from overeating, he still had the unmistakable bearing of a leader. His alert blue eyes seemed to miss nothing.

Henry briefly repeated for his sake what had happened. "Was anyone injured?" Bismarck asked.

"There were injuries, Your Excellency, but I don't think anyone was killed."

"Did you see anyone who might have done it?"

"No, sir."

"The mine could have been set days ago, Your Excellency," General Fremmel explained. "It was—"

"Of course it could have been," Bismarck interrupted. "I am familiar with mines. Does this mean I will be unable to take the waters this evening?"

"I consider that highly inadvisable," the general replied. "You should stay inside the house at present."

Bismarck eyed him coldly. "Very well. But tomorrow I will be going out. I did not come here to be a virtual prisoner in my own house." He turned and left without another word.

A little while afterward, a carriage rumbled up outside and deposited on the steps the burgomaster and the chief of police of Bad Kissingen. Bismarck granted them a short interview, to convince them that he was unharmed, and later that evening, after dinner, Henry and Richard went outside to inspect the defenses around the house.

Henry paused a long while to survey the rock outcroppings on the hill behind the house. "Do you have any men posted up there, Richard?"

"No. I sent a platoon up the hill this morning to look around, but they saw nothing suspicious—not even footprints or places where the leaves had been disturbed. If someone intended to use that hill as a vantage point, he would look it over first."

Henry's silence indicated he was not convinced.

Richard became defensive. "I can't put a man on every rock up there, Heinrich! In my opinion, the greatest danger is the road between here and town, and I've posted men in the trees at intervals, to make certain no one hides there in ambush. That leaves me with less than two platoons to guard the house. One does what one can."

"I suppose you're right." Henry walked to the back door with his friend. Complete protection against an assassin was virtually impossible, he knew, especially when the intended victim refused to remain in seclusion. Still, before he reentered the house, Henry looked back at the hill. Attempts on his own life had made him doubly cautious and suspicious of places where danger might be lurking. And he knew that if he were in charge of the conspiracy against Bismarck, he would choose the hill as the best place from which to attack.

*   *   *

Early the next morning, when Henry went downstairs, he found that Richard had already been up for hours. While the two of them shared breakfast in the kitchen, Richard explained that he had checked all his guards, and since nothing had happened on the road during the night, he had withdrawn several men from there and sent them to check the edges of the meadow around the house.

After finishing their breakfast, Richard and Henry went outside, and the sergeants of the guard reported they had seen nothing out of the ordinary. Henry was standing on the flagstone terrace near the back door when several servants walked past him, carrying linen and tableware. He watched as they set a single place on a lawn table in a corner of the garden.

"That doesn't seem very wise," he commented to Richard. "Couldn't he have breakfast inside?"

"I heartily agree." Richard called over one of the servants and spoke to him, but the man insisted that the Chancellor always had breakfast in the garden. When Richard suggested the routine might be changed, the man looked panic-stricken and retreated inside, calling over his shoulder that the Chancellor would never permit it.

Henry and Richard went inside, to see General Fremmel coming down the hall, his eyes bleary and his temper short from too little sleep and too much brandy the previous night. He listened impatiently as Richard tried to explain what he and Henry had been discussing, then cut him off brusquely. "Must I tell you a solution that would be obvious to a recruit, Major?" he barked. "Post men at the edge of the meadow and on that hill up there! And be quick about it—the Chancellor will be downstairs presently!"

Richard was red-faced. "There may be some delay, sir," he replied evenly. "I don't have sufficient men to anticipate and provide protection for the Chancellor's every movement."

"I've never met a commander who *did* have sufficient men," the general returned with ill temper. "You are fully aware that the Chancellor refuses to be guarded by more than a company. It would give the impression that he lacks courage or that Germany is a lawless nation."

"Perhaps," Henry put in, "the Chancellor could have breakfast in the dining room, at least for this morning."

Fremmel was about to reply when Bismarck appeared. The three military men stiffened to attention, and Bismarck, who always slept poorly, muttered something grumpily and started to push past.

"I beg your pardon, Your Excellency," the general said apologetically, "but it is inadvisable for you to dine outside. I believe it would be safer to—"

"I will have my breakfast where I always do!" Bismarck shot back. "I told you that I refuse to be made a prisoner in my own house!"

"Then please allow me to post dragoons around your table, Your Excellency," Richard pleaded.

"No!" Bismarck threw up his hands in exasperation. "How can I enjoy my breakfast with soldiers hovering about?" He turned to Henry. "Could you enjoy breakfast under such circumstances, Captain Blake?"

"With all respect, Your Excellency," Henry replied, "I would prefer that to being shot. But if you don't wish to dine inside, sir, at least let me put on your coat and go outside before you do."

The Chancellor blinked in surprise, then eyed Henry's trim, muscular build. "If an assassin has such poor eyesight as to mistake you for me, Captain, then he couldn't hit his target in the first place."

General Fremmel laughed dutifully. "The point is well taken, Your Excellency, but the suggestion is worthwhile. You and I are more of a size, so please allow me to wear your coat outside."

"Very well—but do it now." Bismarck unfastened his coat and handed it to the general, who took off his own coat.

Henry preceded Fremmel to the door. "It isn't necessary for you to go outside as well, Captain Blake," the general said.

"It was my idea, sir," Henry replied. "And two pairs of eyes are better than one."

The garden was colorful with flowers in the bright

morning sunshine. Birds were singing cheerfully, and two white-coated servants were standing at readiness near the table. Yet despite the peaceful scene, Henry felt uneasy. As he followed General Fremmel toward the table, he gazed up from under his hat brim at the rocks on the hill. Immediately knowing his earlier instincts had been correct, he swore under his breath as a movement caught his eye and he saw the glint of sunshine on metal.

Reacting instantly, Henry shoved the general to one side and threw himself to the ground as puffs of gunpowder smoke rose among the rocks. The general's grunt of surprise was choked off as bullets ricocheted from the flagstones and, an instant later, the solid boom of Mauser rifles carried across the distance. Henry's cheek was stung by a sharp fragment of slate, but both he and the general managed to scramble to the shelter of a row of hedges. Richard stormed out the door, bellowing orders at the dragoons who were rushing around both sides of the house.

He ran toward Henry in alarm and knelt behind the hedge with him and the general. "Is it a serious wound, Heinrich?" he asked worriedly.

Henry dabbed his bleeding cheek with his handkerchief. "No, it's only a scratch. I've counted five rifles."

Richard shouted to a platoon that had taken up position behind a stone wall. "Keep them pinned down! Don't let them escape! First squad, remain where you are. The rest of you prepare to follow me!"

Richard drew his saber and pistol, then jumped up and ran toward the trees at the base of the hill. "Follow me!" he shouted, beckoning with his sword. "Fire at will!"

A thunderous fusillade of rifle fire erupted, and the men began running after Richard. Henry and the general joined them. From the rate of the return fire, Henry estimated that the riflemen on the hill were indeed pinned down. But although they could not flee, they had chosen a well-protected place and were not giving up without a struggle.

They seemed to be concentrating their fire on Richard, for bullets slammed into the ground all around him. One struck his plumed helmet with a metallic clang, knocking it off his head, but he staggered only momentarily and reached the temporary shelter of the trees.

The gunfire took its toll of the other dragoons, however, and three of them fell. Henry dragged to safety a man who was shot through the leg, and the general helped another.

After relieving the man of his rifle, Henry climbed the hill with the dragoons, holding his fire until he was close enough to make every shot count. The hidden gunmen kept up a withering fire, and bullets ricocheted through the trees on the slope.

From behind, Henry could hear General Fremmel puffing heavily, trying to keep pace. Ahead, he caught sight of Richard and sprinted to catch up with him, then passed him. Bullets were whizzing down the slope to his right, and Henry finally had a clear view of one side of the rocks where the assailants were hiding. He steadied his rifle against a tree, drawing a bead to where he could see a rifle barrel protruding. He fired and quickly worked the bolt to reload.

Fragments exploded from the edge of the rock where his bullet struck, and as the rifle barrel swung toward him, a man's head momentarily came into view. Henry squeezed the trigger again, and the bullet hit the man in the neck, knocking him back out of sight.

Henry reloaded and darted up the hill to another tree. Richard blew his whistle as a signal to the squad back at the house to cease firing, then shouted at his men to spread out and encircle the rocks.

At the same moment, one of the assassins suddenly stood and aimed at Richard. With certain capture or death only moments away, the man was determined to take someone with him, but Henry fired first and shot the conspirator through the heart. The man's rifle discharged into the air as he sprawled backward.

The general, still far down the slope, shouted breathlessly at Richard that he wanted some of the gunmen taken alive. As Richard called to the soldiers to cease fire, Henry kept his rifle aimed. The dragoons quickly obeyed, and the gunfire from the rocks also stopped.

Richard cupped his hands around his mouth and called

to the gunmen to give up. A moment later, a frightened voice that Henry recognized as Bauer's replied that he surrendered, and a rifle was tossed over the rocks. Henry and Richard started forward cautiously, with several of the dragoons following them and others closing in from all sides.

They found Bauer huddled behind the rock, trembling in terror. Mueller was lying near him, wounded, and the other three were dead. Recognizing Henry, Bauer gaped at him in astonishment. "Kauptmann!" he exclaimed.

"Hoffmann!" Mueller said in surprise at almost the same instant.

The dragoons seized the men and began to search them. Richard said dryly to his friend, "It appears that you are well-known here, although I didn't realize you had so many names."

General Fremmel, panting and sweating profusely, finally appeared, and the dragoons moved aside so that he could look at the prisoners. "Are these the ones you saw in Bern, Captain?"

"Yes, sir." Henry turned to Bauer. "You told me once that you and the others were being assisted by a high German official. What was his name?"

"Hermann Bluecher," Bauer answered promptly, glancing in fright from Henry to the general. "He sent information and instructions to Herr Gessell, who—"

"That will do for now," Henry interrupted. "Mueller, you work for Bluecher, is that not so?"

Mueller stared stonily at Henry before he answered. "Yes, that is so. I will confess everything."

"Good!" Fremmel took Henry's arm and drew him aside. "We will quickly have an end to this affair now, and I shall see to it that your government is made aware of your vital contribution, Captain. But we had better get a doctor to attend to that wound on your face. Major Koehler"—he beckoned to Richard—"have your men bring the prisoners and those bodies to the rear of the house."

Henry started down the slope with the general. "I will immediately go into town," Fremmel told him, still half out of breath, "and telegraph Berlin. Herr Bluecher will be put under arrest and tried for conspiracy in an assassination attempt against the Chancellor. He will never bother us again."

"Let us hope so" was Henry's cautious reply.

But Hermann Bluecher was not at his house, nor even in Berlin. Having Mueller take part in the assassination, instead of only guiding the others, had been an all-or-nothing gamble, and Bluecher was prepared for the consequences should the bet fail.

Wearing nondescript, slightly seedy clothing, he was seated in a train station telegraph office in a small town north of Berlin. At his feet was a scuffed valise that contained a fortune in gold and precious gems, documents on his Swiss bank accounts, and other indispensable papers. Bluecher was waiting for a telegram from an informant in Bad Kissingen, a message that would send him either back to Berlin in triumph or on his way out of Germany.

Never a patient man, Bluecher had found his temper tried severely by the wait in the telegraph office. He had endured hunger, discomfort, and humiliation, for in this provincial town people were quick to ridicule a fat stranger. Bluecher had to keep reminding himself that, for the moment at least, he was not a powerful government official but a simple business traveler, waiting for instructions from his company.

The telegraph machine began clacking, as it had many times during the past hours, and Bluecher craned his neck and looked hopefully toward the source of the sound. The hunger pangs he felt were almost overcome by the agonizing tension that gripped him. At length the machine stopped, and the clerk processed the telegram with the well-practiced indolence of minor officialdom.

"Beutler!" the man said at last, stepping to the counter.

Relief flooded through Bluecher, and as he hefted himself from his seat, children in the room laughed and pointed. Ignoring them, he stepped across the room and reached for the telegram. The clerk jerked it back. "Identification!"

Bluecher produced forged papers, and the man studied them suspiciously before handing them back. But when Bluecher reached for the telegram again, the man jerked it away once more. With deliberately slow, insolent movements, the clerk folded the telegram, put it in an envelope, sealed it, then opened the register book, which he pushed in front of Bluecher. "Sign here."

Taking the pen, Bluecher resolved that if the telegram contained the news he hoped for, he would delay celebrating his victory until he saw to it that the telegraph clerk was put to a slow, painful death.

At last Bluecher ripped open the telegram. After reading the sentences several times and turning paler each time, he clutched his valise and shuffled out, having forgotten entirely about the clerk.

In the waiting room, Bluecher passed the restaurant entrance, oblivious to the scent of food wafting through the doorway. He went straight to the train schedule posted on the wall.

His pursuers would first block the border crossings, then alert the police in Bremerhaven and Hamburg, the main ports. They might also have Kiel and Lubeck watched because passenger ships called there as well. But Bluecher meant to head northeast, to Stettin, a freight port and the last place that would be considered as an escape route.

After checking the train schedule, he sat down and reread the telegram. It was long and detailed and named those who had been involved in foiling the plan. With sickening precision, all the facts now fitted together. Bluecher knew that the man in Bern who had called himself Kauptmann was the same man who, the previous year in Darmstadt, had called himself Hoffmann.

That man, Henry Blake, had become Bluecher's nemesis. Not only had he twice survived attacks by skilled assassins, he had also turned the tables and killed his intended killers. Too many times he thwarted plans that Bluecher had carefully devised, and now he had even made Bluecher a fugitive in his own country. And the man wasn't even a German, but an American!

Sitting there with the telegram in his hand, Bluecher wondered where he had gone wrong. Not until his train pulled into the station was he brought back sharply to reality. He had forgotten to buy a ticket, and he would have to purchase one on board. Puffing heavily, he wedged himself through the door of a dirty third-class carriage and found a seat on an uncomfortable wooden bench.

The distance to Stettin was relatively short, but the trip seemed to take forever, with the train stopping at every small village. By the time he had found a grimy room near the city's waterfront, Bluecher was light-headed with hunger. He ate a greasy meal in a tavern crowded with noisy, drunken sailors, and before going to bed he bought a newspaper to look at the shipping notices. All of Europe was closed to him, for he would inevitably be found and extradited to Germany for trial. He became despondent as he read one scheduled departure after another, all of them listing European ports as destinations.

Only one entry gave him hope: The *Seppel*, a freighter with limited passenger accommodations, was scheduled to depart the next day for Piraeus, near Athens. From there it would be easy to get anywhere in the eastern Mediterranean.

The next morning, however, Bluecher's slender hopes again faded when he saw the *Seppel*. An old ironclad steamer with stubby masts, she showed more rust than paint and even from a distance smelled of grease and urine. But Bluecher had no alternative, so he walked up the creaking gangplank.

On deck, a rumpled, unshaven man laughed in his face when he asked for the purser. "I suppose that's me," the man said. "I'm the first officer and the only officer besides the captain. What d'you want?"

"I want passage to Piraeus."

The man fingered his stubbled chin, eyed Bluecher's valise, then beckoned him to follow. He threw open a door and pointed. "There's your cabin, and the fare will be two hundred and twenty-five marks."

Bluecher stuck his head in the door and looked at the tiny, dirty compartment. The money meant little to him, but he resented being cheated. "That's far too much. I could go on a luxury steamer for half the price."

"But you chose to come to Stettin to take passage on a tramp steamer instead." The man gave Bluecher a smug, knowing smile. "Two hundred twenty-five marks, or get off the ship."

Bluecher took out his wallet and counted the money. "When will you leave?"

"This afternoon," the officer replied, pocketing the cash. "We're hauling pig iron, so you should feel right at home." He laughed and ambled away.

Controlling his temper with great difficulty, Bluecher squeezed through the doorway into the airless cabin and sat on the narrow bunk. The food on the vessel would undoubtedly be vile, and even though he had time to go ashore and buy a stock of delicacies, he knew it would be a wasted effort. He always became violently seasick on any vessel, even a riverboat, and the *Seppel* would shortly be setting out into the stormy Baltic.

Bluecher hugged his valise against his stomach, and it gave him some comfort. At least his escape was now assured, he reflected. And besides money, he still had his most valuable asset—his intelligence. Somewhere and somehow, he would build another life and become more powerful than ever, and then he would seek revenge against the man responsible for all his troubles. The last battle in the war between them had yet to be fought, and Bluecher would not settle for simple victory.

XVI

Lanterns flanked the courtyard gate in front of the Casita de Extasis, affording Toby Holt a good view of those coming and going as he lay concealed in brush across the road. He watched a luxurious carriage pause at the gate for a cursory inspection by the two armed guards. It was the fifth carriage Toby had seen in the past hour, and the guards had checked the occupants of each one.

Walter Stafford tapped Toby's shoulder and pointed to a man approaching on a spirited palomino. The silver trim on the saddle and bridle sparkled in the moonlight, and silver studs gleamed on the pistol belt around the man's waist.

The guards stopped the rider at the gate, and a minor argument in Spanish ensued. The horseman sounded drunk, but after a while he unbuckled his pistol belt, pulled his rifle from its scabbard, and handed them to one of the guards, who took the weapons into a gatehouse.

Inside, a small band struck up a gay tune. Toby motioned to Walter that they had seen enough and could leave.

During the day, Toby had carefully examined the compound from a nearby hill through Walter's binoculars. A ten-foot adobe wall, topped with embedded shards of broken glass, encircled the grounds, which comprised a rambling, two-story building, stables set off to one side, and a courtyard. Besides the stable hands, Toby had observed four armed guards—the two at the front gate and two posted at the rear wall. Apodaca had a lucrative business and was taking no chances on being robbed.

The lights of Mexico City glowed brightly to the

south as Toby and Walter crept back to where they would meet Sergeant Lyons, who had been watching the guards at the rear of the compound. He was waiting for them.

"They haven't budged," Lyons reported with a grin. "They're still sitting there, smoking and talking. If one of my troopers ever acted like that on guard duty, I'd have him court-martialed. Like I said, a saddle blanket and a boost is all I need to get over that wall."

"Good," Toby approved. "Let's go back to the men and get started."

After the three of them had crossed the wooded hills to the valley where they had left the others, about a mile away, the men gathered around Toby in the moonlight. He explained his plan.

"Just remember," he emphasized in conclusion, "there will be no unnecessary gunplay. We're here to get those women out, not to kill people, so shoot only in self-defense. I'll personally deal with Señor Apodaca, the owner. Any questions?"

The men shook their heads, and Toby exchanged a few words with Sergeant Lyons, who picked two men and rode off. Toby gave them a ten-minute head start before he and Walter rode with the rest of the men out of the valley. The troopers at the rear of the column led the extra horses for the women.

When they reached the road, about a quarter mile from the bordello, Toby halted the men and continued ahead with Walter. The music from inside was louder now. Riding side by side, Toby and Walter laughed and acted drunk as they approached the gate. The two guards stepped forward, and one of them spoke curtly in Spanish, saying something about weapons.

Edging their horses closer, Toby and Walter fumbled with the buckles on their gunbelts. Before the guards knew what was happening, Toby had slipped his Colt from its holster and leaped off his horse, slamming the pistol down on the nearer guard's head and knocking him unconscious. The other guard cursed and raised his rifle, but Walter jumped on him, quickly dealing with him as Toby had done.

Wasting no time, they dragged the guards behind the

gatehouse, where they bound and gagged them. Sergeant Lyons and the other two soldiers appeared only moments later, to report that the guards at the rear wall had been similarly taken care of. As agreed, Walter led Lyons and the two other soldiers to the stable, where the customers' horses and carriages were kept, while Toby took one of the lanterns from the gate and swung it in a circle, as a signal to the other men.

Soon he heard the distant rumble of hoofbeats, which was joined by the sound of the horses being shooed from the stable and courtyard. Walter, Lyons, and the other two soldiers dodged and waved their arms until all the horses had been herded out the gate and scattered down the road. All the while, the music from the building continued uninterrupted, those inside totally unaware of what was happening. Toby and Walter silently directed the arriving troopers to tether their horses outside the front wall, and guards were posted.

Toby extinguished the gate lanterns to discourage any additional customers, and after repeating his warning about avoiding unnecessary gunplay, he led the way to the front door. He knocked and stepped aside, and as soon as the door swung open, he barged in, bowling over the heavyset bouncer before the man could reach into his shoulder holster. Toby barely kept out of the way of the avalanche of soldiers behind him, who finished subduing the bouncer with pistol handles and rifle butts.

The soldiers followed Toby through the vestibule to the inner door, which opened into a lavishly furnished reception room, where the bored-looking musicians, occupying a small stage, were still playing. Some twenty scantily clad American women were seated on couches or dancing with men in front of the stage.

The woman nearest the door, a tall, slender redhead, was wearily going through the motions of dancing with an elderly man three or four inches shorter than she. Her air of grim resignation changed to alarm as she saw Toby and the others barge through the door, all heavily armed, and bearded and dusty from the long ride south.

Conversation abruptly ended, and the music faded into broken, discordant notes, then stopped. Toby glanced around to make certain there were no armed guards in the room, then motioned to Walter and Lyons to block the other doors. "Everyone remain quiet—*silencioso*."

Despite his orders, however, exclamations of disbelief or exultant joy rose from several of the women, who apparently realized that the newcomers represented their salvation. More than one of the women burst into tears, while others threw themselves at Toby's men and hugged them. "Let's keep order, please," Toby announced more loudly. "We've got to get you ladies out of here quickly, and it'll be a great help if you'll get the others together. I also need to know where Apodaca is and if there are guards anywhere inside the building."

"I'll show you where he is," the tall redhead volunteered. "He always has two guards, but they're the only ones in the building." She put her hand against her dancing partner's chest and sent him reeling across the dance floor. "I'm Amy Harkness."

"Toby Holt—pleased to meet you, ma'am." Toby instinctively tipped his hat, then raised a hand for quiet. "The sooner you ladies gather the others, the sooner we'll leave. You men give them a hand. And round up all the customers in the place and bring them in here."

The women rushed toward the stairs, while Amy Harkness led Toby to the doorway where Walter was standing guard. Sergeant Lyons and some of the men started herding together the customers already in the room.

"I'll give you a hand with Apodaca and the madam," Amy offered, reaching for Toby's Colt. "She's upstairs, and—"

Toby put his hand on the pistol before the woman could get it. "I understand your feelings, ma'am, but you'd better let us handle this."

Amy did not argue but swiftly led the way through the door and down a hall. "Apodaca's office is around the corner," she whispered when they were near the end of the hall. "You'd best be careful. They might be wondering why the music stopped."

Toby drew his pistol and motioned her back. "All right. You rejoin the other ladies."

Amy hurried back to the reception room. Toby handed Walter his rifle, cocked the pistol, and stepped to the corner. As he did so, he heard heavy footsteps approaching, and suddenly a tall, muscular man strode into view. Looking at Toby in shock, he wheeled around and reached into his coat.

Toby leveled his pistol. "Don't try it."

The guard froze only for an instant, then went for the weapon. Toby squeezed his trigger, and the reverberation of the shot was deafening in the hallway. The bullet slammed into the man's shoulder and knocked him to the floor. Toby snatched up the unfired pistol, which had clattered to the floor.

A quick glance around the corner sent Toby ducking back as the second guard, in the doorway beyond, fired. Toby poked his pistol around the corner and squeezed off two shots in reply.

The guard howled in pain, and Toby darted in a crouch around the corner and aimed. But the man had dropped his pistol and fallen, shot through the leg. The door clicked closed behind him, and Toby heard a key turn in the lock.

Not hesitating an instant, Toby rushed the door and slammed into it with his shoulder. It crashed open, and swiftly recovering his balance, he pointed his pistol at a balding man in an expensive suit who was standing behind a desk, reaching into a drawer. No one else was in the room.

"Don't give me an excuse to kill you, Apodaca."

The Mexican wisely lifted his hands, which sparkled with diamond rings. "If you need an excuse," he returned in English, "then I won't give it to you."

"That's too bad." Toby motioned Walter to guard the doorway. "In case you haven't heard, your friend Calusa Jim is dead. Your days of dealing with him are over."

Apodaca actually smiled. "I'm sorry to hear that. Our arrangement was profitable. I'll have to find another supplier."

The Mexican's insolence enraged Toby, and his finger tightened on the trigger. As much as he longed to end the man's life, however, he was unable to kill in cold blood.

Noticing a large safe in a corner, Toby thought of another way of dealing with Apodaca, who no doubt valued money more than human life. "Let's see just how profitable your arrangement with Calusa Jim actually was. Open that safe."

The Mexican's smug smile disappeared, and his steely eyes revealed fear for the first time. "No. You can kill me, but you can't make me open my safe!"

"Yes, I can." Toby glanced back toward the doorway. "If I give those women a few minutes alone with you, you'll be glad to open it. I don't have time to argue with you, so do as I say or I'll get them in here."

Sweat broke out on Apodaca's brow, and Toby could tell he was torn between avarice and terror. He hesitated only a moment, then crossed to the safe and began twirling the combination dial. An uproar from the reception room carried along the hall, and Toby could hear furniture breaking, women shouting in rage, and a harsh female voice—the madam's, he guessed—cursing in Spanish, then screaming before being stifled. Apodaca opened the safe, and Toby shoved him aside.

In addition to a shelf filled with stacks of peso notes, there were two bags of gold coins, worth tens of thousands of dollars. Toby removed the bags and began tossing the bundles of bills onto the floor. From the doorway, Walter commented that Apodaca apparently distrusted banks.

"Yes, it looks that way, doesn't it?" Toby glanced at the bordello manager. "We can divide the gold up among the ladies. It won't make up for what they've been through, but at least it'll be something."

Sergeant Lyons appeared in the doorway. "We got them all collected together and the ladies outside," he reported. "Though I had a bit of trouble getting our womenfolk to keep their hands off the madam. They found her hiding under a bed."

"Yes, I heard." Toby used his foot to sweep a pile of bills toward the curtained window. "Walter, take Apodaca outside, if you will, and get those wounded guards dragged out, too. Mr. Lyons, I'd appreciate it if you'd put these bags of gold in my saddlebags."

The lieutenant handed Toby back his rifle, then seized

Apodaca's collar and shoved him out the door. As Lyons hefted the heavy bags, Toby took a match from Apodaca's desk, struck it against the safe's door, and threw it atop the stacks of bills beneath the curtains. Toby and Lyons watched the flames begin to leap up the draperies.

Then they hurried back to the reception room, where Toby was surprised to see a large pile of trousers, boots, coats, and shirts in front of the stage. From the smell, the mound had already been soaked with liquor. The bordello's patrons, along with the band members, were huddled near the door, barefoot and clad only in their underwear.

Sergeant Lyons put down one of the bags and took a match from his pocket. "We was thinking along the same lines," he explained with a grin. "I just wish I could hear them explain to their wives what happened to their clothes."

Toby laughed appreciatively. "They'll have plenty of time to come up with excuses. It's a long walk back to the city."

The men were herded out the door, and Lyons lighted the match and tossed it onto the clothes, then picked up the bag and followed Toby to the door.

Outside, the women were already mounted up, and all the employees of the bordello who were not badly wounded, including Apodaca and the madam, had been tied up and locked into the adobe gatehouse.

"It wasn't easy fitting all of them in there, Sergeant—I mean *Mr.* Lyons," one of the troopers reported, pocketing the key. "And we had them take off their clothes, too, seeing as it's so hot. They'll feel right at home, I reckon."

Lyons commended the man for his initiative, and when everyone was mounted up, Toby took his place at the head of the column. "All right, ladies," he announced, "we're headed for home!"

A chorus of cheers rose in reply, and several women called out in derisive farewell to Apodaca and the madam. The disrobed customers and the band members were already nearly out of sight, stepping gingerly down the road in their bare feet.

A half hour later, from atop a hill many miles to the north, the rescue party paused briefly to look back. The bordello was a distant beacon, fully enveloped in flames.

After descending the other side of the hill, Toby turned the column off the road. Following the escape route he had planned, he led them into a gravelly riverbed, where their tracks would be difficult to follow. After several miles, he turned onto a branch of the riverbed that led north.

Toby felt sure that the women would be willing to endure the hard, steady pace he wished to maintain, and they did not disappoint him. The hours wore on and the moon set, but the women remained uncomplaining as the column continued north at a rapid canter. By dawn they had reached the ravine where Toby had left two troopers with spare horses, food, and other supplies.

After a quick meal, most of the party settled down to rest, while Toby and Walter climbed a hill overlooking the route by which they had come. They scanned the countryside with binoculars, but there was no sign of pursuit.

"Well, it appears our worries are over," Walter concluded. "I'm sure you'll be happy when this business is finished, won't you, Toby?"

"Yes, I will." Toby had already determined that Bill Hawkins's wife, Sarah, was among the women, and that knowledge had helped set his mind at ease. His expression became suddenly thoughtful. "For several months, Walter, I've been putting off an important conversation I intend to have with someone. But I reckon I can't put it off any longer."

"What sort of conversation?" Walter asked. "Or is it a personal matter?"

"It's very personal," Toby replied. "But I don't mind talking about it. The someone happens to be an especially beautiful young lady named Alexandra Woodling. And I intend to ask her to marry me."

Standing on the same pier where she had said goodbye to Marjorie White months before, Cindy Kerr watched while a boat was lowered over the side of the steamer *John S. Carver*, which had just come to anchor. As the small boat drew nearer, Cindy was shocked to see the change in her friend, who looked pale and exhausted.

The moment the boat touched the pier, Cindy was

there to help Marjorie up the ladder and to embrace her. "Thank you so much for being here," Marjorie said, clearly touched by Cindy's presence. "I can't tell you how grateful and pleased I am."

Cindy kept her arm around her friend as one of the sailors in the boat helped a small, well-dressed native boy up the ladder. The boy gazed around, clearly frightened but also curious, and Marjorie introduced him to Cindy as her friend, Harry. He stuck close to Marjorie, who took his hand and explained to Cindy that he spoke little English.

A crowd of reporters and curious onlookers was waiting outside the shipping company office at the foot of the pier. Cindy told Marjorie that she had the use of Gilbert Paige's house and that his carriage was waiting, if they could get to it.

Leading the way, Cindy shouldered a path through the noisy, milling crowd. Marjorie was barraged with questions, and Cindy, trying to protect her, was jostled from side to side. The carriage driver, Paige's gardener, seeing what was happening, elbowed and shoved his way through to help. In the process he bowled two of the reporters off their feet.

A boatload of sailors had come ashore, and the reporters, giving up on Marjorie, turned their attention back to the pier. The driver helped the two women and Harry into the carriage.

During the drive to Paige's house, Harry had his head craned out the window nearly all the way, while Cindy tried to cheer Marjorie. It was late afternoon when they drew up in front of the red cottage, where the housekeeper, Mrs. Carlson, came out to greet them. Cindy helped Marjorie and Harry get settled in their rooms.

At dinner Cindy noticed that Harry, at least, was adjusting quickly to his new surroundings. Unlike Marjorie, he ate heartily, and although he spoke little, he seemed to understand everything that was said to him. Cindy tried to keep up the conversation, but it was a quiet meal.

Marjorie did talk about the boy, briefly explaining why he was with her, and Cindy wondered what she intended to do with him. Certainly he needed a settled home life and an education. Later, when Harry was in bed and Cindy was sitting with Marjorie on the back porch, she broached the possibility of sending the boy to Toby's ranch in Portland. Marjorie thanked her but declined.

"One of the officers on the whaler took a liking to him," she explained, "and wants to take him in. But the man felt that he should discuss it with his wife first. If she's agreeable, Harry will live with them."

Cindy asked about the whaler's officers, and for the first time, Marjorie seemed eager to talk. She described how close she had become to all the *Beluga*'s crew and how much she would miss them. She also spoke fondly of Edward Blackstone, who she said had stayed on in New Zealand, with plans eventually to visit an uncle of his in India. When she fell silent and thoughtful again, Cindy asked her about the photographs she had made on the voyage. Ordinarily Marjorie needed little urging to talk about her photography, but to Cindy's surprise, Marjorie merely replied that she had some good pictures. A short time later she excused herself to go to her room. It suddenly occurred to Cindy that, on the ride back from the *Carver*, Marjorie had not taken her camera cases with her, which was extremely unusual, since she hardly ever traveled without them.

The next day Cindy and Marjorie walked along the shore. The Maine coastline had a primitive beauty in the warm, late summer months, and Marjorie seemed to appreciate it. Cindy was still concerned, however, that her friend appeared to have lost all interest in her work. She hadn't even shown a reaction when her equipment arrived from town in a wagon that morning, and the only topic she had expressed any feeling about was whether the *Beluga*'s crew would have another ship.

That point was resolved the following day, when the whaler's captain came to visit Marjorie. Cindy found Isaac Tench a very pleasant man, and Marjorie seemed greatly pleased when he broke the news that the entire crew had been paid a bonus in compensation for the hardship they had suffered and had been offered to sign on another whaler currently being refitted.

Later that same afternoon, Cindy was gathering a bouquet from the flower garden when a buggy drew up in front of the house. The short, thin man who stepped out of it appeared to be on his way to a funeral. His expression was grim, and he was wearing a high, starched collar and a severe, old-fashioned black suit. He doffed his hat stiffly to Cindy, then turned to help a woman out of the buggy.

Completely unlike her escort, the woman was graceful and statuesque, some three inches taller and at least fifty pounds heavier than he. She was wearing a bright yellow summer dress and a matching hat that was very becoming on her, and with her rosy complexion, smiling lips, and twinkling blue eyes, she fairly radiated a sunny disposition.

The pair stepped along the path to Cindy. The man doffed his hat again and spoke in a commanding voice. "I am Horatio Cade, ma'am, and this is my wife. Is this where Marjorie White is staying?"

"Yes—yes it is." Put off by the man's blunt tone, Cindy wasn't at all sure that Marjorie would wish to see this particular visitor. "I'm Cindy Kerr, Marjorie's friend."

The man looked away stonily and fell silent, but his wife extended a hand. "We're delighted to meet you, my dear," she said warmly, shaking Cindy's hand. "My name is Henrietta, and you must be the young woman who came all the way from Paris to be with Marjorie, isn't that so? She's had a grievous loss, but there can be no greater blessing in life than to have a friend like you."

The sincerity in the woman's voice made her words doubly flattering, and Cindy felt embarrassed. "You're too kind by far, Mrs. Cade."

"Please call me Henrietta. And here, let me help you with those flowers. There's nothing like flowers to brighten the house and dispel sadness, that's what I say. I love flowers so much, don't you?"

"Very much indeed." Cindy politely tried to include Mr. Cade in the conversation. "Do you like flowers, Mr. Cade?"

"No. I've never found any that are fit to eat."

Cindy gave up the attempt to communicate with the man and led Henrietta toward the house. "Marjorie is in the parlor."

Inside, Henrietta did not wait for her husband to

introduce her but greeted Marjorie warmly, hugged her, and graciously expressed her condolences. When at length she fell silent, her husband stepped forward and shook hands with Marjorie. "I hope you're bucking up. It doesn't do a hand any good to mope about."

They all sat down, and Cindy was about to suggest they have refreshments, when the back door slammed and little Harry came running into the room. A wide grin transformed his face the instant he saw Horatio Cade, and Cindy realized, with some surprise, that the Cades were the couple who were considering adopting the boy. She was startled to see that Cade's gruff face had thawed to a smile and that his icy blue eyes had become warm. The boy turned anxiously toward Henrietta, who came to him and, kneeling down, hugged him to her. Watching them, Cindy concluded that Harry had indeed found a home.

Refreshments were served by Mrs. Carlson, and the Cades visited for another hour. Henrietta wanted to take the boy home right away, and Marjorie agreed. Cindy's throat felt tight as she listened to Harry give a little farewell speech to Marjorie in his broken English, and for the first time she realized how deeply attached the two of them had become. Outside, both Marjorie and Harry cried as they waved good-bye.

For the rest of the day, Cindy was concerned about how the boy's absence would affect Marjorie. Indeed, Marjorie seemed even quieter than usual, and at dinner that evening she hardly spoke, as if she were deep in thought. The next morning, she did not appear for breakfast, nor was she in her room, and Cindy looked for her with growing alarm. She finally found her in the small back room where her photographic equipment had been stored.

She was sitting beside an opened crate of glass negatives, holding one up to the window to examine it. Cindy, relieved that her friend was showing interest in her work again, stepped into the room. Without comment, Marjorie held out the negative so that Cindy could look at it.

Unaccustomed to the dark, reversed image, Cindy studied it in some confusion before she could make it out. Finally she realized it was the portrait of a fearsome Maori

warrior. "He looks like a savage brute. Is he one of those
from the village where you were held?"

"He was the chief," Marjorie said, her throat con-
stricted. "His name was Te Pomore, and he was the one
who killed Ted."

Cindy did not know what to say. "Perhaps you should
put that one aside and look at others, Marjorie," she
finally suggested.

Marjorie wrapped the glass plate in waxed paper and
replaced it in the crate. "No, looking at it doesn't make
me feel worse than I already do," she said, taking another
one from the crate. "I detest him, of course, but it's an
excellent negative." She unwrapped the second plate and
held it up to the light. "This one is, too. Considering the
conditions I had for developing, these negatives are exceptionally good."

"They must be very valuable as well. There can't be
many photographs made by someone who was captured by
Maoris."

"These are the only ones," Marjorie replied absently.
She studied the negative, then rewrapped it and replaced
it in the crate. "I'm sure the demand for these will be
much greater than it was for my slides of the Great Chicago Fire. They're much more exotic. Is breakfast ready?"

"Yes, dear."

Marjorie stood and straightened her dress. "Well,
after breakfast, I'd like to go into town, to see if there's a
studio in Waverly or Belfast where I can make proofs of
these. It's about time for me to get back to work, I
suppose. I have a lot to do."

Taking Marjorie's arm, the two young widows walked
to the dining room.

After a maddening delay of two full weeks, during
which time he met with various German officials and the
American ambassador, Henry Blake finally left Berlin.
Bluecher's escape remained a bitter disappointment to
him, but at least the trouble the man had been causing
was finished, and he was not likely to show his face again
in Germany.

When Henry reached Grevenburg, the von Kirchberg

carriage was waiting for him. He felt a comfortable sense of homecoming as he was driven up the road to Grevenhof, and he looked forward with eager anticipation to seeing Gisela and little Peter. He would have several free days before returning to his official duties, and he intended to enjoy every hour to the utmost.

The instant he stepped into the mansion, however, he knew that something was wrong. The butler was unusually somber and merely glanced at the bandage on Henry's cheek before informing him grimly that the baroness was in her rooms.

"Is she ill?" Henry asked anxiously.

"Yes, sir."

"Is it—?"

"Yes, it is her illness, sir."

Icy fear gripped Henry as he bounded up the stairs and rushed through the sitting room to her bedroom. Gisela was propped up in bed, and her face was pale and drawn with pain. Dr. MacAlister was standing at the window.

Gisela smiled and lifted her arms as Henry moved to her. Seating himself on the edge of the bed, he gently took her into his arms and kissed her. She touched the bandage on his face. "What happened to you, loved one?"

"It's nothing." He looked up at MacAlister. "How long has she been like this?"

The doctor started to reply, but Gisela interrupted him impatiently. "Heinrich, I must know what happened to you!"

Henry's temporary annoyance swiftly faded. "A piece of rock hit me. I was fortunate, however, that it struck my head. I have lived so long among Prussians, you see, that it merely bounced off." He lifted her hand and kissed her palm. "The wound is almost healed, Gisela. Now are you satisfied?"

Still frowning, Gisela fell silent, and the doctor answered Henry's question. "The onset was three days ago, Captain Blake."

"Three days!" Henry could hardly restrain his anger. "I telegraphed yesterday from Berlin that I was returning. Why was I not informed?"

The feisty Scot reddened. "Because, sir, the baroness forbade me to tell you!"

"I thought I would feel better before you arrived," Gisela explained. "And now that you are here, I am so happy that I'm certain my illness will pass quickly. That wound will leave a scar on your handsome face, won't it? That is too bad, but I suppose such things are unavoidable for a soldier."

Henry walked to the window and spoke to the doctor in a lowered voice. "How bad is this attack, compared with other times?"

MacAlister shook his head. "Her condition is not improving. I consider it very serious, Captain Blake."

"The most serious that she's had?"

"Yes, I consider it so."

MacAlister's tone and manner were grim, holding out little hope, and Henry realized that the time he had been dreading for years had finally come. He thought about Dr. Robert Martin and Janessa Holt, and what John Lawrence had told him concerning the operation they had performed.

"Can she travel?"

"It would be unwise." MacAlister frowned, obviously knowing what Henry was contemplating. "She needs undisturbed rest, and a long journey would be very dangerous for her."

Henry was well aware of the obstacles involved, not the least of which was Janessa Holt's hatred of him. Yet the old doctor and the girl were his only hope—Gisela's only hope.

He looked at Gisela, who had overheard the doctor's last words. "Long journey?" she repeated. "What long journey? What are you two talking about behind my back?"

Henry had never told Gisela what he had learned from Lawrence, but now, seeing the pallor of her features, he knew that he could no longer withhold the truth. The distance between Germany and Oregon was vast, and not an hour more could be wasted. He only hoped that it wasn't already too late.

Coming in Spring 1989
WAGONS WEST
VOLUME XXIII
OKLAHOMA!
by Dana Fuller Ross

The great American epic continues in volume twenty-three of the landmark series that has made publishing history with more than 25,000,000 copies in print.

Intrepid Toby Holt, frontiersman and businessman extraordinaire, is called upon to bring peace to an Oklahoma town torn apart by violence and greed . . .

Meanwhile, the other daring men and passionate women whom millions of readers have come to love will pursue their destinies from the expanse of the West to the distant corners of the world—as the American pioneer spirit takes them on far-flung adventures that will stir the heart and quicken the imagination.

Don't miss the next volume in this bestselling historical series. Read OKLAHOMA!—wherever Bantam Books are sold.

★ WAGONS WEST ★

A series of unforgettable books that trace the lives of a dauntless band of pioneering men, women, and children as they brave the hazards of an untamed land in their trek across America. This legendary caravan of people forge a new link in the wilderness. They are Americans from the North and the South, alongside immigrants, Blacks, and Indians, who wage fierce daily battles for survival on this uncompromising journey—each to their private destinies as they fulfill their greatest dreams.

☐	26822	INDEPENDENCE! #1	$4.50
☐	26162	NEBRASKA! #2	$4.50
☐	26242	WYOMING! #3	$4.50
☐	26072	OREGON! #4	$4.50
☐	26070	TEXAS! #5	$4.50
☐	26377	CALIFORNIA! #6	$4.50
☐	26546	COLORADO! #7	$4.50
☐	26069	NEVADA! #8	$4.50
☐	26163	WASHINGTON! #9	$4.50
☐	26073	MONTANA! #10	$4.50
☐	26184	DAKOTA! #11	$4.50
☐	26521	UTAH! #12	$4.50
☐	26071	IDAHO! #13	$4.50
☐	26367	MISSOURI! #14	$4.50
☐	27141	MISSISSIPPI! #15	$4.50
☐	25247	LOUISIANA! #16	$4.50
☐	25622	TENNESSEE! #17	$4.50
☐	26022	ILLINOIS! #18	$4.50
☐	26533	WISCONSIN! #19	$4.50
☐	26849	KENTUCKY! #20	$4.50
☐	27065	ARIZONA! #21	$4.50

Prices and availability subject to change without notice.

- -

Bantam Books, Dept. LE, 414 East Golf Road, Des Plaines, IL 60016

Please send me the books I have checked above. I am enclosing $_____ (please add $2.00 to cover postage and handling). Send check or money order—no cash or C.O.D.s please.

Mr/Ms _____

Address _____

City/State _____ Zip _____

LE—8/88

Please allow four to six weeks for delivery. This offer expires 2/89.